High Valley Home
KATRINE

High Valley Home
KATRINE

JOSEPH DORRIS

iUniverse®

KATRINE
HIGH VALLEY HOME

iUniverse books may be ordered through booksellers or by contacting:

iUniverse
1663 Liberty Drive
Bloomington, IN 47403
www.iuniverse.com
1-800-Authors (1-800-288-4677)

ISBN: 978-1-5320-2005-6 (sc)
ISBN: 978-1-5320-2006-3 (hc)
ISBN: 978-1-5320-2007-0 (e)

Library of Congress Control Number: 2017905151

Print information available on the last page.

iUniverse rev. date: 05/08/2018

To my wife, Susie,
and her four Swedish grandparents who came to America,
Carl and Olga Anderson and Elof and Mary Stromback

Acknowledgments

As FOR ALL my books, I owe many people special thanks for their help and support. In particular, my family has always been my source for inspiration to write about days gone by, the country where I grew up, and the people who lived in those times. My wife, Susan, and children, Scott, Tim, and Krystle, in particular, picked up the pieces while I put this story together. Without them, none of this would be possible.

My sister Linda helped me research the history of Boise City and early Idaho settlements and gave good insight into the story line and characters. My daughter, Krystle, tried to make sure I had the views of a young girl right. (I alone am to blame if I'm off in any significant manner.) I especially owe my wife, Susan, my gratitude for sharing her Swedish ancestry with me for these past nearly forty years as well as for reviewing the manuscript and suggesting inputs throughout the story, especially on nineteenth-century clothing and Swedish meals. My Chicago cousin, also Swedish, Jay Anderson, was a great help in reading the manuscript and reviewing Swedish language and customs. I found Mike Cannon's and Jack Chamberlain's perspectives on the old ways of farming greatly beneficial. Most of the information on mining and Native Americans comes from my passion for studying this time and learning their way of life. My family in Idaho supported me whenever I could make trips home to do my research, especially my sister Ann Giberson and sister Karen Morrow. Finally, I owe thanks to my classmates who grew up with me in Long Valley and brought bits of Scandinavia and Finland with them. Their Finnish ancestors were the people who settled the area in the late 1890s.

Many others have helped and supported me over the years with my writing and artwork. I do not have the space to acknowledge everyone. One special group is my Thursday Night Improv writers. They are wonderful people who just enjoy writing and sharing. The cover is from my oil painting titled *High Valley Black Bears*, and the line drawings are my pen and ink sketches.

Author's Notes

I GREW UP in McCall, Idaho, and as a teenager spent much of my life wandering the mountains and canyons of the wilderness that surrounded my home. Although I have based the Sheepeater Indian series on gold mining and the Native Americans of the nineteenth century, my mother's family was predominately ranchers and farmers. I became fascinated with how my pioneer family in Montana and others were able to carve out livings for themselves far away from towns and without modern implements. Additionally, I have come to appreciate the many nationalities that came to America, particularly during the nineteenth century, to seek opportunities. Foremost they were Americans, but they brought with them their traditions and culture that have enriched our country.

Katrine: High Valley Home tells the fictional story of a young Swedish girl who has come to America and has been separated from her family (*Sheepeater: To Cry for a Vision*). As such, this novel does not have the strong historical ties as do my previous novels. It is set in a fictional valley based on Long Valley, Idaho, where I lived; however, there was no significant Swedish presence in Long Valley during the early 1860s.

Long Valley had a substantial Finnish settlement during the late nineteenth century when farming, logging, and mining were the area's main industries. Otherwise, the Scandinavian people, predominately Norwegians and Swedes, settled more in the northern parts of the state and in several agricultural communities on the Snake River Plain. Not as well recognized were the Nordic people who arrived earlier as lumbermen, fishermen, farmers, and miners but generally without families. Some of these people figure in my other novels. During the time of the Finnish settlements in Long Valley, over a quarter of Idaho's population was Nordic. The Nordic settlers of Idaho's high valleys were adept at cool-weather farming and ranching and were also miners and loggers. The Nordic peoples also brought with them many of their traditions—for example, their churches, saunas, and skis. It is little wonder that the tiny town of McCall, at the head of Long Valley, has produced a high number of Olympic skiers.

I was influenced by my Swedish heritage through my wife's family to write Katrine's story. I have tried to depict what it would have been like by basing my story on those solitary farmers and miners of whose stories I am aware and how they brought Sweden to America. In the early 1860s, there were several operational gold placers, sporadic way stations, packers, and trappers in Long Valley. There were also a few scattered farms to the west in the Weiser drainage as well as along the lower Payette River. After the discovery of gold in Boise Basin, farms became established near Garden Valley. A road did not reach Long Valley until approximately 1880, and then, as I have depicted, it was rarely passable.

My characters are fictional but set within a geographical and historic time. The trails north and east from Long Valley are accurate. The Sheepeater Indians, Nez Perce, and Shoshoni are depicted as known. Jeffrey's Road, which became known as the Goodale Cutoff, and the massacre at Devil's Gate are based on historical happenings. The original Fort Boise had been destroyed by floods on the Snake River and during the Civil War was reestablished at the current site of Boise. A few people were in the area, but true efforts to build the new fort began in 1863, the same year as the establishment of Boise City and the creation of Idaho Territory.

This novel takes place to the southwest of Sheepeater country and Erik Larson's story in *Sheepeater: To Cry for a Vision*. Samuel Chamber's story from *Sojourner of Warren's Camp* and *Salmon River Kid* is set to the north of this region. Samuel's trail into the Salmon River country is to the west along the Weiser River through Council Valley. The characters from these novels will be brought together in the depiction of the Sheepeater War of 1879.

Katrine: High Valley Home
Principal Characters
Autumn 1862, Fort Boise site, in the then Washington Territory

Children's ages as of autumn 1862

Jon and Ruth Larson (missing)
Erik   13 (missing)
Katrine 9 (with the Olafsons)

Sven and Margret Olafson
Katrine 9
Mia 7
Torsten   Born 1863

Nils and Astrid Adolphson
Lars 11
Ingrid 9
Pelle 7

Anton and Emma Wikstrom
Anna 12
Björn 10
Linnea 7
Laurens 3

Gustaf and Olga Andreasson
Jens 10
Barbro 7
Joran 5

Magnus and Louise Lundgren
Harald 10
Emma 7
Oscar   Born 1863

Hans and Ulrika Eklund
Robert 1 1/2

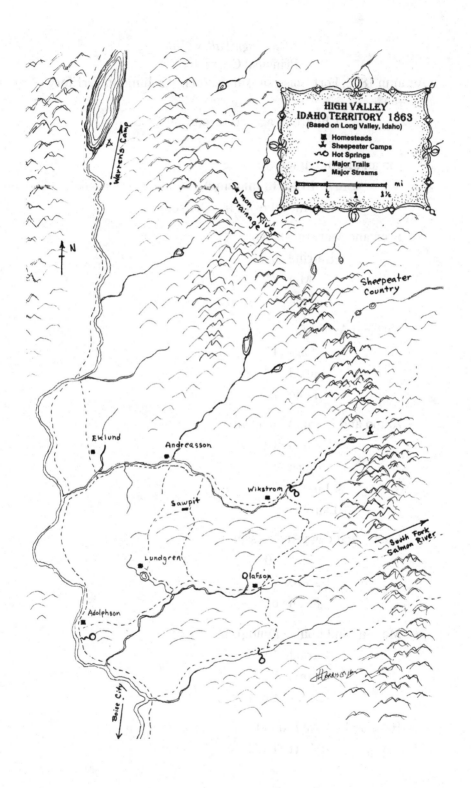

HIGH VALLEY
IDAHO TERRITORY 1863
(Based on Long Valley, Idaho)

🏠 Homesteads
⚔ Sheepeater Camps
∿ Hot Springs
⋯ Major Trails
Major Streams

0   ½   1   1½
mi

N

Warren's Camp

Salmon River Drainage

Sheepeater Country

Eklund

Andreasson

Wikstrom

Sawpit

Lundgren

Olafson

South Fork Salmon River

Adolphson

Boise City

WINTERING 1862 AT FORT BOISE

Chapter 1

KATRINE LARSON'S HEART quickened. Soon they would be overlooking the Boise River and coming into camp. She hastened her step, her bare feet kicking up dust in the dry short-grass prairie. Faint smoke rose from the valley that lay hidden beyond the sagebrush-dotted hills. Sandstone buttresses capped the crest of the hill that the wagons slowly ascended.

"I'm going to climb up and see," Katrine hollered and began running for the outcrop.

Mia Olafson raced after her. "Wait for me."

"You girls watch out for snakes," Mia's father, Sven, called after them from where he walked alongside the mules, leading the wagon.

Katrine hesitated and glanced back. Mia's mother, Margret Olafson, watched with a worried look from the wagon seat.

"Yes, snakes like the rocks," Margret called out. She tightened the reins and shifted herself as the wagon lurched over a rock.

Katrine hated rattlesnakes. Even though it was autumn, the last week had been warm and dry, and they had seen a rattlesnake on the trail the day before. Two people had been bitten during their journey. But her wish to be the first to see their destination overcame her fear.

"Come, Mia. We just have to watch where we put our hands and feet." Katrine remembered her papa's advice. A dull ache briefly washed over her. She had not seen her parents or her brother, Erik, for nearly a month, not since they left them behind when the wagon train headed north on the old Jeffrey road. Katrine didn't understand all the reasons the men decided to leave her family. She knew some feared the illness that her mother had—several people had died, and some believed her mother had the same illness and would cause others to become ill. Others said it was the impending bad weather. In the end, her father had sent her ahead with the Olafsons. She swallowed. Surely her family would soon catch up, maybe a day or two after they reached Fort Boise, now just beyond the rise. Soon everything would be all right again, wouldn't it?

Katrine dashed ahead, skimming over the sharp stones and thorny brush. When she reached the sandstone, she scrambled upward. At nine years old, she was quick and strong. She pushed a wisp of light blonde hair away from her eyes, trying to tuck it back into her braid. Her papa had always told her she had unruly hair. "But that's to tame those blue eyes and freckles of yours," he said. "Otherwise some boy will come courting you, and you won't be Papa's little girl any longer." Her mama told her to wear her bonnet to tend her hair, but Katrine rarely did. Shortly, she stood bouncing on her toes in her green-checkered dress atop the rock, straining to see.

"Can you see? Can you see?" the younger, seven-year-old Mia called from the foot of the rock.

"Yes! I can see." Joy flooded Katrine. White canvas tents and a couple of log buildings stood scattered along a broad, silvery river. And there were trees! Trees everywhere. Most had lost their leaves with the changing season, but some still shone green and gold and orange.

"I want to see." Mia began climbing up, her slender hands and feet finding a grip along the cracks, hoisting herself up like a pine squirrel.

Katrine took Mia's hand and pulled her the remaining distance to the top. Mia's bonnet had become askew, and Katrine promptly helped her retie it. Similar to Katrine, Mia wore her hair in a single blonde braid down her back. She had fewer freckles than Katrine had, but that was because she always wore her bonnet. Mrs. Olafson frequently reminded Katrine of that as well.

"There, see." Katrine spun Mia around, jumping up and down, pointing out the vista. Mia danced with her.

"We can see the camp!" Katrine shouted, waving back toward Mia's parents. "There are tents, and mules, and people."

Sven waved. "You girls just be careful." Similar to most of the Swedish men, Sven was broad shouldered and built solid. "Don't you go falling off."

Katrine liked Mia's parents—Mr. Olafson with crinkly lines beside his watery blue eyes, light sandy hair, and rugged hands, and Mrs. Olafson with her slightly darker sandy-blonde hair. Similar to the other Swedish women, she wore it braided and pinned up. Mrs. Olafson was stouter than Katrine's mother was, but then Katrine's mother was slender and had been ill. Just as her mother did, however, Mrs. Olafson often hugged Katrine and Mia to her ample bosom.

4

"We shall be there one day soon—just you wait and see," Margret always encouraged.

Katrine gazed in awe at the panorama that unfolded beyond her perch. Columns of smoke rose into the late-October air from the camps that spread under a line of trees bordering the sparkling river. Golds and russets painted the hills above. Deep purple and blue shadows marked the trees and hollows. An endless blue sky spread above her. Miraculously, from an empty sagebrush desert, they had emerged onto a wooded river valley.

The Olafsons' wagon reached the sandstone outcrop and passed below Katrine's vantage point, the mules plodding on, following the faint wagon trail that angled downward toward the valley. The Eklunds' wagon followed closely behind with Mrs. Eklund holding baby Robert. Other wagons crept into view, topping the sagebrush-covered hills farther behind, steadily heading toward camp on the Boise River.

Katrine scrambled back down, helping Mia down the last few feet. They chased after their wagon.

One of the outriders came trotting back toward them, shouting, "There she is, folks. Fort Boise!"

Sven Olafson waved his broad-brimmed hat and cheered as the man rode past toward the line of wagons behind. "We be coming in now, Mama." He waved at Margret and gathered the two girls to himself as they came running up.

Cheering rippled down the line. Mules surged against their traces, and the wagons jerked forward at a quicker pace.

Katrine hurried along, anxious and excited, and then she paused, plagued by memories of the past months. At first the journey had been exciting—a grand adventure. Her family was one of thirteen Swedish families that had joined a larger wagon train headed west. At first, the Swedes had talked excitedly about Washington Territory and the high mountain valley to where they headed. "You will believe you're back in Sweden," Nils Adolphson, the man who had found the valley, had written to them. But their excitement had been tempered by the journey, and for Katrine it had become a lifetime of trials.

She had endured the journey. Five months was incomprehensible to her at the beginning. She had no concept of the distance or the difficulties they would face. Her new home was always just beyond the horizon. It was always the next valley. But always at the end of the day after the wagons had camped, there remained another day's journey ahead.

Katrine and the children, including her brother, Erik, had helped along the way wherever they could. They had fetched water and gathered buffalo chips or twisted grass to burn; they had gathered greens and berries for the evening meals; and they had tended fires and watched the livestock. They had also played when they could. They had captured small animals—mostly the boys did, little grass snakes and toads—and tried to keep them as pets. One time the children had come across a fox den. While the wagons lumbered past, they had watched the kits tumbling about in the grass, nipping at each other, chasing their tails, until the line of wagons had passed from view. Then the children ran to catch up. One of the outriders met them coming back and gave them all tarnation for dillydallying. "Wild Indians could have scalped you. Or worse, they could have carried you off and made you their slaves."

The adventure had clouded when a family lost its wagon at an early river crossing and had turned back. Katrine still remembered the saddened faces of their two children. Shortly afterward, some families began losing livestock—oxen, mules, cows. Her papa explained that it was expected, but when her family lost one of their oxen, it became necessary to dump most of their possessions and lighten the load. It saddened Katrine to see their belongings left alongside the trail. Moreover, with the remaining ox and their workhorse pulling their wagon, her family frequently fell behind. Her papa had talked about getting mules when they neared their destination, but it was never to be.

Fort Boise was not the wagon train's final destination. Katrine understood they would meet Mr. Adolphson there, and he would lead them north to the high valley. Although Katrine had become good friends with his three children, she had never met Mr. Adolphson. She was curious to see the man who had convinced everyone to come west.

She shivered. They should have arrived at Fort Boise a month ago and would have except for the bad weather and illnesses that had overtaken the train.

They reached the outskirts of the camp. Katrine knew not to expect much. Mr. Adolphson had written that there were at most a few tents and a handful of prospectors in the area. However, this meant little to Katrine. She bubbled with excitement. She could see horses and wagons and other families. Voices drifted to her ears. There were a couple of log buildings. Dogs barked, and the odor of something wonderful cooking wafted to her.

The captain of their wagon train, Jack Slade, rode back along the line of wagons.

"Turn out here where we still have grass for the stock. Much farther, there won't be any."

Katrine knew feed for the stock was always a concern—that and water and wood. She and her brother had become accustomed to helping their papa find good areas with water and grass to picket the stock. She now helped Mr. Olafson do the same.

Slade stopped in front of Sven Olafson. "I'm taking the rest of the train across the Snake River in a few days. If you Swedes are still insisting on heading north, I'd think hard on it. I can help you find a camp nearby for winter, but I wouldn't chance going north, not with the recent snow."

Sven ran a hand through his bleached hair and reset his sweat-stained hat. "I'll consider what you've said, Mr. Slade," he said. The trail miles now etched Sven's face, and as was true for all the emigrants, he could stand for some decent meals.

"Wintering here will be difficult," continued Slade. "There isn't much in the way of provisions. Your cattle and mules are going to have a go of it."

"*Ja.*" Sven nodded. He glanced around, squinting. Sagebrush and short grasses covered the hills. "I wager it's better here for the stock than where we've been the last month on that lava rock."

"But not better than the Oregon country." Slade tightened his reins. "That valley you're so set on can't be much different from the farmland farther west."

Sven shrugged. "It's up to the others." He nodded at some of the Swedish families that were now pulling their wagons out around his.

"Think on it," Slade countered. He turned his horse and continued riding down the line of wagons.

Harald Lundgren and Jens Andreasson, two of the Swedish boys about a year older than Katrine, ran toward her.

"Come with us," hollered Harald.

As did all the Swedish boys, they both wore light wool trousers and long-sleeved, banded-collar shirts with suspenders. Harald also wore a dark brown vest and a flat cap. Both boys were barefoot and would be so until the ground froze.

"We're going to have us a look around," said Harald. He chased after Jens in the direction of the buildings.

As if the boys were pied pipers, Katrine grabbed Mia and chased after them. Of the boys who were nearest to Katrine in age—Harald, Jens, and Björn—she liked Harald the best.

"You girls, mind your manners," Margret called out.

"Yes, ma'am," said Katrine. As had her own mother, Mrs. Olafson watched out for her. Katrine swallowed at the memory. Jens's bobbing blond head brought another image. Erik had light blond hair and vivid blue eyes, more vivid than her own. Katrine blinked. She could still see her brother waving *adjö*, standing back on the windswept plain with Papa, growing smaller until she could no longer make out either of them except as small black spots next to their wagon. She missed her brother—almost thirteen now. He had watched out for her most of all.

Katrine shook her thoughts and followed the other children as they wandered about the camp, greeting the people they met. They slipped into one of the low-slung buildings.

"You folks just arriving?" A rough-cut man with scraggly whiskers greeted them. "You must be that emigrant train that was stranded for a while."

"Yes, sir," Harald promptly replied.

Harald seemed older than his ten years and was always quite proper. Unlike the other Swedish children who were blond haired and blue eyed, Harald had darker hair and hazel eyes. Katrine credited Harald's mother, who was English.

"You're mighty lucky you went the direction you did on the old trail. Savages attacked some settlers and burned their wagons near Devil's Gate. At least ten people were murdered."

Katrine stared at the man, swallowing hard. The *old trail* was Katrine's nightmare. That was when her mama had become ill and her family had been left behind.

"'Course it wasn't as tragic as the Utters and Van Ornums a couple of seasons ago. After savages murdered a bunch of them, some that escaped, starved to death. The survivors resorted to eating the dead ones just so's they could keep themselves alive. Ten out of forty-four souls made it."

Katrine trembled. She and the others had heard the stories. This man seemed to be taking delight in trying to scare them.

"No, sir, if you hadn't of followed that old trail, you might have

8

been the train that got attacked. The main Snake River route ain't safe anymore. Maybe when more soldiers get here, come spring." He scratched his whiskers, squinting. "Yes, you folks are mighty lucky."

Katrine squeezed her eyes shut, trying not to remember. Maybe the same Indians who had murdered the settlers had found and killed her family. Maybe that was why Mama and Papa and Erik had not caught up. Her world darkened into blackness.

"Now what kind of goods can I show you?" The man drummed his fingers on a barrelhead and stared directly, it seemed, at Katrine.

"N-nothing, sir," Katrine mumbled. She began backing away, pulling on Mia. There was nothing in this man's store. It did not hold dresses or hats or shoes. Instead, it held a strange assortment of gear, which mostly looked like cast-off items that he had found along the emigrant trail, and it now held a terrible nightmare from *back there*.

Still trembling, Katrine ran into the other building. Harald and Jens had already found their way inside.

This man seemed more pleasant and welcomed them. "Be sure to tell your folks I still have supplies. Won't be much come a couple of days though. I'll be heading out myself."

Katrine could smell some foodstuffs, although the odor was not rich. There were a couple of near-empty crocks of pickles and a few eggs. Shriveled potatoes covered the bottom of a basket. Beside it was another basket with half a dozen apples. A few onions lay among loose husks in a third container. Despite the dismal showings, Katrine's mouth began to water. Anything would be a welcome change from cornmeal and beans, and compared to what remained in their wagons, the food was considerable. There were also bags of flour and canisters of sugar and chunks of lard—all staples that they would need.

Katrine's heart caught. She squeezed Mia's hand and pointed. Near a kerosene lantern stood a tall glass jar that contained a dozen or more sticks of brightly colored candy. She sighed. It was doubtful that the Olafsons would buy her a piece, and even if her parents had been there, they could not have afforded such a luxury. She hoped that one of the children would get a piece and share it with the rest of them. She shivered. Of all she had seen, the candy made it seem that they had returned to civilization.

9

Chapter 2

BACK AT THE wagon, Katrine and Mia bubbled with excitement at all they had seen. Margret, now wearing her patchwork apron over her gray dress, busied herself with supper, nodding as the girls talked. After a time, Sven came into the firelight and gave Margret a quick kiss.

"You're later than usual." Margret pushed a spoon through the thick stew.

"We had much to discuss, and I had to check on the stock." Sven sat near the fire. "Even with a number of travelers around, there seems to be more Indian activity. A few settlers have lost horses, and there have been attacks on the main trail. I understand now why Mr. Slade wanted to go the old northern route. A few days after we turned north, some wagons were attacked, and a number of emigrants were killed."

Katrine paused with the dishes and cooking utensils that she and Mia carried from the wagon box. The flood of unsettling images was rekindled. Trembling, she set down a plate next to a cup that Mia had placed.

Sven smiled. "You two make me wish I had a son to help me with *my* chores." He raised his eyes and nodded. "Mama, you have life too easy."

Sven held out his arms for a hug, and Katrine and Mia fell into them.

"Ah, but my son wouldn't be as pretty as my little angel." He ran his finger down Mia's nose.

A pang washed over Katrine. Her papa had called her his little sunshine and poked her dimples.

Margret handed Sven a plate of stewed turnips with pieces of beef. "And we're thankful to have Katrine for a while as well."

Katrine caught the look in Mrs. Olafson's eyes. No one talked about Katrine's family any longer, but now her family would be along shortly, wouldn't they? An ache rose inside her chest.

Sven sopped up some of the stew with some biscuit. "It is mighty good to have something besides beans and corn bread, it is."

Presently, he sat back. "Mr. Slade has some concerns."

Margret set aside her plate. "Should the girls be listening?"

"They can hear." Sven glanced at Katrine and Mia.

Something strange moved inside Katrine's stomach.

"As you can see, there's not much here yet. The real effort will take place come spring. All they have are some city blocks laid out next to the fort—Boise City they're calling it." Sven laughed. "I assure you, it will be a long time until that day."

Sven filled and lit his pipe. "Some of our party wants to continue north to the valley, but Mr. Slade is hard over that if we go this late in the season, we will be inviting disaster. He offered again to take us with the rest of his train west to the Oregon country, but if we don't accompany his train, he advises we winter here." Sven clenched his pipe. "There are no supplies here to speak of, and the cost is high for what there is."

Katrine did not understand all the reasons for heading west, but she understood that they had started late in the season, considerably later than the other wagon trains. She remembered that the men argued about leaving, and they may not have done so except that her father had told them that it made no difference if they starved in Minnesota or starved out West.

"As much as my heart is set in going north, I see Mr. Slade's wisdom," Sven said. "Even if the weather warms and we have a couple of weeks, we won't be able to build cabins and get in enough hay to see our stock through the deep snow."

"Then we shall wait to see what Mr. Adolphson thinks," Margret said.

"Except by the time he gets here, Slade may be gone."

Sven raised his arms for the girls and pulled them close. "Are you two willing to stay here this winter so we can go to the valley next spring?"

Faintly, Mia nodded her head.

"Yes!" shouted Katrine. She knew Mia didn't fully understand, but she guessed that Mr. Olafson was not really asking Mia. If they went on to Oregon, there would be no chance of Katrine reuniting with her family.

Margret wiped her hands on her apron. "But how do we survive the winter any better here?"

"We have a little coin that I put aside for supplies. We can hunt and fish. Slade says there should be sufficient graze for the stock a short distance upstream. Come spring, more packers and soldiers will be here. They'll be bringing in goods and working on the fort. At that point, we can resupply to some extent." Sven shook his head. "For sure it shall not be easy."

Margret bit her lip. "Are any of our party going on to Oregon?"

Sven slowly let out a puff of smoke. "I believe the Nilssons and Öbergs are going."

Katrine swallowed. She knew their children.

Margret's lips tightened. "I do pray Mr. Adolphson arrives soon so we might have a better idea."

The following day, a tall man with unkempt blond hair and a scraggly beard and wearing a wide-brimmed black hat and coat rode into camp. He led a couple of heavily packed mules. Katrine wondered at the ruckus until the man swung down and boomed out, "Now where's that Adolphson family?"

Nils Adolphson, the man who had convinced the Swedes to come west, his washed blue eyes darting around, had arrived at their camp.

Never had Katrine seen such joy. Astrid Adolphson kept hugging and kissing her husband. His children, Ingrid, who was Katrine's age, and seven-year-old Pelle, jumped and danced around for his attention. Only Lars, who was eleven, stood off a bit, fidgeting, seemingly not certain of his father whom he had not seen for almost two years. Lars had helped bring his family's wagon across the country, although another man, Jon Stromback, had been hired for that purpose.

Lars reminded Katrine of her brother, Erik. Unlike the other children, Lars seemed more serious and stuck to his tasks. Both Lars and Erik had just begun growing out of boyhood. People already said Lars would be tall and slender like his father.

At last, Ingrid and Pelle began settling down, and Mrs. Adolphson, who was also slender and taller than most of the women, backed away from her husband. Mr. Adolphson embraced Lars and said how proud he was of the job he had done. An ache rose inside Katrine. Her brother had done much the same for her parents. Why could this not be her papa and mama and Erik?

She squeezed her eyes, trying to see them but caught only fleeting glimpses. It scared her.

There was general good celebration in the camp that night. Katrine heard some talking about continuing to the valley again. Surely they could reach the valley before the heavier snows came.

Nils cautioned them. "It's at least two thousand feet higher, and I came through some pretty good drifts about halfway down the canyon. It's going to be difficult getting our wagons up there as it is, much less getting them up there through snow. Besides, the rest of winter is fast on its way, and that valley will get six feet."

He continued in a preacher-like voice, "No, we'll be safe here. There are soldiers about, and they should dissuade any Indian attacks."

"What, half a dozen men?" questioned Carl Isberg.

"More will be here come spring. They're coming in to protect the wagons coming across the Snake River route. They are also to watch for Southern sympathizers attempting to take gold out to the South."

"Have you looked around? There's nothing here to get us through a winter," said Klas Jonasson. "What makes you think things will get that much better by spring?"

"I've seen more gold seekers and settlers in the last month than in the entire time I was in the valley. A rush is on. Up north there have been strikes in Pierce, Elk City, and Florence. Now I'm hearing news of a major strike northeast of us in a place called Boise Basin." Nils straightened his hat. "Mark my words. Men and supplies will be flooding through here all winter. We're here at the right time. We'll have plenty to get us through. This winter will pass in no time, and we'll be on our way before you know it."

The Swedes turned about to each other, nodding. Katrine's spirits rose. It was decided. They were wintering, and the best thing—it would only be a matter of a few days until her family would be along.

"So what have you been doing all this time? Did you get our cabins built?" Gustaf Andreasson asked, laughingly. Mr. Andreasson was a rather large, gangly man with deep-set eyes. Except for his children, he struck Katrine as someone to avoid.

"No, Gustaf, but I've been about the valley checking out what I think are the best tracts. Later, I can show you a map I've drawn up and explain what I think."

Cheering abounded. "So who gets first choice?"

"I was thinking of Jon Stromback for getting my family out here. And as I understand, he's been a help to all of you." Nils nodded toward a young man standing nearby.

Jon nodded. "Thank you, sir, but I won't be needing you to set aside a tract for me." He pushed nervously at his hat. "I've been thinking. I was sure pleased to help bring your family across and to help out where I could, but I think I'll be heading north to the goldfields."

Silence descended on the group. Katrine's heart sank. Mr. Stromback had been a favorite person whom she had come to care for. Not only did he help the Adolphsons, he had helped the Olafsons and her family as well, especially when they lost their livestock.

"I didn't want to push off until you got here, Mr. Adolphson, but I hear they're finding good gold in the Salmon River country. I figure now's my chance to get some ground before it's gone. You will understand."

Adolphson tightened his jaw but nodded. "If you are certain about this, go, but with the snow, I recommend you cross the Snake and then cross back into the Salmon River country. No one goes down the Snake River canyon unless it's by raft. It's got to be over four hundred miles for you to go around."

"I've done some studying on it," Jon replied. "I still figure I'll be there long before you get to your valley."

"Maybe so," Nils said quietly. "I'll be sorry to see you go. You should know I had a fine piece of land picked out for you." He reached out and shook Jon's hand. "It's not too late."

"I'm obliged, but I've always had a hankering to try my hand at finding gold, and this seems to be my chance." Jon glanced around in the gathering dusk. "Mostly I just don't favor sitting here all winter. I wish you all well."

Katrine hung her head. Although he was eighteen or nineteen, Mr. Stromback sometimes called her his little sister. Now he was leaving them. Another knot grew in her belly. The joy of seeing Mr. Adolphson rejoin his family had suddenly evaporated.

Jon must have noticed. "Hey, little sister," he called to Katrine. "Come here."

Slowly she walked up to the man. At this moment, he acutely reminded her of Erik. He had always seemed to be looking out for her, like Erik had done, but especially after her family separated from the train.

"You just take care of everyone for me, now won't you?"

She nodded and gave him a hug.

"Maybe I'll visit sometime to see how you're all doing. Would that be all right?"

"When you do, I'll make you some rose hip tea." Katrine smiled.

She watched as Mr. Stromback turned his horse and mules away. Katrine remembered he had offered to stay back with her parents, but they had declined. Papa had said the others needed his help more.

Chapter 3

KATRINE WOKE TO see Mr. and Mrs. Olafson bundled up and seated near the fire a few feet from the shelter. They talked softly, but she could clearly hear their words in the crisp night air.

"I won't accept that this is a mistake," Sven said quietly. He patted Margret's hand. "Each day we have new problems, but each day we always solve them. We've come this far, you and I. We can go on."

Margret shook her head. "We've been blessed, Sven. But the others? How will they fare? Maybe we should all go on to Oregon as Mr. Slade has suggested. We wouldn't have to winter."

Katrine felt her world going black. She thought again of her family.

Sven slowly shook his head. "Look, I know we're relying on one man's word, but at least he has been true to his word. It wasn't Adolphson that made things go bad in Minnesota. Had we stayed, we would have been little more than indentured servants, owing our souls to Warling, relying on him to feed us and for hand-me-downs. I want my own life. Adolphson has been to the valley and says how fine it is. This will be a real opportunity to have land and to provide for ourselves since we've come to America."

"It didn't give the Backstroms a new opportunity … or the Stiles … or the Larsons," Margret said softly.

Katrine swallowed. A sickness had overtaken them near the Jeffrey cutoff. All four of the Backstrom family had died; Erik's friend, Mark Stiles, had died; and then her own mother had become ill.

"I do not disagree, but I have to believe there is purpose in God's plan, and that is why Katrine is with us." He glanced toward Katrine. She quickly closed her eyes.

Sven continued in a lower voice. "We all knew what we were up against before we left Minnesota. The Larsons and the others wanted this opportunity just as much as we did, and our misfortunes are no different from the others who have come this way. Rather, we have fared better than most."

Margret shook her head. "I just don't know, Sven. I can't help but fear that we will soon come up against something we can't overcome. And then what?"

Sven laughed softly. "Keep in mind, with the good Lord's blessings, you and I have managed to overcome everything we've come up against thus far. What, ten years together, you and me?" He leaned over and kissed Margret. "I'd say that gives us a good chance of facing the future."

Margret glanced in Katrine's direction. "Well, for Mia's sake and for Katrine's sake, I pray you are right."

"Margret, *älskling*, my dear, on this one I'm right." Sven rose. "Let's get us some sleep. We have much to do tomorrow."

In the morning, fourteen wagons continued west toward Oregon. Katrine watched as the Nilssons' and the Öbergs' wagons lurched into the line with the others. Eight of the original thirteen Swedish families remained near Fort Boise. They moved upriver for protection from the wind and to find better grass for their livestock. There they began constructing winter shelters. According to those who knew the country, there would be little snow, but it would be windy, and temperatures often dropped below zero.

Katrine surveyed the surrounding, stark hills. A few trees grew along the river and ran for short distances up the draws. The largest were cottonwoods with splintery wood and gnarly branches that clutched a few dull bronze leaves. Some alders and mountain maple grew intermixed with the cottonwoods. Thick clumps of willows choked the river bends and reached to seven or eight feet high, making it difficult to walk any distance along the river, especially for the children. Sagebrush carpeted the hills above the camp, its blue-gray hue contrasting with the pale amber grasses. Dense stands of dark fir, spruce, and pines covered the steep, snow-covered mountains farther above. She gazed toward the mountains. Come spring, that was the direction they would be headed.

Suitable timber for a cabin was scarce in the river bottom. Katrine helped drag brush to where Sven constructed a shelter against some downed cottonwoods. He draped it with the wagon cover. The floor was sod but soon turned to packed earth. It afforded moderate protection from the wind and recent rain and snow. It reminded Katrine of living in a brush pile. The other families were little better off, except for the

Adolphsons. They had found the remains of a trapper's cabin and fixed it up.

A couple of soldiers making their rounds visited the Olafsons and had coffee with them. One suggested to Sven that he improve his shelter.

"We get bad wind here, even in this valley."

The younger soldier introduced himself to Katrine and Mia and accompanied them while they gathered wood. "I'm Mathew. I come from Chicago."

"That's almost as far as us," Mia said. "We came from Minnesota."

Mathew whistled. "Yes, you've come a long way."

Katrine guessed Mathew could not be much older than seventeen or eighteen, maybe a little younger than Jon Stromback.

"Don't you wish you were back in Chicago with your family?" Katrine asked.

"With my family, yes, but not back East. I'd probably be fighting rebels somewhere. Besides, I like the frontier."

"We want to go to a valley where we can build cabins," Mia said. She pulled on a long piece of willow that was stuck in the mud.

Mathew grabbed it and pulled it free. "I 'spect you do." He laughed, studying Katrine and Mia. "You know, I have a sister who looks just like you two. Your parents are blessed to have such beautiful daughters."

Katrine blushed. "I'm not Mia's real sister. I don't have any sisters, but I might still have a brother." She cautioned herself from expressing any more hope.

Mathew raised his eyes. "*Might* have a brother?"

"Katrine's brother and parents are lost," Mia said.

"Oh." Mathew glanced back to where his companion sat with the Olafsons. "So these aren't your folks? You all look so very much alike."

"All Swedes look alike," Mia said. "We're all Nordic—blond hair and blue eyes, you know. Except the Lundgrens. Their mother is English."

Mathew laughed. "Yes, I suppose." He stood. "Please excuse me, ladies. I shall return to my business."

Katrine watched as he walked back toward the shelter. She wondered why she had told him about Erik. The soldiers visited for a while longer before saying goodbye.

"Our job this winter is to check on travelers," Mathew explained. "It won't be very difficult if we have such friendly families as yours."

After he left, Katrine whispered, "They should have been here by now."

Mia nodded. "Maybe in a little while."

Katrine's chores included gathering wood and bringing in water. Sometimes she went with Mr. Olafson to check on the stock. She did so, much more frequently than did Mia. Katrine believed it was because she was the oldest. Although they were always working, their tasks were somewhat easier than some of the other families'. The Olafsons had lost two mules and their cow on the journey and had fewer animals for which to care. Their surviving stock consisted of a riding horse and four mules. The horse was a mare named Boots. Two of the mules, Ornery and Jack, were riding mules, with Jack being the more difficult of the two. The other two mules, Olga and June, were strictly work animals but had been plow broken. Although nearly all the families had lost livestock, a few still had some cattle and chickens and even a couple of dogs, all of which needed to survive the coming winter and the forthcoming trip to the valley. But once there, Katrine knew those families would then have milk and butter and eggs. The Olafsons would not. However, Mr. Olafson never allowed the lack of stock to dampen his spirits. He just said, "I'm more of a farmer. I can grow what we need to eat. We'll get another cow in proper time."

On Sundays, Katrine joined with the Olafsons and the others at the Adolphsons'. The men had added a lean-to under which everyone could gather. Nils led the group in a prayer and then read a passage from the Bible. They sang a few Swedish hymns, and then the women set out a communal dinner, often the most food offered at one meal for the entire week.

Not everyone contributed the same to the dinner, but everyone brought something. Katrine was proud when Mrs. Olafson brought a duck or fish that Mr. Olafson had caught in addition to her *knäckebröd*, crisp rye bread. Katrine and Mia sometimes brought peppery-tasting yellowcress that they gathered near a small spring along the riverbank.

After dinner, they shared stories, and on days when their spirits seemed the lowest, Magnus Lundgren brought out his violin and played lively Swedish melodies. Magnus had a lighter build than most of the Swedes and a clean, angular face. He walked with a limp from having been kicked by a mule. It didn't keep him from tapping his foot in time to his music. His wife, Louise, was a brunette, which is why their two children, Harald and Emma, had brown hair and hazel eyes. Katrine thought both Harald and Emma seemed more reserved than the other children, but they spoke the clearest English and were always the best dressed.

Tonight, Harald and seven-year-old Emma sang "Uti vår hage" ("In Our Pasture").

Uti vår hage där växa blå bär
Kom hjärtansfröjd!
Vill du mig något, så träffas vi där
Kom liljor och akvileja, kom rosor och salivia!
Kom ljuva krusmynta, kom hjärtansfröjd!

In our pasture grows blueberries
Come joy from the heart
If you need me for something, we will meet there!
Come lilies and aquilegia, come roses and salvia!
Come sweet crisp-leafed mint, come joy from the heart!

The others soon joined in. Katrine loved the song. It made her think of the valley to where they were headed and of the berries and flowers that she and Mia would soon be gathering.

And then Magnus, limping about in the circle, would take up a livelier tune. The Swedes soon had no choice but to get up and dance.

After the songs and dancing, Nils Adolphson brought out a bottle of *brännvin,* a distilled drink from grain or potatoes, and passed it among the men. He always offered the first sip to Gustaf Andreasson and then quickly retrieved the flask and passed it along. Andreasson protested.

"Ah, Gustaf," explained Nils, "too much of a good thing lessens a man's appreciation and fosters disdain."

"Whoever decided that has never met me," Gustaf loudly complained.

Mr. Andreasson frightened Katrine a little. He was a gangly man with dull blond hair and bushy whiskers. He had heavy eyebrows with deeply set eyes that reminded her of a scraggly wolf. In contrast, his wife, Olga, was small and somewhat plump with a small, round face and darting eyes. Unlike them, their son Jens was slender with dusty blond hair and bluish-gray eyes. Similar to most of the children, he had freckles strung across the bridge of his nose. He was quiet and often glanced around nervously as if he were about to be scolded for something. The Andreassons' other two children, a girl, Barbro, and a five-year-old boy, Joran, were like any flaxen-haired, blue-eyed Swedes. Both were talkative imps.

Katrine and the children frequently gathered under the lean-to and allowed the adults room inside the cabin where they could talk. They played games and told stories about Swedish trolls and elves. Anna Wikstrom, who at twelve years old was the oldest of the Swedish children, seemed to know the most stories, and everyone insisted on her taking an extra turn. Katrine envied Anna. She had long, reddish-blonde hair and blue-green eyes. Everyone blamed Mrs. Wikstrom's auburn hair for her children's reddish tint. In turn, Emma Wikstrom blamed the Vikings. Katrine liked how Anna sometimes braided her hair above her ears. Maybe she appeared more beautiful than the other girls did because she, like Lars, was growing up. Anna treated Katrine kindly, and Katrine tried to emulate her.

Katrine whispered to Mia, "Anna can help teach us when we get to the valley. She knows a lot."

Mia agreed. "Björn knows good stories too."

Katrine glanced at Björn, Anna's younger brother. He was a couple of months older than Harald and Jens. His blond hair had the same reddish tint as Anna's, but his eyes were vivid blue, reminding Katrine of her brother, Erik's, eyes. Björn also had high-arching, dark eyebrows, probably from his father, Anton, who had thick, bushy eyebrows that accentuated his chiseled face. Björn's eyebrows gave him the impression of being pleasantly surprised and interested in whatever someone was saying, whether true or not.

"Björn knows them because of his mother," Katrine said. She liked Mrs. Wikstrom because she remembered so much about Sweden; however, Mrs. Wikstrom always ended her stories with, "But here in America, you can do all of that and much, much more."

This day, Emma Wikstrom cut up and shared a couple of withered apples with the children. "Soon we will be in the valley and someday have our own apple trees. Remember the story about the apple tree." She smoothed her apron and sat back against the side of the Adolphsons' cabin.

"In Wärmland there was a poor farmer boy whose family had but one apple tree. Each year the apple tree blossomed and grew many apples. Each autumn, as his wise mother had instructed, the boy left hanging an apple for the birds, an apple for the barnyard elf, and an apple for the tree. When the boy brought in the apples, his mother would say, 'These are wonderful, bright red apples. Did you remember to leave an apple hanging for the birds, and for the barnyard elf, and for the tree?' 'Yes, Mother, I have done so,' said the boy.

"But one autumn there was even less food. The boy was very hungry and picked all the apples. His mother asked if he had left an apple for the birds, an apple for the barnyard elf, and an apple for the tree. 'Alas, Mother, we are very hungry. I picked all the apples.' The mother was very sad. 'The birds will be hungry and not come back and sing. The barnyard elf will not watch over our animals. And the tree will forget how to grow its fruit.'

"The next spring, the tree put out but three blossoms and set but three apples. The boy and his mother were very, very hungry, but the boy left the three apples hanging on the tree: one for the birds, one for the barnyard elf, and one for the tree. The mother and the boy ate mice and spruce needles and drank birch tea. In the spring, the apple tree was again filled with dozens and dozens of blossoms, and that fall there were many wonderful bright red apples. From that winter on and forevermore, the boy left three apples hanging, one for the birds, one for the barnyard elf, and one for the tree. This is why today you see on apple trees in Sweden three apples after the autumn harvest."

Katrine squeezed Mia to herself, whispering, "When we have apple trees in the valley—and we shall—we will be sure to leave three apples."

Mia asked, "Will we have a barnyard elf?"

"For sure. I think they are riding with us in the wagons and just can't wait to get to their new home."

Mia giggled.

In her mind's eye, Katrine could see the white and pink apple blossoms filling dozens of trees in the magical valley where they were heading. She sniffed the night air, making herself believe it was the fragrance of apple blossoms and not the sting of snow. How she longed to bite into a bright red apple and taste its snappy flavor.

Days later, the wind bit sharply as Katrine wandered along the river. She watched the water rushing over a fallen log. A pair of ducks busily paddled around in the eddy, dipping for food. She felt happy to be in camp near the others, but there also remained a hollow feeling, made worse by the fact they were here and her family had not caught up. Surely they would soon reach them. Each day she expected her family to come into the camp, but each day ended in empty disappointment.

Lars approached Katrine. She thought that he looked and acted

21

much like his father. He was tall for his age and more direct in his mannerisms than the other children. He also had darker eyes and darker hair, perhaps because he was a little older.

"My father and Mr. Olafson are looking to speak with you, Katrine."

He sounded more somber than usual. Katrine's heart began racing. She wondered why. Maybe she had become too much of a burden for the Olafsons, and they had other plans for her.

She followed Lars back toward the Adolphsons' cabin.

Sven sat with Margret on some freight boxes, clasping her hands in his, nervously kneading them. Nils Adolphson and Anton Wikstrom stood nearby, quietly talking with two soldiers. No one noticed Katrine.

"What would they have hoped to gain by going north?" Nils asked.

"Either Jon was confused or he was trying to shake the Indians," Anton replied. He snugged his coat.

Katrine stopped, frozen in her step. Her breath caught in her chest. Lars hesitated as well. He glanced at Katrine.

"Going north, they would have eventually run into the Salmon River. No one's gone that route." Nils turned in Katrine's direction, widening his eyes when he noticed her. He frowned but beckoned her to come forward.

Katrine forced her steps forward and reached the soldiers and the Olafsons. Their strained eyes sought hers.

Nils introduced one of the soldiers. "This is Sergeant Brönhaus."

The man straightened and bowed briefly to Katrine. He cleared his throat. "One of our tasks is to assist travelers and see to their safety. You should know, Miss Larson, that a small detachment of men rode back to search for your family."

Clammy ice swept over Katrine. The sergeant's eyes had already told the story.

"I'm sorry, Miss Larson. We found where your party split up. The markings were still there. We found where your family's wagon turned north. We spent several days searching. Where your family was headed ... toward the Salmon River canyon ... They could not have made it." Sergeant Brönhaus glanced down.

Stinging needles washed over Katrine. She choked, unable to breathe.

"You have our sincerest condolences."

Sven beckoned to Katrine to come near. "You should know this, Katrine: we love you. We will always love you."

Katrine could not bear the look in the Olafsons' eyes. She could not move toward Mr. Olafson. She stared at the dirt. The hope she had nursed over the past weeks splintered into nothingness and skittered away into a black void. Everything good she had tried to imagine now seemed utterly foolish.

Katrine did not believe she was crying—she had cried until nothing remained inside her after realizing her parents and Erik were gone, but now she noticed tears splashing onto her hands. She trembled, unable to speak or move.

She felt Mr. Olafson's arm about her shoulders. "We want you to stay with us, Katrine."

"B-but they didn't find our wagon," she choked out.

"No, Miss Larson, we didn't," Sergeant Brönhaus replied. "We know that country. It would be impossible."

"Then Mama and Papa and Erik might still be out there." Her sobs filled the air. "E-Erik said he would come for me. H-he promised."

She quavered, shaking against Mr. Olafson's strong arms as he clasped her into himself, squeezing until she calmed.

"There was another thing, Miss Larson. I am very sorry. Please try to understand. There were pony tracks along the trail ... Indians."

Images of Indians swarming over her mama and papa and Erik, cutting them to ribbons, like the man said they did to the settlers on the emigrant trail, washed over Katrine. She shook harder, a throbbing pain filling her, until she choked out her words. "But no one found them," she whispered. She refused to give in. The images blurred into a dull red light. She tried to focus on Mr. Olafson. "M-maybe they're wintering like we are. They'll find us in the spring."

"My condolences for your great loss, Miss Larson. If there is anything else for which we can be of assistance, please inform us." Sergeant Brönhaus bowed slightly, replaced his headgear, and with the other soldier, turned away.

"Katrine—" Sven began but quieted. "You will always have a home with us for as long as you shall wish."

Margret pulled Katrine to her bosom, smoothed her hair, and held her into her warmth. "God heals all things, Katrine. This too, he shall heal."

But Katrine believed this would be impossible, even for God.

Chapter 4

INSTINCTIVELY THE OTHER children tried to console Katrine. Even at a young age, children accepted that people died. A few had lost parents. Some had lost one or more siblings, usually as babies. They knew the Backstrom family had all died and that the Stiles had lost a son, which was why the surviving Stiles family had continued on to Oregon. None of the children mentioned Katrine's parents or brother, now presumed dead. Instead, they went about trying to find fun and helping their own parents wherever they could.

Katrine withdrew into a world of blackness. She did her chores while shrouded in numbness. She had to live. She knew she was blessed. She had Mia for a sister, and the Olafsons were her parents. Other orphans never again had families. She looked in the direction of the Olafsons to where they busied themselves with dinner. She would always try to be grateful. She would address them as Mama Olafson and Papa Olafson, but they were not *Mama* and *Papa*. Despite what the soldiers had said, her real parents and brother might still be out there.

She found peace when the families gathered on Sundays. The songs and stories helped. She dreamed of the valley where they would build a cabin. Something told her she would grow up there, and occasionally she pictured her real Mama and Papa and Erik meeting her there—a little something like heaven. Instinctively she knew it was not good for her to harbor such dim hopes, but her hopes comforted her.

During Sunday meeting while the children played, the adults gathered under the Adolphsons' lean-to discussing how everyone fared. The cold, not the lack of food, was their greatest concern. They had sufficient beans and cornmeal, and there was abundant game—mule deer, ducks, and trout. The deer came to the river each evening, and it was not difficult to kill one of the curious creatures.

But wild game had no fat, and everyone knew they needed fresh vegetables. The stems and leaves of cow parsnip and salsify had withered, making it difficult to find and dig roots or bulbs. When able, the children picked some remaining rose hips and gathered yellowcress.

Katrine took Mia and wandered up a sunny draw near the camp to where withered rose bushes were yet covered with bright red-orange pods.

"There are oodles and oodles," squealed Mia. She plucked the bright pods and gathered them into her apron pockets.

"We might even make jelly," Katrine said. "Not all of them have frozen. Some are plump and fat." They reminded Katrine of tiny reddish-orange apples.

They picked until the sun was low and then hurried home to the shelter. Margret excitedly hugged them. "We shall be able to make tea every night and still have some to share." She fixed her apron. "We shall start preparing them at once."

Margret sat at the makeshift table and dumped the rose hips into a large pile. "First, we pinch off the stems, and then we split each one and take out its seeds. After we get them all done, we can lay them out in the sun to dry. Of course we will boil some of them up for *nyponsoppa*. We don't have many potatoes, but I can spare some of the turnips. It will be a fine soup."

"I can't wait!" exclaimed Mia.

"What about jelly?" Katrine asked. Rose hip jelly with corncakes was better than rose hip soup.

Margret shook her head. "Perhaps next season. We need to save our sugar for our tea." She split open a rose hip and carefully scraped out the yellowish seeds. Katrine and Mia joined her, taking the rose hips one by one, splitting them, and laying the red-orange husks aside in a small growing pile. Before they had even finished a few dozen tiny pods, the daylight had faded.

"The rest will have to wait until morning," Margret said.

The fading light was also the signal for supper. Katrine was responsible for tending the cooking fire and bringing in water. She left the shelter and surveyed the diminishing woodpile, shaking her head. Cottonwood burned rapidly. Sagebrush burned even more quickly. Neither made good coals for cooking. Dead willow burned the longest, but she could rarely find a piece larger than two inches thick. She walked upriver a distance and finally found a dead clump and dragged it back.

It had grown dark, and Katrine shivered. Stars speckled the horizon. Papa Olafson had still not returned from whatever kept him. As usual, a cold wind had kicked up, bringing with it the smell of wood smoke mixed with musty pine and river water. Each evening, the wind gathered upriver and then came rushing down, buffeting their shelter, testing the fire, and filling the shelter with smoke. Katrine threw some of the willow wood onto the fire. The fire was too far from the shelter to bring much warmth, but if it were closer, the smoke would be unbearable.

Mama Olafson came outside with her green shawl wrapped about her shoulders and put the teakettle on to heat. "Where is your wrap?" she asked. "You had best move along inside, Katrine. It's getting chilly."

Katrine knew the shelter was not much warmer inside. Despite that Papa Olafson was a skilled carpenter, without wood and almost no time, he had been able to do little more than erect a crude brush structure and cover it with their wagon canvas. And despite the layers of brush that Katrine had helped weave into the shelter, it did little to halt the cold wind. They shivered even on sunny days.

Sven came into the shelter and pulled off his coat. "It will be a cold one tonight, it will." He stamped his feet.

They had a few precious candles for light at night and burned them only briefly to see while they ate their evening meal. Winter darkness came early at this latitude and lasted more than fourteen hours. With no light by which to see or do anything, they went to bed. Katrine took solace in knowing the summer would have longer light.

This evening, they heated some river rocks and rolled them to the foot of their blankets. The wind had died down, and Katrine curled up with Mia. Still she felt chilly. About midnight, Mia woke Katrine with her shivering and complaining that she was cold. Katrine tried to bundle her closer to herself but with little improvement. The cold seeped up from the ground, increasingly intense until finally she could no longer sleep. She huddled shivering, watching the stars through the gaps in the shelter.

"Can't you sleep?" Margret asked. She must have noticed from where she and Sven lay on the other side of the shelter.

"N-no, I'm cold." Katrine's teeth chattered.

Margret came to her bed with some meal sacks. "Here, these might help a little."

Katrine scooted back down next to Mia while Mama Olafson laid the sacks over her and patted them down.

"Better?"

"It's the ground," Katrine whispered. "The cold comes from the ground."

"Slide them under you."

Wriggling around, Katrine got the sacks underneath her. "It's a little better. Thanks."

Margret returned to Sven's side. Katrine listened to them whispering for a moment but could not make out what was said.

Katrine woke in the morning with her head throbbing. The sky was gray and overcast.

"Snow clouds," Sven said.

By midmorning the wind kicked up and the snow began. It blasted against the side of the shelter, whistling as it pushed through the gaps, piling snow in areas across the floor. The four of them huddled together.

"Well, Mama, on a day like this, I'm figuring you won't be able to cook. Maybe it will pass quickly."

"We shall have cold corn bread then," Margret said.

"Can't we build a fire inside?" Katrine wondered.

"If we can keep from getting smoked out and from catching the shelter on fire, we might," Sven said. "The Indians have fires inside their tepees."

"I think it is worth the risk," Margret said. "We'll just be freezing otherwise."

Sven pulled on his coat. "We shall try. I'll get some wood and water."

"I can get the water." Katrine took the wooden pail. It was her chore. She followed Papa Olafson outside into the biting wind and snow. She pulled her scarf about her nose and ears, but the wind whistled through.

"Nippy, isn't it?" Sven pulled his own scarf tighter and headed upriver.

Overnight, ice had locked most of the river into a silent sheet of greenish gray. Snow scudded in twirling bursts across its surface. A small opening remained below a rock where the water ran quick and curled back on itself in white bubbles. Katrine tried to push the lip of her bucket down to catch the water. It suddenly caught and quickly filled. She pulled back and slipped, sliding partially into the water. Frantically, she sat back, pulling free. The bucket bobbed onto its side. Dismayed, Katrine watched as it floated beyond her reach and wedged against the far side of the opening. She had to get it. She shivered from the stinging cold. Her dress was soaked and now beginning to freeze. She found a willow and reached for the bucket, tapping it, agonizingly coaxing it closer to where she could reach it. It held only a couple of inches of water.

She quickly scrambled back to their shelter with the near-empty bucket, her hands shaking from the numbing cold.

"You're wet!" Margret exclaimed. "Get your shoes and dress off. Mia, grab those blankets."

Shortly, Sven came inside with a bundle of willows. He smiled and began laying a small fire. "Got more water than you intended?"

Katrine nodded from within her blanket cocoon, her teeth chattering.

Sven built a small fire inside a ring of rocks. "Pray to the Lord that this works."

Initially the smoke billowed out, curling about the floor, sending everyone to coughing, but as the room heated, it rose to the canvas ceiling and seeped out along the edges.

"I've noticed we aren't the only ones with a cooking fire inside," Sven said, rubbing his hands.

Margret prepared some hot cornmeal porridge and some rose hip tea. Katrine shook while drinking the tea. Nothing had tasted or felt so good.

The following day, Sven added more brush to the sides and top of the shelter. He brought in some armloads of sagebrush. "If the ticks don't wake up, this should make for a warmer bed. Just break off the smallest branches. We'll burn the rest."

Katrine began helping and arranging the sagebrush. It had a wonderful tangy fragrance.

"There, girls, you should find this a mite warmer." Margret spread the meal sacks back over the top.

That evening while Katrine dragged a few pieces of wood back to the campfire, she overheard Mama and Papa Olafson talking.

"I don't think the Andreassons are going to continue with us next spring," Margret said. "Maybe some of the others won't as well."

A numbing ache filled Katrine. She thought of the Andreasson children—Jens, Barbro, and Joran. She could not imagine them going back. She stood listening outside the firelight.

"They have nothing to go back to," Sven said. "None of us do."

"But none of us have anything here either."

"Then there is no difference. We can look forward to the valley."

Katrine came forward with her wood.

Margret looked up and frowned. "It shall not be that bad, Katrine. We just worry about getting through this winter."

"All of us do," Sven said. "Maybe we will get some snow. It is never as cold when there is a nice blanket of snow."

Katrine found that the shelter was warmer that night but not by much. She still shivered and clung close to Mia. Maybe a blanket of snow *would* help.

Christmas came. The day began crisp and clear. Even the wind had stilled. Ice had seized the river where it quietly meandered across the valley floor. Black zigzags marked the few places where the river ran too quickly to freeze. The little snow that had fallen had blown into a few drifts, leaving most of the frozen ground barren.

"I thought we would be in the valley by now," Sven said. "I wanted to give you this when we arrived there." He handed Margret a canvas bundle. When Margret opened it, her eyes quieted. She smiled and pulled out some calico with a small yellow and blue print and some light wool.

"Oh, Papa," she whispered and hugged and kissed him. "I could have been making clothes already with this, but I'm glad you waited. I will have something I can sew on until spring."

Katrine and Mia each examined the cloth.

"It feels so nice," Katrine whispered.

"And of course both of you can help me. How shall that be?" Margret said.

Katrine could not help a gleeful squeak, and she grabbed Mia and did a little dance.

"And for my little angel, this is for you." Sven ran his finger down Mia's nose and handed her a small package.

Inside were two pale yellow hair ribbons. Mia grabbed her father about his neck, squealing.

For a terrible moment, Katrine thought she was going to be left out. Well, she should not be surprised. The Olafsons did not know they were going to have another daughter for Christmas.

But Sven smiled and handed a second package to Katrine. It contained two similar hair ribbons but sky blue. They would match Katrine's blue dress that she wore for special days. She stared and swallowed.

Katrine looked down. "We didn't get you anything, Papa Olafson."

"Come here, girls." He scooped them both to himself, covering them with his big arms. "When we get to our new home next spring, you shall have time to make special things for presents. You both being here is present enough for Mama and me. Isn't that right, Mama?"

"Oh, this has been a blessed Christmas to have both of you," Margret said.

"Now we are going to go visit the Adolphsons. Everyone will be there. We'll have some Christmas songs and something to eat together."

They pulled on their coats and scarves, bundling up against the frigid cold, and headed downriver. Katrine looked forward to seeing the other children. They had been confined to their shelter for far too long.

Chapter 5

ALTHOUGH THE SNOW did not accumulate in the river valley as it did on the hills, the valley was colder and less protected. Northwest winds continued racing through, bringing stinging, icy needles. Each day, the men chopped ice to open up water for their livestock. They stripped cottonwood bark and cut willow twigs for feed. They gathered or cut wood for the insatiable fires. Even the stoutest fire did not seem to keep the cold away. Katrine told Mia spring would soon be on the way, but she knew the worst of winter would soon be upon them.

The families gathered under the lean-to at the Adolphsons to mark the new year. Despite attempts to celebrate, Katrine could not help but overhearing the adults' hushed talk. Some families had lost more livestock. Their provisions had dwindled. They wondered aloud if they would survive to see spring.

The women and children crowded into the Adolphsons' cabin. Some of the boys remained outside, tending a fire around which the men gathered. Katrine listened to the men.

"For certain it would have been foolish for us to continue," Magnus muttered.

"I wonder sometimes," Anton said. "Maybe the timber and the valley would have offered more protection."

Magnus shook his head. "We wouldn't have had enough feed for the stock. Even if we had been able to cut and cure some hay, it wouldn't have been enough."

"Ja." Gustaf pulled his coat tighter. "But trying to survive here is no better than staying another winter in Minnesota."

"But keep in mind, starting from here come spring, we will not have as far to travel," Nils said. He brushed snow from his long black coat. "We will have time to plant crops and get a harvest in before the winter."

Gustaf glanced darkly from under his heavy brow at the blowing

31

snow. "It would make no difference. We will still have to wait until June to get there, considering what you say about how deep the snow gets."

"The valley will start clearing in April," Nils said. "We'll have high water and snowbanks to contend with on the route in, but I'm confident we can get crops planted as soon as we can prepare some ground."

"Is the road to get there well traveled?" Carl Isberg asked.

Nils frowned and slowly shook his head. "It is not much more than a trail."

"Wagons have been across it, ja?" Carl stared stonily at Nils.

"*Nej.*" Nils shook his head. "I did not wish to discourage you. I've scouted the route. We'll have our work cut out in a canyon just south of the valley, for sure, but we can do it."

"So there is no road."

"If need be, we'll build one," Nils said. "It is the reason for an early start."

Blowing snow whistled about the men as Nils's words sank in.

"We shall get the wagons there. It will take work is all," Nils said.

Silence met him.

"Remember why we're here," Nils continued. "We want our own land. We want a place like Sweden where we can have our own community. A place where we can celebrate Santa Lucia and Midsummer's Eve without getting looked at cross-eyed." He spread his hands. "To have our own church and school. That's my dream."

A gust of wind twisted some snow into the air and moved across the camp.

"That is my dream as well, Nils," Sven said quietly. He glanced at the others. "I'm for going on, come spring. If we can survive a winter here, we can survive a winter anywhere."

"It'd help if we had some brännvin," Gustaf said. "What'd you do with that bottle anyhow?" He eyed Nils.

Nils laughed. "I say we wait a bit. I don't see many freighters coming through bringing whiskey. When I do, we shall have our *snaps.*"

Lars threw some more wood on the fire. Katrine had heard enough. Shivering, she reentered the warmth of the cabin.

Snow driven by a blustery early spring wind bit Katrine's cheeks. Gray clouds scudded across a horizon cut by naked cottonwood fingers. Smoke drifted from the several emigrant cooking fires along the river as the evening light dimmed. Katrine had heard the news that Mrs.

Wikstrom was ill. She wanted to visit, but no one knew if her illness was contagious or not. She worried for her friends, especially for Anna.

Margret went alone to visit. Upon her return, she muttered, "They have a worse place to live in than us. I don't know how four children and two adults can fit under that shelter, let alone stay warm. And with this weather, they have to stay inside all cooped up. It's a wonder they aren't all ill."

"Mia and I should go see Mrs. Wikstrom," Katrine said. She needed to see that she was all right.

"I believe that would be proper, Katrine. Tomorrow you take her some of the rose hips that you and Mia picked. I think they might be good medicine."

When Katrine and Mia reached the Wikstroms' shelter, Mr. Wikstrom came out to greet them. His shoulders sagged, and his eyes were pained. Katrine drew back. He explained that it would be best not to bother Mrs. Wikstrom.

He took the rose hips and thanked them. "I'll be sure to tell Mrs. Wikstrom you were here. She says she hopes to be well soon." Anton ducked back into the shelter.

Anna, Björn, and Linnea came outside. Linnea was the same age as Mia, and sometimes they played together, but today, the wind was cold, and they just stood around not saying much. Anna held her arms about herself. Björn kicked absently at the ground.

"If you want, you can come to our place and visit," Katrine suggested.

"Maybe sometime," Anna said quietly.

Katrine caught worry in Anna's voice. Even Björn did not have his ready smile. She and Mia said goodbye and trudged back to their shelter. The frozen ground crunched under her feet, and an uncomfortable feeling filled the pit of her stomach. She tried to sound cheery. "Mr. Wikstrom liked the rose hips, Mia. We'll let Mama Olafson know."

Whenever the weather warmed, the Swedes' hopes rose. Then another storm moved through. It was another Sunday meeting during such a storm that Katrine listened to Mr. Adolphson repeating his stories, attempting to rekindle their hopes. He promised they would reach the mountain valley that reminded him of Sweden—the valley where the grass whispered against a cow's belly, where they could grow barley and rye, and where the hot springs flowed from the mountainsides. Katrine closed her eyes and tried not to think. She wanted for winter to be done

33

and for spring to arrive. She wanted to be on their way to the valley. This day, the Wikstroms were absent from Sunday meeting.

New fallen snow clung in feathery clumps on the grass and trees. The bucket sloshed water against Katrine's leg as she slipped in the mud on the riverbank. At least some of the ice was melting. Spring was finally on its way, although there would still be deep snow in the high valley to where they would head.

Katrine carried the water into the shelter. Mia helped as she ducked through the fabric door.

"Thank you, girls," Margret said. She hardly looked up but continued mixing cornmeal.

Moments later, Sven came through the opening, a strange look on his face.

"We should all have a seat," he said softly. "Maybe fix us some hot tea, Mama."

"What troubles you?" Margret moved the teakettle from the coals and took out the bag of dried rose hips.

Sven sighed. "There is no easy way of saying this. You all know Mrs. Wikstrom has been ill. She died last night."

A rush of blackness enveloped Katrine. She fought to get a breath.

"She passed quietly in her sleep. Nothing could be done."

Katrine pictured her own parents and brother who were lost and presumed dead. She could feel it happening all over again.

"The poor soul," Margret whispered. She pulled Mia to herself. "Those poor, poor children."

It did not matter that Katrine had lost her own parents; she could not shake thinking of how her friends now felt. "Poor Anna," she whispered. "Poor Björn. Poor Linnea." Laurens, who was but three, was probably too young to understand.

Days later, they buried Emma Wikstrom near a stake that had been driven into the prairie soil to mark the location of the future cemetery for Boise City. Two other persons had already been buried there from previous misfortune met on the trail. Their bodies had been near enough to bring them in rather than to bury them along the Snake River.

Katrine recounted that they had buried six people during their journey. Mrs. Wikstrom was the first to be buried in a cemetery. Maybe Anna and Björn would feel better knowing that their mother was buried near where a city would soon be built.

She watched her friends. They stood silently. Anna held Laurens close to herself. Linnea stood on her other side, holding onto Anna's dress. Björn especially appeared lost. His face held a look Katrine had never seen but recognized as bewilderment and grief, strangely out of place with his expressive eyebrows. Perhaps Katrine knew what they felt more than anyone else who stood at the gravesite. She knew their hurt and emptiness, and she knew there was nothing that could be done to change either.

Nils Adolphson, in his dark Sunday-meeting coat, his eyes strained, removed his hat and said a prayer. The others tried to sing a psalm. They shoveled dirt into the grave. The hollow sounds it made thumping onto Mrs. Wikstrom's body was more than Katrine could endure. She covered her ears and squeezed her eyes closed, shaking.

She recalled her last visit with Mrs. Wikstrom. She had told about a Swedish elf that must have gotten lost because she was certain she caught sight of him near their camp. "It was just like the elf I saw back on our farm in Sweden," Mrs. Wikstrom had said. "It has to be Jeppe. You should watch for him. He wears a pointed hat with feathers."

Anna had said, "I miss Sweden. Why did we come here, Mama?"

Her mother had paused and then explained. "Oh, Anna, America is opportunity. None remained for us in Sweden. We will have so much more here in America. We will have our own land and our own home. Here you can dream of great things and make them happen."

Katrine smiled to herself. Ever since the story about Jeppe, she and Mia had kept their eyes open for him—especially Mia.

Katrine understood death. Inside she was hurting. Mrs. Wikstrom was at peace, but she ached for Anna and Björn and Linnea and young Laurens. Already she wondered if she would ever see Anna smiling again.

The others whispered that Anton Wikstrom would now turn around and take his children back to Minnesota. He appeared beaten, and his eyes appeared strangely detached from his bushy eyebrows, like the lost and bewildered looks on Anna's and Björn's faces. Katrine wondered how it would be possible for him to care for his children and to build a farm in a remote mountain valley.

The sun finally began to linger. The grasses along the river began greening, and the cottonwoods and willows began unfurling their leaves. The families talked about resuming their journey. The valley was two weeks north of them. Katrine found it difficult to accept that it was still not free of snow. Impatient as they were, the Swedes took the opportunity to fatten the surviving livestock on the new grass and to mend gear. With each passing day, the excitement grew, much like that which Katrine had felt before leaving Minnesota.

Katrine walked along the river, feeling the warmth of spring and feeling hope. Swollen with the snowmelt and spring rain, the river seemed to be bringing life from the high country. Ducks, halted in their migration north, had gathered in an eddy, jabbering at one another. She watched them bobbing about, chasing around before she caught sight of a pair of hawks soaring above the cottonwoods. She dreamed with the hawks as they rose on outstretched wings and circled in great arcs on the warm updrafts.

She reached down to pick some blue flowers with bright yellow centers—the colors of Sweden. She caught sight of old skeletal willow leaves among the rocks near the river's edge—lacy and mysterious. She pushed at them in the moist soil, now quiet memories of life that had passed. Once green and vibrant, they had turned golden and fallen to the earth where the winter had turned them to feathery skeletons— much like the memories of her family. She shivered. Were they now also skeletons? She tried not to think those thoughts, but she could not shake the dreadful feeling inside.

She thought of Mama and Papa. She thought of Erik, who would now be thirteen. She closed her eyes, trying to see him, seeing his shock of blond hair, his freckled face, and his vivid blue eyes. She pushed at the leaves with her toe. New leaves would replace these. But nothing could replace her family. She fought the bitter memory as a breeze buffeted the overhanging gnarled cottonwood limbs, scraping them together like brittle bones.

In the rattle, Katrine heard her brother: "You have my sacred word, Katrine. No matter what happens, I'll come and find you." That promise had accompanied her each day since *back there*. If Erik lived, she knew that he would search for the valley of which Mr. Adolphson had spoken.

Katrine picked up a couple of the skeleton leaves and, cradling them gently in her hand with the flowers, headed toward their shelter.

The images of Erik and her parents began fading. She fought to resurrect them, her eyes stinging.

She saw Papa Olafson heading in her direction, waving.

"It's a good day today, Katrine, it is." He carried an empty pail. "You should be helping Mama and Mia get things finished for packing rather than spending time picking flowers." He winked.

"Yes, sir," Katrine whispered. She let the flowers and leaves fall to the earth. She took the pail and headed toward the river for water.

A couple of robins fluttered about through the willows. A male perched on a cottonwood limb and sang its song: *Cheerily, cheer-up, cheer-up, cheerily.* Another male staking out his territory farther away sang an answering call.

She watched the river rushing by. She wondered to where it went—down to the Snake and then to the Columbia and then out to the ocean. Sometimes she wished she could go with the river—to see all the sights, the cities, the people.

Katrine filled her pail and turned for the shelter with the water.

Mia was running toward her. "What keeps you? Mr. Adolphson's at the shelter. Tomorrow we're going!"

A warmth, warmer than the day, flooded Katrine.

1863, THE TRAIL IN

Chapter 6

THIS WAS THE day! They were heading out. Katrine trembled with excitement but also with worry. Papa Olafson had explained that only gold seekers and packers had been along the old Indian trail that followed the river to the north. Theirs would be the first wagons to attempt the route.

No one expected Anton Wikstrom to continue. It would not be easy to farm in the high valley, miles away from any settlement, but especially so for Mr. Wikstrom with just himself and his four children. A knot rose in Katrine's chest. Anna was her best friend. Now she and her two brothers and sister stood watching as Katrine helped the Olafsons pack their wagon. The knot grew more intense.

Abruptly, Anton threw his coffee into the grass. *"Åt helvete!"* he exclaimed. "We're going." He grabbed some tools and carried them toward his wagon.

Anna and Björn broke into cheering and ran about gathering their belongings. Katrine, her heart nearly bursting, grabbed Mia and ran to help.

"Are you sure about this?" Nils approached Anton. "You have your children to consider."

Anton stood stiffly, pulled his ragged coat more tightly about himself, and arched his bushy eyebrows. "Which is precisely the reason we're going. We have nothing to go back to."

Nils smiled and nodded. "You shall have a good tract of land then, my friend. I'll see to that."

By midmorning, six wagons were packed and headed out. The Jonassons' and Isbergs' six young children stood beside the trail watching as they passed. Despite Mr. Adolphson's encouragement, the two families had decided against the valley and instead would travel to Oregon. Katrine recalled their continuous grumbling, but she still wished they were coming. Mr. Adolphson had told them that if they did not find land, they would be welcome to come back.

The men led the wagons. Ulrika Eklund, hardly eighteen, rode with her baby, Robert; otherwise, everyone walked. The surviving livestock, three cows, a heifer, and the Adolphsons' young bull, trailed behind. Several cages of squawking chickens were strapped onto the spare mules. Among the families, there were also a couple of dogs, often following one group of children and then another.

As before, Katrine and Mia and the other children explored and played games. No one feared Indians north of the Snake River Plain, but they remained watchful and stayed close to the wagons. Katrine watched the mountains ahead and tried not to be impatient. They seemed so terribly far in the distance. It was going on a year since they had left Minnesota.

Nils Adolphson initially took the wagons west toward the Snake River, following the main Oregon Trail. A day and a half later, he turned east along one of the rivers, explaining that he believed it to be the correct one. The major rivers flowing from the north—the Boise, Payette, and Weiser Rivers—all turned west to enter the Snake.

"Correct one?" questioned Gustaf. "Don't you know?"

"I wasn't interested in taking a wagon into the goldfields when I first went there," Nils said. "Coming back, I knew I could cut across the mountains to Fort Boise and save time."

"And what if we're not on the correct one?" Gustaf demanded.

"It's the right one," Nils countered. He set his jaw and pushed ahead, following the broad, racing stream.

By the day's end, Anton and Sven insisted they double back. "We must be certain," Anton explained.

"Fine, so be it," Nils said. He hiked up one of the bluffs above the river.

Coming back down, he smiled and pointed. "There, see that grassy ridge with the snow? That is where this river turns north and leads us straight to the valley."

"You're certain?" Anton asked, pushing at his hat.

"As certain as God is in his heaven and I'm on his green earth, I am."

In another day, they turned north. The trail quickly became little more than a muddy, rocky track that followed the swift-flowing river. Men and mules struggled to haul the wagons, but each mile took them higher into the now-timbered hills.

This country was far different from the grassy, sagebrush-covered hills that Katrine had grown accustomed to near Fort Boise. Across the river, thick trees and brush carpeted the steep slopes. The side with the trail had fewer trees, but she could see the thick timber and rock outcrops seemingly blocking the route ahead.

That night, the families huddled against the cold around a campfire near the junction of a tumbling creek and the main river. A few snowbanks clung to the north side.

"We chose the right time," Nils said. "To have delayed a week, we would have had high water, and trying a week earlier, all of this would still be buried under snow."

The next day, they reached one of the major river crossings. The river crashed noisily against rocks strewn across the channel and spilled into a deep pool below. The men unloaded the wagons and packed what gear they could across by mule. They next hitched six mules to each wagon and, one at a time, began pulling them across. Katrine watched, terrified.

Hans Eklund put baby Robert into a basket and strapped him to his back and crossed on horseback. Similarly, Anton threw four-year-old Laurens into the saddle in front of him and held him fast in his big arms as he crossed. The oldest children also forded the river on the mules, but the others rode with their mothers in the wagons.

Katrine's heart was pounding by the time the Olafsons' wagon entered the water. The mules struggled to budge it against the current. It shuddered and then locked up, wedged against submerged rocks. The water pounded the sideboards, spilling through the gaps. Katrine stared at the rushing water and clung tightly to Mia, trembling as the wagon began filling.

Sven and Anton rode into the river and grabbed the lead mules on either side. Shouting and cursing, they dragged the animals forward. The wagon began sliding downstream. The mules heaved and floundered but suddenly broke the wagon free and hauled it up the bank, water straining from its bed.

"Praise the Lord," Nils proclaimed.

"If we have many crossings like that, we might not make it," Sven muttered.

The following day, they began up a steep grade adjacent to the river. The lead wagon soon became mired in snow and mud. Below the trail, the river danced, wild with whitewater.

Nils and Gustaf stood quietly, examining the trail. Half the trail had washed into the river.

43

"What made you think you could get a wagon up this?" Gustaf spat, scowling. He pushed a hand through his scraggly hair.

"Most of this hillside was still up here and not down there when I came through," Nils replied, nodding toward the pounding waters.

The river had cut into the slope, and a raft of conifers had slid into it. The other men came up to examine the situation.

"At this rate, we will not get there in time to put in any crops," Magnus said.

"Ja, I had hoped we would fare better," Nils said, shaking his head. "Unfortunately, I agree. We are running out of time. We can spare a few days to fix this cut, but now I see no other choice. I propose we leave three of the wagons. We'll get three to the valley so we can begin planting. We can retrieve the others later."

"And who is lucky and gets a wagon, and who doesn't?" demanded Gustaf. "You cannot farm without a wagon."

"Draw straws. It doesn't matter," Nils quietly replied. "We'll share equally of the wagons until we can come back."

"You knew this country before writing us those letters," Gustaf said. "I think you knew we couldn't get wagons up here." He clenched his fists.

"You have brought us to face this?" Magnus said. He removed his hat and moved up to where he could view the cut, limping slightly.

"I said it would be difficult, I did, but we can do it." Nils tightened his jaw. "We just have to commit to three wagons from this point."

Grumbling ensued. Men consulted with their wives. Sven took Gustaf and headed down toward the river. Katrine decided they must have come to some agreement because when the two men returned, Gustaf proclaimed he was willing to go on.

Shortly, they had unloaded three of the wagons and moved them off the trail. They packed what farming implements they could on the remaining wagons. Sven packed his carpentry tools. Cooking wares, clothing, and food stocks took up the remaining room. They packed other gear on their riding horses and spare mules. Everything else was left behind, some with plans for retrieval, some forever abandoned.

They filled the cut with rocks and logs and widened the track sufficiently to pull the three wagons through it. They moved on, following the increasingly narrowing gorge, winding their way around rockslides and across steepening benches. Two days later, they emerged onto a canyon where the river pinched between fractured black granite walls and ran booming white through a narrow crevice. A party of miners with fully packed mules had stopped ahead of them beside the river.

One of the packers greeted them. "Didn't think this trail could be done with wagons." He eyed them as they struggled to bring the wagons up. "I've been this way a half-dozen times, and I can hardly get my mules through here."

"You're right, my friend," Gustaf loudly agreed. "We're on a fool's mission. We've been on a fool's mission since leaving Fort Boise." He turned toward Nils. "So it is now that we turn back."

Nils shot Gustaf a look and studied the river below. At length, he said, "I believe we have no choice but to bridge it. We can pull apart the wagons and carry them across."

"Ja, I'm not turning back now," Sven declared. "We are over halfway there." He pulled his ax, rolled up his sleeves, and headed toward a massive spruce tree.

The packer shook his head. "Now that's what I like." He hollered to several of the men below. "We got us some Swedes here who are willing to fell trees. Let's give them a hand."

The men who were struggling with the mules near the river cheered.

Two days later, they had built a serviceable bridge and began leading the horses and mules across, carrying the disassembled wagons, piece by piece. Katrine walked ahead of the mules with Mia, refusing to watch until they were safely across.

"You folks have gotta be believing that valley up ahead is gonna turn to pure gold for you," one of the packers said. "I can't totally disagree. Best country I've seen for raising horses and cattle, even sheep if you like. Grass is best I've seen. I'm not sure it's farming country though."

One of the other prospectors muttered, "Don't wanna disappoint you, but I'm a thinkin' the winter's gonna best you and send you all packin' back. Better hope this bridge stays intact."

Katrine didn't want to ever go back. Whatever lay ahead was going to be her home. Erik knew where they were headed. How would he find her if they went back?

The packers said farewell and continued along the riverbank, heading upstream with their mules.

"We're across. Now what do we do?" Gustaf asked, eyeing the thickly forested canyon walls. "We don't exactly have a road up out of here."

"We build a road," Nils said quietly. "When we get to the top, we reassemble the wagons."

"I'm done," Magnus said. "My missus and I can farm near Boise City. Someday they'll need a teacher there. I see no need to continue on."

"Magnus is right," Gustaf said. "I'm for taking my mules and heading back for one of the wagons and returning to Fort Boise."

"I'm still willing, but I have to face some truth," Hans said. "My baby boy and Mrs. Eklund aren't taking to this much anymore."

"We all must be of heart," Nils said. "We have only to cut timber up this ravine to get us back onto the trail. As long as there is room between the trees for the mules to get through, they'll pack out the wagons. They can haul anything."

The men did not move.

Nils tried again. "In a week at most, we'll be in the lower part of the valley. If you're not happy with what you see, we'll take a vote. We'll all turn back. It makes no sense going on with only a couple of families. None of us would survive."

Magnus turned abruptly and limped quickly toward Nils, his fists clenched. "Don't put that one on us, Adolphson. You'll survive without us just fine."

"Look," Nils said, "I apologize. I may have made a fool's decision, but I think not. Decide for yourselves when we reach our new homes. For now, let's get there."

That night after they had camped, Nils and Sven began notching the trees, marking them for cutting. At first light, all six men and Lars began clearing timber. They felled trees and moved the logs and rocks to either side of the route, slowly traversing up out of the canyon bottom until they intersected the trail.

The following day, they loaded the mules and began climbing the newly cut track. When they reached the trail, they released the loads and headed back down into the canyon for more. Some of the men worked on reassembling the wagons. The boys led the livestock. Katrine and Mia helped carry the bedding. Margret lugged up her iron kettle. No one traversed the newly cut road without carrying something out of the canyon.

Early the next morning, they were again struggling along the faint trail, occasionally cutting trees to get the wagons past. The Olafsons' wagon

46

was in the lead, and Katrine kept near Papa Olafson. He often walked ahead of the wagon, blazing the trees for the wagons to follow. They pushed through some scattered timber. In near disbelief, Katrine found herself staring across the expanse of a broad meadow.

"I'll be a troll's uncle!" Sven exclaimed. He ran a few steps into the meadow and spun around. "Grass. Timber. Water. To blazes, look at those geese. And there ... you can see fish rising up." He laughed and shouted back toward Adolphson, "You were right, Nils, you were right. It's better than your stories, by gum." He threw his hat into the air.

Katrine began dancing about, spinning, taking in the view, laughing. Mia and Mama Olafson joined her.

"I can see steam, Papa." Mia pointed.

"Must be one of the hot springs," Sven said. "Maybe we'll get a cabin near one, and we can have hot baths every week. What do you think about that?"

Mia shrieked with glee and began jumping up and down. Katrine shivered, happy at the thought of such a luxury.

"From the looks of it, Nils, we could sure stop here," Sven shouted.

Nils and the others came up to talk. Children chased about, laughing.

"This is a fine spot, for sure, Sven, but this is just the beginning. Up north is better land, I should think."

Sven shrugged. "I can't think of a spot any finer," he said, "but I'm willing to see."

He tugged on the mules. They plodded forward, pulling the wagon, now rolling easily across the grassy meadow.

Katrine could not get over the sight. She was familiar with farming and the rocky, muddy fields of Minnesota, but this country was unlike any farmland she had seen. Thickly timbered mountains, capped in snow, surrounded the valley. A deep river meandered lazily across it, overflowing into the meadows and collecting in ponds, forcing the trail to take to one side. Wildflowers bloomed, particularly a blue one, which carpeted the meadows. She realized one of the blue ponds in the distance was in fact an expanse of the blue flowers.

"I thought it was a pond." She pointed it out to Mia.

"What kind of flowers are they?" Mia asked. "They're everywhere."

"I'm figuring it's what the Indians call camas," Sven answered. "They use the bulb like we do a potato. We can try some if you like."

Katrine thought about it. "I hope the Indians don't come here."

"Could be they do, but we'll be just fine," Sven explained. "What I understand is these aren't like the Snake Indians. As far as what's known, these Indians don't cause trouble. They're known as Sheepeaters, partly because they hunt mountain sheep."

Katrine liked that. One reason they had gone over the Jeffrey cutoff was to avoid the Indians. A knot grew in her stomach at the memory. She returned her gaze to the powder-blue flowers in the warm, grassy meadow and tried to think happy thoughts.

It was late afternoon the second day after they had entered the valley. They followed a sweeping bend in the river and crossed a small tributary. To the east, a hot springs steamed into the sky. Its waters trickled down from a bluff into a series of mud pots and pools. Beyond, a shabby cabin stood near the river. Aspens clung to a hill behind it.

"Well, Astrid, there's home," Nils announced. "That's what I built for you."

Katrine thought it resembled one of the shelters in which they had spent the winter on the Boise River.

Astrid Adolphson frowned; she gathered her skirt about herself and headed toward the ramshackle structure. "Come, children. I can see we'll have our chores ahead of us now." Their black dog, Anka, bounded toward the cabin with them.

Nils swept his arms about, addressing the others. "What do you think? You see the hot springs here. There is another one up north. There's good land. There's timber. There's water. There's game. We will all have good homes."

General cheering abounded. A surreal sensation flooded Katrine. They were done traveling. They had reached the high valley. She wandered toward the aspens with Mia following behind her, intending to explore. The men could ride out and decide where the other cabins would be. She liked this hill and the deep, meandering river nearby. Now she intended to find some of those blue camas flowers and maybe dig some of the bulbs.

The High Valley

Chapter 7

WHILE PAPA OLAFSON was with the men scouting out possible land, Katrine explored near the Adolphsons' cabin. Gentle rolling meadows dipped or rose from the pattern caused by the small streams and hills until the land rose upward at the valley's sides and eventually ended in snowcapped granite peaks. Katrine was struck by how the valley resembled a broad trough scooped out by a giant hand with smaller finger troughs jutting downward from the mountains into the valley. Tall, thick grasses, speckled with spring flowers, blanketed the valley floor. Aspens and stands of timber covered the small hills that rose like islands from the floor or ran in stubby fingers from the mountains.

When Sven returned, they repacked their gear with the Lundgrens' into one of the wagons and headed east, following an old Indian trail along a deeply flowing stream. At about a mile and a half, Magnus turned up the first tributary.

"Adolphson says there's a large pond and level fields about half a mile up this direction," Magnus said. "I'm thinking it will be a good piece of land."

"Ja, God's blessings to you, Magnus. We made it."

Magnus nodded. "Many times I had my doubts. Now the work begins, but at least the work will be in the same spot come morning." He laughed.

Katrine waved goodbye to Harald and Emma as their family turned up the smaller, gently flowing creek, the heavily packed wagon cutting tracks through the deep grass. Their chickens were strapped on back, and their cow trailed behind.

Sven continued eastward, leading their mules, following above the stream for another mile and a half to where he topped a small, aspen-cloaked hill.

"What do you think?" Sven wrapped his arm about Margret's shoulders. Katrine and Mia came up to look.

51

A small creek descended from a low ridge to the north and joined a larger creek that drained the eastern ridge. A sunny knoll rose between the two branches.

"This land shall grow oats and barley like no one's seen. And with a little trouble, I can cut a ditch across the bottom of that small hill and put in an orchard."

Mia clapped her hands. "Will we grow apples?"

"In time we will, angel."

He waved toward the small hill. "The cabin shall be there where it catches the morning sun and where the creek forks. There's a good bench for a corral and garden for all sorts of vegetables."

"Potatoes and turnips?" Mia asked.

"And beets, and peas, and onions. All sorts of vegetables."

"And cabbage?"

"Especially cabbage," Sven replied. "Why, in this country, we'll grow cabbages the size of your head."

Margret clasped Sven's arm, a worried look.

"Yes, Mama, I know," Sven said. "We have much work to do, but it's ours. All ours." He waved his arms about. "We'll put in the garden first. Our tent has served us well for this long. It will do for a while longer. Then I'll build a cabin. Afterward, I'll worry about getting in some oats for the livestock. The horse and mules will need them for the winter."

Sven gestured toward the timber. "There is plenty of timber, and with fair weather, we should have plenty of food come winter for you and the girls and the little one." He smiled and patted Margret's tummy.

Margret frowned. Katrine had guessed. Now it was official. She and Mia laughed.

"And now we have no time to waste. After we unload these mules, I'll go back for what's still in the wagon. Mama, you and the girls can find a place for making dinner but not too close to the creek. I don't like the mosquitoes."

Katrine could not resist the temptation to explore beyond the cabin site while Mama Olafson began making dinner. She followed the faint trace of the old Indian trail up the hill until she could see the rising mountains beyond. A heavily timbered ridge ran toward the southeast with rocky outcrops littering its crown. High to the northeast, Katrine could see an old burn scar. The fire had left blackened stumps and snags and patches of brush. One of the stumps began moving. She caught her breath—*a bear.* The animal was much too far away to be of any danger, but it made her realize that they lived on the edge of wilderness, unlike the others who had cabins out in the valley.

She turned to head back to the cabin. A smooth granite boulder resting near the center of a small opening in the timber caught her attention. She climbed onto it and sat, gathering her dress underneath. It was a secluded spot from the trail but from where she could see the valley below. Spruce and aspen trees framed the view. The river sparkled blue and silver in the far distance. On the far western side of the valley, dark green conifers blended into grayish blue and then purple as they rose into gentle mountains that were still capped by brilliant snow. A low, aspen-covered hill ran south of the cabin site. If people came from that direction, they would cross that hill and then come down to the creek and up again to the old trail she had followed. Maybe Indians had recently used it. Katrine shivered. Then she thought of Erik. He would be coming from that direction looking for her. She wrapped her arms about herself, thinking of her parents and thinking of Erik, rocking and trembling. This was where they were supposed to be—all together as a family, but now it was only her.

She noticed some scattered white spots beneath the shade of the spruce trees below. She jumped down and stole under their dark canopy. A multitude of flowers of a kind she had never seen spread across the forest floor. Three bright green leaves grew close to the damp earth with a solitary stalk supporting a waxy white flower with three slender petals and a bright yellow center. Joyfully, she picked several and hurried down to where Mama Olafson had built a fire and was preparing dinner.

"I found these," Katrine said. "There are dozens and dozens under the trees. They look like three-pointed stars."

"I believe these are called trilliums," Margret explained, handling one gently. "We can put them in water and enjoy them for a few days." She found a clay mug. "These are special flowers, Katrine. See the three petals? They remind us of the holy Trinity."

Mia examined them. "One is sort of purple."

"Yes, I brought one that was purple. A few are purple, but they seem old."

"And these are flowers of hope," Margret continued. "They bloom in the spring under the trees where it is dark."

Mia said, "I believe they are dresses for fairies and elves. We should go and see if any are dancing."

"You should not go too far," Margret cautioned.

"Yes, I saw a bear on the mountain," Katrine said, remembering.

"You did?" Mia exclaimed.

"It was a long way away where a fire had been."

"See, they live among us," Margret said. "You must always be careful."

The first few nights, they again slept under their canvas tent. It had become so shredded, it hardly covered them. Katrine slept uneasily and woke early, catching sight of a sleek animal with a long tail flashing through the timber behind them. Boots and the mules set up a nervous racket. Sven said it was probably a mountain lion but not to be frightened. The horse and mules would scare it away, and now that they were camped, it would likely leave. Mountain lions were secretive animals that hunted by night and rarely bothered humans.

A night later, Katrine woke to a scream. She grabbed Mia, who was already sitting up, shaking.

Sven and Margret stirred from their blankets nearby. Sven threw wood onto the campfire coals and grabbed his rifle.

"What is it?" Katrine asked, her voice cracking and heart pounding. "It sounded like a girl screaming."

"It's all right. It's all right," Margret whispered, coming over. "It's a mountain lion."

"Will it get us?" Mia shook.

"No, darling," Margret replied. She stroked Mia's hair. "Papa has his gun, and the fire will keep it away."

Something about the cat's sound had penetrated Katrine deeply. It was as if a cold, clammy thing had crept inside of her and would not let go. She could not stop shaking.

"I don't like mountain lions," Katrine whispered.

"It will be all right, sweetheart. Papa's going to build us a cabin. And maybe somebody's dog will have puppies, and we can get us one. A dog will keep mountain lions away."

Katrine and Mia bobbed their heads, still clinging to each other. "I want one now," Katrine said.

By the end of the second week, the settlers had planted rudimentary gardens and had turned their efforts to raising their cabins. Each family leveled the ground, felled trees, and dragged logs to their respective building sites. The men squared the logs and notched them in the familiar Swedish style for tightly fitting them, something they had mastered against the Swedish winters.

When the materials for the basic shell were ready, each family sent out word to the others for help in raising the cabin. Customarily, the women put together a dinner for those who came to help. In this manner, as each cabin was put up, the small community came together for a day and a meal. When it was Anton Wikstrom's turn, Margret helped Anna prepare the meal. The men lifted and fitted the heavy logs into place. When the walls reached about four feet high, they set up a hoist and pulleys to swing up the upper logs. They then laid in a pitched roof.

Of all the home sites, Katrine especially liked the Wikstroms'. Steam billowed from the hot springs a short distance up the trail above the cabin. Although tempted, she and the children avoided going swimming. There was little time for playing while they put up the cabins. Instead, they gathered small limbs and the largest rocks they could carry and brought them to the cabin site. Katrine made it a point to collect her limbs and rocks from as near the hot springs as she could so she could view the cascades of steaming water gushing from the hillside.

Katrine was particularly proud of the Olafsons' cabin. Papa Olafson had spent days with the broadax squaring off the logs so that they fit snuggly. No mountain lion could get in through the logs, except that the door was presently a flap of canvas from their tent. Anything could easily come right through it.

The cabin was about ten by twelve feet. A small loft on each side gave room for some storage. They strung a curtain across the room at night for Katrine and Mia to sleep on one side while Sven and Margret slept on the other. Katrine helped Mama Olafson and Mia make mattresses from flour sacks that they stuffed with meadow grass, and Papa Olafson built bed frames with rope lacing to raise the mattresses off the dirt floor.

"When the geese return this fall, I'll be filling these meal sacks with soft goose down," Sven explained. "Then you girls can sleep nice and warm and comfortable." He nodded toward Katrine, who was once again trying her best to fluff up the meadow grass in her mattress.

"Maybe some aspen fluffs would be better," Katrine said.

"Ja, they might be, but you would have to spend a week and a half to gather enough."

They had no other furniture, having had to leave it behind. Instead, Sven fashioned a crude table from closely spaced aspen poles. They used stumps for chairs. Sven promised he would build some three-legged stools as quickly as possible, but until he had time for real carpentry work, the stumps would have to do.

A few days after they had moved into the new cabin, Magnus Lundgren drove up with his wagon. Eleven-year-old Harald was with him, brown vest over his white shirt, wearing his flat cap, looking neat and proper as usual. Katrine and Mia raced into the yard to where Papa Olafson already waited.

"Nils and I agreed you should share this wagon with Anton," Magnus announced. "I shall be using Nils's wagon until we can retrieve yours." Carefully, Magnus climbed down, swinging his lame leg clear. After his accident, he was unable to bend it much.

"Thank the Lord," Sven said. "I've been waiting to haul rocks for a proper fireplace."

Harald jumped lightly to the ground, his darker brown hair catching in the breeze. He greeted Katrine and Mia and began helping with the harness.

"How's your mama doing, Harald?" Katrine asked. Both Louise Lundgren and Mama Olafson were expecting babies. Having that in common kept each close with how the other fared.

"Mother is bigger is all," Harald replied. His dark eyes flashed as he untied the leads.

Katrine liked Harald, but all the children had grown close. She wished Harald's sister, Emma, had accompanied him. They could have played for a while.

"It's all yours, Sven," Magnus said as the mules were freed. "I only hope Nils doesn't forget he's now sharing his wagon with me. Every time I think I've become situated, I'm looking around for a wagon for hauling something or another."

Sven laughed. "Ja, if Nils forgets, send Harald back up to get this one."

"And with my luck, he will find you've lent it to Wikstrom," Magnus said. "We should have picked cabin sites based on who would have the wagons and plows."

"Ja, I'm still spading a suitable garden, planting a little as I go. Wikstrom is plowing."

While Margret prepared a small noon meal, Katrine gave Harald a tour of their farm. She proudly pointed to the garden where a few leafy tops showed.

"We don't have as big a garden yet," Harald said. "I've been digging and digging, but we don't have a plow either."

"But you have a fireplace for cooking, I imagine," Katrine said.

Harald nodded. "We have the best fireplace and best cabin, and we have a good cage for the chickens."

"I wish we had chickens. Papa Olafson says maybe we'll get some next season."

"We don't have many eggs yet. The chickens are still getting used to being here." Harald grinned. "When they're feeling happy, we'll have more eggs."

"We don't have any animals except our horse and mules. You can't eat them."

Harald smiled. "Well, you can eat them, but you don't want to unless you're starving."

Katrine shrugged. "I'm happy we're here. Are you?"

"Yes, but now we have to work all day every day."

Chapter 8

KATRINE FOUND PAPA Olafson in the yard harnessing the mules. Mama Olafson watched from the doorway.

"What do you plan to haul?" Margret asked.

Sven straightened. "I believe the girls and I should get some rocks and build us a proper fireplace. What do you say?"

Katrine and Mia cheered. Margret appeared a little worried. "Should you not put in more crops, perhaps the oats?"

"Nej, a fireplace is more important than having you standing out in the wind and rain cooking."

Katrine and Mia rode with Sven to a spot near the creek where cobbles spilled from a cutbank. Together they filled the wagon, drove it back, and dumped the cobbles into a pile. They made several more trips before Sven took them to another area along the creek where there was some sticky gray mud.

"This is some clay I've found and will work both for chinking between the logs and for the chimney." Sven shoveled as much as possible into the back of the wagon. Katrine and Mia mostly watched. It was too sticky to pick up. When they returned to the cabin with it, they slid it out of the wagon into a pile near the cobbles.

Next, Sven drove the wagon up into the timber.

"We'll need lots of sticks about an inch in diameter and about three feet long. We'll use the clay and sticks to build the upper part of the chimney. Sticks are okay to use on the upper part because they're far enough away from the fire."

While Katrine and Mia busily collected the smaller sticks, Sven cut poles and small timbers. They worked for several hours until the wagon bed was three-quarters full.

"This will have to do for now," Sven said. "Any poles we don't use on the chimney, we'll use for fencing or for firewood. We'll need to fence the entire garden to keep out the wildlife. We don't have a dog to chase away the rabbits and squirrels."

"That's going to take lots of poles," Katrine said.

"The fence will just be a start. We'll need more poles to build a shed and then a pen for when we get a calf."

"Can we get a calf now?" Mia asked.

Sven shook his head. "As soon as we grow enough crops to trade for one, we can. Perhaps next summer."

"That will be a long, long time," Mia said.

"For a little girl, it's a long time. For me, not so much time anymore." Sven smiled.

Around midmorning the next day, Sven came to the cabin.

"This is a special day for all of us, Mama. It's time to take the wagon up to the Wikstroms. You and the girls are coming along to visit."

Katrine noticed Papa Olafson had already tied Boots to the back of the wagon and hitched two of their four mules to the front. One was the riding mule, Ornery. The other was Jack, that Papa Olafson occasionally rode. The mules that were left behind were the working mules, Olga and June.

Neither Katrine nor Mia rode the horse or mules alone by themselves. Papa Olafson rode with them, and then they usually rode Boots. Although Katrine had ridden Ornery, she did not like doing so. Ornery sometimes lived up to her name. Papa Olafson knew this and so took the mule during the day and left the horse at the cabin for Margret and the girls for an emergency.

It was about five miles by way of the trail to visit the Wikstroms. They headed downstream until they intersected the creek that came down from the Lundgrens' cabin. There, they followed up the creek north past the Lundgrens and then over a low ridge and down to the creek that flowed past the Wikstroms' place. The Wikstroms were another mile up from where they intersected the creek.

When they pulled into the Wikstroms' yard, it was as if Pandora's box opened. Anna, Linnea, and Laurens came running into their yard area, laughing and talking excitedly. Björn was not there, but Katrine knew he was most likely in the field with his father.

"We brought you the wagon," Katrine explained. She helped Papa Olafson begin unhitching the animals.

By the time they had finished, Mr. Wikstrom and Björn had arrived.

They exchanged greetings and then gathered about a makeshift table for some bread and potatoes. Margret helped Anna, as she customarily did whenever visiting. Sven explained the plan for sharing wagons.

"I had to go quite a distance to get up past the Lundgrens' place because of the timber. Maybe you and I could take out a few trees each trip and shorten the road."

"I'll take my ax," Anton said, "but you'd think we'd be happy going around after all the timber we cut to get up out of that canyon."

"We can always use the poles," Sven reminded him. He stroked his chin. "Ja, these wagons will be the end of us yet. I'll be glad when we can retrieve the others."

"Nils was right to leave them. We still wouldn't be here."

Katrine knew both Papa and Mama Olafson were wondering how Mr. Wikstrom was doing without a wife to help him build a farm and take care of four children. He answered them without a question.

"Björn is a good farmhand. He and I have a pretty good garden in. We're now plowing. We've broken just about enough sod to sow some rye."

Björn's eyes crinkled to his father's praise. He seemed to have even more freckles now. Katrine decided that for some reason boys got freckles during the summer, not so much the girls, although she had plenty of freckles as well, perhaps because she did not like wearing her bonnet.

Anton gestured at the cabin's rough walls. "The cabin's not much yet, but it keeps us dry. Anna is a fine cook. I wouldn't be able to handle things without her, so I'm not sure about school. I admit I'm not much at taking care of a four-year-old." He held out his big arms. "Come here, Laurens." The boy scooted into his father's lap.

"Now I think you should all come and see the best thing," Anton said, "and I didn't have to do much at all to get it. Come see the hot springs. This winter if we get too cold, we'll all be able to run up there and heat ourselves up."

Anton led the way about four hundred yards up the trail to where a cascade of steaming water spilled down granite boulders and emptied into a good-sized creek that rushed through the gulch on down past the cabin. The creek itself collected in large pools; however, it was icy cold, having carried snowmelt from the surrounding mountains. In contrast, the hot springs were near a hundred degrees. Steam rose in billowing clouds from the hillside above and along the trickles of cascading water.

"We have not had time to do much up here, but Björn and his sisters have started moving rocks for catch basins. There's an upper pool, which is of some size, and then a small cubby down here." He pointed across the way to where Katrine could see the water's gleaming surface.

Katrine marveled at the mountain of boulders and the water trickling over and around them. Similar to the Adolphsons' springs, there was no unpleasant smell, unlike many of the other hot springs they had passed along the Snake River trail.

The area around the springs was devoid of trees. The spruce and fir apparently did not tolerate the hot water. In their stead, clumps of alder and mountain maple swept their lacy branches above the cascading waters. Ferns and delicate blue forget-me-nots grew from among moss-covered rocks. The scent of mint filled the air.

"We can pick some mint for tea," Katrine told Mia.

"Maybe we have mint down by our creek."

"Probably, but we can pick some anyway, and when we get back, we'll hang it from the ceiling."

The lower pool was small, being about three feet deep and at the foot of a gusher of hot water cascading off the rocks above. A faint trail followed the edge of the open area where the springs emerged from the hillside.

"You can follow that trail over the ridge to your place," Anton said. "I walked to the top. It's a good trail, but I wouldn't try bringing a horse across it. This side is pretty steep and covered with blowdown."

Sven studied the ridge. "Ja, it would be a lot closer going over than around the way we came, for sure." He glanced at Katrine. "Maybe you girls can use the trail to come and visit."

Katrine shivered with joy. She was already jealous of the Wikstroms' hot springs. The idea of visiting thrilled her. Only, she was uncertain about what animals or wild Indians she might meet along the way.

They reached the upper pool, which was about two feet deep and eight feet across.

"Today, we don't have time, but perhaps you can swim on your next visit," Anton said.

He spoke too late. Katrine and Mia, led by Anna and Linnea, had begun wading into the pool, balancing on the slick rocks. Björn and Laurens soon splashed around as well. They may as well have been swimming.

Björn reached down and wrestled with a cobble.

"If each time we come here and take some rocks out, it will get bigger," Björn explained.

Katrine followed his example and reached into the water to pull out a cobble. Her dress was soon quite soaked.

Margret had come up the trail and called for them to return to the cabin.

Katrine and Mia fairly skipped down the trail. "When can we come and go swimming?"

"Soon," Margret replied. "We have too much work for swimming now."

The days warmed and reminded Katrine of her birthday. She remembered last year when one night her family had gathered around the wagon and sang a birthday song. Erik had given her a wooden carving of a bear. Katrine had once told the Olafsons when her birthday was, but she had lost track of the days. What could Mama and Papa Olafson give her for a birthday gift anyhow? They had already taken her in. She had a warm home, although when it rained, the roof leaked. Papa Olafson said he still had to finish it. At least the wind didn't come through like it had the shelter on the Boise River.

Katrine decided she would go to the creek to see if there was a pool where she and Mia could wade, maybe like the larger pool at the Wikstroms'. The water was still too cold for anything but wading, but she enjoyed exploring, and she could always gather some yellowcress or dandelion greens for Mama Olafson. Besides, staying in the cabin when the sun was shining was often asking too much of her. Mama Olafson seemed to know this as well and did not hesitate to grant permission when she asked.

On the way, Katrine and Mia passed Sven, who was busy in the garden.

"You two are out, I see. Is there nothing you can't do to help Mama?" He winked.

"She shooed us out," Mia explained. "She wanted us to see if some nettles are growing along the stream."

"Well, that is a fine idea. Some steamed nettles would be nice, though I expect it is still a little early. Maybe you can find where they are beginning to grow. Then you can gather some for Midsummer's Eve."

Katrine's heart caught. This would be the first celebration in the valley. She remembered the festive times from Minnesota. It was a time for singing and dancing around the Midsummer's Eve pole.

"Perhaps later we can all go in search of nettles," Sven said. "Now I would welcome your help on something very important." Sven turned and headed back to where he had been digging in the garden.

Katrine noticed blocks of sod stacked along the edge.

"Do you think you can help me carry these to the cabin?"

Mia appeared dubious but attempted to lift one of the largest blocks of sod. "Ew, there's a worm." She immediately dropped it.

"A worm isn't going to hurt you," Katrine said.

"Nope," Sven replied. He hefted several blocks of sod onto his shoulder and headed the few yards back toward the cabin.

Katrine picked up the piece Mia had dropped. "You can help me, Mia."

Gingerly, Mia grabbed a corner, not very effectively, but Katrine didn't mind.

"We'll make a pile of the sod up here," Sven said, indicating where to put the block.

"But why, Papa Olafson?" Katrine asked. "The garden's back there." She remembered using sod to help make rows and to divert water from the irrigation ditch.

"These are going on the roof," Sven said.

"On the roof?" Katrine exclaimed.

"It will keep the rain out," Sven replied, "and if we ever get some goats, they can live on the roof."

"Like the troll and the goats," squeaked Mia.

Katrine remembered the Swedish fairy tale. She eyed the roof. She would have never thought of using sod on the roof.

Mia frowned. "What about the worms, Papa? Won't they come in?"

"Ja, maybe for a bit. But you and Katrine can catch them, and we'll go fishing. How about that?"

Mia groaned.

They hauled blocks of sod until they had moved them all to near the cabin. By the time they had finished, Katrine's arms were black with soil, scratched red, and felt numb. Mia had been of little help. Katrine didn't complain, but she decided things were much cleaner when she helped Mama Olafson.

Sven began by setting a row of sod along the lowermost edge of the roof. He had built a stout ladder and hauled the other blocks up as needed, laying them in snug rows as he covered the roof. Katrine and Mia climbed up onto the roof with him.

"You just mind where you put your feet," Sven cautioned. He set a chunk of sod down and fitted it tightly against another. "Now when it rains, most of it will soak in, and then our roof will soon look like a meadow with flowers and grass."

"And then will we get goats?" Mia asked.

Sven laughed. "Perhaps someday, little angel." He stepped on an area of the roof and appeared worried. He pushed his weight up and down. "It will just have to do," he muttered.

At suppertime, Katrine noticed only a little dirt had fallen through. Already Mama Olafson had swept the dirt floor clean, and as near as Katrine could tell, there were no worms. She figured there would be after the first rain.

In the evenings, Sven worked on furniture. He began making four stools. He cut round sections from the butt end of a log and, using his auger, bored holes for some legs. He braced the legs with short lengths of wood for which he also bored some holes. The pressure from spreading the legs served to wedge them more tightly into the seat.

"Here, these should do until I have time to properly construct some chairs."

Margret shook her head. "You so amaze me, Papa." She and the girls plopped onto the stools, thankful for not having to sit on stumps any longer.

"And now we can all sit at the table and celebrate."

To Katrine's surprise, Papa and Mama Olafson and Mia broke into the birthday song. So they had not forgotten. Today she turned ten.

> Ja, må hon leva. Ja, må hon leva
> Ja, må hon leva uti hundrade år
> Ja, visst ska hon leva. Ja, visst ska hon leva
> Ja, visst ska hon leva uti hundrade år

> Yes, may she live. Yes, may she live
> Yes, may she live for a hundred years
> Oh sure, she will live. Oh sure, she will live
> Oh sure, she will live for a hundred years

"If I had a fiddle, I'd play for you," Sven said. He hugged Katrine. "By gum, you are getting to be tall. And look at all those freckles and pretty blue eyes. Just like yours, Mia. You two could be sisters."

"We are," Mia said, giggling. "Katrine's my big sister."

Chapter 9

KATRINE FREQUENTED THE garden with Mia, helping pull weeds and pick insects. Potatoes, turnips, beets, and onions were now growing, as were cabbages, spinach, and peas. Mama Olafson now prepared meals inside the cabin without the rain pouring through the roof. The cabin still had a dirt floor, but Katrine knew time was running short for planting grain. Papa Olafson had finally acquired one of the plows and was busy plowing a field northwest of the cabin.

Katrine often accompanied him to the fields, sometimes to pull out and stack stones or chunks of wood, sometimes to carry out water, and sometimes just to keep him company.

Today, she watched as he brought Olga and June to where the plow was sitting. He hitched them up and clucked to them. They lurched ahead, plodded across the meadow. The plow sliced through the deep grass, curling up two lines of dark black earth, flipping them over, one on each side of the blade, turning a black furrow. Papa Olafson had looped the reins about his neck so he could keep both hands on the plow and guide it. It was magic to Katrine that the mules walked so straight.

"How do Olga and June go so straight?" she asked, quickening her step to keep up.

Sven laughed. "It's because I go straight," he explained. "You pick out a point on the horizon and keep your eyes on it. The trick is to get the first cut straight. The mules will follow the path on the next cut."

Katrine followed Papa Olafson for a time. The plow snagged, and the mules protested against their traces.

Sven shoved at the plow. "By gum, this is not easy sod to cut. Too many willows and shrubs growing with the grass. The plow doesn't want to cut the roots."

He straightened the plow and clucked to the mules. They plodded ahead. When he reached the end of the row, he came back to the outside of it, leaving about a foot between the rows. When he again reversed direction, he went up the uncut middle, slicing open a line of dark black earth between the rows.

The blade stuck again. Sven heaved on the handles, pulled his bandana, and wiped his brow. "It's good that it is rich soil, Katrine. But it is stubborn."

Katrine mentally measured the area that Papa Olafson had plowed. She could not stop the question that bubbled out. "How are we doing?" She knew enough to realize that they had little time to grow crops.

"Just pray I can cut enough sod to do us some good. This year we get an acre of oats and maybe some rye. Next summer, we get some barley. That is my aim." Sven smiled.

"I hope so," Katrine murmured. She knew they might be in trouble.

Sven snapped the reins lightly. The mules strained into their harness, springing the blade free from where it had stuck, again pulling it stubbornly through the deep meadow sod.

It took better than a week to plow the acre. Sven harrowed it by dragging a toothed rake across the ground, further breaking up the sod and pulling clumps of willow roots free. At last, he announced it was time for sowing. Katrine helped him sling out the seeds, watching while he spread seeds left and right. She caught places that seemed not to have as many and scattered her seeds. The creamy kernels sparkled in the sun against the damp black earth.

"You and Mia can come and walk all over this," Sven said. "Tamp the seeds down so they get moisture and the birds don't get them."

Sven looked around. "It looks like a goodly amount, Katrine, but this will hardly do for a start. It may be a slim winter for us. However, I shall take whatever I get, and I'll go hunting. It might have been just as well that we don't have a calf."

Katrine did not like to hear about the winter they would face in a few short months. "The Adolphsons have a cow, a bull, *and* a heifer," she pointed out. She hurried to keep up with Papa Olafson.

"Ja, and Mr. Adolphson's going to need a lot of grain to feed them, but he's been here for a season and already had a cabin built and has plowed a lot more ground." Sven turned and took her bucket that had held the oat seed. "Now, every day, you and Mia need to come out and chase birds away. And pray for rain, especially for our oats. Not too much that the seeds get drowned but just enough they get started growing good."

Sven paused and smiled at Katrine. "It's good to have you helping me." He pulled her in with a gripping, one-armed hug. "Now be on your way to the Lundgrens and let Mr. Lundgren know he can come and get the harrow and bring me the plow when he's done. I'll start on some ground for rye."

Every day, Katrine ran to the field with Mia. Usually there were only a few birds, but they dutifully chased them away. At last, they were rewarded with green blades sprouting from the clods of plowed sod.

Sven walked the fields as well. "Ja, ja, this is good. We shall see now if we get some grain before the snow comes."

Katrine stood in the doorway looking south toward the end of their land to where the creeks came together. It was warm enough now that maybe she and Mia could go swimming.

Sven came up from the garden. "Looks like we have some visitors coming." He waved toward the south and pointed out some horses and riders.

For a fleeting instant, Katrine thought of her family, and her heart skipped. Then she caught ahold of herself. Of course it wasn't.

"I shall get some dinner fare and coffee going," Margret quickly said. "Who do you suppose they could be? Travelers always go past the Adolphson place along the river trail." She filled the kettle with water from the barrel near the door.

"I don't see wagons," Sven said. "I was hoping the Jonassons and Isbergs had changed their minds. We'd have a better go of it with a few more settlers."

Katrine caught Papa Olafson's tone. She knew everyone already worried for the winter.

The men were prospectors, and they didn't turn down Margret's invitation to stop. They refused anything to eat but took some coffee. "We can't be taking any of your grub when fixin's are so slim," one of them said.

Margret appeared hurt. That's when Sven shooed Katrine and Mia outside to play.

It was later that evening when Sven talked about their visitors to the girls.

"I suppose it doesn't matter much to us, but we are no longer part of Washington Territory. This country is now known as Idaho Territory."

Katrine thought it was interesting. She did not understand much how the territories were formed. She knew they would eventually become states that belonged to the United States.

"Idaho Territory," Katrine repeated. "That's a funny name. What does *Idaho* mean?"

Sven shook his head. "I'll be a troll's uncle, but that I do not know." He smiled. "Probably nobody does. Maybe it's a word somebody cooked up. But I guess you could ask the same for Oregon."

Katrine shrugged. As Papa Olafson had said, it mattered little.

"More importantly, you should know that group of prospectors happened to be Southern sympathizers. I did not care to share where my loyalties lie, for they were in great spirits. General Lee defeated General Hooker at Chancellorsville in Virginia. They talked of a certain victory for the South and were planning on contributing the gold they were about to find to the cause. You'll recall that one of the reasons soldiers are now at Fort Boise is to help stop the transfer of gold to the South."

Margret busied herself with making some cornmeal cakes. "I do not much care either way, Papa. I just do not like seeing young men die."

"They are dying so that others may be free. We had no slaves in Sweden. For that reason, I support the Union, and I shall honor my new country more when we no longer have slaves in America as well."

"We shall pray," Margret said. "I pray for all the soldiers that peace will soon come."

Katrine swallowed. The war was months away from them; yet it somehow still touched them. Anytime anyone traveled through, others asked for news about the war.

"In other respects, there is good news," Sven said. "They are heading into a new mining camp known as Warren's Camp. It's on this side of the Salmon River rather than north of it. They believe this may become one of the main routes to serve the camps, especially from Boise City. The camp already has a couple of settlements and news of several very rich strikes."

Margret brightened. "That means they will be in need of milk and cream and eggs."

"Ja, and vegetables and beef," Sven added. "Presently, goods are coming in from Lewiston, which as I understand it is the capital of the new territory. It's a supply town on the Snake River at the mouth of the Clearwater River northwest of here."

He offered his cup to Margret for a refill of coffee. "This valley is closer than Lewiston. Supplies should come through here as well." He laughed. "By gum, we might see a settlement here yet." He slapped the table. "At the very least, we'll be able to supply the folks that are coming our way. All we have to do is grow something."

Despite the initial dark news, Katrine felt an uplifting spirit. This would be a good valley in which to live after all. This was going to be a good home.

MIDSUMMER'S EVE 1863

Chapter 10

KATRINE WOKE WITH excitement. It was the first day of summer, the summer solstice, and time to celebrate Midsummer's Eve. She looked forward to seeing everyone again. Except for when they raised the cabins or swapped a wagon or a plow, it was as if everyone had disappeared into their own private worlds. After having spent nearly a year traveling together, it seemed strange that they were so far apart.

Katrine put on her light blue dress, the one she kept nice for visiting and celebrations. Mia wore her pale yellow dress. The girls braided their hair above their ears, as Anna sometimes did for special occasions, and tied on their new blue and yellow ribbons. They finished weaving flowers into the crowns they had made. Margret wore her nicest rust-patterned dress, and Sven had his brightest white shirt and dark gray vest. He polished his boots and jammed on his best and only hat, sweat-stained with a hole.

"You're not wearing that," Margret huffed.

"Ja, until we get there. And what about that bonnet?" He eyed Margret's large floppy covering. Both girls refused to wear theirs. After all, they had crowns of flowers.

Katrine and Mia rode Boots, and Margret rode Ornery. Sven took Jack but only because it was necessary. Jack frequently went where he had a mind of going. They had a single saddle for the horse and rode the mules bareback.

Eleven adults, fourteen children, and baby Robert gathered at the Adolphsons' place. It was much improved from its first sighting seven weeks ago. Nils and Lars had built a lean-to shelter for the gathering and had set up rough wood tables and peg stools.

Katrine caught her breath. In the center of the yard stood the Midsummer's Eve pole all decorated in pine boughs and flowers. It reminded her that Swedes across the world gathered this day and put up Midsummer poles. Midsummer's Eve was a time for a grand dinner, songs, and stories. It was a magical time when all of nature came to life; when the animals talked with one another; and the unseen folk—the fairies, elves, and trolls—came to make mischief and perhaps to dance and sing and celebrate along with them.

Katrine wanted the singing and dancing to begin, but the adults had gathered and were already sharing tea and coffee. The men talked about their land, how their crops were doing, and what troubles they were having with their stock. Katrine overheard Papa Olafson talking about the mountain lion they had heard. It always caused her to shiver. The Wikstroms also had a problem with a mountain lion coming near their mules and had seen several black bears. Katrine told them about the bear she had seen.

"It is because we live near the hills," Anton said. "Mountain lions and bears won't wander into the open valley as much."

The boys began some foolish antics that evolved into a game of chase of sorts around the pole in spite of the Adolphsons' dog, Anka, getting in their way. Their cheering and laughing caught Katrine's attention. They chased after one another, trying to swat each other with willow sprays before they could return to their spot in the circle about the pole. She envied their boisterous play until Anna, who was the oldest and now thirteen, joined in. When Anna did, Katrine did, taking tacit approval from her. At twelve, Lars was the oldest boy. Harald, Jens, and Björn were all eleven, with Björn being the oldest by a few months, a good year older than Katrine. Ingrid was a few months older than Katrine, but the other children were younger.

It was no contest for Katrine to chase the younger boys about the circle playfully swatting them on their legs before they could scoot back to their spot. Then she slowly strolled around the outside of the circle while all eyes remained glued to the ground. She would secretly pass the willow bundle off to another *it* before sneaking back into her former place. She handed off to Harald. All was quiet a moment; the children's eyes began to wander, trying to find the new *it*. Suddenly, the circle erupted, and Harald began switching poor Jens before he even knew what was about. Jens scrambled off around the circle desperately trying to stay out of Harald's reach. Finally back safely to his place in the circle, Jens rubbed where he had been switched. Harald began roaming about the circle looking for a new *it* with whom he could deposit the willow switches.

"Hey, hey," Nils said. "You children should go to the hot springs while you still can. Lars can take you."

74

They promptly dropped the willows and gathered around Lars, who led the way in the direction of the river.

"What if some Indians come along?" whispered Mia.

"There won't be," hissed Katrine. "There are too many of us."

The Adolphsons' hot springs had long been known to the trappers and Indians and now to the miners that passed through. Seemingly, every passing party paused for a swim and paid its dues by adding rocks to enlarge the two pools. The springs seeped from a myriad of locations that covered about an acre. Over the years, humans, and on occasion, animals, had dug individual mud pots that filled with hot water, one connecting to the other in strings of pearls descending the hillside.

Cattails, bulrushes, and horsetail covered the slope in a thick carpet of swords and brown catkins except in the small circular areas where the mud pots and pools were located. Red-winged blackbirds cackled from the nodding cattail stems and flitted away when the children approached. Soon the children were splashing and playing about in the largest pool under Anna's watchful eyes. Lars and the older boys picked a pool closer to the river where they could bathe and then run out into the river to cool down.

Katrine and Mia found a mud pot and smeared the sticky, hot mud over their bodies. They then washed off in the larger pool with the other children.

"I wish we had a hot springs," Katrine said. She had wished that since the first day she had heard of them.

Mia answered, mimicking her mama's words. "We have what the good Lord intends for us to have." She giggled. "Sometimes we can come here, and sometimes we can go to the Wikstroms' whenever Papa will let us."

"The one at the Wikstroms' is nicer. It has gushing water," Katrine said. She swam about in the shallow pool. It had a smooth, clay and sand bottom with very few rocks. One end was deeper than the rest of the pool, and she settled there to soak in its warmth.

All too soon, it was time for dinner.

The men still talked while the women and girls spread out what fixings they could for a shared dinner. Those who had more food had brought a bit more. Katrine noticed that the Eklunds seemed to have brought the least. Hans and Ulrika Eklund did not have any older children who could help with farming. It was just the opposite. Ulrika had baby Robert, who seemed always to require his mother's care.

Katrine was eager to put out the Olafsons' dish of mashed peas in cream. They got the cream from the Adolphsons, but the peas were from their own garden. Katrine had also brought some roasted camas roots that she and Mia had dug. The camas had a smoky flavor and was served with wild onions and trout. The Lundgrens brought a favorite Swedish dish of boiled deep green nettles with salt and butter. The Adolphsons sacrificed a few seed potatoes to substitute for the traditional new potatoes with wild onions and sour cream. The new potatoes were no larger than beans. Nils had checked. "They have good growth, for sure, but nothing is bigger than a pebble. Next year."

Topping the dinner off was the traditional Midsummer's Eve strawberries and cream. Most of the children, including Katrine and Mia, had diligently picked the tiny, wild berries. They filled two bowls with bright red berries and drenched them in sweet cream.

Anton liked them so much that he threatened to transplant some of the strawberry plants into his garden and see if he could get any size to them. "They are better than any I've had in the old country, for sure."

"When they get big, they lose their flavor," Nils said.

"If I get some big as new spuds, you won't care, I think," Anton countered.

Katrine ate and ate. She thought it was the finest meal she had had in all her ten years.

Nils brought out the saved bottle of brännvin. "It's been a long trail here, and we have a lot to celebrate. Shall we?"

He poured a small glass for each of the six men. Each looked the other in his eyes and then, saluting one another, shouted *skål* and took a sip.

They broke into the drinking song, joined by everyone.

> Helan går
> Sjung hopp faderallan lallan lej
> Helan går
> Sjung hopp faderallan lej
> Och den som inte helan trår
> Han heller inte halvan får
> Helan går
> Sjung hopp faderallan lej

Here's the first
Sing, hup fol-de-rol la la la la
Here's the first
Sing, hup fol-de-rol la la
He who doesn't drink the first
Shall never, ever quench his thirst
Here's the first
Sing, hup fol-de-rol la la

The boys took up with the men, singing drinking songs as well, hoping for a small reward of snaps. Lars began another song.

För trillan för trilla ...

Upon completion, the men raised their glasses, shouted skål, and one passed his to Lars for leading the effort.

The boys racked their brains for more songs and sang another and then another, trying to entice their fathers to share yet another sip with them but to no avail.

The men were beyond discussing crops and caring for stock as the brännvin flowed more freely. Their loud jokes and songs must have overwhelmed the women because they now sat in the shade a good distance from the cabin, discussing when the babies would arrive, how everyone's health had been, and the prospects of more settlers coming to the valley. They then took to the tables where they gathered up the plates and leftovers and carried them into the cabin. They returned to their husbands.

"It is time for the Midsummer pole, Olafson. To the pole, Wikstrom." Begrudgingly, the men rose and set aside their glasses.

Katrine and the children had already gathered about the pole. The girls helped each other pin on their crowns of flowers.

"The children first," Anna begged. She took Lars's hand.

"Ja, for sure," Sven agreed.

"Girls and boys," Katrine suggested. They alternated positions and, holding hands, began a dance about the pole. Anka, still not worn out, chased after them. Magnus Lundgren brought out his violin and played in accompaniment of the singing, tapping away.

Katrine danced between Harald and Jens. Both boys were good dancers, kicking out their legs and springing high. Katrine found it difficult to mimic them.

The boys turned to face out of the circle. More challenging now, they still kept ahold of the girls' hands and tried to dance in time with the music and circle around the pole. Someone hollered *switch,* and the circle clumsily began going in the other direction. They switched again, going faster and faster until the circle broke down.

"All together now," Nils said and broke into a song, clapping. The other adults joined in also singing and clapping.

The boys and girls scrambled back and separated into two circles, the girls on the inside. The boys danced one direction; the girls danced the other. The boys backed under the girls, who held their hands over their heads. In three steps, they went to the outside again, this time sweeping their arms over the girls. Katrine concentrated and whispered to herself, "Over, under, over, under," as the boys stepped past her and then back.

Shortly, they were out of rhythm. The dog underfoot didn't help. Katrine found herself first tangled with Jens and then more firmly tangled with Harald. She could not help but notice his hazel eyes and smile.

"We shall show them how to do this," Gustaf boomed. The adults shooed away the children. Magnus Lundgren began playing his violin again, bowing and swinging. Katrine and the other children began singing and clapping. The adults formed two circles, dancing opposite directions of each other and then changing directions.

They stopped, all facing the pole, alternating man and woman. The men snapped their fingers, danced inward, hands to their hips, kicking their legs, returning to their positions. The women twirled inward and twirled back in the opposite direction. The music and tempo increased. By now the snaps had made an impression. The adults, too, fell apart, laughing and joking.

Everyone now breathless, the dancing ended. Katrine could not remember when she had had so much fun.

Back at the cabin, Nils brought out another bottle of brännvin, which he had saved for the occasion. The men toasted their good fortune and their futures. The boys sang drinking songs and occasionally did so well as to again be rewarded. Gustaf, especially, seemed to acquire a larger share of snaps as the afternoon wore long. His slurred voice rose and fell with the boisterous singing.

Louise Lundgren, quite pregnant, gathered the women and girls together under a clump of aspen trees in the opposite direction of the men and boys.

"I think this shall be a wonderful home for all of us," Louise said, and then she produced a small medicinal bottle of whiskey. "I've been saving this for this evening." She took a sip. "We English don't have a midsummer celebration, but I think we should." She handed the bottle to Olga Andreasson. In turn, the other women took a small sip and toasted the valley and their new homes. Young Ulrika did not imbibe, explaining she was still nursing baby Robert.

Margret, also now quite near her due date, boldly stated, "Maybe you should give that baby a sip. Make him strong." She laughed.

Ulrika replied indifferently, "I do hope we get some venison or salmon soon. We certainly need more than corn bread and beans."

All too soon, the celebration ended. Although it was the longest light of the year, the closest cabin, the Lundgrens', was over two miles distant, and the Wikstroms lived nearly six miles away. Night was not a time to be traveling across country on faint trails. One thing the Swedes agreed on was to meet on Sundays as they had done when near Fort Boise.

"We have only each other," Nils explained. "Even if one or more of us cannot make it, my home will always be open. You just come on Sundays. Bring a dish of food, and we'll have a dinner and get together. I may even pour some snaps."

The others vowed they would come.

"Even in the snow."

"Ja, no snow ever stopped a Swede," Sven agreed.

The evening grew long, and the families said their farewells. Sven helped hoist Katrine and Mia back onto Boots and led the way on Jack. Margret followed behind on Ornery.

Katrine, seated behind Mia on the rocking shoulders of the mare, gazed toward the western sky. It now shone yellow, tipped with orange. The orange blended into a green blue and then into indigo.

"Look, Mia, the rainbow is captured in the sky," she whispered. "This truly is a magical time of the year. Tonight the trolls and elves will be dancing with their own bonfires on the hillsides."

"They will?" Mia asked.

"Of course."

Katrine thought of what Harald had said at one time. He scoffed that trolls and elves and fairies didn't exist. She believed it was his English mother's fault, putting such nonsense into his head. *What do the English know of trolls and elves?* Everyone Katrine knew told stories about the little people from the old country. The fact so many people told the stories, there must be something to them, and Midsummer's Eve was truly a special time, a magical time, no matter what.

If there weren't trolls and elves and fairies, how else could it be explained when things went missing and turned up where they should never have been? What else explained the little voice she heard when she was in the woods picking flowers or berries? Of course it was an elf. And she was pretty sure the bear she had seen on the hill behind the cabin had troll friends. In Sweden, the trolls rode on the bears and wolves and raced around the mountains. She hadn't seen any trolls for certain, but she blamed the musty smell near her rock on them. She was not scared. It was only at night when one had to worry about trolls. During the day, they turned to stone. Maybe some of the rocks near the cabin had been careless trolls.

She thought she saw something scurrying near an aspen. She clasped Mia more firmly, thinking of pointing. Instead, she allowed her chin to rest briefly on Mia's shoulder.

"Mia," she whispered, "I think we need to see if we can't find a fairy circle where the elves have danced. Would you like to look with me?"

Mia nodded. "Only if there are no trolls. Promise there won't be trolls."

"There aren't trolls during daylight," Katrine reminded her. "And I haven't personally seen elves or fairies, but they've whispered things to me. I think they came with us from Sweden and were in our wagons on our way out here. Remember Mrs. Wikstrom. She said their barnyard elf, Jeppe, came with them."

"They whispered to you?"

Katrine paused. It wasn't exactly what they had said. It was more the feeling she got. "When we got here, I think the elves told me where the trilliums grew."

Chapter 11

THE HEAT AND drought of summer had arrived. Spring flowers were replaced with daisies, sunflowers, and Indian paintbrush. Margret showed Katrine and Mia some lupine that grew near the garden fence.

"*Blomsterlupin.* There are lots of them coming into bloom. We had them in Sweden." Margret swung around. "Oh, they so much remind me of Sweden. Maybe we'll have some pink and white ones as well."

Most of the pealike blossoms clustered on the tall stalks were blue and lavender.

Katrine was happy something reminded Mama Olafson of Sweden. She was reminded of how often Mr. Adolphson had said the valley was like Sweden—the spruce and fir, the birch-like aspens, the meadow roses and mountain maple, the luxuriant grasses, and the meandering streams. She was too young when they left Sweden to fully appreciate its beauty, but she was beginning to understand why this valley meant so much to the Swedes.

"So this is what Sweden looks like," she whispered. But she was happy this was America.

She gazed at the sparkling creek rushing by. She had not explored much of its length. Maybe there was a larger pond farther downstream. "Come, Mia, it's hot. I think we should go find a place to go swimming."

"We need to ask Mama."

"Of course we will." But Katrine worried that Mama Olafson would say no.

Margret surprised them. Rising from her knees from where she worked in the garden, she said, "I think it is a wonderful idea, but I shall come with you. If we don't find much of a bathing place, we'll tell Papa where to make one."

They soon followed the creek. It pooled in several spots downstream from where it joined the other branch. Beavers had dammed the creek but had seemingly abandoned their ponds. Judging by the lack of nearby willows and aspens, Katrine decided the beavers had moved to where they could find food—either that or something had eaten them. She wondered if mountain lions liked to eat beavers.

Most of the beaver ponds were too shallow for swimming. They had filled with mud, and the largest was hardly two feet deep. Cattails grew around one side. Red-winged blackbirds clung to the old catkin spikes, bobbing in the breeze, calling to each other in their melodic clacking. Dragonflies zipped about in the warm day, stopping for moments in midflight, hovering, and then on lacy buzzing wings, darted away. Tadpoles squiggled from the mud, raced in zigzag lines for a few feet, and then sank back into the fine gray mud, releasing tiny bubbles where they burrowed. Spotted green frogs leaped from among the cattails where they sat in the sun waiting for flies and made splashes into the pond, scissor-kicking away.

All that was missing were the elves and fairies, Katrine decided. She liked to believe they lived along the creek as well, maybe riding on the frogs' backs or flying about with the dragonflies.

"Maybe we'll see an elf home," she whispered to Mia.

Mia's eyes grew big. She scanned the cattails and bulrushes. "What does one look like?"

"Oh, it has bluebells planted about with buttercups. There might be toadstools for the elves to sit on. They have tiny beds made from bird feathers and butterfly wing pillows."

Mia searched again. Katrine wished there really were elf homes. She spotted an alcove lined with rocks that she believed could be one, and seeing it, Mia yelped with glee.

They wandered downstream until they reached a much larger pond. It had formed between two narrow cutbanks with steep slopes that rose on either side. Some willows grew at its head. Although the pool was only about eight feet across, the water was deeper than the other ponds, about four feet deep. Several small trout scooted away and settled again, fanning the water, suspended in the current near the outlet.

Soon, Katrine and Mia were splashing about. Margret took off her shoes and, pulling up her dress, waded in and washed her feet.

"You should swim," Mia protested. "It feels nice."

"I'm just fine, watching you two." She rubbed her belly.

Katrine believed Mama Olafson was thinking about the baby who was growing inside of her, much larger now. It excited her to think soon there would be a new life, but she also worried. She knew that sometimes mothers died when their babies were born, or the baby died.

Margret smiled. "I know what you think, Katrine. You know the baby is close. You and Mia are both soon going to be big sisters."

Katrine liked how Mama Olafson called her a big sister.

"Would you rather have a brother or a sister?" Margret asked.

"I'd rather have a brother," Mia quickly replied. "I already have a sister."

A glow washed over Katrine.

Katrine splashed around, glad for the feeling of the water and the fresh air. This was so much better than the wooden washtub they used on Saturday nights.

Margret watched them, a bemused look. "Katrine, you'll soon be becoming a young lady. I am not sure I am ready for either of you two to be growing up."

Katrine noticed Mama Olafson scanning the trees to the south or the hillside behind them. It made Katrine a little fearful. She wondered if the mountain lion was watching them swim, or worse, if Indians were nearby.

Margret suggested they return to the cabin.

When they reached it, Sven stood in the doorway. A worried look etched his face.

"I took the girls to swim in the creek," Margret explained.

Sven relaxed. "I worry about Indians," he explained. "I know we haven't seen any, but a hunting party on its way through would not hesitate to take advantage of women."

Margret started to say something, glancing in the direction of Katrine and Mia, and then tightened her lips.

Katrine awakened to the pale light of morning as Sven left the cabin to tend the stock. He often hobbled the animals at night, explaining he was yet uncertain they would stay, or worse, if they would be stolen. He worked around the yard and garden for a good hour before breakfast. It gave Katrine and Mia a chance to get up and dressed, to put away their bedding, and to take care of things. Margret also rose before daylight. She stoked the cooking fire and began preparing meals for the day. Katrine started her day by bringing in wood and hauling water to fill the barrel.

When Sven came in for breakfast, he splashed water onto his face and gave Margret a kiss and then sat while she brought out the food.

"You sure have a knack for timing, Papa," Margret said. "You must be waiting for the moment I am ready."

"Ja, ja." He rubbed her growing belly. "So am I having ham or eggs?"

"Today I have rustled up some corn cakes and turnip stew. The pig wasn't fat enough, and the chickens haven't come home to roost."

Katrine knew they had no pig to fatten and no chickens. Occasionally they went to the Lundgrens and got a few eggs, but no one in the valley had a pig. If things were good this year, they might get a heifer or chickens next spring.

After breakfast, Sven headed out to the fields to where he was cutting the long meadow grass. In a week or two, he would begin gathering in the cured hay. Katrine and Mia usually tended the garden, doing some weeding or picking bugs. Sometimes they went to the oat field, which was now lush green, and pulled unwanted weeds, particularly thistles.

About midday, Sven returned to the cabin, this time for a noon meal. As always, he hung his hat on a peg, washed his face, and greeted and hugged the girls. After dinner, he frequently rested and then returned to the fields and worked until sundown, which at this time of year was after nine. But this day he returned to the cabin in the early afternoon.

"I don't like the looks of what is rising up in the west. We could have a heavy storm."

Katrine had noticed that the day had been warmer than most and muggy. White billowy clouds had pushed down from the north and climbed into the western sky until they now masked the sun. Their black bellies advanced steadily in their direction.

Margret set a bowl of soup in front of Sven. He quietly ate, glancing frequently in the direction of billowing clouds. Muted thunder drummed across the valley, interrupted by a louder crack, nearer the cabin. Angry clouds began blotting out the sky.

"I better have a look around and make sure things are tied down." Sven left the cabin. When he returned, a blast of wind filled the cabin.

Abruptly, the blackened sky split with flashes of lightning followed by booming thunder that reverberated up the low gully and through the cabin walls.

"Here she comes," Sven said.

Another explosion twisted down from the mountainside.

Katrine huddled with Mia, holding her, flinching. A flash lit up the

84

mountain. Seconds later, a flickering ribbon hit the aspens on the hill to the south, followed immediately by booming that vibrated the cabin. Skittering balls of dazzling light bounced along the ground. Katrine cowered deeper into the cabin. The flashes and explosions marched steadily toward them. There was no place to go.

Thick, heavy rain began pelting down, then thundering down, sending sheets of water from the sky. Water ran from the hill behind and around the sides of the cabin. Rivulets seeped under the log walls and coursed across the earthen floor, quickly turning it to mud. Water dripped from the roof.

The sound increased, drowning out any other sound, although Papa Olafson talked to Katrine but a few feet away. The candle flickered from the drafts of air pushed by the thundering water. Spatters and then muddy showers erupted through the sod roof.

Margret began gathering up the bedding to keep it dry.

Katrine felt as if she was being consumed by the wrath of a mighty being. Another bolt lit up the cabin, followed instantaneously by booming, vibrating thunder.

"When's it going to stop?" Katrine cried. Mia clung more tightly.

No light showed in the sky except that which came from the flickering lightning.

Hailstones began bouncing crazily in the yard, first a few, then a torrent, drumming loudly, gathering into small ribbons of white.

"*Herre Gud*," Sven muttered. He sat unmoving. "The crops ..."

Margret took his hand.

Dread seeped through Katrine. She thought of the garden and the leafy vegetables, and she thought of the tender oats now being shredded.

She held onto Mia for what seemed ages until silence enveloped the cabin—silence that was almost as overwhelming as the torrent of rain and hail. Cascading water leaked from the roof onto the floor.

Katrine feared to look out the door. When she did, an alien winter world greeted her, and a cold chill swept into the cabin. The surrounding land shone white. Trees were stripped nearly naked; bits of twigs and leaves lay scattered across the ice. The creek gushed a muddy, dark torrent of mad water, gurgling and pounding with hailstones.

"It's all gone, isn't it, Papa Olafson," Katrine whispered.

"I fear so, and there is little we can do. Come build up the fire. Let's begin drying things out. We'll have our work cut out for us tomorrow, for sure."

A strong odor of smoke woke Katrine. She had barely slept, her blankets having been wet. She whispered to Mia, "I smell smoke. We better go to see."

She crept from behind the curtain and noticed Mama and Papa Olafson were gone. Their blankets were still on the muddy, earthen floor.

Katrine cautiously looked out. Surprisingly, the hail had melted. The smoke seemed stronger. She gazed toward the aspen-covered hill. Her heart caught. Flickering, orange and yellow flames blazed brightly in what had once been a clump of trees. Other flames crawled along the ground, flaring up when they found brush. Thick white smoke billowed into the still sky.

Sven stepped into sight from down near the creek.

"It's a fire, Papa Olafson. On the hill."

"Ja, Mama and I have been watching."

"Will it come here?"

"Nej, it should go out, but we better get things gathered up just in case."

Katrine could see that Papa Olafson had been cutting a swath of barren earth between the hill and the creek. Mama Olafson stood nearby with a spade in her hands.

They gathered back at the cabin and watched the fire. It had burned much of the aspen grove and the scattered spruce trees within it, and it had blackened an area to the south. It moved slowly along the hillside above the creek toward an open meadow. Beyond was a hillside of thick timber.

"As dry as it has been, let us hope it does not get into the pines," Sven said. "At least the wind isn't up."

"Look, Papa Olafson, some horses." Katrine noticed that two riders approached from the southwest.

Nils Adolphson and Lars rode up.

"Thank the Lord, it is not your cabin, Sven," said Nils. "That lightning was something terrible, it was." Nils and Lars swung down.

"Ja, I think that fire smoldered all night and then took off this morning. It doesn't look like it will go far. Probably it will burn out in the meadow where it's wet before it reaches the timber."

As they continued watching, Anton Wikstrom and Björn rode into the yard. After exchanging greetings, they all stood watching the orange line slowly advance. When it reached the meadow, a line of white smoke began billowing up. The flames dimmed.

86

"Ja, it is too wet," Sven said. "We have nothing to worry."

Margret invited everyone in for some coffee and corn bread. Katrine and Mia tripped over themselves to help. Soon the men were discussing other things, wondering if the crops would recover, wondering if they were prepared for winter, and wondering if anyone new would arrive.

Katrine grew sufficiently brave to lure Lars and Björn away from the table. She wanted to show off their garden and farmyard. They reached the fence. The crops lay flattened, much worse than what Katrine had imagined.

"W-we had a garden."

"It will grow back," Lars explained. "At least the root crops will."

Katrine stood on the railing looking for any hope. The boys seemed less interested in the garden than they did in the creek. They soon had pulled up their trousers and were chasing minnows.

"You should put a dam here and make a pond," Björn suggested.

"We go farther down the creek to bathe," Katrine explained.

"You wouldn't have to walk so far," said Lars. "It wouldn't be like our hot springs, but you could go swimming if you dammed it up."

Katrine became envious. Both Lars and Björn had hot springs. "Well, our swimming place is deep. We can already swim there whenever we want."

"We might build our hot springs deeper," Lars said.

"We might build a *badstuga* sometime," Katrine said. Why she suggested this, she did not know, other than for some reason she remembered the Eskolas' sauna back in Minnesota. Similar to the Finnish, the Swedes had brought the custom to America with them.

Björn waded about in the creek chasing the tiny fish. "I was thinking you should build a pond for fish, but of course, if you wanted, you could go swimming too."

Katrine had noticed the minnows before. "You have a good idea, Björn. Maybe I will ask Papa Olafson."

Björn arched his eyes and smiled. Katrine liked Björn's smile, his deep blue eyes, and his thick freckles, but she was careful not to say anything like that.

The boys climbed out and sat with Katrine and Mia on the bank, enjoying the warm day.

"I'm glad you came to visit," Katrine said.

"We came because of the fire," Lars reminded her.

"Well, maybe you can come sometime just to visit."

"We already visit at Sunday meeting," Lars replied. "Besides, you don't have a hot springs."

The comment stung, and Katrine wondered why she had mentioned visiting.

"If you want, you can come visit us," Björn said.

"We would have to walk. It's way too far," Katrine admitted. "We can't use the horse in case Mama Olafson needs it. Papa Olafson needs all the mules in the fields." The thought of visiting had sent a quick surge through her.

"It's not too far," Björn said. He turned and gestured toward the low hill to the north. "All you do is walk over that hill. I've walked up there from my side, and it's not too far to your side."

"Maybe after the baby comes," Katrine said. The thought of the hot springs tugged at her. Then she remembered the bear ... and the mountain lion. Even after the baby arrived, she was not sure she could brave the trail.

Katrine later told Papa Olafson about Björn's idea to make a pond.

"I have been thinking the same thing," Sven replied. "It's too far down the creek to the beaver pond for you and Mia to go alone, and soon Mama won't be able to go with you."

He stood and brushed off his trousers. "And I think today is as good a day as any to get started. Come, girls, we're going to the Wikstroms' to get the wagon for this job."

He saddled up Boots and then threw the blanket onto Ornery. They took the shorter, upper trail around the hill. Although the men had discussed cutting trees to shorten the road, neither had cut any. The return trip with the wagon would be an additional mile because of it, but Katrine knew how precious time was, and building roads was not as important as tending fields, especially after the hail.

At the Wikstroms', they visited just long enough to say hello. Sven hitched the wagon to the horse and mule, and on the return trip, he stopped where they had gathered rocks for their fireplace.

"We'll need lots of these rocks."

Katrine could not carry a single rock the size that Papa Olafson carried, but he seemed happy with whatever stones she and Mia loaded into the wagon.

Back at their land, they unloaded the rocks below the small pond on the creek nearest to the cabin. But when they had finished unloading the rocks, Katrine could not believe how small the pile was.

"It's going to take a long time, isn't it, Papa Olafson?"

"For sure. Just you remember, the longest day begins with a single moment. It is how you use all those moments that makes the difference."

They took the wagon back for more rocks, and for the next several days, they brought back even more loads. The pile that blocked the creek slowly grew taller.

Finally, Sven stood back. "I may add more rocks in the future, but for now this will do."

The small pond had increased to twenty feet across and about four feet deep.

"By gum, I believe you shall now be able to swim here," Sven said. "And maybe some trout will move up into the pond as well. We can go ice fishing. The real reason I built this dam is for the stock and us this winter. This will make it easier to get water."

Katrine thought they were done, but Papa Olafson took them for still another load of rocks. They began work on what appeared to be a small rock hut below the pond outlet. It spanned the creek.

He began splitting some aspen logs and rough-hewing them flat.

"I shall be glad when we set up a sawpit so I can have some decent lumber," Sven said.

He laid out the rough boards and laid a brace across them. He augered holes through the brace and pegged it to the boards. He fit the finished lid to the top of the rock box.

"There, we now have a springhouse." Sven tapped the top. "Make sure you girls keep rocks on the top of this lid. Some bear will figure out there's something tasty inside if you don't."

He straightened. "Now all we need is a cow so we can put some milk and cream inside." He glanced about the valley. "This is perfect country for raising cows, I should think." He smiled at Katrine and Mia. "Next spring, maybe."

Katrine felt warmed. Papa Olafson was the finest carpenter among the settlers. He had some very nice tools. She watched the water cascading over the rock dam and disappearing under the springhouse. Now they had a pond where she could bathe in the summer and skate in the winter. More importantly, they had a nearby place to get water and a place where they could store their food.

Chapter 12

SOMETHING HAD AWAKENED Katrine. It took a moment for her to place the sounds. It was Mama Olafson. Katrine came fully awake. *It's time.*

"I think the baby's coming," Katrine whispered and scooted under the curtain. Papa Olafson was up and moving about. Mama Olafson was doubled over, breathing hard.

"Katrine, sweetheart," Sven whispered. "You should be in your room."

"It's the baby, isn't it?" Katrine asked. Her eyes were big with the thought.

Margret nodded. "Yes, I thought I had a little more time."

Sven embraced Margret and kissed her. "I can get Mrs. Adolphson. I'll be gone at most two hours."

"The baby might be here by then," Margret whispered. Perspiration wetted her forehead.

Katrine wanted to volunteer. She could ride the horse and knew the way, but something held her back. It was night outside.

"I can help," Katrine offered. "You just tell me what to do." Inside she shook. She had no idea what to expect or how she could help. She had seen calves being born, but this was different; it was a human baby.

"We don't have any choice," Sven replied. "You and Mia can get things ready." Sven shook as he pulled on his shirt, tucked it, and started pulling on his boots. "Stoke the fire. You'll need some hot water." He shoved his hat on, grabbed his coat and rifle, and leaned over. "Take your time, Margret, *älskling*. Just tell our son to wait a bit longer." He smiled thinly.

"Our *son* may be another daughter," Margret whispered.

"Then tell her to wait." Sven ducked out the door. "She's had nine months. A couple hours longer won't matter any."

Katrine knew he was joking. The baby would come whether it was told to wait or not.

90

Margret turned to Katrine. "You do what Papa said. When Mrs. Adolphson gets here, we'll need some hot water."

Mia came into the room.

"Push the sheet back," Katrine said. "The baby's coming."

"Now?" She rubbed her eyes.

"Pretty soon. We're going to be midwives." Katrine had heard the term but had no idea what would be in store.

Margret moaned again. "I should have paid attention last evening when I thought I just felt some kicking."

Katrine stoked the fire. Not knowing what else she could do, she came back and sat near Mama Olafson.

"You can get some cloth ready," Margret said. "I have my sewing kit with a cord and scissors."

Mia knew where it was.

Margret breathed harder. Her face grimaced. "Come, girls. You can feel."

They both placed their hands on Mama Olafson's belly. Katrine felt how tight it was, and she felt the baby move.

"The baby wants to come out," Margret explained.

Katrine wished she knew more what to do. The water was nearly ready. Papa Olafson was a long time yet from being back. She hoped he would hurry. Mama Olafson was hurting, but she had said it was the way it was supposed to be.

Daylight had arrived. Katrine had dozed. The sounds of horses and talking brought her fully awake. Papa Olafson and Mrs. Adolphson came through the door. Things became a flurry of activity.

"How are you doing, Margret?" Astrid asked.

Other niceties were exchanged. Katrine wanted to sleep. She had been awake all night.

"Louise had her baby, and now you," Astrid continued.

"Yes, I heard you went there to help as well."

"He doesn't look Swedish at all. His hair is just as dark as his brother's and sister's. I'm not sure what Mr. Lundgren thinks about that. They've named him Oscar." Astrid patted Margret's head.

"That's a nice name, Oscar."

"Well, now that I'm here, Katrine, you and Mia can play outside. I'll call you when I need your help."

Katrine frowned. Before Mrs. Adolphson had arrived, she was old enough to help. How was it that now she wasn't? She wanted to see.

"Come, girls," Sven called. "We can be outside. The day is nice. We won't go very far."

Torsten arrived the morning of August 6, 1863. When Katrine heard his cries, an inexplicable warmth flooded her. She wasn't really a big sister, unlike Mia now was, but Katrine felt like one. It was a special new feeling in her life.

Katrine and Mia snuck back inside.

"He's a feisty one," Astrid said. "You have a healthy, beautiful son, Margret."

Tears wet Margret's face. She held the tiny infant to her breast. Katrine watched with wonder. A new life had arrived. Torsten pushed hungrily at his mother's breast.

Katrine felt happy but remembered that Torsten was not her real brother. "He's wrinkled," she said.

Sven laughed. "Like all of God's creatures, we start life that way, and we shall end life that way."

Katrine did not like the thought but smiled. Ironically, she recalled Mr. Adolphson's hopes that new settlers would come to the valley. She knew he continued to write letters to his friends back east and encouraged the others to do so as well. Papa Olafson had written some. But no one had come—only the original six families. Now two new settlers had arrived, not from Minnesota or Fort Boise or Lewiston but from among themselves.

Torsten had quieted. His big eyes seemed to catch sight of Katrine. Katrine knew the baby was too young, yet she liked to think that he had sought her. Strange sensations washed over her. It would not be too many years until she would be of age, although she never allowed herself to dwell on such thoughts. What did the future hold for her? Would her future be with Harald or with Jens or with someone who had not yet reached the valley? She thought it would be someone she would yet meet.

"You have your wish, Mia," Katrine said, finding her words awkward. "You have a little brother."

"I'm happy. I now have a sister and a brother."

Katrine swallowed. She found herself trembling, unable to confront her own feelings. A darkness descended. "I have a brother too," she whispered, fighting her thoughts. "I have a brother too," she said more loudly.

Mia stared back, her eyes unwavering. She said nothing, but Katrine knew what she thought. *Your brother is lost, and everyone says he's dead.*

Katrine left the cabin. She wandered into the yard. Her eyes automatically swept to the southern hill and charred aspens, the direction from which she knew Erik must come. *Nothing.*

Shortly after Torsten's birth, Sven took Katrine and Mia down along the creek to near the beaver pond where they had gone swimming and where some willows grew. They cut and trimmed dozens of long eight- to ten-foot willows. Sven bundled them and tied them onto their riding mule, Ornery.

"If we use Ornery more often, maybe she'll give less trouble when carrying you girls around."

Back at the cabin, Sven split some of the willows and trimmed others. He began shaping some into large bows, soaking them in the wooden tub in hot water. He took a section of log and smoothed one side. He cut an oval section, drilled holes along one edge with bit and auger, flipped it over, and drilled four more holes, one at each corner.

Katrine figured out what he was making by the time he began soaking and forming two long willows. She watched him bend and twist one around the other and then attach them to the seat. He drilled holes for smaller spindles across the curved back and laced smaller willows through the spindles.

He drilled more holes and tapped in braces for two arms. He curved some stout pieces of mountain maple for the rockers and attached them to the four legs.

By week's end, Margret's new rocking chair stood ready. Now she had a nice, comfortable chair to rock in and in which to put baby Torsten to sleep. Katrine and Mia climbed onto the rocking chair whenever given a chance, rocking themselves as well.

Sven laughed. "I best start making another one, I see." He stroked his chin. "Where does the time go?"

WIKSTROM HOT SPRINGS

Chapter 13

Every day after visiting the Wikstroms, Katrine had wanted to return and swim in the hot springs, but now that Torsten had been born, she reasoned they would not be able to go for a visit for a very long time. So she was very surprised when Papa Olafson said, "What do you think if you and Mia ride over and visit the Wikstroms? I'm going to help Mama with Torsten today and build a cradle."

Katrine swallowed. She and Mia had ridden several times to the Adolphsons', but they had always been with Papa Olafson. They had not ridden very far by themselves.

"If you go to the hot springs, you won't need to take a bath tonight. Would you like that?"

"Yes." Katrine was thrilled but also a little scared. She was curious as to why Papa Olafson did not want her help. Frequently she held pieces of wood and fetched his tools.

Mia jumped up and down, squealing. "Should we take them something?"

"Certainly," Margret said. She put Torsten down. "Take them some corn bread. And don't spend all your time at the hot springs. Help Anna."

Katrine hugged Papa and Mama Olafson.

"If you aren't back by dusk, I'm coming to look for you," Sven warned.

Katrine knew that would not be good. Mama Olafson would be left alone with baby Torsten.

Sven helped Katrine onto Boots and positioned Mia behind her. He patted Katrine. "You just make sure Boots minds who her boss is."

Katrine knew a horse needed to know who was in charge. That was partly done by a firm grip on the reins at first. Horses liked to go places, however, and Katrine knew after they started out that Boots would likely follow the trail all the way around the mountain and to the Wikstroms' without much pause.

When Katrine reached the trail that cut over the hill, she turned

Boots up it. Instead of following the wagon trail past the Lundgrens', this direction would cut off about a mile.

Boots seemed to know she was expected to be gentle and kept moving except for when they reached a pool of water where she insisted on pausing to drink. Katrine and Mia both almost slid over the mare's neck.

"That was close," Mia said. "We almost fell off."

"We could get back on," Katrine said. "I would take Boots to a big log or something." She had to sound confident for Mia's sake.

They crossed the ridge, dropped down, and forded the creek that came down past the Wikstroms' place. Boots clambered up the bank and turned upstream toward the cabin.

Katrine felt proud when she rode into the Wikstroms' yard. Anna, Linnea, and Laurens immediately spilled out of the cabin and ran to her. She began telling about their ride over. Mia gave Anna the corn bread.

"We'll have it for dinner when Björn and Papa are back," Anna said. "You can help me."

Katrine visited with Anna and helped her prepare dinner while Mia and Linnea explored. They fixed up some steamed nettles and some salt pork along with the corn bread.

Shortly, Anton and Björn came in from the fields. Both greeted them happily. Anton held out his big arms to give them a hug.

"What a nice surprise. How is your mama doing, and how's that new baby brother?"

"He's feisty," said Katrine, remembering what Mrs. Adolphson had said.

After noon dinner, Anton glanced around, smiling. "Well, this beings Saturday, I think Björn and I have done enough. I imagine you would all like to go to the hot springs so you can be ready for Sunday meeting tomorrow."

Katrine shivered with excitement. She knew that would be what he would think, and soon they were all headed up to the springs. The girls unbraided their hair and splashed about in the upper pool. Katrine noticed there had been some work done to it. The water that fed this pool cascaded from a short distance above them across a flat rock and sprayed down into the water. Katrine sat under the spray.

"My pa and me have been working on it, making it bigger," Björn said, arching his eyes. "We've been moving rocks out of the bottom and piling them on the sides."

He reached down and, straining, pulled up a fair-sized rock. Katrine took ahold and helped him roll it toward the edge. They moved a couple more, but most were too heavy to lift.

"I'll wait for my pa on the bigger rocks," Björn said. He sat back in the water. Katrine sat next to him, allowing the water to wash over her.

After a short while, Björn led the way to the lower pool where he again began moving rocks. Katrine tried to help. A couple of spots were quite deep.

"We haven't been able to make this one much bigger, but it's a lot deeper," Björn admitted. "Anna washes our clothes here because it's hotter—especially where it comes out of the ground here." Björn reached up and touched the gushing water coming down from above them.

Katrine reached into the water. She quickly pulled her hand away, surprised at how hot it was.

Björn laughed. "By the time it drops down here, it's cool enough." Björn sank down into the pool again. "Come, maybe we can move some more rocks."

They both moved a few more rocks before tiring from the work and then made their way back to the upper pool.

Katrine liked the upper pool better. Although not as deep, there was more room, and she could see the trail that wound its way toward the cabin below. She turned and studied where the trail disappeared above them.

"Anna, do you know where the trail goes?" Katrine asked.

"Papa says it goes over the mountains into the Salmon River country. He said Indians used to use it."

"Have you seen any Indians?" Mia asked, her eyes big.

"No, but someday we might," Anna replied. "Papa says to always be on the watch."

"Do you think they'll come back?" Katrine asked.

"Probably sometime."

Katrine shivered. She wondered what they would look like and if they would be murderous. The trail near their cabin was similar. Papa Olafson had said the same thing—that it used to be an Indian trail and that it might still be in use.

Katrine found herself scooting closer to Anna and Linnea. She didn't want to think about Indians. Instead, the girls talked about sewing new dresses. Anna was jealous that Mama Olafson had cloth for making dresses.

"I have to patch Björn's trousers again, and I don't have any extra material," Anna said.

"When we come again, I'll bring you some," Katrine said.

"Maybe you should come to our place. Mama will help you," Mia suggested.

Björn and Laurens had left the pool and found a large, flat rock to lie on in the sun.

Anna noticed and suggested it was time to go.

Katrine lingered. She was happy in the warm water. It felt silky. She waved her hand through the crystal water in front of her, her fingers snaking through the dappled light that shined through.

"It's time." Anna waded to the side of the pool where Katrine reluctantly joined her. They helped each other braid their hair and then dressed.

"You'll get sunburn," Anna called to the two boys. "We best go."

At the cabin, they began making some supper. It was some soup and the remaining corn bread. It was a lighter meal than the noon meal. Katrine hated that the day had gone so quickly.

Anton helped Katrine and Mia back onto Boots. He said much the same as Sven had said. "Now, you just make sure you let that horse know who's boss."

When they had headed back along the trail, he hollered after them, "Tell your folks hello and come whenever you would like."

Katrine shivered. "Maybe we can come swimming every week," she whispered to Mia.

After she and Mia had made it back home, she thought long about the Wikstroms and the hot springs. Mostly she thought about Björn and how much fun she had with him. It had been like playing with Erik. Her stomach clenched. Well, she did have a brother now, but he was only a few weeks old.

Chapter 14

THE ASPENS TURNED golden, and the tamarack began to glow yellow amid the black spruce on the mountainsides, their spindly limbs appearing as if they were fiery Christmas trees. The low huckleberry shrubs and red osier dogwood turned bright red. The willows changed from bright green to various shades of rust and pale yellow.

The autumn foliage did not remain long. A cold storm blew through, blanketing the surrounding peaks in white and scattering a dusting throughout the valley. Cold settled in behind the storm, and each morning, frost carpeted the meadows. Sven cut the oats, to what extent they had ripened, and brought them in.

Katrine helped him stack them under the lean-to out of the snow.

"We won't have any meal or porridge, but the horse and mules won't care," Sven said. "To them, this will be dessert." He pitched more of the loose oats onto the pile.

Katrine wanted to try to get some grain but decided Papa Olafson was right. "What about the rye?"

"What little I got planted will grow all winter. Next summer we should have a small crop."

The harvest was complete. The men gathered at the Adolphsons' place with what little crops they could spare for trading at Boise City. Katrine helped gather a few potatoes and onions. Three men—Nils, Gustaf, and Magnus—were shortly headed down the river with the crops as well as with some butter, milk, and eggs.

Going on three weeks, the men returned to the Adolphsons' where they distributed the goods. Nils explained he was able to arrange with a merchant to take credit against their future crops. The merchant was pleased with what they had brought in, especially with the potatoes. The spuds helped convince him that they were worth the risk. As a result, they brought back additional staples for the six families—salt, wheat flour, cornmeal, beans, and salt pork. They also brought back some sugar, coffee, and tea.

Almost as important as the staples, they brought back news. Nils shared that a bloody battle had been fought at Gettysburg, which resulted favorably for the Union. General Lee was turned back from the North. In the western territories, the mines near Boise City were now booming, and local goods were coming into the area. Boise City was the main supply point for the gold strike in Boise Basin. Lewiston remained the main supply point for the mines to the north in the Salmon River district. All the mining camps needed fresh goods, and the packers taking in the goods were doing well, selling everything at premium prices.

"Which means we could sell everything we produce and then some," Nils concluded.

"But we also have to have enough to feed ourselves," Hans said.

"Ja, I promise it will not be like this forever," Nils said. "Next season we grow more, and soon we will have all the produce and beef they will want. We will all be doing very well."

"At least we had a good trail," Magnus said. "The river was low. Our bridge was still there."

"Ja, we were not thinking. If we had had more mules and proper harness, we would have tried to get back another of the wagons," Nils said. "All three are still where we left them."

A few days later, Sven began cutting trees on the hill behind the cabin. He hitched Jack to the new logs and snaked them down into the yard where he began smoothing them. Katrine helped by handing him tools as he worked. Using the adze, he chopped notches along the top, the length of each log. Then using his broadax, he cut and trimmed off the notches, creating a rough but flat surface. He positioned each log across a couple of braces and then planed and smoothed the flattened surface until it was soft and even.

"What do you think, Katrine?" Sven ran his hand down one of the smoothed logs.

Katrine ran hers down as well. It felt silky smooth. "It feels nice."

Sven entered the cabin and began moving things from one side to the other. "I'm building a floor," he announced.

Katrine had guessed that was what he intended, and she and Mia were soon carrying items temporarily outside.

Sven cut into the earthen floor and began laying the smoothed logs, one next to the other.

Katrine and Mia bounced barefoot on each as he placed and leveled it. When Sven had laid half the floor, he moved everything to the finished side. Margret mostly watched from her rocking chair while taking care of Torsten.

"There," Sven remarked as he tapped the final puncheon plank into place. "I'm sorry I had to wait until now to do this."

He stood and dusted his hands. "It's not much, but it will do until we build a real house with real floors."

Margret tucked Torsten into his cradle and hugged Sven. "It's wonderful, Papa. Just wonderful." She twirled with him across the floor.

Katrine and Mia clapped and danced about as well.

Margret paused and kissed Sven. "Remember that even God did not create the world in a single day. No man could do more than what you have already done."

The following morning, Katrine woke to Papa Olafson packing some gear. Boots was in the yard, as were two of the mules.

"I best be doing some hunting," he explained. "I'm heading north with Mr. Wikstrom and Mr. Andreasson to see if we can get a deer or two. You and Mia can help me smoke it. How's that?" He tied his bedroll behind the cantle and lashed his rifle on top.

Katrine knew the men needed to do some hunting. No one yet had pigs or cattle to slaughter. Some families had already harvested deer. The older boys had earlier discovered the best fishing holes and were occasionally excused from some of their farm duties to go fishing. Those families who lived near the river had run nets for whitefish and trout. They pickled some of the smaller fish, similar to pickling herring back in Sweden. They smoked the larger fish. Katrine and Mia fished the pond Sven had built near their cabin, but the trout were small. He promised he would take them to the river for salmon when they began running.

As he headed out, Sven called to Katrine, "You take care of Mama and baby Torsten. Say a prayer that I'll be bringing back some meat."

"Of course, Papa Olafson." Katrine stood with Mia and Mama Olafson holding Torsten and watched him heading toward the Wikstroms'.

Four days later, he was back with Anton and Björn, an elk packed onto the backs of the two mules.

Katrine and Mia danced about. "You got us one," Katrine said.

"Ja but just. We saw nothing until we got to the high country north of the big lake," Sven said. "Then we got lucky. A herd of six cow elk walked out in front of us. I got one, and Andreasson got one. We're sharing mine with the Wikstroms."

Shortly, Margret, Katrine, and Mia had the large pots outside filled with water and a fire going. The men hung the elk, skinned it, and began cutting the meat into thin strips for brining.

Katrine helped Björn drag aspen poles into the yard for building a large smoke tent. As the meat soaked in the salt brine, Sven and Anton erected the poles and wrapped a canvas about them, forming a tepee. Björn and Katrine began cutting green aspen and willow wood for the smoke. Sven and Anton strung twine near the apex and built a small fire underneath. When the fire had burned down to coals, Margret and Mia hung the meat from the twine. Björn and Katrine threw on chunks of green aspen logs and closed up the tent. Billowing white smoke seeped from the top. The smoke tent was finished.

While the smoking was in progress, Margret fixed a dinner of fresh elk steaks, potatoes, and gravy.

"I don't know what the reason for raising cattle will be if we can get an elk every season," Anton said, shaking his head.

"You forget we tramped over half the country to find them," Sven said and laughed. "We got lucky."

"Ja, I would not depend on the elk, but it would be good to get at least one each year."

"I'm not done hunting," Sven said. "Maybe a few deer won't go over the mountains and down into the canyons."

Anton agreed. "But when do any of us have time for hunting?"

The settlers had expected Louise Lundgren to teach school, but there was little effort to begin. Louise's baby, Oscar, who had been born shortly before Torsten, was yet shy of eight weeks old. Instead of teaching, Louise passed out the few readers and arithmetic books to the older children and assigned them the responsibility of instructing their younger siblings as they were able. At Sunday meeting, she gathered the children together, and they compared notes with what they had learned.

Otherwise, the children helped their parents prepare for winter by picking berries and harvesting the remaining vegetables from their gardens. Mostly the boys helped their fathers bring in hay, build fences, and construct shelters. There was little free time for school or for play.

Each night brought frost, and ice formed on the pond's edges. A skiff of snow covered the ground. Katrine helped Sven bring some of the cured hay from a loose stack in the field to the lean-to near the corral where it would be easier to access when the snow deepened.

While they worked, it began snowing. Katrine brushed it from her hair, watching it fall from the sky.

"Before the end of winter, Mr. Adolphson says we will have six feet," Sven reminded her.

Katrine shivered. She could not imagine six feet. Standing tall, she would still be buried by nearly two feet.

"Ah, it won't come all at once, that's for sure, but some days you might think so." Sven leaned on his pitchfork. "We had deep snow in the old country. Of course Mia wouldn't remember, and I don't know what part of Sweden your family came from. If I remember, your pa said Wärmland. There was not as much snow where your family lived." He winked and threw more hay to the back of the shed.

"I remember snow. I don't know how deep it was. Erik told me it was deep."

The snow that had begun softly now increased to a fury. Thick flakes swirled out of the sky. This was unlike the first scattered snowstorms that had dusted the high country. Katrine had never experienced a storm like it—not in Minnesota and certainly not last winter at Fort Boise.

"The size of goose feathers," Mia remarked.

"Frozen goose feathers," Katrine said. She worried. All day the day before, it had snowed. Today it snowed. Nearly two feet had accumulated.

"We better start praying this roof holds," Sven murmured.

Margret nursed Torsten, rocking gently, and glanced quickly to where Sven looked.

Katrine caught her look. "It will hold, Mama Olafson. We did a good job building it." Katrine recalled when she and Mia had helped Papa Olafson cover the roof with sod.

Deep within, she was disappointed that it was snowing. Just before it had begun, Papa Olafson had promised to take her to the Adolphsons'. They wanted to get some supplies for Christmas, and she had seen some pale blue cloth. She told Papa Olafson it would be a very nice Christmas present for Mama Olafson, but it would be better if she had it early so she had time to make things.

Sven had said, "That's a strange present. We give her a present so she can make presents."

"When I'm older, that's what I would like," Katrine said. Of course she hoped she could help with the sewing.

"I suppose that would be like someone giving me a nice piece of cherry wood so I could make bowls," Sven said. "By gum, you are right. I think it would be a very nice present."

They had waited for the baby to arrive and for the crops to be done. Winter was a time for indoor work. Now it was time, but with all the snow, Katrine wondered if they would ever be able to go.

"Perhaps I should begin working on respectable chairs," Sven mused. "I should have had you girls bring in some more saplings. When the snow stops, we'll all gather some."

Margret cradled Torsten, taping him gently, rocking softly. "I would like some chairs."

A loud crack filled the cabin, and a raft of snow slid through the ceiling, skittering across the floor.

"Up, up," shouted Sven. He pushed Mia away from the cascading snow.

Katrine and Margret scrambled to the back of the cabin.

Another crackle erupted, and more snow slid into the cabin. Then all was quiet.

"Maybe she'll hold," Margret whispered, holding baby Torsten closely.

"For sure it will." Sven continued eying the ceiling. "It was that one spot that always concerned me."

CHRISTMAS 1863

Chapter 15

On a clear late-November morning, Katrine and Sven headed downstream toward the Adolphsons'.

"It may be our best chance," Sven explained.

Katrine followed on Boots as Papa Olafson broke trail with Ornery in the lead. The horse never seemed to mind following the mule, but frequently, the mule protested if expected to follow the horse.

Katrine was excited. Mama Olafson would be so happy to have the blue cloth. They also needed other supplies, having gone short already on salt because of brining the elk.

The Adolphsons always seemed to have lots of things, mused Katrine. Their cabin had become a stopping place along the trail for those going into the mines to the north. Occasionally someone would leave a newspaper or relay news of happenings in Idaho Territory and the war. Any news was a source for discussion during their Sunday meetings. Now with the snow beginning to pile deep, Katrine knew fewer of the families would be able to make the trips on Sundays. She was happy they were going.

Katrine enjoyed riding across the sparkling snow. Everything glittered and danced. Ice particles materialized in front of her and gleamed in the bright air. Boots clambered through the snow, steam venting from her nostrils. The mare seemed to enjoy the snow as well.

"Keep your eyes on the dark trees," Sven warned. "This bright snow can blind you."

She followed Papa Olafson as he worked his way off the trail along the apron of some trees where it was less bright.

"I best make us some goggles for next time," he said.

Except that it was not as bright under the trees, Katrine did not care for riding under them. Sudden hollows and dips made it dangerous footing for the horse and mule. Sometimes buried brush broke loose as they crossed and flipped up against the animals' hocks. Snow dropped from the branches onto Katrine's head and back. She was happier when they broke out into the open again, but now she squinted against the bright sun.

Katrine spotted the steam rising from the hot springs well before they reached the river. When they arrived, everyone came running— Mr. and Mrs. Adolphson, Lars, Ingrid, and young Pelle. Since the heavy snow of a couple of weeks ago, Katrine had not seen any of them.

Katrine felt overjoyed to get the blue cloth. Papa Olafson picked up the other supplies and also bargained for some dried peaches. Katrine shivered. She knew Mama Olafson would make a pie.

"Do I have credit?" Sven asked.

Nils replied, "Ja, but if you have the time, maybe you could make us a rocking chair. All I hear from my missus is how much she wants a rocking chair like Margret's."

Sven glanced strangely toward Astrid.

"Not for that reason," Nils quickly said.

"Ah." He laughed.

By mid-December, snow had blanketed the valley in a thick mantle. Gentle, shadowy folds showed the twists and turns where the creek flowed underneath. Occasional jagged black lines revealed the faster, open water. The stock had cut trails from the clumps of aspens where they liked to gather and down to the larger creek. The animals no longer wandered out trying to graze but stood patiently near the rail fence that surrounded the lean-to for hay to be thrown out.

Sven broke trail with Jack, heading to the Adolphsons' for Sunday meeting; Margret carried three-month-old Torsten all bundled up in a thick blanket in front of her on Boots; and Katrine and Mia rode Ornery. The sky was bright blue, but the cold nipped at Katrine. Both she and Mia wore long scarves, wrapped about their mouths and noses.

The lean-to-like barn where they all gathered at the Adolphsons' and had their dinners had three open sides with one log wall. Recent visits had shortened, depending on the weather. After dinner and before returning to their own homes, they warmed themselves inside the cabin. They visited for three or four hours and then were back on the trails before the early darkness could catch them.

"Maybe next season, we can build a church for a proper school and meeting place," Nils suggested. "At the very least, we can build that sawpit and start cutting boards to put sides on this lean-to."

Katrine was happy to see that everyone had made it to the Adolphsons'. They had all brought fixings for a special dinner. The Adolphsons had affixed a canvas to cut down on the wind. The women and the youngest children stayed inside in the warmth of the cabin and prepared the dinner. The men gathered outside and visited near a large fire that Lars and the older boys tended. Some of the other children chased each other and threw snowballs until it was time for Saint Lucia. Then everyone gathered under the lean-to. Anna played the role of Saint Lucia, dressed in her white bedclothes, wearing a crown of fir boughs and kinnikinnick with lit candles affixed. Anna walked among everyone, passing out sugar-sprinkled wheat rolls with dried wild currants.

This was a special moment for Katrine. She remembered the story of Saint Lucia who visited the leper caves and wore a crown of candles for light so she could free her hands to hand out the bread.

The sun settling in the western sky sent long rays across the snow. They sang a Santa Lucia song.

> Sankta Lucia, ljusklara hägring, sprid i vår vinternatt
> glans av din fägring
> Drömmar med vingesus under oss sia, tänd dina vita
> Ijus, Sankta Lucia
>
> Saint Lucia, bright clear mirage, spread in our winter
> splendor of your beauty
> Dreams with wings rustling over us prophesy, light your
> white candles, Saint Lucia

Nils said a prayer. Then he reminded everyone, "Soon the days will grow longer and light will be with us. Before we are ready, it will be time for Midsummer's Eve."

Katrine shivered. Looking out at the snow, now blue with shadows, and feeling the gripping cold, it was difficult for her to imagine the summer's light and warmth. They now faced winter's quiet isolation and cold.

The men and older boys remained outside talking for a while, a leg thrown over the other, smoking their pipes, gathered near the fire. One occasionally directed one of the boys to toss on another piece of wood. Katrine and the women and younger children kept warm in the cabin with cups of hot tea.

The sun slipped below the horizon, and the evening darkness gathered quickly. The families bundled up and headed back across the snow to their homes, miles away.

Sven led the way with Jack picking his way back across the trail. The snow lit the countryside well enough that they could see the trail. Having come across it several times, the stock easily pushed through.

Margret whispered to Katrine and Mia, "This is like Joseph and Mary going to Bethlehem, don't you suppose?"

"Yes, Mama Olafson," Katrine whispered. Stars spread frozen in the black canopy above. She hugged Mia. It had been a wonderful Santa Lucia day. Soon it would be Christmas.

Then she paused. She could not help but think of her own parents. She accepted that they now watched down on her. She thought of Erik, maybe somehow still alive, looking up at the same starry December night. She imagined him in a cabin somewhere safe, maybe thinking about her.

Chapter 16

A SEVERE STORM accompanied the arrival of 1864. It was little comfort to Katrine knowing that the days were slowly lengthening. The snow continued to pile up and now came up to the edge of the roof. She and Mia walked over it with little trouble. The cabin was like a cave inside a snowdrift.

Sven kept trails cut between the cabin and the lean-to where the hay was stored and near where the horse and mules huddled. He had cut and stacked wood against the side of the cabin. As the stack shrank, more of the cabin walls became exposed to the snow and cold.

Katrine's most demanding chore was to bring in water each day. She also brought in wood, making sure a good supply remained near the hearth. Some would always be drying for easier burning. She kept a small amount of kindling in the corner in case the fire went out and had to be relit.

The weather remained bitter cold, and one snowstorm chased after another as the snow continued to pile. It now filled the valley to a depth of four feet.

"I should be making skis," Sven muttered. "No horse can get about in this snow. Maybe after it packs down some but not like this. I guess we won't be making any Sunday gatherings." He had begun work on a *proper table,* as he called it, from pieces of wood he had brought in last autumn.

Katrine and Mia worked on a rag rug, braiding strips of discarded cloth and sewing the pieces to an ever-growing spiral.

Margret tended to Torsten and began sewing with the blue cloth. "We should just do what we can do."

"Ja, the only trouble I see with this snow is that it comes without much daylight. About the time the sun comes up, and things warm up a bit, the sun goes down again," Sven said.

"Yes, and now I think we are about out of light, unless you wish to light a candle," Margret said.

"Nej, save the candle. We can go to bed." Sven hammered on the table, fitting a peg to hold a piece of wood.

"Maybe tomorrow you girls can go outside and play in the snow now that it seems to have stopped snowing," Margret said. She began putting up her work.

Katrine tucked the rug away. It would be a good thing tomorrow to leave the cabin. These last few days locked up in the snowstorm were telling on everyone. But even outdoors they were confined to the packed trails. She got up and put Torsten into his cradle. She pulled the sheet across the cabin, and she and Mia changed into their nightclothes. Katrine decided at the last minute to look out, just to make sure the snow had finished falling.

She pushed open the door. It took a moment to see anything in the dark. Strange lights flickered across the snow. She looked behind her, puzzled. The fire was low. She glanced back across the meadow. Unmistakably, soft, glowing colors flowed across the snowy landscape.

Katrine turned toward the north and recoiled, stunned by the sight. Billowy curtains of light green and blue, like shimmering waterfalls, blazed behind the northern mountains behind her, casting their colored light across the snowy peaks and the landscape below. *The northern lights.*

"Come quick, come quick." Katrine stuck her head back into the cabin. "Look at this."

"What is it?" Margret asked as she and the others came quickly to the door.

"It's the northern lights!" Katrine exclaimed. She waded into the snow, gazing upward, mesmerized by the lights until her feet began stinging from the cold. She then ran back in and shoved on her shoes. She grabbed Mia and tugged her outside where they began dancing together in the snow. Katrine waved her arms and spun about with her head back, drinking in the incredible sight.

Mia laughed and twirled as well.

They danced together, arm in arm, in the deep snow. Margret and Sven hugged and laughed at the show above them.

Bright, billowy greens and blues with tints of rose hung suspended across the sky, dancing and flowing outward, waving in and out among tendrils of pale greenish light, filling the sky, wave after wave.

114

Never had Katrine seen anything like it. It was magic, truly magic. Her breath caught, and ice nipped in her nose, but the glorious lights held her fast.

"It's like the fairies are dancing," she said softly.

"Ja," Sven replied, "that is what they say back in Sweden, the snow fairies. For sure, they are dancing. Can you remember them so beautiful, Margret?"

"No, and we used to see them so often in the old country. Only once did we see them in Minnesota, and they were pale—not anything like this."

Katrine could not tear her eyes away. "They are so beautiful, Mia. And to think anyone who is out tonight can see them, wherever they are."

"Even the Wikstroms and Adolphsons? I hope they see them," Mia said.

Katrine thought of her brother. "Dear Lord," Katrine whispered, "if Erik lives, tell him to look up at the sky tonight. Tell him I'm out here watching the snow fairies dance, just like Mama and Papa said they did back in Sweden."

She turned back toward the mountain. The colors had begun to ebb. The feathery tendrils began waning as if the dance was ending and the snow fairies were tiring. Slowly, the glowing lights dimmed and faded from the black sky. Flickering fingers remained glowing on the northern horizon, rising up occasionally and then fading back. Soon only their memory and a myriad of quietly blazing points of light frozen high above remained.

Because the snow had been so heavy, the Olafsons and Katrine had not attended a Sunday meeting at the Adolphsons for two weeks. When they finally gathered, the news was not of the northern lights, but it was sorrowful news about the Eklunds' baby. Hans and Ulrika were absent. Harald explained he had heard the baby was sick. His mother had gone to their place a couple of times to try to help, but then the snow had come, and she had not been back.

"When she got there last Friday, it was the most terrible scene," Harald said. "The baby died. Mrs. Eklund was still in her bedclothes and hadn't taken care of herself for days. Mr. Eklund was fraught with despair, trying to help, but Mrs. Eklund threw a knife at him and cut his arm. When my mother tried to go inside, Mrs. Eklund was like a possessed troll and just kept screaming and screaming. Mother told me the dead baby was still in their bed."

Katrine's breath caught in gasps, and a clammy knot grew inside her. Robert had been two. During the entire trip from Minnesota, people had worried for him. When they had finally reached the valley, they believed he would be fine and grow stronger. Katrine's vision blurred. Now the boy was dead. Oscar and Torsten had been born. Baby Robert had died.

It was two weeks later when they again gathered at the Adolphsons' for Sunday dinner that Katrine overheard the others talking about the Eklunds. Mr. Eklund had to fight to take baby Robert away from Mrs. Eklund so he could bury him. He dug a hole through the snow on the hillside behind their cabin. His wife screamed at him and grabbed for the baby the entire time. Later Mr. Eklund thought some wolves or coyotes had tried to dig the body up. Only it wasn't wolves, it was Mrs. Eklund. Mr. Eklund almost had to tie her up to keep her from going to the grave and digging up the body again.

Hans soon talked about leaving. Nils and Astrid Adolphson visited. Nils shared some words of comfort from the Bible. Astrid tried to reason with Ulrika but could not connect through the fog of her grief. Hans began saying that coming west was the biggest mistake of his life.

"I can take Ulrika to Minnesota. She has a sister there. I can't do it and hope to still have any cabin or fields by the time I return," Hans said. "If I go, it means leaving all of you."

"Until the snow melts, there is nothing you can do," Nils reminded him.

"I can feed her and help her with necessities, but I can't do any other work," Hans admitted.

It was clear that Hans now only waited for the snow to leave the trail so he could take his wife from the valley.

Chapter 17

THE SNOW RECEDED, and a few prospectors and packers began traveling the river trail past the Adolphsons'. The Swedes gathered at the Adolphsons' to see the men off to Boise City for badly needed supplies.

Hans was there with Ulrika and his fully packed mules. Ulrika was bundled in her coat with a gray shawl over her head, unmoving. Hans steadied his horse. Katrine knew he would not be coming back. A knot welled inside her.

"You're welcome to my chickens, Mr. Adolphson," Hans said. "With luck, I can get my old wagon from below the gorge and get back to Fort Boise with it."

"You don't have to go, Hans," Nils said.

"I have no choice," Hans confessed. "I have to take care of my missus."

"Ja." Nils nodded. "You are young, Hans ... How old?"

"Just now twenty."

Nils handed up a coin pouch. "Here, this is what we could gather together for you. After the resupply, the men may have something additional. No matter, we'll see you have good supplies."

Hans stared for a moment at the proffered pouch before taking it. He turned away, shaking his head slowly before straightening and turning back. "It is not because of any of you here, you understand, Mr. Adolphson. It ... it was more my dream to come here than it was Ulrika's."

"Well, the good Lord willing, Ulrika will come around. Likely so when she sees her sister again. You may have your family yet," Nils said. "Godspeed to you."

Hans looked away again. "My wife ... she didn't have the strength of the rest of you. Baby Robert was all she had. I—"

"You do not have to explain, Hans. We all think highly of you. Maybe encourage others to join an expedition and come here to join us. You've seen the valley. You know we can make good lives here."

Hans nodded and nudged his horse toward the trail. Ulrika's mule followed with the other pack mule tethered behind her.

Katrine thought that Mrs. Eklund resembled a person possessed, the way her eyes appeared from under her gray shawl. They stared unfocused without recognition from one person to the next, even when she gazed at Mr. Eklund.

"You wait at Fort Boise for a good train going back east," Nils demanded. "Promise me you will."

Hans glanced away. "Ja, I have no stomach for facing Indians alone. You can be sure we will not strike out until we have a good company."

Sven rode toward Nils. "I'm ready," he said. "Do not forget we are bringing back the wagons, so give us a full three weeks before you come looking for any of us."

Nils nodded. "Just you keep your eyes on Mrs. Eklund. That's the least we can do."

Sven clucked to Boots and moved to the lead in front of Hans and Ulrika. Magnus and Gustaf fell to the rear behind the Eklunds with the fully loaded string of horses and mules.

Katrine held Mia's hand, waving with Mama Olafson as Papa Olafson led the procession downriver until he passed the bend near the hot springs and disappeared from sight. She kept watching until the last mule disappeared. An uncomfortable knot grew within her. It would be up to her to help Mama Olafson while he was gone. She hoped Mr. and Mrs. Eklund could get back to Minnesota. She wondered why they just didn't stay in the valley with their friends. Mrs. Eklund would get better in time, wouldn't she?

Katrine helped Mia climb back onto Ornery with her and followed Mama Olafson with infant Torsten back toward their cabin. Papa Olafson had taken the rifle but had left his pistol. Katrine knew how to use it, but he had told her to ride to the Wikstroms' if there was any trouble. Mr. Wikstrom had stayed to work his fields and to keep an eye on everyone who remained behind.

No one anticipated trouble, at least not from Indians or drifters. Their biggest trouble would be taking care of themselves and possibly some severe weather.

The first night, Katrine felt terribly alone without Papa Olafson asleep in the cabin. She woke to pale moonlight filtering through a slot in the cabin wall and glanced to where Mama Olafson and Torsten slept. Now nine months old, Torsten slept through the night. Katrine spotted a mouse scurrying across the puncheon floor in and out of the moonlight. It ran toward Torsten and then scurried around his bedding. Katrine wished they had a cat. Nothing could keep the mice out. Maybe that was what had awakened her—the mouse running across her face. She shivered.

She lay awake for a long while listening to the sounds of the night— the aspens whispering in the breeze, the clatter of something against the side of the cabin, the squawk of a sleepy bird, and Ornery and Jack moving about in the corral. Mostly it was the wind buffeting the cabin. It was May, but it was cold. She could smell rain. She rolled over. The small leaves and dried grass in her bedding crinkled with her movement. She thought of the night animals, particularly of the cougars. The mules would let her know if a mountain lion came about. They were probably lonely as well. Olga and June were with Papa Olafson, camped somewhere on the trail going to Boise City. She thought of the good things the men would bring back. Mostly she hoped Papa Olafson would bring back a heifer.

The morning brought sunshine, and Katrine was thankful to see the world as it had been. Outside, she glanced toward the mules' corral. Ornery swished her tail and Jack cocked his ears as if saying good morning. Katrine dipped some water from the barrel by the door and brought it in for breakfast. Already Mama Olafson had risen and had the fire going. Sven had built a hearth and a place for pots to sit on rocks between which Margret could scrape some coals for cooking. They talked of getting a stove someday. Maybe he would be bringing one from Boise City during this trip.

Margret dished up some wheat porridge with a few dried apples. She cut a small piece of salt pork into three pieces. Margret offered Torsten some of the porridge. He made a face.

"He'll soon learn to love it," she said. "It would be so much better with milk or cream … or butter." She gazed out the small window, an open square in the side of the cabin that they covered at night with a blanket, or in cold weather, heavy wooden shutters.

"Is Papa going to get us a heifer?" Mia asked.

"He thinks there's a good chance," Margret said. "Last fall, Mr. Adolphson made arrangements with a merchant for seeds and some livestock."

"Mr. Adolphson's cow had a calf," Katrine said. "If it had been a heifer, maybe Papa Olafson could have traded for it."

"Only the Wikstroms and we don't have a calf," Mia said.

Margret laughed gently. "We will have what the good Lord intends for us to have. Papa will do his best, but he is also a very good farmer. We can always trade crops for milk and butter."

"Well, when Papa Olafson gets a heifer, she will have a calf with the Adolphsons' bull, won't she?" Katrine asked. "Just like Harald's and Jens's cows did."

"We sure hope she will," Margret said. A smile tugged at her lips.

"Then there will be no more going to the Adolphsons' or Lundgrens' for milk. Life will be happy," Mia said.

"Maybe by next summer," Margret agreed.

"But what if Papa doesn't get a heifer?" Mia asked.

"Do not worry, Mia." Margret pushed a strand of Mia's hair back into place. "There are so many good things for Papa to get. He may get chickens instead, and then we'll have eggs. And if we don't get a calf this spring, maybe we can get one this fall.

"It is like the story of the spinning woman, Cecilia, in Dalland." Margret said. "You will recall she never had enough flax but always saved a small amount for her work the following day. 'I shall always have some work if even a small amount for a piece of silver for my bread,' she always said. And then she had something to look forward to."

Margret raked some coals into the gap between the rocks and pulled the kettle over them.

"One morning she found extra flax for her spinning. She wondered and wondered from where it came. She spun her flax and sold her yarn but still saved some flax for the next morning's work. And again in the morning light, there was even more flax to be spun. This went on for some time, and Cecilia soon had silver enough for her bread.

"One night she stayed awake to see from where the flax came. She was surprised to see an old elf spinning flax, singing a song to himself, 'Today you may not have enough flax, tomorrow either, but by and by you shall, unless you become greedy and sell it all.'

"Presently Cecilia saw a beautiful dress that she decided she must buy, and so she spun all of her flax for the needed silver. She had no flax and no work to look forward to, but she had wanted the dress. Alas, the next morning there was no new flax and none thereafter."

Mia nodded. "So someday we will get a cow as long as we do our work today."

Margret nodded. "It's the best way, although sometimes in spite of your best effort, your dreams won't be met. For sure if you don't put forth the effort, no dreams will be met." Margret pulled the boiling water off the fire and added some rose hips for tea.

Katrine sipped the sweetish tea, enjoying the tangy flavor. "We should do some knitting," she said, thinking about the story.

Margret laughed. "While Papa is gone, I think we should spade up more ground in the garden. He would be more pleased if he could plant a few more potatoes."

Katrine tried to keep her mind off Papa Olafson's absence. She did her best to keep up her chores and to help take care of baby Torsten. And like Mama Olafson had suggested, they spaded a new section of garden, working some on it each day.

Later, Katrine quietly slipped away to her favorite spot on the rock in the clearing above the cabin. There she could be alone and look down on the cabin and the valley and think. Often she had anxious thoughts, but today she tried to be happy.

The snow had newly melted and left patches of muddy brown grass. A few trilliums bloomed in the shadows of the spruce trees. Kinnikinnick spread its bright green leaves under their canopy. A few withered red berries still clung to the sprawling branches. Catkins spotted the spindly aspen limbs.

Katrine gazed across the valley toward the snow-clad mountains. She thought of Papa Olafson and the others who were heading toward Boise City. She hoped they could get down the trail through the mud and snow. Mostly she hoped they could bring back their wagon and a heifer.

She shook her head as she gazed about. This was a huge, empty country that swallowed the few settlers in the valley. She climbed from her rock and headed back, dragging a dead aspen. Always she brought back wood for the fire.

"I was just going to send Mia to look for you," Margret said. "I do hope you were not too far away. The bears will be coming out now, and they will be very hungry. A young girl would be just the right size for a springtime meal."

Katrine shivered. "I just go to the rock on the hill." She pointed. "I can see the cabin from there." She decided until Papa Olafson returned that maybe she would stay nearby.

Chapter 18

PAPA OLAFSON HAD been gone a month. Katrine knew that Mama Olafson worried, but Katrine knew in her heart that he was safe. He worked harder than anyone she knew. He was a good farmer and a good carpenter. He traded some of his carpentry work for things they needed. He built a cradle for Mrs. Lundgren's baby boy. He had built a sled for hauling firewood across the snow. He wanted a better one but needed good lumber to do so. Nevertheless, Katrine could not help but think of all the livestock the Adolphsons and the others had. She could not help but wonder why some people got everything and others did not.

This day, Katrine and Mia walked to where they had a better view of the trail to the south.

"Do you suppose today they'll be back?" Mia asked. "They've been gone a long time."

"If they have heifers and shoats, it will take longer," Katrine said. "They have to walk all the way, and they might be very little."

"I walked all the way, and I wasn't very big."

"And we took over three weeks."

"Only because the wagons got stuck all the time, and we had to build a bridge and a road."

Margret came to the door. "You girls should come inside. Help me with this dough. If Papa comes home today, he would be pleased with some hot bread."

"Mama Olafson, will they do good trading?" Katrine asked, turning toward the cabin. "No one speaks Swedish in Boise City. Mr. Andreasson thinks they were cheated last year. They should take Mrs. Lundgren because she's English."

"Now, I wouldn't worry about your papa and the others. They speak English just fine, and they know how to cipher. Prices are always very high on the frontier, and many times no one has what farmers need."

"No, they have what miners need, like whiskey." Mia shook her head.

Margret laughed. "Well, we shall see."

Katrine took one last glance to the south, expecting to see nothing, but there was Papa Olafson coming over the hill. Her heart jumped.

"Mama Olafson," she cried, "he's coming."

But something was wrong. They were going to bring up their wagon. And there was no heifer.

"Does he bring anything?" Margret came running, carrying Torsten. She shielded her eyes, looking toward the south. "Where's the wagon? There's only one mule." She hurried down the trail. Katrine rushed after with Mia on her heels.

A knot in Katrine's stomach tightened. A lot could have happened in four weeks. She had looked forward to hearing about the trip and seeing what Papa Olafson had brought back. Now she was scared.

Papa Olafson and the mule came closer down the hill and crossed the creek. Boots seemed fine. The mule named June seemed fine. Olga was missing.

Then Katrine spotted a small creature with big ears trotting over the hill, bringing up the rear. She stood on tiptoe to see.

"I see something with him, I do!" she cried. "It's a calf."

"For sure?" Mia asked, straining to see.

"For sure. I can see its big ears. We got a heifer, Mama Olafson."

Katrine grabbed Mia and danced around. But then they quieted, reminded again that there was no wagon and only one mule.

Sven waved and smiled weakly. He slid from the saddle, first hugging and kissing Margret and then hugging and kissing Mia and Katrine. June came to a stop, blowing and jangling her head.

The calf came into the yard. Sven gestured toward her. "She's a beautiful creature, is she not?"

"I think we should name her Trillium," Katrine declared.

"Trillium? Whatever for?"

"The trilliums are blooming. And she has a white spot on her face that looks like one."

"Trillium," Sven said. "By gum, that is a fitting name. Now let's get her some water and show her to her pen. She's had a very long walk."

The young calf hardly made it inside the pen before it collapsed in the straw. Katrine had remembered to get a bucket of water. Trillium ignored it.

"Is she all right?" Katrine asked.

"I'm sure she will be fine," Sven answered. "I'm starved, Margret. You girls help me get these packs off June, and I'll be in."

"Where's Olga and the wagon?" Margret demanded.

Sven frowned. "I'll tell you all about it. Just be glad I'm here to tell the tale." He turned to release the packs from June. "We best have some tea as well."

Katrine tagged after Papa Olafson, helping where she could. She could tell he was troubled. Boots went immediately to the creek for water. June followed as soon as her packs were removed, shaking and quivering. Katrine could tell there was very little in the packs.

"Let's carry these things in." Sven handed Katrine his bedroll. He hoisted one of the packs over his shoulder. Mia carried a smaller bag.

It should have been like Christmas with Papa Olafson's return. It wasn't. Katrine didn't know what it felt like.

Margret set a plate of potatoes, venison, and greens in front of Sven.

"Mr. Andreasson nearly drowned," he said at last. "I nearly did as well."

Margret sat; her hand immediately went to Sven's.

"We should have never tried to get those wagons back up the canyon. Now I think about it, we were the luckiest greenhorns ever to set foot on the face of the earth last spring when we headed up this way. If those miners hadn't helped us build that bridge, we wouldn't have gotten any of them up here."

Sven pushed back from the table.

"The bridge was still there on the way down. It was all but gone on our return trip. We should have realized on the way down not to try it. We could tell then that high water had damaged it.

"Andreasson tried to get the mules to cross just below it with the wagon. The wagon got stuck halfway across. He got impatient and thought he could break it loose. We got eight mules on it, including ours and two of Wikstrom's. The wagon filled with water. Instead of cutting the animals loose, he continued whipping at them, trying to get them up the bank. The wagon pulled everything into the river. The two wheel mules were lost, including Olga."

Sven emptied his cup. "I kind of feel bad now for naming her Olga. She was mean, but she didn't deserve to drown."

Margret put a slice of pie in front of him.

"Ah, that's what I needed." Sven took a bite.

"You'll remember, Margret. I've told you this story. Olga was my first girlfriend, or so I thought. But then what does a twelve-year-old lad know? Olga pulled some mean tricks on me. When I got that mule, she reminded me of Olga with some of her shenanigans. The name was a natural for her."

Sven turned toward Katrine and Mia. "Let me give you some advice about boys."

Katrine thought he was looking more at her than at Mia.

"I hate to admit it, but boys aren't as smart about girls as you might think. Don't expect too much. But when it comes to work and providing a nice home, they'll do anything they can to take care of you.

"Now when one of them comes noticing you, then you let me know. I'll figure out if he's good for you or not."

Katrine gulped. There were three boys, all a year older than her—Harald, Jens, and Björn. None of them was noticing her, and she certainly wasn't noticing any of them—not at ten years old, she wasn't.

"Oh, Papa, stop that," Margret demanded. "You girls will not have anything to worry about for a very long while. You just worry about being girls for the time being. Now what happened to Mr. Andreasson?"

Sven shrugged. "He went in for the mules and finally cut them loose. He went under. I went after him and got tumbled about a bit. Wikstrom pulled me out. We fished Andreasson out after he had floated down the river a couple dozen rods or so. He had enough brännvin in him; I think that was the only reason he didn't drown."

Margret shook her head. "That's becoming his demon as well, I fear."

Sven glanced toward Katrine and Mia.

"I think it should be said, Papa. These girls are old enough to know some of the evils of brännvin."

"And I won't disagree, but this country can get the best of you. It's not a bad thing to have some snaps now and then. For sure during Midsummer's Eve you'll see me outbest Andreasson."

Katrine began feeling uncomfortable. Papa Olafson normally would not talk in this manner in front of her or Mia.

Margret sighed. "So that was our wagon that was lost."

"Ja, and our mule. The other mule was Wikstrom's. He didn't need that." Sven shook his head. "I don't know how he and his children are going to make it. They had a wicked go of it last winter as it was, and now this." Sven ran his hands through his hair.

"But the good news is we did get his wagon across. We did it the way we should have done it in the first place. We repaired the bridge, took apart Wikstrom's wagon like we did the others last spring, and we hauled it across, which is why it's taken us a month to get there and back."

Sven eyed the girls. "Now let this be a lesson. Sometimes being in a hurry only puts you behind. If it works the first time, don't be all too ready to change things."

Margret tightened her lips. "I think the girls and I shall pay the Wikstroms a visit. Maybe we can help Anna a bit. Anna's still but a girl, you know."

Katrine perked up. She enjoyed visiting the Wikstroms and playing with the children. Besides, they had the best hot springs.

"Well, I best finish taking care of things. We got our heifer at least." Sven rose and headed back out into the yard.

Later Sven told more about the trip. They learned about some new farms upstream on one of the tributaries north of Fort Boise. The homesteaders intended to do as the Swedes were doing and raise vegetables for the miners in the Boise Basin. An area farther east where some Chinese were putting in crops was already being referred to as Garden Valley.

"Maybe if Adolphson had gone that route, we'd be homesteading there instead," Sven said. "It's lower elevation, more crops can be grown, certainly more fruit trees. But then if he had gone that route, he might have been the one discovering the gold and none of us would care about growing crops." He shook his head. "Or he might have been the one killed by Indians. George Grimes was his name. That was the fellow we heard about that first winter in Fort Boise. If so, we wouldn't be here at all. It is strange the ways in which the Lord works.

"We didn't make it to Boise City with all of our goods. A fellow setting up a supply center bought all our root crops, the eggs, and the butter. He paid us in gold. We continued on to Fort Boise and traded the furs. There were very few stock animals. Fortunately, the man Adolphson had contacted last fall came through for us. He said if we hadn't showed up when we did, they were going to sell everything the next day. We got our heifer, and so did Wikstrom. Andreasson brought back a shoat and some chickens. Lundgren found himself a dog. It's white as snow."

Katrine felt a little jealous. A dog would let them know if bears and mountain lions were about as well as when strangers approached.

"I was amazed at the dozens and dozens of miners going through, whites and Chinese. We ran into two pack trains of at least two dozen mules each. I believe there will be a thousand people in the Boise Basin shortly, if not already. That country is booming."

"Perhaps it is good then that we are here," Margret said. "We can take our goods to Boise City, but maybe we should take them to the Salmon River mines as well."

"Ja, we are halfway between both areas," Sven said. He smiled and reached out and patted Margret's hand. "I am glad to be home. With all the people down below, I was feeling out of sorts."

"Was there any news of the war? Of our friends in Minnesota?" Margret asked.

Sven shook his head. "There were no letters for Adolphson despite those he has written. The war is ongoing with little activity during the winter. General Grant is now commanding. I hope he fares better than the others fared. I should like to see our country united again. I should not like seeing our sons being forced to go to war."

"Will they come looking for men here?" Katrine asked.

"It is possible," Sven said. "Both sides are conscripting soldiers."

Katrine always thought of the war as being very far away. It did not seem as distant this day.

Chapter 19

THE SOIL HAD warmed. Sven began working the fields and planting the garden again. He had plowed and sowed an acre of oats. Presently, the rye from last season was rapidly growing and a vibrant green. Katrine and Mia helped him in the garden by spading and raking the ground for the vegetable seeds such as the peas and turnips. They cut a long row about an inch deep, placed the seeds, and covered them with a thin layer of soil.

When it became time to plant the potatoes, Katrine gathered those from the root cellar that were the most wrinkled and had white, wormlike shoots sprouting from them. She cut them into pieces, ensuring that each piece had a few shoots. She liked their sweetish, starchy smell.

Sven dug two trenches and formed the dirt into a long mound between them. Every foot or so, he dug a depression into the mound. Katrine and Mia placed two or three potato pieces into each hole, pulled the dirt over them, and tamped it down.

"Potatoes love this northern light," Sven explained. "Most of Sweden does not grow potatoes this well. Probably nowhere on earth grows potatoes this well." He leaned on his shovel and smiled. "The people in Boise City were surprised at the size of those we had to sell."

They next planted the remaining onions, some now mushy flesh in paper husks. Sven dug a long, narrow trench. Like the potatoes, the onions had begun sprouting. Katrine placed them in the trench and buried them one by one.

"If we are lucky, a few of these will blossom and put out seeds. The bulbs will also grow small side bulbs." Sven pointed to a section of bulb attached to a large, withering onion. "Pick these off and plant them by themselves, and they will grow into large bulbs."

Within a day of planting, chlorophyll began returning to the ghostly shoots, turning them bright green. A few days later, new green spears pushed upward. Katrine loved watching the garden each day.

Other crops began to grow. The beets and turnips were sending up leafy tops. The cabbages had two or three purplish-green leaves. Some peas were unfurling, pushing their crooked necks out of the warm earth, sending out the first few leaves. Sven had driven a small row of stakes into the soil, marking them. Katrine and Mia had helped push forked branches into the ground between the stakes to support the pea vines.

Katrine glanced up from their work in the garden.

"Look, Papa Olafson. Some men are coming." She had caught movement near the aspens on the trail south of the cabin to where some men on foot had appeared.

Mia strained to see. "They look strange."

Sven straightened and reached for his rifle. "By gum, they look Chinese." He shaded his eyes. "I'm sure they are, just like the ones we saw near Garden Valley."

The Chinese drew nearer; each carried a pole suspended across his shoulders to which two large wicker baskets were tied, one balancing the other. They wore large, conical hats. One of the men waved.

Katrine noticed their toothy smiles. "They seem happy."

"I do not believe they are a threat," Sven said. He set down his rifle. "Katrine, you best tell Mama she might have some company for dinner, but I'll be a troll's uncle if I know what to feed a Chinaman. Maybe Mama knows. We sure don't have any rice."

Katrine ran and told Mama Olafson. When she returned, the Chinese had gathered around Papa Olafson, setting their baskets of belongings aside. They chattered noisily, although Katrine could not catch a single word of English. Most curiously, all four of them had entered the garden and were walking down the rows with Papa Olafson, examining the growing plants, pointing.

Katrine hoped they would not help themselves to the vegetables.

"Would you like something to eat?" Sven asked, turning to one of the men.

All were dressed similarly with loose-fitting tunics that had large, open sleeves and necks, loose-fitting trousers, and cotton slippers. Frequently, they smiled and bowed to Sven.

"They sure are a friendly sort," Sven murmured. "Go back and help Mama bring something out. Maybe some boiled potatoes."

Katrine and Mia raced back to the cabin.

"Come, girls. I've rustled up some things. Mia, you take and spread this blanket for the food. From what I understand, they prefer to sit on the ground."

She handed Katrine a plate with venison, a bowl of potatoes, and some onions. "You take these out."

Margret followed, carrying Torsten.

The Chinese grinned broadly when everyone had gathered about. They all seemed drawn to Torsten and chatted excitedly to him. Margret sat him down beside her where he withdrew behind her dress.

One of the Chinese said, "You have vehlie nice boy."

The oldest appearing Chinese clasped his hands and bowed repeatedly. "I am Wong Shing. Thank you for food. I have food."

Sven nodded toward the others. "What about them?"

"We all have food," Wong Shing said.

One of the men had taken out some small crocks and a kettle. A third began a fire. Soon they had a small pot of water on the fire.

"You join us," Wong Shing said, gesturing and bowing. "We eat together."

It was the first rice Katrine had ever seen, and there was lots of it. The youngest Chinese heaped some onto her plate and then scooped a vegetable relish on top. "You like?" he questioned.

Katrine tentatively tasted it and then nodded. She did like it. "It's very good."

The young man smiled broadly. "I am Sun Xie."

"I'm Katrine." Except for when they addressed her or her family, they spoke Cantonese, a singsong rapid-sounding language. She liked listening.

Soon they were sharing food around. Margret could not let the Chinese outdo her and brought out some strawberry preserves and corn bread. That brought more smiles.

And then there was tea. Sun Xie served it in an assortment of tin and ceramic cups. It seemed to be his task to serve the others.

Sven asked to where they were traveling.

"We go to Warren's Camp," Wong Shing replied. "Other Chinese there have good strike. We will all get rich." He laughed. "Lei Min has brother there." He nodded to a third man.

Lei Min grinned. "We come to find gold. Maybe send some home to families. Maybe soon we go home to them."

It occurred to Katrine that the Chinese were much like other miners going through. They were in search of riches but indicated no desire to stay.

130

Wong Shing asked something of the fourth man. The man rose and rummaged through yet another pack and then returned with several bundles and squatted with them, smiling and nodding.

"This is Sang Yune," Wong Shing explained. "He is gardener, much like you. He does not speak English, but I can tell you what he says."

Sang Yune opened some small packets, revealing a wealth of different seeds. He gave the names in Cantonese, talking rapidly about the seeds and appearing quite proud of them.

He handed some to Sven, talking and pointing.

Wong Shing interpreted. "Here are Chinese radish seeds. They grow vehlie fast and are like big turnips. You should try some."

Then Sang Yune pulled out some damp leaves from a cloth bundle and, pulling them back, revealed a few fibrous tubers with wilted green leaves. They emitted a slight onion smell. He handed several to Margret.

Wong Shing explained. "These are *gau tsoi,* Chinese chives. They are much like onions but use the leaves and flower buds. Use for good flavah. They are for long life and good health."

"Oh, I can't accept these," Margret said, shaking her head. She bounced Torsten in her lap.

"Vehlie good medicine for family," Wong Shing explained. "You vehlie good woman. Reminds Sang Yune of his mother in China."

Margret blushed and thanked Sang Yune. "I might not be able to grow them. So please don't be disappointed if I can't."

Wong Shing interpreted, and Sang Yune spoke rapidly for a moment.

Wong Shing explained. "He say you already grow fine children and good garden. He say he know these will grow like your children. You are good woman."

Torsten reached for the plants. Margret took them and handed them to Katrine. She seemed flustered. Sang Yune bowed. To Katrine's delight, Mama Olafson bowed tentatively in return.

Shortly after the exchange of seeds and some potatoes that Sven gave them, the Chinese packed up their belongings and headed up the old Indian trail that went toward the Wikstroms'.

Katrine remarked, "They were very friendly. I had no idea. You hear stories."

"They look funny," Mia said.

"Well, I suppose you look funny to them," Katrine said.

Margret hunted around for a bowl to use for the chives. "I don't have anything spare to grow any plants in."

Sven shook his head. "Those chives will remain good for a few days. Girls, I need you to find me an aspen stump that is hollow. I can fix wood to its bottom. That should make a fine planter."

Katrine thought she knew exactly where to go for an aspen log. Many of the aspens seemed to become hollow in old age. She had already seen where some bluebirds were nesting. Although she would not use one of their trees, she knew another should be nearby. "Come, Mia, we should go right now."

MIDSUMMER FLOWERS 1864

Chapter 20

AT SUNDAY MEETING, the news of the Chinese quickly spread. Everyone wanted to know how they looked and talked.

"I can't explain how they talked," Katrine said. "They use lots of *oh's* and *ah's* and *sing's* and *sang's*."

Björn laughed. "And their eyes are narrow." He pulled at the corners of his eyes, his dark eyebrows accentuating the look.

"Well, to them, our eyes are round."

"I hear they cut up each other with cleavers, and they smoke opium," Lars added.

"These all seemed friendly to each other. They served dinner all around just like a family."

"I k-kind of wish I could go with them. I w-would like to visit the goldfields someday," Jens murmured.

Katrine noticed Jens's stutter, which sometimes he did. He was generally quieter than the others were, as if he were unsure of things.

"There's more gold that grows in the ground than what lies beneath the ground," Björn replied. "That's what my pa says. Gold comes and gold goes, but a garden always grows."

"Not when it's hailing or snowing," Katrine reminded him. It was a good saying, but in truth, the land sometimes did not yield a bounty.

"Just the same," Jens continued. "I-I'd like to see things someday."

"You're no older than I am, and I'm twelve," Björn said, arching his eyes. "But maybe we can go to Boise City with the men next time."

"We can't all go," Harald said. "We have to leave somebody behind in case of Indians."

"No one has seen any Indians."

"My father says some of the miners coming through saw some."

"Ja," Lars replied. "An emigrant train near Devil's Gate was attacked. Remember, we turned north before there."

"That's not up here," Björn countered. "They only come here to go hunting, and now that we're here, they might not come any more."

Katrine thought about it. "There's an old Indian trail that goes over the mountains behind our cabin, and your papa said there were shelters on the trail behind your place. They'll probably come back sometime."

"We've been here two summers," Björn said. "No one has seen any."

"Oh, they're here all around us. If they don't want to be seen, you won't see them. You don't see them until it's too late," Lars said. He stabbed a stick into the ground as if it were a knife. "Best we always keep a watch."

Katrine shivered. She often sat alone on the boulder in the meadow. It was near the trail. Maybe Indians did watch her but didn't want to hurt her.

The Andreassons were hosting Midsummer's Eve. Katrine had never been to their farm. She looked forward to seeing the Andreassons' place and visiting Jens, Barbro, and Joran, although Mr. Andreasson scared her a little.

The Andreassons were about four miles north of the Adolphsons and along the creek that came down past the Wikstroms' place. The Wikstroms were an additional two miles to the east. Katrine and the Olafsons went over the ridge near the Lundgrens', however, which made it a distance of about four miles.

When they grew near, Katrine eyed the Andreassons' cabin. It appeared less well built than the Olafsons', but then Papa Olafson was a good carpenter. The fields were not as nice either. They contained scattered granite boulders and were cut by gullies. However, a well-built fence surrounded a nice garden near the cabin.

Now Katrine could see some of the children already playing. Her heart caught. She spotted the Midsummer pole. It stood near the cabin, decorated with flowers and greenery. Katrine was sure that Jens and Barbro had mostly been responsible.

Katrine found Jens near a small hut constructed of woven willows with a roof of sticks and sod. Mr. Andreasson was examining a hole in the coop, frowning. Chickens ran about.

"It's a fox for sure." Gustaf stared darkly at Katrine. "This is Jens's job to build a proper chicken pen. He plays too much. Maybe someday when we have no chickens because a fox got them all, he will learn how important it is to do his work first."

Katrine

Gustaf shoved a stick into the hole and walked away, shaking his head.

Katrine swallowed. Papa Olafson would never say something like that in front of her friends.

Jens shrugged. "Rainy broke it." A gray-spotted mongrel, wagging her tail, had come out to meet Katrine.

There were no hot springs at the Andreassons'; instead, there were two ponds along a small creek adjacent to the cabin. Most of the children went there to swim before the Midsummer's Eve dinner was ready. Harald and Jens chased small fish in the shallows while Katrine and the other girls chased tadpoles in the mud near the cattails. Rainy kept them company, barking and romping in the mud as well.

Gustaf and Sven found them covered in mud, chasing around.

"I thought you came here to clean up, not to get muddy." Sven laughed. "Better wash up. The dinner is nearly ready."

Katrine and the others waded out into the clear stream, splashed water on themselves, and then dressed before racing off up the bank toward the cabin.

Dinner was a sight. There were plenty of new potatoes with creamy butter, some cheese, and some boiled eggs. The main dishes were trout and venison. Of course there were steamed nettles and wild strawberries with cream. There was also some wild asparagus and a heaping bowl of blue serviceberries.

"Maybe next season we can have beef or ham for Midsummer's Eve," Magnus said.

"For now, we will have milk cows, not beef," Nils said. "However, it may be wise to raise beef cattle for the nearby mines rather than worry about farm crops."

"Ja, or sheep," Sven suggested.

"Nej, I shall have a ham from our shoat we are raising. You others worry about beef cattle or mutton," Gustaf exclaimed. "Now it is time to sing and dance."

They gathered around the Midsummer pole and began dancing the same exuberant dances they had danced a year ago. Magnus played his fiddle. The children tried to outdo the adults and as usual ended in a giggling heap. The adults tried to outdo the children with similar results. They danced and sang until they had run out of familiar Swedish Midsummer's Eve dances and songs.

Afterward, Gustaf Andreasson brought out a bottle of brännvin and began passing it around to the men. The women and girls began clearing dishes. As always, the boys sang drinking songs and attempted to entice the men to a sip of snaps. Lars, who was now thirteen, seemed to be the most successful.

Gustaf led the singing in a boisterous voice. No matter what the song, he soon took over, singing and dancing, slapping and stomping. Sven and Anton joined but to a lesser extent. Gustaf stumbled and cursed then laughed as he toppled into the grass.

Jens ran to his father. Katrine, returning from the cabin with some tea, saw what was happening.

"Wha' you think you're doin'?" Gustaf yelled at his son.

"Helping you."

"I don' need help. What? You think you're a man now?" Gustaf struggled to his feet. He took a swing at Jens, but Jens dodged away.

Katrine gulped, feeling a knot tighten in her stomach.

"*Helvete*," Gustaf yelled. "Worthless." He took another drink.

"Let him be," Sven said. He waved his hands. "Who's got another song?"

Harald began the drinking song.

Helan går
Sjung hopp faderallan lallan lej
Helan går
Sjung hopp faderallan lej

Gustaf, bottle in hand, stumbled around, singing just as loudly as before.

"I think that is enough," Sven finally said as he took the bottle and gently sat Gustaf down. "We will sing till the sun sets, my friend."

The others turned away and talked or dozed. Katrine played tag with the other children, with Rainy chasing after them. Jens sat watching, chin on his knees, his arms clasped about them.

Katrine went and sat next to him but said nothing.

"H-he gets like that s-sometimes," Jens stuttered.

"Thank you for letting us visit," Katrine said. "You have a nice cabin. I like your chickens and your dog."

"Ja." Jens nodded. "She's a good dog, she is, and she lets us know whenever someone is coming."

The sun began settling toward the horizon. The women rose first, reminding their husbands of the distance home and of the youngsters that still had a fair bit of traveling to do.

The Olafsons returned over the hill east of the Lundgrens'. When they crested the ridge, Katrine caught her breath. The meadow spreading below down to their creek was caught in the golden afternoon sunlight. Then she remembered.

"We have to pick some flowers, Papa Olafson!" She started to scramble from the mule.

"What?"

"We have to pick flowers. We didn't do it at the Andreassons'."

Sven pulled up and laughed. "I guess this is as good as any place to take a rest." He took Torsten from Margret's arms and helped her down. They sat on the ridge in the grass watching as Katrine and Mia ran about looking for flowers.

"You remember, don't you?" Katrine asked Mia.

"Of course I remember," the younger girl said and nodded vigorously.

Katrine picked her first flower, a blue lupine, Mama Olafson's favorite flower. "And they should not be the same ones I pick if you can help it."

Mia found a yellow prairie coneflower.

Katrine found a scarlet Indian paintbrush.

Every few steps, they spied another. "They all have to be different," Katrine said. "You need seven."

"Of course."

Soon they were each up to six. The seventh blossom eluded them. Every time they thought they had found a different one, it turned out to be one of the ones they held in hand.

"Here's a little bitty one," said Mia. She had stooped low and was examining a tiny plant under the leaves of a chokecherry shrub. "It's a violet."

"One that an elf would like," Katrine said. "Maybe we should both pick one so we each have seven. Is that all right?"

Mia nodded.

"We can go now, Papa Olafson," Katrine said, running toward him, her flowers in hand. She noticed that both he and Mama Olafson sat together bouncing Torsten, watching them and smiling.

The light had faded before they reached their cabin. Hardly able to keep their eyes open, Katrine and Mia dutifully washed up their hands and faces.

"I wish we had a hot springs," Katrine whispered. She unbraided her hair and then helped Mia. Maybe someday Papa Olafson would build a badstuga. That would be much better than splashing cold water onto her face before going to bed at night.

Katrine pulled the curtain across the room and slipped into her nightclothes.

"Remember, Mia."

But already Katrine noticed that Mia had pulled away her pillow and placed the seven flowers underneath.

"I hope I dream of Pelle," she whispered.

"I'm not going to tell you who I hope to dream of," Katrine said. She knew she was far too young for marriage, but every Swedish girl knew that on Midsummer's Eve if you placed seven different flowers under your pillow, you would dream of your husband-to-be. At first, Katrine had thought of Lars, but everyone knew that Lars and Anna would someday marry. She hoped she would dream of Harald.

Chapter 21

AFTERNOON THUNDERSTORMS PUNCTUATED the hot midsummer days. Sven had cut the meadow grass, and it now lay curing in the warm sun. The rye that he had planted last season was ripe.

Katrine had risen and already brought in water and wood. Mama Olafson was up with Torsten underfoot, preparing their breakfast. The sun streamed through the door as Papa Olafson came inside, his face and hands still wet from washing. He tousled Katrine's hair and ran his finger down Mia's nose. "How are my two girls this bright and shiny morning?"

"Hungry," they both replied.

"And my beautiful wife and baby boy?" Sven reached an arm around Margret and hugged her while she tried to get a kettle off the coals. He picked up Torsten and swung him around. A giggle escaped from the boy.

"How is it that you are joyful this morning?" Margret set some steaming porridge with butter and a plate of salt pork on the table.

"I'll be a troll's uncle but that we shall soon be having *limpa* bread with this porridge. The rye is ripe. I'll begin harvesting immediately."

"Praise the Lord. Now we must pray for no rain."

Sven took a bite of salt pork. "Yes, soon we'll be threshing and winnowing rye and grinding it for meal." He eyed Katrine and Mia. "What do you think about that?"

Katrine and Mia squealed with happiness. It had been a very long time since Katrine had had any rye bread.

They finished eating. "You girls be good. Help Mama." Sven swallowed down some coffee and then was out the door.

It struck Katrine that Papa Olafson never paused during the day's work, sometimes not even for noon dinner, especially when he was plowing or harvesting.

"I'll take water and go to help if I may," Katrine said.

"Of course. It will be a hot day today," Margret said.

Katrine often went to the fields to help Papa Olafson. Each time, she was eager to see the work he had done. There was a good feeling to be able to look around and see a plowed field when it had been broken stubble before, or better yet, to see a carpet of sprouting oats or rye after sowing a field.

She took the canteen and a piece of corn bread with butter that Mama Olafson had wrapped in a cloth. Katrine found Papa Olafson walking through the ripened rye, swinging his cradle scythe, cutting a swath, following the perimeter of the field, working his way toward the center. He had already cut a large area around the field. She caught up to him. Mama Olafson had been correct—the day was already uncomfortably warm.

"Ah, it is good to see you, Katrine." Sven didn't pause swinging—always to the left, so the grain fell in a neat row and the heads aligned in the same direction. "How about you meet me at the aspens?"

Katrine followed, watching him swinging, swinging, his shoulders bunching and relaxing under his long shirt with his sleeves rolled up. He walked slowly, steadily. She wondered how he managed. The dust and chaff from just a short walk tickled her nose and throat. She coughed.

When Sven reached the aspens, he pulled his bandana from around his neck and wiped his face. He took the canteen, sat, and patted the ground next to him.

"It's a hot one today, it is."

Katrine sat and stretched her legs out in the shade, watching as Papa Olafson took a deep swallow. Usually she would say, *Maybe it will rain.* But any rain while harvesting could be disastrous. "Maybe some clouds will come but just while you're cutting."

"Ja, maybe." Sven had another swallow of water and took a bite of corn bread, which he quickly chased down with more water.

He rested a moment before scrambling back to his feet. "I guess I best get at it. Come a day or two, you can come out and help sheave the rye. Thank you for the water."

"I'll bring some more later," Katrine said. "Mama Olafson is making a nice noon dinner."

Sven glanced at the sun. "About two more hours." He began swinging again—cutting, swinging back, cutting. Bundles of rye stalks fell, flashing in the sun. Bits of dust and chaff hung in the air.

142

A few days later, when Katrine again accompanied Papa Olafson to the field, the cut rye was ready for bundling. Sven began cutting again while Katrine began gathering the rye into bundles and tying each sheaf with a few strands of rye straw. When Katrine had several sheaves, she stood them up in a shock, the grain heads upward. She laid a sheaf across the top of the shock in case of rain.

Before noon, Mia came out with the water and some bread. She helped for a while, but she soon tired of the work and returned to the cabin.

Katrine worked hard but could not keep up with Papa Olafson. When he had finished a good portion of the field, he came back to where Katrine was and helped her some more.

"We need to remember to keep a sheaf for the birds this winter," Katrine said.

"Ja, of course we shall." Sven racked up some more sheaves into a large shock. He worked rapidly, frequently eyeing the sky.

He pointed to the bank of thunderheads building on the western horizon.

"That is my concern," he said, pointing. "Today we should be okay. A quick summer rain won't hurt, but hail could." He grabbed and twisted some more strands of rye. "Just pray we have a few more dry days, and then we'll bring the rye into the lean-to." Sven smiled. He glanced at Katrine. "And then …?"

"Threshing," Katrine finished.

"And then …?"

"Rye meal and limpa," she almost shouted.

"And *knäckebröd*," Sven added.

"Of course." Katrine laughed.

Their harvest was interrupted only by Sunday meeting. Katrine knew if the weather had not held, even on a Sunday they would be working in the field, probably with Mama Olafson and Mia also helping.

The Wikstroms did not make Sunday meeting. Katrine listened in on the men talking, attempting to learn what was happening. Apparently, he had gone north along the trail into the Salmon River country. She was not surprised. Even Papa Olafson had wondered if it was more practical to take goods into the mines to the north than to take them south to Boise City. However, she didn't understand why Mr. Wikstrom went alone. She wished Anna had been around. Anna would have told her.

A few days later, Sven awaited the wagon for gathering the rye. Katrine dressed Torsten, now nearly eleven months old and almost walking. He pulled himself along quite nicely, not really crawling, but he would reach the wood box or a chair and pull himself up, standing there, beaming as if he had invented the most marvelous thing. He would sway for a moment and then plunk down on his rear, surprised but unhurt. Then squealing with glee, he would crawl quickly away to the next object by which he could draw himself up.

"He will be walking inside a week." Sven beamed. "Just now you girls keep him from that fire and what's cooking. That shall be your job."

Katrine had him cornered near where she and Mia slept where he busily investigated some wood shavings, putting them into his mouth, deciding if he should chew them or spit them back out.

Voices came from the yard. Nils and Astrid Adolphson had arrived, bringing up the wagon.

Mia ran out into the yard to greet them. Katrine kept ahold of Torsten until they had come in and seated themselves at the table. Margret busied herself with the coffee.

"Did you hear the news?" Nils asked, eyes wide, hands pushing across the table, pausing.

Everyone's eyes caught his.

"Wikstrom is back, and he's brought a new wife with him."

"I'll be a troll's uncle!" Sven exclaimed. He juggled his coffee, spilling some.

Margret stopped in midpour. Katrine froze, holding Torsten, knowing that she and Mia should go outside. Instead, she tried to slip farther into the shadows.

"He said he was going to do that when he left here—go all the way to Lewiston, if necessary, by gum," Sven said, "but I didn't give him a chance in blazes of doing so."

So that was the real reason he went north, Katrine realized.

Nils shook his head. "Seems he had just crossed the Salmon River and was heading downriver in the direction of Lewiston when he ran into a troop of ..." he lowered his voice, "hurdy-gurdy girls."

"Hurdy-gurdy girls! Herre Gud!" Sven slammed down his cup.

"Ja, and somehow he convinced one of them to come back here with him." Nils laughed loudly, nodding.

"But is he married?" Margret asked, voice trembling.

Nils glanced her way. "That is the miracle. He heard about a preacher that was sometimes up at Slate Creek—a Reverend Weatherspoon, I believe is his name. I got Wikstrom to confess that much, beings I have some say in the spiritual goings-on around here. Anyway, he rounded up a couple of prospectors to be witnesses and the reverend married them right then and there on the trail."

"So he wasn't married in the church," Margret whispered.

"Now, Mama, don't be so harsh. This was the Lord's doing, it was," Sven said. "If it wasn't, how was it to be he'd just meet a likely woman and find a traveling preacher?"

"Perhaps," Margret said, frowning.

"Ja, I do believe the Lord had a hand in it," Nils said. "Otherwise he might have had a long wait to make things proper."

"I doubt he would have waited," Astrid said. Everyone laughed.

Margret glanced toward Katrine, startled. "I thought you two were outside. What you heard, you should not have."

Katrine shrank back, somewhat scared, clutching Torsten. "W-we're sorry." Rarely were they scolded.

Astrid must have realized the position Katrine and Mia were now in. "I for one say the good Lord would not have minded either way. Those Wikstrom children need a mama. But for sure this is the Lord's doing; otherwise, that Wikstrom would not have met those girls *or* Reverend Weatherspoon."

"Maybe so," Margret replied. She still seemed skeptical. "Perhaps we should not judge so quickly. I'm sure she will be a fine wife and mother."

"Her name's Frieda," said Nils. "She's German."

"German!" shouted Sven. He raised his hands. "The other—being a hurdy-gurdy—I could accept, but *German*? How could Wikstrom have gone and done such a thing?"

"It is the devil's work," whispered Margret, apparently changing her mind about God's involvement. She spun toward the girls. "Off with you two. Forget what you have heard this day."

But Katrine knew she could not forget. "Come, Mia. We'll go to the garden." She started slowly for the door, still hesitating so that she might hear more. She wondered how a German mother would be any different from a Swedish one, but based on Papa Olafson's tone, she had become a little worried for Anna and the children.

"She hardly speaks English," Nils continued. "And for sure she doesn't speak any Swedish."

"Oh Lord, preserve us," Margret whispered.

Mia pulled back. "Let me get Torsten."

Outside, Katrine paused. She could not help herself and stepped back inside.

"What's a hurdy-gurdy girl?"

The adults appeared thunderstruck. Katrine stood patiently in the doorway, wondering why what she had said was bringing such a strange reaction.

Sven sputtered and tried to explain. "They're women who ... who ... You explain, Mr. Adolphson."

Nils shrugged. "They're women who work in saloons. They play music on a crank organ and serve whiskey. Sometimes they sing for the men and dance."

"It's the devil's work," whispered Margret again. This time Astrid nodded.

"Oh," Katrine said. That did not seem so bad. She had heard of saloons and knew some of the Swedes sometimes drank too much— Mr. Andreasson, for example. Some of the men had talked about Mr. Andreasson. Mama Olafson whispered about it and then had sternly told her, "But we never talk about it. Especially not around his children."

Katrine knew this was something she would not talk about either, but she would whisper about it to the others, except maybe to Anna and her brothers and sister, of course. She bubbled at the thought of meeting Mr. Wikstrom's new wife.

Chapter 22

KATRINE WAS IMPATIENT to meet the new Mrs. Wikstrom. She was greatly surprised when Papa Olafson suggested that she and Mia take the trail over the ridge to do so. It was about two miles by going over the ridge instead of the four miles around. Mama Olafson said she was fine with watching baby Torsten. She would have the horse if need be, and she could summon Papa Olafson by putting spruce boughs in the fire.

"Be sure not to act oddly with the way she talks. Remember your manners. Invite them to Sunday meeting so we can all meet her," Margret commanded.

"Of course, Mama Olafson," Katrine said.

"Here, let me get you some of the Chinese chives. Tell Mrs. Wikstrom to put them with eggs or potatoes. They are different from what she is familiar with." Margret wrapped a few up and handed them to Katrine. "And you might find some raspberries growing higher on the ridge this time of season. Maybe you can pick some and take them to the Wikstroms as a thank you."

"How about raspberries for us?" Mia wondered.

Margret laughed. "On the way home, if it is not too late, you can pick some for us. How's that?" She smiled.

As Katrine headed up the trail, she became nervous. The trail ran over the hill to the north and crossed through aspens and fir trees in the direction from which they had heard the mountain lion. Papa Olafson had told her if she ever ran into one not to run. "They're like cats. If you turn your back on them, they will pounce. Have you ever seen a cat go after a mouse? As long as the mouse doesn't move, it's fine. The moment a mouse turns to scamper away, the cat has it."

Katrine remembered all too vividly. She had watched a standoff between a mouse and a cat before. The cat just watched, twitching its tail. But then the mouse turned and began sniffing at something, and the cat grabbed it. *Stupid mouse,* she remembered thinking, recalling the cat pawing and chewing the creature into a ball of wet fur before commencing to eat it.

Papa Olafson said they had chased all the mountain lions back into the mountains. Mr. Adolphson had killed one last winter while it tried to get their calf. Mr. Adolphson said he had never seen one so bold that it came into the yard and the calf pen. Besides, they need not worry about mountain lions now. It was full daylight. Mountain lions came out at night.

Nevertheless, any movement, any birds flitting from the shrubs and trees, caught Katrine's attention.

At first the trail followed a trickle of water for a short distance up a draw before it entered the scattered aspens and shortly afterward, towering ponderosa pine and firs. The July heat pulled the fragrance of the conifers into the air. The heat also plastered Katrine's dress to the nape of her neck, and sweat trickled into her eyes.

"I wish we had water," Mia mumbled.

"We will soon," Katrine said. She was thirsty as well. The heat beat on her. The air was quiet, not moving, and she felt trapped.

Near the top of the ridge, the timber pulled back, revealing an open, gravelly knoll. The faint trail wound its way up along the ridge for a distance and then in and around some granite boulders.

"What a beautiful place this is, Mia," she said, turning to look down toward the valley. "The sky and water are so blue, and the valley is so green." She spun around, gazing in all directions.

"It's wonderful," Mia agreed.

"I wonder what Mrs. Wikstrom is like," Katrine said.

"Nobody knows. She hasn't come to the Adolphsons' for Sunday meeting."

"That's because she's embarrassed she was a hurdy-gurdy girl," Katrine said. She skipped ahead down the faint trail. "We mustn't say anything to Anna or Björn or Linnea about it though."

"N-o-o, we mustn't," Mia said, shaking her head slowly.

They neared the open area.

"I wonder where the raspberry bushes are," Mia said.

"Near the boulders, I think." Katrine decided to check around the rocks a few yards above the trail. Raspberries liked sandy, disturbed areas. She immediately recognized the spindly shrubs farther uphill.

"Yes, there's one," Katrine said. "And there's lots of raspberries. I can see them."

Mia began picking. None went into the pail but instead went straight into her mouth. "Thank goodness."

Katrine plunked many of the ones she picked into her mouth as well, thankful for the sweetness and the moisture.

The raspberries grew thickly around and above them as far as Katrine could see. Some dead timber, scorched by fire, stood angry and splintered in the barren glen. This was the burn scar that she could see from the hill behind the cabin. It extended upward, cutting a swath through the timber for a distance along the mountain flank. Elderberry, mountain ash, willow, and mountain maple shrubs were crowding back into it. Only a few small conifers had begun growing. Grasses and flowers were thick.

Mia stood looking uphill. "Goodness, there are lots and lots of flowers. Yellow ones. White ones. What are they all?"

"I don't know much about flowers, but there's some fireweed," Katrine said. "Remember, Mama Olafson showed us some near the cabin. 'Just like Sweden,' she said."

Swaths of light lavender pink highlighted the high points of the scar, masking the downed logs and broken granite.

Katrine was particularly drawn to another flower. Tiny white stars were gathered into pointed globes on top of two-foot tall stalks that rose from grassy clumps. She examined one fragrant dancing globe after another. Like sentinels, the beargrass flowers marched up the hill, scattered about with the fireweed.

"These are beautiful," Katrine whispered. "They look kind of funny. We should pick some and take them to the Wikstroms."

Soon both girls had wandered higher off the trail into the burn scar, picking fireweed, some blue lupine, and some beargrass spikes.

A muffled grunt brought Katrine to her senses. A black shape, not registering at first, materialized above them and began growing nearer. *A bear.*

Katrine froze, unsure of what to do, afraid to tell Mia in case she screamed and ran. The animal had not noticed them. It seemed intent on raking raspberries from the shrubs into its great maw. It paused and looked in Katrine's direction. She remained motionless until the bear resumed its foraging. Then she saw another smaller brown shape come tumbling into view. *A cub.* Usually bears had two cubs. Frantically, she searched for the second one, but there was none.

Mia had gone silent. She had noticed the bears as well. Very quietly, Katrine touched Mia's shoulder and began stepping back down the hillside, her heart hammering like a wild drummer. She felt Mia shivering. Bears were like mountain lions. She should not run, but everything in her body screamed at her to do so.

Slowly, with sweat stinging her eyes, she continued down. It was then when Mia whispered and pointed. Katrine saw Mia's bundle of carefully gathered wildflowers lying on the log.

Gently, she pressed her own flowers into Mia's hand and tugged at her to keep backing away. The sow and her cub disappeared from view behind logs and shrubs, but Katrine knew they were still there. She knew if the sow decided to attack, it could be on them in a few bounds. She now turned and walked quietly back down toward the trail. She said nothing. Mia tagged along at her heels. When she intersected the trail, Katrine continued for many more yards before finally pausing.

"Probably only black bears," Katrine whispered. Her heart continued pounding hard, aching. "They don't bother people very often except when you bother their cubs. I'm glad they didn't see us."

"She looked huger than a black bear." Mia could hardly talk. "I don't want to go to the Wikstroms' anymore." Tears had sprung into her eyes.

"It's all right," Katrine said. "We'll be just fine. Maybe when we go home, we will go the long way. Would you like doing that?"

Mia nodded, tears glistening.

They did not pick any more raspberries but hurried on toward the Wikstroms'. By the time they began descending the ridge above the hot springs, the bundle of flowers had wilted and disintegrated into a few scraggly lavender fireweeds and drooping lupine.

The trail came out above the hot springs and then turned down the creek to the cabin. At the yard, Katrine shook with relief. She could hardly believe they were safe. Anna, Linnea, and five-year-old Laurens came running out to greet them. Katrine looked for Mrs. Wikstrom.

"We saw a mama bear and her cub," Mia explained, breathless.

They recounted their experience, tumbling over their story, reliving every detail.

Anna ran into the cabin. "Mama Frieda, Katrine and Mia are here. They saw a bear."

A young woman, clearly younger than the other settlers' wives, in her twenties, came outside. She seemed a bit nervous but smiled and waved. "*Hallo, hallo.* I'm Frieda." She wore a red dress with a green top with lacing. She had a cream-colored apron about her waist. Katrine remembered it had been Emma Wikstrom's. Frieda had missed the point about the bears.

Katrine decided that Frieda was pretty. She had bright blue eyes and wore her blonde hair in a long braid down her back. She had a smallish nose and somewhat high cheeks. She acted a little strange.

"Vi såg björn och björnunge. We saw a bear and her cub," Katrine said. Frieda appeared further confused.

"She does not understand Svenska very much," Anna explained.

Katrine swallowed. For some reason, she had forgotten that Frieda was German, maybe because she looked like all the other Swedes.

Katrine tried in English. "Hello, I'm Katrine. This is my sister, Mia. Well, she isn't really my real sister. I don't have any, but I'm living with her now."

Frieda appeared a little less confused and replied, "Willkommen."

Katrine laughed. Both she and Mia understood that word. "*Välkommen* and *willkommen* were very similar."

About then, Anton and Björn came up the trail. That prompted retelling about the bears. Frieda finally began to understand, and she frowned, glancing nervously at both Katrine and Mia.

"Der Bär?"

"Ja, björnar."

"O güte. Güte. Goodness."

Anton held out his arms and hugged the girls. Katrine gave Frieda the chives. Anna helped explain how to use them. They had some biscuits, and then Anna asked about swimming.

Björn insisted he should go with the girls. "We're too close to the cabin for bears to come, but I better go just in case." His eyes took on a serious look as he obtained and checked the pistol.

Katrine was not sure about swimming now with bears around either, but with Anna and Linnea, things took on a new perspective. Soon the girls and Laurens were splashing about. On any other day, Björn would have joined them, but true to his word, he walked up the trail and began whittling on a piece of wood while he stood guard for the bears.

They swam in the upper, larger pool. Plentiful water gushed from the hillside directly above and bounced off the rock ledges into curtains of water, streaming into the pool. The pond was now about twelve feet across and oval in shape. The deepest part was over three feet deep where the water cascaded into it. Most of the water spilled out over one of the ends, which Katrine realized could be dug out and expanded a little more if someone desired to do so.

Katrine loved the water's silky feel and clean smell. It was almost too warm.

All too soon, it was time to go. They got out and began drying off.

Björn came down the trail. "You were all making too much noise for any bears to come," he explained. He showed them his carving of a yule goat.

At supper, they talked about the bears again.

"You could have stayed with us tonight and rejoined your family at the Adolphsons' tomorrow," Anton said.

Both Katrine and Mia looked up. "Maybe we still can."

"Nej, your folks would be terribly worried if you didn't come home. They'd come looking for you," Anton said. "I don't think you'll run into the bears, but if you would like, Björn can go with you and meet us at the Adolphsons' tomorrow."

Katrine felt a flutter inside her. It was funny. *Björn* meant bear. The *bear* would protect them from the bears.

"Would you do that, son?" Anton glanced at Björn.

Björn shrugged and smiled. "I'll go." Everyone knew that what the father asked, the son would deliver.

Katrine felt so much better going back over the ridge that she fairly skipped. Only when they reached the burn scar did she become nervous.

"There they are," Björn abruptly said, squinting and pointing. The sow bear was near a downed tree; she and her cub were ripping apart a stump.

"She's big," Björn whispered. Although he packed the pistol in the back of his trousers, his hand never moved toward it.

Katrine watched the bears ripping at the stump, rooting around with their noses, and then moving on through the shrubs, nudging and stripping berries.

"Do they ever stop eating?" Katrine whispered.

"Until they hibernate, both of them will be eating demons." Björn pushed his hands down his trousers. "Maybe me and my pa should come and shoot her. She'd render a lot of grease and meat."

Katrine had not thought of that possibility. Until Björn mentioned it, she had only considered herself and Mia as becoming meat.

Sven and Margret were surprised to see Katrine and Mia in the accompaniment of Björn. He smiled and explained, "They ran into a big sow bear and her cub. I walked back with them."

That night, Björn made his bed near the girls. Katrine felt overwhelmingly that her brother had come home. More and more, Björn seemed like Erik; only that Björn was two years younger. The feeling was unsettling. She closed her eyes, trying to see Erik's face. In its place was Björn's freckled nose and blue eyes framed under his dark eyebrows.

In the morning, they rode to the Adolphsons' for Sunday meeting. Shortly after they arrived, the Wikstroms showed up. Everyone immediately gathered about to meet Frieda. Anton asked Björn if they had encountered the bear again. He explained they had. Sven, Anton, and Björn discussed hunting it because it was such a large bear. No one except the Andreassons had any livestock for butchering. Like last winter, they planned on hunting and harvesting wild game. A bear would go a long way.

Katrine and Mia visited with Anna and Linnea. They talked about Mr. Wikstrom getting married. Anna admitted it was a little strange, but she liked Frieda. Frieda was nice to them.

She then quietly admitted that except for bread, Frieda was not the best at cooking. "Of all things, she's best at making bread. I'm even learning from her. But for everything else, I'm the one teaching." Anna laughed. "It's not easy because neither of us understands the other very well. I'm insisting we both speak English."

Lars walked past and smiled toward Anna. Katrine caught Anna smiling back.

She blushed. "I think Lars and I might marry someday. He comes to visit whenever he can. He says it is to visit the hot springs with Björn, but I know he thinks about me."

"He's only thirteen," Katrine said.

"He's almost fourteen, but I'm not saying now," Anna hissed. "I'm thinking in a few years."

"Of course in a few years," Katrine quickly replied. "When he can build his own cabin and plow his own fields and take care of a wife and a family."

Anna appeared crestfallen. Katrine grew angry with herself for having said such a silly thing. When you were a young girl, you could imagine such thoughts about marrying. She had spoiled Anna's dream. But she also knew a man had to make a living before he could marry, and that would not be for some time for any of the boys in the valley.

Chapter 23

KATRINE HELPED PAPA Olafson gather the rye shocks into the wagon and bring them to the shed. There they began threshing and winnowing until the first small crop had been finished. Proudly, Katrine brought the first bag of grain to Mama Olafson.

"Oh, Papa, I'm so thankful," Margret exclaimed. "Now, girls, you can help me make *knäckebröd*." She promptly set up the small hand mill and started grinding.

Katrine and Mia watched with glee as a thin stream of coarse meal flowed out and into a bowl.

Margret added some water and a little salt, mixed it, and handed the bowl to Katrine.

"You girls take turns beating it until it's light and fluffy."

Katrine started beating the mixture, trading off with Mia until the dark brown paste had lightened to a rich reddish brown.

"Now for frying." Margret took a large ball of the dough, patted it into a thin cake, and formed it into the bottom of the iron skillet. Katrine used a small, round biscuit cutter and cut out the center.

Margret fitted the lid onto the skillet and placed it on the coals. Immediately, the rich aroma of rye bread began filling the cabin. In a few minutes, she pulled the skillet out and flipped the bread onto the table where it steamed, nice and crisp.

When all the cakes were baked and had cooled, Katrine and Mia threaded them onto a long willow. Katrine hoisted Mia up to where she could wedge it across the ceiling.

"There," Katrine said. "Now no mice will get them."

"And we'll have knäckebröd all winter," Mia said, clapping her hands.

On another day, Margret sent Katrine and Mia to the hill behind the cabin for huckleberries. Katrine had been looking forward to when the huckleberries were ripe. They were her favorite. She asked if Mama Olafson would make a pie.

Margret laughed. "I doubt you can find enough for a pie, but we can use them like Swedish lingonberries for toppings or a sweet sauce."

"We'll get enough," Katrine said, nodding, "but not if Mia eats them all like she does raspberries."

"Me?" Mia glowered.

"I'm sure you'll both eat your fair share." Margret shooed the two girls out. "Try not to go too far. If you see any bears, come back immediately."

Katrine knew bears liked huckleberries better than anything else except for maybe a freshly caught salmon.

Huckleberry bushes grew lower on the mountain along the fringe of timber. Some even grew scattered under the open timber on the hill behind the cabin.

Grasses had seeded, and late summer flowers now carpeted the open areas. A breeze carried the scent of pine and fir. Squirrels chattered from the tops of the trees, and the huckleberry bushes were thick with bunches of purple-black berries.

Katrine bent to pick her first berries when something whistled past her and smacked the ground. A deep purplish-green pinecone bounced and rolled a short distance, stopping. A couple dozen cones littered the floor under the ponderosa pines.

Katrine shot a look up the tree. A squirrel clung to the end of a branch where the cones grew, bustling about, swaying in the wind, cutting another cone.

"Don't you have manners?" she called loudly and laughed. "You're supposed to say, 'Look out below.'"

"Maybe that's what they're chattering," Mia said.

The squirrel barked at them, swaying high up on the limb, its tail jerking.

"They're cutting cones. When they have enough, they'll dig holes around the tree trunks and bury them for winter," Katrine explained.

Another cone whistled past, hit with a thud, and rolled to Mia's feet.

"Are they good for eating?" she asked.

"All pine seeds are good. My mama sometimes used them. They're hard to get out of their shells though. You have to break them with a stone and then pick them out. They're really small."

"We should ask Mama if we should get her some."

"Well, the squirrels will get them all if we don't hurry," Katrine said. Another cone whistled past. She stepped farther away from the tree to avoid being hit, looking up.

"Let's get some," Katrine impulsively declared. It seemed fun where the squirrels were in the tops of the trees. She grabbed one of the lower branches and pulled herself up.

"It's easier to pick up these," Mia said as she began gathering some of the cones that littered the ground.

"I'm going to get my own," Katrine said. For some reason, maybe watching the squirrels running about, she just wanted to climb the tree. And for once she wished she had trousers to wear like the boys did. It was not because girls couldn't climb trees, as most boys believed, but it was because girls' dresses got in the way that they didn't.

Steadily, Katrine climbed upward, keeping her feet next to the trunk, pulling herself up one limb at a time. It was not as easy as it had appeared from the ground. The tree began swaying. The squirrels launched themselves into the neighboring trees, scolding loudly and escaping the invader.

Reaching a spot where she could see some cones far out on a branch, Katrine stopped.

"I-it's really high," she called down.

"Maybe you can reach that one near you," Mia suggested.

Katrine spotted two purple cones on the end of a branch and began reaching toward them, trying to keep her balance. The tree swayed. A bit of dizziness hit her, and she grabbed ahold, her heart pounding.

She could see the top of the cabin, the yard, and the garden. The view calmed her.

She reached for the cone again. Some blue jays began squawking.

Katrine looked for them and froze. Three Indians rode directly toward the cabin.

"Indians," she hoarsely whispered. An iciness washed over her.

Mia turned toward the cabin, squinting. "I see them. What do we do?" Her face was pinched.

Katrine began climbing down as quickly as possible, catching a branch in her side, skinning her hands as the bark and twigs gave way. She dropped the last few feet to the ground.

"A-are they going to hurt Mama?" Mia asked. Her hands twisted in her dress.

Katrine brushed herself off, trying not to think of the terrible things that could happen. "We have to fetch Papa Olafson."

"Maybe they killed him already." Mia's voice cracked. Tears welled in her eyes.

Katrine knew she could not give in to her own desperate feelings. She peered toward the cabin. The Indians had dismounted and now approached the cabin, partially visible through the trees. One stood to the side, cradling a rifle.

They were brightly dressed, and feathers fluttered about their heads, yellow, white, and black. Faces stoic, they were bronze-chested and wore breechcloths with fringed leggings. Their spotted ponies wore bright blankets. In spite of Katrine's fear, the men were somehow impressive.

"We have to help," Katrine whispered. She headed down the hill, instinctively keeping to the cover of the trees.

"W-wait for me," Mia cried from behind her.

"We got to find Papa Olafson." Katrine noticed that the man with the rifle scanned the hillside in their direction.

White smoke billowed from the cabin. An icy jolt coursed through Katrine until she realized that Mama Olafson had thrown spruce boughs into the fire so that Papa Olafson might see her signal.

Two of the Indians had reached the door. Heart pounding, trying to move her feet forward, Katrine saw Mama Olafson appear in the doorway with Torsten on her hip.

Katrine froze.

One of the Indians gestured wildly. Margret cradled Torsten a moment before setting him down. She gestured and waved them down. The three men remained casually standing outside the cabin. Margret disappeared back inside.

Relief washed over Katrine. "I think they're friendly," she whispered. She changed course and headed toward the cabin, determined now to help Mama Olafson. Still she shook. It could be a trap, but whatever was about to happen, she had to be with Mama Olafson. Mia followed closely behind her, breathing hard.

The man with the rifle looked up and stiffened. He took a step in their direction, holding up a hand and gesturing. Whatever would be, he had seen them. Trembling even more, Katrine walked into the yard toward the man.

He spoke words she did not understand. The tone was choppy and gruff but seemed nonthreatening. Katrine pushed past him and, with Mia closely following, slipped into the cabin.

"Girls," Margret said loudly. Her eyes darted over them, relieved.

"What do they want?" Katrine asked.

"Why, I do believe they are hungry."

157

"What are you going to do?"

"I shall do as I would do for any visitor." Margret smiled. "We're going to give them a meal."

Katrine swallowed. Mama Olafson intended to let them visit. Would they do terrible things afterward?

"Now quit looking like you've seen a ghost and get me some of the dried apples. Mia, you get some knäckebröd down. I'm dishing up some stew."

Katrine shook her head. Of course they would give the Indians a meal.

Soon Katrine and Mia carried out bowls filled with turnip and venison stew to the three men. They had seated themselves cross-legged under an aspen near the creek. They gestured and grunted loudly as they each received a bowl. Torsten watched them with big eyes. Katrine recoiled from their odor. The smell was a mixture of smoke, old game hides, and sweat. She backed away.

Immediately, the Indians began scooping the stew with their fingers, eating noisily, nodding their heads, all the while watching Katrine and Mia.

One took the crispbread, submersed it into his stew, and swept it into his mouth.

"I guess they must be part Swede," Margret whispered. "They sure seem to like turnips."

Katrine almost laughed, but this was real. Maybe after the Indians had eaten they would kill them, or do worse things. She had heard stories. Their copper-colored bodies looked sinewy and strong. None appeared very old. After getting past his feathers and animals skins, one appeared to not be much older than Lars was. He had been the one holding the rifle, which was decorated with dangling white animal skins. It lay to the side now, as did the other two Indians' rifles.

Their ponies stamped and nickered nearby, pulling at the grass. Two were gray with white rumps and black spots. The other was white with black spots. They had long, flowing gray and white manes.

Katrine thought about all the stories she had heard. She wondered now. None of what she saw proved any of them. Bewildered, she watched as the men ate, clearly appreciative.

Curiously, they turned their bowls over when finished. They stood and wiped their hands on their leggings. Then without saying anything further, they gathered their ponies and mounted up. Quickly they rode past the cabin toward the eastern peaks in the direction of the old Indian trail.

When the youngest brave passed Katrine, he smiled and patted his chest, loudly saying things Katrine didn't understand.

"I think he was telling you that you would make him a good wife," Margret said. A smile tugged at her lips.

"No," Katrine sputtered. "Never."

The man turned and laughed loudly, making a whooping noise as he again shouted at Katrine. He turned his horse for the trees and galloped after the other two men.

They began gathering dishes about the time Sven came riding Ornery into the yard. He had his rifle trained in the direction that the Indians had gone.

"Is everyone all right?"

"Yes," Margret said. She picked up Torsten, who still seemed mesmerized by the Indians. "We just had some visitors is all."

"Smelly ones," Mia added.

At Sunday meeting, the talk was all about the Indians.

"I believe they were Nez Perce," Sven said. "Katrine said their horses had spotted rumps. That's the appaloosa horse they breed."

"I didn't know Indians bred horses," Gustaf said.

"These do."

"From what I understand, they don't often come here," Nils said. "They are usually west along the Little Salmon River and the Snake River, and then up into the Clearwater country where some of the mining is now going on. Most of the Nez Perce are northwest of Lewiston across the Snake River."

"They are a long way from home then," Magnus said.

"I imagine they come through here to trade with other Indians, maybe those southwest of us," Anton said.

"Or to get out of the snow," Nils said. "I told you these Indians wouldn't bother us."

"But I don't need any unwelcome guests either," Sven said. "They now know we have horses. To them, unless you're riding it, a horse is free for the taking. Not so much the mules."

"What's wrong with mules?" Gustaf asked.

Magnus laughed. "They want horses that can catch buffalo, not mules for carrying them."

Chapter 24

THE HAY HAD cured. Sven and Magnus took the wagon and their four children and started bringing it in.

Katrine and Harald helped rake the loose-cut hay into small piles that Sven and Magnus then pitched up onto the wagon. Mia and Emma helped push it down into the back of the wagon. When they had gathered a full load, Sven drove the wagon to a place where they loose-stacked it from where they would feed the stock during the winter. Some they took to their respective sheds for when the snow forced them to corral the animals. Sven stored some under the lean-to on one side of the oat and rye straw.

"You've done better than I have at enclosing this shed," Magnus remarked.

"Ja, I still have work, but I keep adding one pole here and another there to block out the rain and snow."

"I have to go farther for my poles." Magnus glanced at the timbered ridge behind the Olafsons' cabin. He pitched some hay into the corner of the shed.

"You are welcome to come and get a load," Sven said.

Katrine and Harald helped pack down the hay, making room for more. Katrine liked jumping on the hay with Harald, but it got stuck under her dress and down her neck, and it scratched and itched. More and more she wished they lived near a hot springs.

Most of the fieldwork was now complete. Katrine was excited. Mrs. Lundgren's baby was old enough that she was going to start teaching school. Last season, she and the others had studied from their readers and arithmetic books and helped each other. Sometimes they had met for a short while with Mrs. Lundgren during Sunday meetings.

Now Katrine joined six girls and six boys at the Lundgrens' cabin and lean-to. She guessed that when the weather got bad they would all crowd into the cabin. For now, they huddled under the lean-to.

Katrine looked forward to attending school with the other children. Each day, they recited or read from their readers as requested, as long as the Lundgrens' white dog, Sir, did not pester too much. Sometimes Katrine and Anna assisted with the younger children. Mostly Katrine helped Mia at night when they were doing their assignments. Sometimes they memorized paragraphs; other times they read aloud. Reading was the best part of school because Katrine could see things in her head while the others read. The world was not just their high valley.

Katrine liked Mrs. Lundgren. At first, everybody whispered what was Mr. Lundgren thinking, marrying her because she was English. Katrine believed things must be all right because they had three children. The only differences that Katrine could ascertain were her dark hair and brown eyes. She also dressed nicely and often wore a long indigo dress with a high collar. Without question, she spoke proper English and acted more proper. *English*, the others said with slight disdain.

Of course Harald and Emma were the best at speaking and writing English. Harald told Katrine that his father said it was important because they were Americans now. They would need to write and speak English well in order to be successful.

Mama Olafson had explained that Mrs. Lundgren came from New York where she had met Mr. Lundgren after her parents had died. As the Olafsons had done, Mr. Lundgren took his family to Minnesota for land, but when that did not work out, he joined the wagon train west. Mrs. Lundgren said she always wanted to live on the frontier and try teaching school.

The only problem that Katrine could see with school at the Lundgrens' was that Mr. Lundgren liked to borrow Harald from time to time for work. More than once she had overheard Mrs. Lundgren giving him all tarnation for taking Harald out of school. "I don't allow the other children to skip school. Our son won't skip school either."

But everyone knew that sometimes it was necessary to miss school, especially for the older boys. Farm work never ended, and sometimes there were problems that needed fixing. School could wait. It was the same for bad weather.

Katrine noticed that Harald also regretted missing school. He seemed to be the smartest of the boys and knew the most interesting things.

Even though the hay was in, work never ceased. Papa Olafson greeted Katrine when she returned from school.

"Today we'll start building a stock shed for Trillium," Sven announced.

Of course Katrine helped. Mostly she fetched things.

"The horse and mules can huddle under the trees out of the snow, but the calf needs a better shelter."

They rode to the timber where Sven began cutting poles. Katrine held them as he lashed them to the mules and dragged them back to the yard until he had a large pile.

The next day, again after school when Katrine could help, Sven began digging holes. "I don't have lumber, so I build what we used in Sweden. It's called a pole shed."

Sven set pairs of poles at four points where the corners of the shed would be. He set additional pairs midway along the length of each side, except for the door. Here, he set two pairs of posts about five feet apart.

"Trillium won't understand a narrow door," Sven explained.

As Papa Olafson erected the poles, they reminded Katrine of a strange fence. Once up, he began inserting aspen poles into the slots formed by the matched posts. Katrine helped him hold them while he fitted one end into the slot and then slid the other end into place. Eventually, he formed a loosely stacked wall of poles about six feet tall. He laid poles across the corners of the box for a short distance and then shorter poles spanning the newly formed corners. In that manner, he closed in a roof.

"If we don't get too heavy a snow, this roof will work just fine," Sven said.

Next, Sven built a fence around the stock shed, as well as the lean-to and Trillium's pen.

"Boots and the mules can come over to this side near Trillium's shed where we can also feed them, but now they can't break into the pantry and help themselves." He laughed.

Katrine could see that now the horse and mules were fenced out, but they still had access to the creek and open range. Trillium also had plenty of room to range for pasture.

When Sven finished the feedboxes, Katrine and Mia brought in the straw and then an armload of hay.

"Let's see how Trillium likes her new home." Sven led the six-month-old heifer into the pen. It took only moments for her to find the hay.

The girls approved.

"She can go inside when the weather gets bad, just like a barn."

"But there's only room for one cow," Mia said.

"Each year I can add to the shed."

It had grown dark. Katrine followed Papa Olafson and Mia back to the cabin, thankful for its warmth and the light from the kitchen fire. They lit the kerosene lamp and began supper. Afterward, Katrine and Mia studied from one of the readers. Both had assignments they were to read the following day. Torsten was asleep in his cradle. Mama Olafson fixed some hot tea.

A scream pierced the quiet. Icy needles raced down Katrine's back.

Sven straightened. "Mountain lion. Probably the same one we've heard before."

Katrine remembered all too well, hearing the lion last fall.

"Now we may have trouble. That cat may think Trillium is her next meal." Sven grabbed the rifle and checked his load. "Now that Trillium is inside that pen, the lion may think the calf's trapped."

Sven took up the kerosene lamp. "Come, Katrine, let's go see if we can find it. You carry the lamp."

Katrine's heart began wildly thumping.

Trillium rolled her eyes at them when they checked on her. She was up near the shed. Although she was a good-sized animal, not the small calf that Sven had brought to the valley several months ago, she was still no match for a mountain lion.

Sven walked about the perimeter a bit. Nervously, Katrine followed, trying to hold the lamp out in front of them. She wondered how it would be possible to see the mountain lion.

"Hold your light high and wave it slowly around. I'm trying to catch its eyes," Sven whispered.

Katrine trembled as she raised the lamp. What if they did see the mountain lion's eyes? Would it attack?

"What are we going to do if we do see its eyes, Papa Olafson?" Katrine whispered.

"Shoot at it. Otherwise, there's not much we can do tonight. I think the horse and mules can fend for themselves, but if that cat figures out the calf can't run, we're going to have trouble."

Sven raised the rifle. "Plug your ears." He fired a shot in the direction of the scream. "Let that lion wonder about that."

Katrine trembled like a leaf; her ears rang.

No one slept well that night. They did not hear the mountain lion again, but Sven remained awake for a good while.

All were relieved to find Trillium still alive in the morning and with no evidence that the mountain lion had come any closer.

"I guess I have no choice but to fix a gate and lock Trillium up at night."

When Katrine returned that day after school, she saw that the gate was finished. Papa Olafson had fashioned a door out of more slender aspen poles that he had pegged to a stout frame. He placed the door across the opening and barred it into place.

"I will sure be pleased when we get a sawpit and I can cut some boards," Sven muttered.

The next day at school, Katrine and the children took turns reading aloud their assignments. The day was warm compared to the previous few days, and the thirteen children all sat cross-legged in the dust near the lean-to. The Lundgrens' dog, Sir, came out to greet them, but after it realized the children were not there to play, it went back to keeping guard over the cabin.

Several children shared readers, depending on what level they had achieved. The very youngest were huddled aside with Anna, practicing writing their letters on the slates.

"I would like Jens to read the next section, please," Mrs. Lundgren announced.

Katrine watched as Jens stood up, taking a reader from Harald and wetting his lips.

"What is the first rule for reading?" Mrs. Lundgren asked.

Katrine and the older children answered in unison: "You shall keep your head up and pronounce every word clearly and separately."

Mrs. Lundgren stood patiently.

Jens wet his lips again and began.

"Th-this is the continuing story of Sir Anderson when h-his river boat capsized during his African expedition.

"'When I opened my eyes, I was m-met w-with th-th-the m-most splendid sight. God's sun shone with favor upon my face. I was so taken by its beauty, I had scare-scarcely noticed that the true miracle was the life He had graced me with.

"'I caught sight of the remnants of my boat. It appeared at once that I was the sole sur-survivor. Mr. Jerome's lifeless body had washed ashore near my feet.

"'However, instead of a flood of thanksgiving and gratitude for my life, a moment of great anger overcame my being. Alas, I cussed my creator. It took but a moment to realize my blasphemy, and I quickly beseeched Him for forgivenance.

"'God had pre-pre-served me, but for what purpose and for what end?

"'Shortly thereafter, I began to realize my true peril. Without Mr. Jerome's knowledge and skill of navigation, I was at peril of finding my way. Now I prayed with fervor for true deliverance.'"

Jens lowered his book.

"Stand for a moment, Jens. Please look at the word, *cussed*."

Katrine heard some muffled giggles.

Jens glanced at his reader and then looked back toward Mrs. Lundgren, frowning.

"The word is *cursed*. Do you see the letter R that you missed?"

Jens glanced down again. "Y-yes, ma'am."

"Otherwise I believe you read well. Did anyone else catch other errors?"

Katrine had caught *forgivenance* for *forgiveness*; however, she was not willing to point it out.

"Very well," Mrs. Lundgren said. "Continue reading your assignments aloud at home, Jens, and work to improve your enunciation and clarity. Speak your words more slowly."

"Yes'm," Jens replied and sat down.

Mrs. Lundgren closed her reader. "I believe that shall be enough for now. Enjoy recess for a few minutes."

Clapping books and chattering erupted as everyone began scrambling to their feet.

"Quietly," Mrs. Lundgren reminded them.

The boys raced away from where they had been seated and immediately began a game of chase. The Lundgrens' dog joined in.

Katrine migrated toward Anna and the other girls, who talked about girl things.

After a few moments, Katrine noticed Jens and Harald had come up nearby, panting from having been running.

Harald eyed Jens. "You stutter a lot when you read," he said. "You're funny."

Jens stood still. He frowned. "You m-m-make m-mistakes too."

Harald laughed. "See, you did it again. You should do as my mother says and practice eh-nun-ci-ate-ing your words."

"Y-you wouldn't say that except your mother is our teacher."

"No, it's true. Isn't it, Katrine?"

Before Katrine could answer, Jens rebutted, "W-well, y-y-you d-dress funny. A-all English-like."

Harald laughed louder. "Now you're getting angry. You stutter even more when you get angry."

Jens screwed up his face and suddenly shoved Harald. "So, you still d-d-dress f-f-funny."

Harald stepped back in surprise, readjusted his cap, and then launched himself at Jens.

Both boys were in the dirt, rolling and pushing and hitting. Katrine watched in dismay.

"Fight!" Björn called. The others came running.

It lasted but a moment before Lars waded in and grabbed Jens and pulled him away.

Björn grabbed Harald. "Quit, Harald, before we all get into trouble."

They were too late. Mrs. Lundgren stamped her feet, arms crossed. "Enough, children."

Jens and Harald stood apart, fuming, staring at each other. A trickle of blood ran from Harald's nose. He wiped at it.

"You wait," he said and breathed sharply.

"Enough, Harald," Mrs. Lundgren said. She stared at Harald and then at Jens. "Your fathers will hear about this. There is to be no fighting."

Jens's face paled. "P-please d-don't, Mrs. Lundgren," Jens stammered. "N-not my pa. P-please don't."

Harald stood aside, his face smug.

Jens kicked at the dirt. "H-Harald st-started it," Jens said.

"I did not. You pushed me."

"*Both* of you were fighting. There is no reason to justify it, Harald," Mrs. Lundgren said. "Both of you will have additional assignments due tomorrow, and you shall both see me after classes today."

Katrine could not remember Mrs. Lundgren appearing more disgusted. She was happy that she was not involved.

"Class shall resume."

Subdued, the children returned to their places in the dirt, legs crossed, readers in their laps.

Salmon Fishing and the Sheepeater Camp

Chapter 25

THE CROPS THAT could be harvested were done, and as they had done the previous season, the men turned to hunting to supplement their food. Both Sven and Anton each killed a deer and smoked it. No one had seen any elk.

Although Sven and Anton now owned heifers, they owned no other livestock except their horses and mules. Nevertheless, they would slaughter their heifers if necessary to survive. Breeding the heifer would be much more valuable for when it had its own calf and began producing milk.

"We'll eat coyotes if we have to," Sven said. "I won't give up having milk and butter next year."

"You have high hopes on Adolphson's bull." Anton laughed.

"And so should you."

"No elk this year. I say we go fishing," Anton said. "Adolphson says the salmon are running."

In another day, Sven and Anton took their families to fish for salmon at the lake that was several miles north of the Eklunds' former farm. Tall grasses and brush already filled the Eklunds' yard, and shreds of canvas snapped in the black jaws of the old doorway.

"He was young. He should have braved it longer," Anton said.

"Ja, but then I cannot blame him with his wife going crazy on him like that," Sven replied.

There were no more comments until they had passed the abandoned cabin. Katrine thought of baby Robert and then of Torsten, who now rode sitting in front of Mama Olafson.

The trail wound its way alongside the river that tumbled in large steps of whitewater across shelves of gray granite. Willows, chokecherry shrubs, and whortleberry bushes, now in their fall colors of muted yellow, maroon, and bright flame orange, grew under the scattered pines and sparse spruce. Tamarack stood like golden torches on the timbered hillsides. A broad section of broken granite littered the river as if some giant had scooped it from the mountains and flung it into a heap at the outlet of the lake.

"It looks like one of those lakes in Sweden where the ice pushed everything out and just left piles of rock," Sven said.

Katrine stretched herself up off Boots, trying to get a better view of the lake. Like a magical jewel, it crept into view, silvery and still, lying between two rocky arms that enfolded it. Towering crags abruptly rose from its waters at the far end. Heavy black timber that fringed its shoreline fell away, rising into rolling, timbered hills. Patches of yellow and orange from autumn foliage reflected from the quiet waters. Beyond, snow-spattered granite spires with sawlike teeth lined the horizon.

Below the outlet, the water broke into sections of whitewater that cascaded in four- to six-foot falls that plummeted into a series of pools among the granite shelves. The pools shone red with swarming salmon.

"I've never seen such a sight," Sven said.

Both Sven and Anton quickly made their way down to one of the pools with their pitchforks to where the salmon crowded each other in an attempt to go up the falls.

Katrine watched one scoot upward under the fast water and then disappear into the black depths of the lake beyond.

Sven stabbed at the water, scattering the salmon. He stabbed again. The pool emptied of fish. Katrine decided that harvesting salmon might not be easy.

Anton waded in a short distance and swept his pitchfork through the water. He speared a salmon and flung it onto the bank where the nearly two-foot fish lay flopping.

"Pretend you're a bear," Anton said. "Swing at them like you have paws."

Sven began swinging and soon pitched a salmon onto the bank.

Katrine was a bit squeamish trying to catch the flopping fish. Björn and Anna came along and clubbed it and then took it to where Frieda and Margret had begun cleaning the first one.

Soon they had several. Many were ripe with bright orange eggs.

"Like caviar," Sven said. "Sure might try some."

Katrine decided she didn't want to. The fish smell was strong. It clung to her and everything around her. She and the others were soon covered in mucus and blood and strong salmon scent.

Katrine decided she had had enough of the salmon and led Mia,

Linnea, and Laurens up to the lake to explore. The water was low, leaving a pristine white sandy shoreline. A few isolated boulders jutted up through the sand. They began chasing each other, running through the soft sand, squishing it up through their toes. They ran about until weary and then flopped in the cool sand.

"This is so beautiful. I wish we lived here," Katrine said.

"You can't farm here," Mia quickly replied.

"At least we live nearby. Maybe we can come back during the summer just to visit. Do you suppose we could go swimming?" Katrine rose and walked to the waterline, looking out over the mirror surface. Mia followed.

"I don't know. I guess it's always cold," Mia said. She stuck her toes into the water. "Brrr." She quickly pulled them out.

"Maybe it's warm in summer." Katrine turned and picked up a small flattened rock and skipped it far out into the water, breaking the surface into repeated ringlets of silver and blue.

Mia tried to skip a rock as well, but it plunked instead.

Laurens and Linnea joined them. Soon the lake's quiet surface was pockmarked with sprinkling pebbles.

Katrine took Mia and wandered along a tiny creek with a gravelly bottom in search of more flat stones. She soon found herself in a small clearing where the creek meandered through. It was a beautiful place with a level floor, the creek spilling across its bottom, collecting in small, crystal pools before entering the lake. She noticed strange, skeletal structures made of poles and tree limbs along the fringe.

"Look at the shelters." She pointed toward them. An eerie feeling enveloped her. "They look old. Do you suppose they're Indian shelters?"

"I think they are. Are there Indians here?"

"I don't believe so." But the hairs on Katrine's neck rose. Her eyes swept the timber for signs of any. "It doesn't look as if anyone's been here for a while."

The structures resembled brush piles more than they did a home. Decaying hides flapped in the breeze from some of them, and Katrine caught the lingering odor of dead things. Stones were set in rings outside the shelters—old campfires, she presumed.

"We better go tell Papa Olafson and the others."

A bit scared, Katrine took the younger children and made her way back to the group where they were still fishing. Presently, Sven, Anton, and Björn followed Katrine and Mia back to the Indian campsite. The women remained with the other children at the falls, cleaning the salmon.

"Will the Indians come back?" Mia asked, biting her lip.

Sven walked among the lodges. "I don't believe so. The people who built these haven't been here for some time. This camp looks more like it has been abandoned than used."

"Are these Indians murderous?" Björn asked.

"I doubt it." Sven squatted near the opening of one of the shelters. "I'm guessing these are Sheepeater Indians. As I understand it, they generally avoid whites."

Björn stooped down and entered one of the lodges. "These aren't very big." He pushed at the poles overhead.

The earth had been scrapped away in the center of the shelter and formed a shallow bowl. Rocks were stacked around the perimeter. Slender poles had been shoved into the earth and leaned against each other, forming a cone of poles and brush.

Presently, Björn reached down and picked up a glassy black fragment. "Look, an arrow point."

Anton examined it. "It's volcano glass. I'm guessing they traded for it. I've never seen anything like this around this country."

Katrine began searching for more obsidian. She found some pieces, one pretty good but nothing as complete as what Björn had found.

Another shelter held some stone bowls.

"Do you think Mama Olafson could use one of these?" Katrine asked.

"She probably could, but I see no reason for taking one," Sven replied. "If these Indians come back, they may want to take them with them. Even if they aren't here now, it would be like someone coming into our cabin and taking one of Mama's bowls."

"Yes, sir." Katrine felt a little embarrassed.

Björn picked up a hook-like spear. "I judge this is for catching salmon. They wouldn't have left something like this if they weren't planning on coming back." He made a stab with the spear at an imaginary target.

Sven shook his head. "Maybe they intended to return, but now that we have farms nearby, they've decided against it."

Katrine began feeling uneasy again, as if they were being watched. "It feels as if spirits are here," she whispered to Björn.

"Maybe," he replied. He arched his eyes and smiled slightly. "Spirits can't hurt you though."

Katrine hoped he was correct. "Maybe we should go now." The feeling became more unsettling.

Sven laughed. "Ja, we know where this place is. Now we need to keep watch in case the owners return."

They made their way back to the falls where the others were finishing with the salmon. Quietly, Sven and Anton informed Margret and Frieda of what they had seen.

"Thank the Lord this place is not nearer to us," Margret said. "I think they come here to go fishing, just like we did."

They packed the salmon into canvas bags, strapped them onto the mules, and headed back.

Katrine felt even more unsettled when they rode past the Eklunds' abandoned cabin again. She thought again about baby Robert. Was his spirit still here?

Arriving back at the Wikstroms' cabin, the men immediately began working on setting up another smoke tent. Similar to the one they built last fall, they built a frame from aspen poles and covered it with a large section of canvas. After the fire burned to a bed of coals, they piled on aspen and willow chunks and hung the salmon over twine near the top of the tent.

Both Frieda and Margret cornered the children. Frieda said, "You smell of der fish. All of you. To the hot springs. Und wash your clothes before you dare to come back."

"This salmon smell is not so bad. You should smell *surströmming*," Margret said.

"Vhas ist surströmmink?"

"It is the most vile, stinking stuff on the face of earth."

"And you eat it?"

"Don't you tell Sven I said so, but we Swedes eat it only out of respect for our ancestors. It's tradition. They were starving and had to survive on eating rotten fish. Sven insists it's not rotten; it's just soured like sauerkraut."

Frieda nodded. "Well, maybe it ist not so bad then. Sauerkraut and pickled pigs feet ist very goot."

"The sour part is its only resemblance," Margret said. "It is vile, foul-smelling, evil-tasting, rotten fish, it is."

"You keep it then," Frieda said.

"I pray Sven always grows good crops and gets game. I should never like to see surströmming again as long as I shall live," Margret continued.

"You do not honor your ancestors very well."

"I come from the south part of Sweden."

Soon Katrine and the others had climbed to the lower pool where they began taking turns scrubbing their clothes in the hotter water, rubbing them between their hands and over the rocks. Anna helped Laurens with his. When they had scrubbed as long as their arms could take it, they wrung them out and laid them on the boulders and bushes to dry. While their clothing dried, they all joined in the larger pool, splashing and swimming about. Björn busied himself at one end of the pool trying to roll out more rocks. Katrine scooted over to help as she had done before.

"Thanks," Björn said. "Pretty soon it'll be deeper with all these rocks piled up."

Katrine enjoyed working with Björn. He made her feel appreciated.

During the following Sunday meeting, Sven and Anton told the others of the abandoned camp.

"Ja," Nils said. "For sure they are Sheepeaters. I saw a small hunting party the first time I came through the valley. They wore furs and hunted on foot—no horses. Another fellow with me pulled his rifle, but the Indians were more interested in disappearing than visiting. They are mostly peaceable. It's the Snake Indians you have to watch for."

"It will pay to keep our eyes open," Gustaf said. "All Indians are thieves. If given a chance, they'll have your horses in no time."

Although the Sheepeaters were said to leave the whites alone, Katrine remained skeptical. She did not go back to her rock in the meadow for several days, and when she did, she took Mia.

RYE SHEAF AND SKIS

Chapter 26

THE TREES HAD shed their leaves, and frost now carpeted the meadows in the mornings. The families gathered at the Adolphsons' to see off Nils, Anton, and Gustaf to Boise City for trading and supplies. Sven had given them his list of items for which to trade, mostly cornmeal and salt pork, some salt and sugar, and some household necessities such as canvas and kerosene oil.

While awaiting their return, Katrine helped Papa Olafson as she always did. He began plowing fields for next season. He also dragged more poles to the yard for improving the corral and shed.

"I have a bad feeling that the mountain lion isn't going to forget where Trillium is."

The men returned in twelve days, bringing in their fully packed string of fourteen mules.

"We hit it right. The river was low, and the work we've done on the trail is paying off," Anton said.

"Ja, the time for crossing the river is in the fall when it's low, not the spring," Nils said. "But I will say, every farm around is taking in its crops during the fall. If we can save some over to spring when the mining camps really need them, we could sell them for much more."

"I think I just do what I can, if I ever have crops enough to sell," Sven said and laughed. He hoisted a pack up onto Jack and tied it.

At their cabin, Sven began unloading the mules. Katrine helped.

"Judging by the sky today and the way the air feels, it won't be long until a good storm comes through."

Katrine glanced up. High, thin clouds had muted the deep blue. She bit her lip.

"Now don't you worry, Katrine. We'll be all right. We did fine last winter, did we not?"

Katrine shivered, thinking how soon the snow might come.

"For sure we now have a heifer to feed along with the horse and mules, but we have hay and oats."

That evening for supper, Margret fixed stew with knäckebröd and some newly acquired dried peaches.

It had grown dark by the time the dishes were stowed.

Sven pulled out his pipe. Torsten sat in his father's lap, playing with his suspenders. Sven picked him up and carried him about the cabin, laughing. Presently, he carried the boy to the door, set him down, and peered out. "Come, girls. You should see this," he said and stepped out.

Outside, the cold bit at Katrine's cheeks and nose. Stars glittered in the indigo sky.

"There on the horizon, can you see?"

A faint light silhouetted the trees along the mountain range to the east, and a white haze hung in their branches.

"There shall be a ring around the moon this night," Sven observed. "For sure, a storm's brewing."

Katrine shivered as she watched an arc of purplish-red and gold light brighten along the horizon, like a faint rainbow. Soon the moon's shimmering edge broke into the night sky and slowly ascended. Katrine's breath hung on the cold night air.

She thought of the nearby warm cabin with plenty of wood and plenty of food. They had worked every moment for the coming winter. It was almost as if they had been readying themselves for battle. Now the enemy was foretold by the shimmering halo of light that surrounded the rising moon. They were ready.

"Take one more look around tomorrow," Sven said. "If there's anything that needs to be brought in or picked up, we best do so. I expect whatever's left out tomorrow night might as well be forgotten until spring. Mother Nature is about to put this entire valley to sleep."

Katrine wondered how Papa Olafson could be so certain. What had he sensed that told him a storm would soon be upon them?

The following morning, Katrine woke to frosty cold and a gray sky. Papa Olafson was outside taking care of stock. Katrine began helping Mama Olafson at the tiny stove that Papa Olafson had brought back from Boise City. It was an iron box about eighteen inches wide and long with a metal chimney that inserted into the mud and twig chimney. She heard horses coming hard and looked out to see Mr. Adolphson and Lars coming fast into the yard. All talked loudly as they dismounted and headed toward the cabin.

Banging their way inside, she caught bits of Mr. Adolphson's words.

"They got two of my horses. They got Andreasson's two horses as well. I haven't heard from Wikstrom. Apparently, they passed you and Lundgren up."

Indians, Katrine realized. Her heart caught.

"To blazes, they did," Sven said. "I'll go with you to get them back of course." He glanced at Margret.

Margret's eyes flashed, but she immediately began packing some rations.

"Andreasson's going as well. Maybe Wikstrom will join us. We'll head over to his place and meet up over there. The tracks were headed north."

Sven grabbed his muffler, heavy coat, and rifle. He handed the pistol to Margret. "They won't come back through here, but just in case, be ready." He glanced at Katrine and Mia. "You girls take care of the stock while I'm gone, but go together and keep your eyes open. Don't go anywhere else. Understood?"

Katrine nodded. Mia held tight to her.

"If we press the Indians hard enough, they may release one or more of the horses," Nils said.

Lars had said nothing but watched quietly. Katrine wondered if he was going.

"I wished we had more horses to follow with," Sven said. He checked his ammunition pouch. "Horses will move faster than mules."

"Mules will go longer," Nils replied. "And ours are better fed. At least that's how I understand."

"We're about to find out." Sven grabbed his bedroll and the bundle of rations. He kissed Margret and squeezed her. "I'll be fine, Mama, *älskling*," he said. "Those Indians won't want to fight us. Not with four rifles facing them."

The men rode out of the yard before Katrine could fully comprehend what was going on. Lars remained behind. They stood looking at each other.

"What happened?" Katrine asked.

"Sometime last night they ran off two of our horses. I thought I heard something, but we were too slow to stop them. Then Mr. Andreasson came by this morning and told us he had lost two of his horses. That's when Pa told him to get up to the Wikstroms' to see if he had been hit. We came this way to check on you and the Lundgrens."

Katrine could hardly believe what had happened. "Do you suppose it was the Indians that visited us last summer?"

179

Lars shrugged. "Maybe. They knew we had horses."

Katrine swallowed. "But why? We were nice to them and gave them some food. Why would they take our horses?"

"It's a game with them. They always try to steal horses from one another. One minute they act like your friends, and the next, they have your horses. That's why if my pa and the others chase them hard, they might let the horses go. But you can figure they'll try again, if they do."

That evening, the storm that Papa Olafson had predicted pushed into the valley. Three to four inches of snow soon blanketed the ground. Slushy ice formed on the pond. Katrine looked around somewhat in disbelief. A day ago, it was autumn. This day, winter had returned.

Katrine took care of Trillium, making certain she had feed and hay. The heifer always seemed happy to see her. The mules were fine without much tending. They were quite able to forage from the hillside and meadows. She carried in wood and filled the water barrel.

A week passed. Katrine began feeling troubled. She knew Mama Olafson worried, but she spoke cheerily. Neither expressed their fears. Katrine and Mia quietly helped with some sewing and knitting, and of course, they played with Torsten. Each day, they stared out the window at the snow-covered ground and wondered. No one visited. It was as if the remainder of the world had ceased to exist.

A day later, Katrine spotted Papa Olafson coming over the hill. He waved when closer to the cabin. She ran out to help him with the horse and then, with Mia on her heals, followed him to the cabin to hear the news.

Margret kissed and hugged Sven. "What happened? Did you get the horses back?"

"We're all fine." Sven sat and began pulling off his boots. "We got one of Andreasson's horses back and an Indian pony, but that was all. We were so far north that we began to fear we'd run into more Indians than we would care to meet. Signs of them were everywhere. And the snow was worse, so we called it off."

"An Indian pony?" Margret poured him a steaming bowl of soup from the pot always ready on the stove. She buttered some pieces of knäckebröd.

"Yes, I think one of the Indians let it go in favor of one of the other horses. We left it with Adolphson since he lost two of his horses."

Sven broke the crispbread into his soup. "Ah, this is what I've missed." He took a bite.

"What's the pony look like?" Katrine wondered.

"He's a red roan, but we aren't sure if it will be any good. It was pretty skittish."

"Maybe Lars can train it," Katrine said.

"Probably not much, but Mr. Adolphson thinks he can either sell or trade it." Sven sipped some of his soup.

"Anyway, we followed them north to the Little Salmon River to where they turned west and crossed into the Snake River country. The other side of the Snake is Oregon. I didn't realize how close we were to the border."

He sat back.

"I saw a lot of country, some fit for farming, some not. We saw no other settlers and no miners. It makes me glad we're here together with others in our own valley."

"Will the Indians try for some more of our horses or come back for their pony?" Margret asked.

"I fear saying it, but they may. It was pretty easy for them to get the three horses they ended up with."

"Was it the Indians that camped at the lake?" Katrine asked.

Sven shook his head. "No, we rode through there. No sign of anyone having returned. It wasn't Sheepeaters in any respect. They don't own horses."

Katrine felt a little happier about having the Sheepeaters as their neighbors.

"These could have been our visitors from last summer, but I doubt it. Likely, it was a hunting party that could not believe its luck. I'm pretty certain they were Nez Perce. If they were Bannock or Paiute, they would have returned south. We may never know who they were for sure. We just have to keep our eyes open." He glanced at Katrine and Mia. "Am I correct, girls?"

Katrine nodded.

"Now I'm a couple of weeks behind with work, but it was the right thing to do. Next time it could be my horse." Sven emptied his bowl and pushed it toward Margret for more. "Very good. Thanks."

At Sunday meeting, they talked about the Indians, ignoring Jens who excitedly told anyone who would listen that they had slaughtered their pig. It had finally gotten cold enough and stayed cold enough to do so. Katrine was envious. The Andreassons now had lard and salt pork and ham and bacon. She knew Papa Olafson wanted to raise pigs as well. They all did. But they needed lots of crops for raising pigs. At present, a cow that produced milk, cheese, and butter and ate grass was far more important than a pig that got slaughtered in the fall. Of course they would trade with the Andreassons for some lard and ham if they could.

Katrine went to see the Indian pony, which was still corralled near the Adolphsons' cabin. She thought it was very beautiful. Its reddish coat glowed in the afternoon sunlight as it moved away from her.

"He's still pretty skittish," Lars said. "It might be he never settles down, but he might be good for breeding." Lars had come to the fence and stood watching.

Some of the other children gathered around to see the new horse as well.

"I wager I could train it," Björn said.

Winter storms continued, and the snow deepened. Katrine and Mia followed Papa Olafson to the Lundgrens' for school while he broke trail.

"If it's too much by this afternoon, I'll be back to see you home," Sven said.

But they had no trouble, and after they had returned from school, Katrine noticed that Sven had brought in some lodgepole pine saplings that he had trimmed.

"I believe it is time I began making us some skis."

Katrine and Mia laughed.

"Ja, soon skis may be the best way to get around. Boots and Ornery aren't going to be liking much more of this snow. You girls can get to school. I can get over to the Adolphsons' if need be. Even Mama can get around."

Katrine didn't think Mama Olafson could get around on them, but Papa Olafson seemed convinced. He began working on the skis that night and every night for several nights thereafter. He split the logs, forming crude boards, and planed them smooth. He next boiled water and immersed one end into the water, adding more water and stoking the fire to keep it boiling. When he removed the boards, he bent the tips back and tied them into place while they slowly dried. Afterward, he carved and smoothed the tips. He then replaned and sanded the bottoms, continuing to smooth them.

"We must get out all the bumps or they won't slide very well, even with some beeswax on the bottoms."

Finally, he stood a pair up for Katrine and Mia to see.

"See, girls, if we want to visit anyone before May, we have to do like in the old country or be happy sitting like bumps all winter. I had enough of sitting like a bump last winter."

Sven fixed leather straps to hold their shoes in place. He found a couple of willow poles, fashioned some small pegs onto one end, and put a leather strap on the other. "These are for balance, although sometimes they get more in the way than they help."

When Sven had finished a second pair of skis, they took them outside to try them. Sven tramped around, packing a trail. Katrine tried to walk with the skis, slipped, and immediately fell. Chuckling, Papa Olafson helped her up. She shuffled and fell again. It was not as much fun as it appeared when Papa Olafson slid about. Katrine used the poles to help her stand back up and keep balance. She finally managed to shuffle along the track and back, sometimes sliding a bit, without falling. Papa and Mama Olafson and Mia cheered.

"See, you get the sense of it," Sven said. "Now when I finish Mia's, you two can ski to school."

"What about when it snows really deep?"

"I will go and help pack a trail like this one," Sven said. He took off, tramping and sliding a distance on the snow, using his poles only occasionally.

Katrine tramped around a bit more, sliding. It was fun, but Mia was clambering to get the skis. She helped Mia get into the skis. Mia quickly began sliding around, squeaking with glee.

Sven cheered. "Mama is next. I'll build us all a pair."

Margret frowned. "I have Torsten to care for, remember?"

"Ja, we just throw Torsten into a pack and sling him onto your back, and then off you go."

"You sling him onto yours," Margret replied.

"By gum, I will. Just you see. Come, Mama, we Swedes know what to do in snow."

After the first time that Katrine and Mia skied to school, the other children decided they needed some skis as well. Sven was soon busy crafting additional pairs. Nils copied a pair and helped Lars build some, but Sven had the proper tools and was the most skilled. Before Christmas, everyone tramped about the valley on their own skis, visiting one another, pushing and sliding across the snow from one neighbor to the next. After all, there was little else to do in the winter other than to try to stay warm and feed farm animals.

At Sunday meeting, Anton suggested, "Sven, you should make a sled with skis instead of that box you drag around for firewood."

"This summer for sure," Sven replied. "For now I am tired of making boards out of logs. We will get a saw from Boise City and build a sawpit, and then I can get all the lumber I want."

"Ja, I could use a sled as well," Nils added.

As Christmas approached, Katrine remembered to set out the rye sheaf that she had saved back for the birds. No sooner had she and Mia stood it up than nuthatches and chickadees began flitting down from the sky, alighting on the straw and pecking for grain.

Katrine loved watching the birds, in particular the chickadees with their black caps, white cheeks, and black bibs. The tiny birds were most inquisitive, bustling about on the sheaf, flitting from the garden fence back and forth, making their high-pitched call: *chick a dee dee dee*. She also enjoyed watching the red-breasted nuthatches as they scurried up and down the sheaf as if it were the trunk of a tree. They sounded their *yank yank* call as they darted about chasing one another. Occasionally a gray jay with its arched eyebrows or a blue jay with its black topknot came around, but Katrine did not care for them chasing away the smaller birds.

Katrine just knew their barnyard elf would appreciate the birds and would now do his best to help care for their animals through the winter. At least this is what she told Mia.

They skied to the Adolphsons' for Santa Lucia. Ingrid Adolphson, who was now twelve, was Saint Lucia and wore a wreath of fir set with tallow candles. The cakes were a little larger this year and were again laced with wild currants and sprinkled with sugar. The men toasted each other a little more exuberantly. The women talked about their children and about sewing new clothes. What made it most special for Katrine were the songs they sang and the stories they told.

The Olafsons celebrated Christmas quietly a few days later at their cabin. They exchanged small gifts. Katrine and Mia had knitted socks. Margret had made mittens. Katrine decided that Papa Olafson, of course, had made the best gifts. They were the skis with which everyone could now get about.

Chapter 27

DURING THE LONG winter nights, Katrine could not avoid gloomy feelings from the darkness pressing in around her. The sun hardly shone before it disappeared and the world again grew shadowy and silent. Each day, the family rose in the dark, lit a candle, fixed a breakfast, and at the first hint of light, set about doing daily chores. Sven took care of the stock, pulling down hay, and chopping ice. More than once he reported mountain lion tracks near Trillium's pen. He expressed how lucky they were that the cougar hadn't been bold enough to go after one of the mules or Boots. On several nights, Katrine had awakened when the animals had set up a ruckus.

"If I don't try to trap it, I may live to regret it," Sven said. "Lundgren and Andreasson have traps." He set his rifle back. "Well, the cat hasn't been able to figure out Trillium's pen. For now we'll just keep alert."

Katrine worried. She knew that if they lost Trillium, they would likely never have their own milk and butter.

Evenings came early and pressed down on them. Margret fixed supper earlier in order that they could see. They then quietly sat in the cabin, keeping a small fire going for its warmth and flickering glow. Infrequently, they lit the kerosene lamp or a candle.

Each night before bed, Katrine checked the night sky for the northern lights. They had seen them only that once. Now the moon began rising, round and creamy bright over the landscape, sending its long light across the sparkling new-fallen snow and chasing away the dreary darkness.

Like tiny jewels everywhere, Katrine thought. "Come, Mia, let's go and watch the moon."

Mia wrapped on her scarf and began putting on her coat.

"I'm going with you girls. Put on your skis. We're going out into the meadow," Sven said.

Katrine wondered what had gotten into Papa Olafson.

Soon they were tramping across the snow, packing it down as they skied. The full moon rose, suspending itself behind a naked spiderweb of aspen limbs and long ponderosa needles. A thin line of clouds cut it into fantastic shapes.

"Look, Mia. It looks like a long-necked goose."

The moon illuminated the clouds, became quenched behind the thicker layers, and then reemerged as a shimmering luminescent orb.

They continued sliding through the snow. Sven led the way down into a thicket of willows and aspens toward a tall, dark spruce.

Katrine began worrying about the mountain lion but said nothing.

"This is the time of the goblins and trolls," Mia whispered. "We should keep our eyes out for them."

"Perhaps, little angel, but this is not a goblin." Sven stopped near the large spruce. "Listen."

Softly, the hoot of an owl filled the night.

"Oh," Katrine whispered. "An owl."

"Listen to what he says."

Mia stood near Katrine, shivering. Katrine didn't feel cold. Her breath hung on the still night air.

The owl's call filtered down to them again. Another call seemed to come from the timber across the meadow.

"I think it's another one," Katrine said. "They're talking to each other."

The owl in the tree nearest them called out again, a low-throated *whooo*. Moments later, the other owl answered.

Katrine listened to their back-and-forth calls, eerily piercing the quiet.

"The woods have their own night music," Sven said. "In summer you hear the bullfrogs and crickets. Now you hear the great horned owls."

The moon quietly freed itself from the uppermost tree branches. Gliding silently, it filled the sky with brilliant light, bathing the meadow in a luminescent glow, painting the shadows pale blue and the snow a faint lemon.

"We should go," Mia whispered. "I'm cold."

A shadow filled the sky above them as the owl launched itself silently and dropped downward from the spruce and then out and across the meadow. It ascended into the far tree, and the night sounds ended.

"I guess they found each other," Sven said, and he laughed. He kicked his skis around, and the girls followed, tramping back up toward the cabin in the magical moonlight.

After stowing their skis, they lit the kerosene lamp and sat down at the table. Margret served them some hot tea. "So what was the purpose of all that?" she asked, smiling.

"Many folks have never been out on a night like this in the deep snow with only the music of nature about them. I thought it might be good for the girls to see a different world."

Sven turned to them and asked, "Did you have fun?"

Both nodded. Katrine said, "It's different. The owls are out there now, but they won't be there in the morning."

"Ja, I've had to come home at night a time or two and have learned to listen carefully to things around me. You can learn a lot by listening."

"Pshaw," Margret said, laughing gently.

"Does that mean you would like for me to show you?" Sven said. "Come then." He grabbed ahold of Margret. "The girls can watch Torsten and make us more hot tea for when we come back."

Margret protested, but Sven got her out the door. Katrine heard her laughing, and then their voices dimmed.

"The owl will be gone," Mia said.

"The moon won't be," Katrine answered, amused.

Hints of spring began tripping about the valley. Daylight began lingering, and the sun began inching north. The frosty nights warmed more quickly into sunlit days.

Katrine wanted to get out of the cabin and do something. They had been snowbound for too long. She thought about visiting the Wikstroms and the hot springs. Papa Olafson agreed that if they really wanted to do so, they could ski over.

"You must be watchful of the weather. Start back early in case something goes wrong. That will give me time to come and look for you."

Katrine now hesitated, realizing the danger, but the thought of visiting was too strong. "We'll be sure to start back early."

Katrine and Mia started out, tramping across the snow, carrying a pack with some food and a blanket in case of an emergency. They went up the same draw east of the Lundgrens' where they had crossed to the Andreassons' for Midsummer's Eve. Katrine slipped a little, trying to get up the hill, but soon found she could step sideways up the steeper parts. When they crossed over the ridge, they entered more dense timber.

"We have to follow the trail here between the trees," Katrine explained. She could have angled farther to the northeast, but she worried she would not be able to ski down and cross the creek. Closer to the Wikstroms' cabin, the creek flowed through a narrow, rocky draw.

"Once we make a trail going there, it will be easier going back home," Katrine said.

She peered about. To the west, the country opened in unbroken snow and isolated trees and willows. Toward the east, the trees pressed in, forming a thick, dark carpet on the ridge that rose above them.

They skied along following the general direction of the trail until they reached where the creek emerged from the draw. Mia kept close behind.

"We'll have to cross down to the other side now," Katrine said. She worried about crossing the creek. It was March. She wondered if ice still spanned the creek, and if so, would it hold? She began thinking they had not been very wise in trying to ski to the Wikstroms'.

She came out above the creek and breathed more easily. An unbroken blanket of snow stretched across, marked by a deep dimple that showed where the creek flowed beneath. Farther below, a couple of black holes showed rushing water.

"You let me go first," Katrine said. "It looks scary, but I'm sure the ice is sturdy."

She slid carefully down toward the creek, packing the snow as she went, and crossed the dimple. When Katrine believed she was safe, she turned and called to Mia.

Slowly, Mia slid out, following in Katrine's tracks.

"I'll be glad when it's summer," Mia murmured.

Katrine laughed. "You don't make a very good Swede. Papa Olafson says Swedes get along just fine in the snow."

"I like snow. I just don't like skiing across when there's water underneath."

They turned up the trail toward the Wikstroms' cabin. It was heavily packed with recent signs of use.

Katrine loved visiting the Wikstroms. Mr. Wikstrom always gave them a big hug and asked how his other girls were doing. They had also come to love Frieda. She fussed over them. It was almost as if Frieda had not only adopted Mr. Wikstrom's four children, but she had also adopted Katrine and Mia. And of course they loved visiting with Anna and Linnea and Björn and Laurens and visiting the hot springs.

Everyone piled about them as they made their way into the cabin, except for Anton and Björn, who were tending chores. Katrine recognized that farm life at the Wikstroms' during winter was much the same as at their place. The men tended the stock, chopped ice, and cut firewood. Today, moments after they had arrived, they came stomping inside, arms full of wood. Björn immediately told Katrine about some mountain lion tracks.

"My pa says those cats should be over on the Salmon River drainage out of the snow. There aren't any deer here, and they like deer."

"What bothers me more are the wolves," Anton said. "Have you girls seen any?"

Katrine shivered and shook her head.

"There's a big gray one and a black one," Björn said.

"If it's a mating pair, they may have pups in the spring," Anton said. "I don't like that. It won't take long for a pack to get going."

"We have to be careful when they're around," Björn said. "They could run the stock."

Katrine swallowed. She began thinking about the distance back to their cabin. "I'm not sure about wolves, but we have a mountain lion near our place."

"I'd rather have mountain lions," Anton continued. "Wolves can gang up on livestock. A mountain lion goes it alone."

"Where are the wolves?" Katrine asked nervously.

"North of our fields," Anton said. "We heard them a couple of times. They might be considering that our mules might make a good meal."

Frieda was busily slicing potatoes. "Oh, now don't you worry about wolves. They won't come around this close."

"I'll shoot them if they do," Björn said. He squinted along an imaginary rifle and pulled the trigger.

"Come then," Anna suggested. "We should go to the hot springs before noon meal."

Finally, Katrine thought. They immediately headed for the door.

Björn jumped up to follow.

"A moment, Björn. I need your help," Anton said. "You and I need to fix that door on the calf's shed."

"It's broken?"

Anton nodded.

"Aww," Björn protested.

Katrine was disappointed, but she knew boys needed to help their fathers.

Katrine was surprised to find that a lean-to had been built with walls and a wood floor for them to change under and leave their clothes.

"Papa and Björn built it for during snow," Anna explained.

Katrine was thankful. It was cold the few steps to the springs but then wonderful when she slipped into the hot, steaming water. She scooted over to where the water slid into the pool off the rocks.

"This is so nice," Katrine said. "I so hope we get a badstuga someday."

"We'll come over when you do," Anna said. "I like the hot springs, but sometimes in winter, it's too cold to come up here."

"I like it when it's cold," Mia said. "Your hair gets all crusty with ice. Then you just duck under." She disappeared under the water.

All too soon, it was time to get out. When Katrine did, the wind bit cold against her, freezing her hair as well. She was even happier for the lean-to. They decided to wait to rebraid their hair back in the warmth of the cabin.

For dinner, they had twisted bread, boiled potatoes with butter, and some venison. Frieda fussed, making certain that they got all they wanted. Katrine recalled what Anna had said about Frieda's cooking. The potatoes were acceptable, but the venison was a little charred. Indeed, the bread was the best—different from Mama Olafson's and somehow lighter.

It was early afternoon, but Katrine knew it was time to leave. She started thinking about the wolves again. She wanted to get back while the sun was still up. Four miles was not really that far, but now it seemed an impossible distance.

"Maybe we should take Björn with us when we go home," she suggested. "He can go to the Adolphsons' with us tomorrow."

Anton laughed. "I should not have talked about the wolves. You will be just fine with it being nice and bright out."

"You just stay really close," Katrine said to Mia when they got started. "We can't get out of sight ever."

"N-o-o," Mia said. She shuffled along close behind Katrine.

Katrine could tell Mia was scared. Even though Mr. Wikstrom had said not to worry, Katrine could not help it. She watched every bush and tree for hidden wolves. She started skiing faster.

Soon her breath came hard. She heard Mia struggling behind her, but Mia didn't complain. Katrine knew she was thinking the same as she was. She forced herself to slow down and allowed Mia to catch up. She

190

peered into the scattered trees. There were no wolves, yet she shivered with fear. She imagined them bounding out, heading toward them. They could do nothing against them if suddenly they should appear. A panic washed over her. They could never outski a wolf even if it was in deep snow.

"We're doing good," she said, encouraging Mia. She began skiing again toward their cabin.

They reached the summit and crossed over the ridge. Katrine remembered this was where she and Mia had picked flowers last summer during Midsummer's Eve. Now it was a frozen blanket of glistening snow, cut only by their earlier tracks leading up from the creek. Before heading down, she looked around again to be sure no wolves followed.

When they reached the main trail and turned up it, Katrine breathed more easily. They were just a mile away from their own cabin. Late afternoon shadows crept over the trail. Soon she could smell the wood smoke, and then the cabin roof came into sight. She shivered with relief. She looked again for wolves. There were none. Nevertheless, she could not shake the feeling.

She told Papa Olafson about the wolves being near the Wikstroms'.

"That means they are near us as well," he said. "Worry not. They shouldn't bother us. They might want Trillium, but to be safe, we will wait until the wolves are gone or the snow is gone before you visit the Wikstroms by yourselves again."

Katrine wished she hadn't said anything, but maybe it was for the best. She worried that Mia could be hurt.

A warming wind came through the valley, melting and evaporating the deep drifts. They heard the wolves on a few nights before they mysteriously quit howling and disappeared. Their greatest threat became the mountain lion again. It seemed to return after the wolves had ceased howling. For some reason, the lion never closely approached Trillium. Katrine believed it had come to respect Papa Olafson's rifle.

Chapter 28

THE SNOW RECEDED to the draws and shaded areas. Geese winged their way back north. The warm sunshine and greening grass made Katrine and the other children want to run through the woods, play tag, and visit the hot springs—anything but to sit still for school.

The men began their third season of plowing and planting, continuing to expand their acreage toward the required five acres needed to prove up their claims. They sowed rye, oats, and barley. The older boys and Katrine were now frequently called upon to help in the fields. Louise Lundgren protested but to little avail. Katrine, herself, was torn between attending lessons and helping Papa Olafson.

Prospectors and pack trains loaded with goods and equipment began trickling through along the river trail heading into the Salmon River mines. Nearly all stopped at the Adolphsons' place. Nils traded for or sold goods, and Astrid served meals, charging travelers a dollar per plate. Often as not, the travelers also paused for a bath in the hot springs. Astrid expressed concern for the children who liked to swim there as well. Nils sent Lars with a rifle to accompany them.

Now that the trail was open, the men gathered to take goods to Boise City to trade for seed and stock. They had some remaining root crops, eggs, butter, and bread. They had no beef for trading, although it was now a matter of time. Three calves had been born this season, and two were bull calves.

Katrine watched as Papa Olafson headed out with Mr. Wikstrom and Mr. Andreasson. They took every mule and horse that could be spared, and all were heavily packed. It was unspoken that they would never take wagons down the canyon or bring one up again until a decent road had been built. There were no ferries along the trail, and the bridge they had built had again washed away.

Nils said that for now it did not matter. "If miners can pack in stamp mills and bridge cables on mules, we can pack in plow blades and harrows."

192

Katrine hoped someday to go to Boise City, but the country in between remained wilderness. There were no homesteads except a trading station, which was a few miles up another river near Garden Valley. She was also a little afraid of the city. Multitudes of people now streamed in, including Chinese and hundreds of prospectors, all heading into the Boise Basin.

Over three weeks passed before Sven returned. Katrine could not believe the sight. He came over the hill with four crates of squawking chickens balanced on two of the mules. Mama Olafson was beside herself. Katrine and Mia helped him gently set the crates in the shade. Torsten tried sticking his fingers into one of the cages.

"You might get pecked," Katrine said, pulling the boy away.

Sven laughed. "Only once," he said. "I'll put these chickens in the calf pen and use these crates for them until I can build a proper chicken cage."

Sven eyed Katrine and Mia. "Now when we get our puppy from the Andreassons, we'll have a dog about that can keep the foxes away from the chickens."

"A puppy?"

"Ja, the Andreassons' dog had four puppies. We're getting one when they get a little older." Sven began hauling the chicken cages over to the calf pen.

Katrine laughed, and Mia squealed with joy.

"That will be in a few weeks. For now we best take care of these chickens ourselves."

Sven found a bucket for water and released the chickens near Trillium's pen.

Katrine counted nine. One was a brown-and-red rooster, and the others were varied colors of rust, yellow, black, and gray. They scooted about the yard and immediately began pecking for bugs and scratching the dirt. Several gathered around the water bucket, pecking at the water and then jerking their heads back so the water could run down into their gullets.

Torsten eyed them as if not sure what to think and held fast onto Katrine.

When the chickens had settled, Sven brought out a carefully wrapped bundle. "These are special."

Unrolling the canvas, the young shoots of trees came to light.

"I have two dozen apple trees. Think of that!"

Katrine and Mia clapped their hands.

"Mr. Wikstrom and I had these brought up from Oregon. If they grow, we'll have all the apples we want for making pies and feeding to the livestock. And when the trees get old, I may even have some wood for carving into furniture."

"But will they survive the winter up here?" Margret asked.

"For sure. They've been bringing apple trees into this country for some time now. Some years the frost might get the blossoms, but most years we should have some fruit."

"This year?" Mia asked.

Sven laughed. "They need some growing first, but perhaps in a couple years. There will be only a few apples at first, but each year afterward, we will have dozens and then hundreds."

At the noon meal, Sven shared other news. "You girls may be too young to fully understand. There was much celebrating in Boise City. The war's over. The Southern Insurrection has been put down. Last month, General Lee surrendered to General Grant." He paused. "Unfortunately, the South exacted revenge. President Lincoln was assassinated. I heard they caught and hung the scoundrels, but still it is a dark spot in our history." He spread his hands. "We should all be thankful for one thing. There will be no more slavery in this country. Those people will now have opportunities to make their own livings."

Sven paused and took Margret's hand. "That's why we came to this country, Mama. We came here for land, for our own home, and a chance to make a life for ourselves." He looked about and then at the girls. "We have that now. Remember that when things seem bad."

Margret nodded. "I will always praise God and be grateful," she said. "For the girls ... for our son." She touched each of them, looking into their eyes and smiling.

Sven smiled. "And now we should see more people coming west to homestead. And I think more will be coming in our direction. Boise City is the new capital of Idaho Territory. Hundreds of people are swarming about, and the mines are booming. It is only a matter of time before some shall join us in this valley. Maybe Adolphson's dream will finally come true."

Katrine and Mia helped plant the apple trees. Sven dug deep holes, setting the soil next to each one and then lining the bottom with a few pebbles. As Katrine held a tree upright, he pulled the soil back into the hole, and he and Mia tapped it down. He formed a small depression around each tree for trapping and holding moisture.

"The most important thing will be to keep the deer out of them," Sven said when they had finished.

On the uphill side of the garden, he began setting varied-length poles into the earth like slender pickets of a fence. He spaced the poles a few inches apart but unevenly. When done, the tops of the poles were from four to six feet tall.

"A deer looking at this fence won't jump it. It confuses them," Sven explained. "You girls can keep filling the spaces with smaller limbs. Then the rabbits are less likely to come inside as well."

Each day after the trees had been planted, Katrine carried out a wooden bucket full of water, and she and Mia diligently dipped water onto them. Papa Olafson had said it was necessary until the roots were established.

Anxiously, Katrine looked forward to Midsummer's Eve, which would be held at the Lundgrens' place. Katrine was pleased. The Lundgrens were about two miles away, less if they crossed over a small hill and walked directly there instead of following the bend of the creeks.

Katrine and the others loved Louise Lundgren and her children. Harald and Emma knew the woods and fields about their cabin and often had something to show to Katrine whenever she visited.

A small stream fed a large pond near the cabin. Similar to the Olafsons, they had built a spring box at the outlet below the pond.

One day, Harald had showed her a muskrat lodge. Two muskrats swam out toward it, cutting Vs in the water.

"I've been watching them. They have babies," he explained, his eyes sparkling.

"They might get into your garden."

"If they do, we'll sic Sir on them or trap them. They make good fur."

Along with the traditional boiled potatoes, nettles, and wild strawberries with cream, roast goose, ham, and salmon made Midsummer's Eve dinner special. There were the traditional dances and songs about the pole. The children again tried to outdo the adults, and again the adults made fools of themselves in their attempted response.

They played silly games. Everyone participated in three-legged races. Katrine roped up with Harald and raced Linnea, who was roped up with Jens. Katrine and Harald tripped before the finish line and ended up a heap on the ground. Jens and Linnea hugged, congratulating each other.

Mr. Adolphson poured some snaps for the men. Katrine noticed when Mr. Adolphson took Mr. Andreasson's glass from him. She felt bad for Jens and his sister and brother.

Katrine thought the best thing about Midsummer's Eve this season was the news that Frieda was going to have a baby. The men joked that Anton did not waste any time. For Katrine, it was exciting to think her friends would soon have another brother or sister. It was also exciting to know that another child would soon arrive in the valley.

BUILDING THE SAWPIT

Chapter 29

KATRINE ACCOMPANIED SVEN when he trailed Trillium to the Adolphsons' for breeding. She was not sure what to expect and was a little surprised when all they did was turn Trillium out into a corral near Mr. Adolphson's bull. Mr. Lundgren and Mr. Wikstrom had already brought their cow and heifer in.

"This is a lot of animals for me to be watching," Nils said. "Expect a visit from Lars as soon as business has been taken care of."

They laughed.

Katrine looked around to see if she could spot the Indian pony. She didn't see it. No one talked about it except to say it made it through the winter just fine, and it was fitting in better.

That was when she noticed Mr. Andreasson and Jens heading in their direction. They were leading their cow.

Sven nudged Nils. "It appears you now have another cow to watch."

Nils watched, shaking his head.

Jens waved and smiled at Katrine. He glanced around furtively.

"I'm glad you're here," he said. "H-here, I was going to give him to your pa."

Katrine could not help but squeal when Jens handed her a squirming tan and black and white puppy.

"What are you going to name him?" Jens asked.

The puppy began licking Katrine's face. Its ears pointed straight up. "I think Nisse, for elf."

Jens smiled. "That's a good name."

Katrine could not wait to show Mia. All the way home, she held the squirming puppy in her arms—their very own dog.

Nisse quickly adopted himself to Torsten, following the boy wherever he went.

"That might be good," Margret murmured. "If we can keep sight of at least one of them, we'll find the other." She tossed Nisse a scrap of gristle. "In the meanwhile, Katrine, I want you to teach the puppy to leave the chickens alone."

Katrine was all too happy to do so.

The men began building a sawpit. To this point, they had gotten by with splitting logs with their axes and wedges and smoothing the split sides. The rough wood was suitable for cabins and puncheon floors but not for furniture, barns, or houses. For that, they needed studs and lumber.

They had chosen a site below the Wikstroms' place partly because they had a hill into which they could dig the pit, but more importantly, they had access to the heavily timbered ridges to the south.

The men dug a cut into the hill that was about twenty feet long by eight feet deep. They buried six posts upright into the ground, notched the tops, and fit beams across the pit. On top of the beams, they built a rough platform on which to rest the logs for sawing.

Sven showed Katrine the saw. It was shiny, bright steel with two handles about eight feet long and eight inches wide. He explained how the teeth were angled so it cut on the downward stroke but not when it was being pushed back upward.

"The top sawyer has the brunt of the work, pushing the saw down," he said, "but the pit man has the worst of the job because he gets all the sawdust falling on him." He laughed.

Katrine shivered, thinking of sawdust in her hair and down her neck.

"As the men cut the log, the top sawyer also hoists it along these saddle blocks so more can be cut." Sven tapped some wooden stubs that were fixed to the platform. "They can cut about a ten-foot board in this manner."

The day after the pit had been completed, the women and girls brought food for a community gathering. Katrine and Mia stood with Margret and almost-two-year-old Torsten, who was as excited as anyone to watch. The older boys, Lars and Björn along with Harald and Jens, had worked alongside their fathers in constructing the pit and begged for the first chance to try it out. Björn and Jens won the opportunity.

The men skidded a seasoned log out onto the platform and wedged it into place with the saddle blocks. The two boys pulled off their shirts.

"You take the lower handle," Björn suggested to Jens and climbed onto the top of the platform. Jens scrambled underneath.

"Now, we gotta do this," Björn said quietly. "Don't let Lars and Harald outdo us."

Jens nodded. "I-I'll try." He flicked his eyes nervously about while the men positioned the saw.

Katrine figured Björn had enough strength for pushing the saw, having grown up used to driving a mule team and cutting wood. She was uncertain about Jens, who had a slighter build and seemed to find hunting and fishing more to his abilities.

Their fathers took bets. Nils Adolphson said, "Go."

Björn shouted, "One," and shoved the blade begrudgingly downward, spitting sawdust. Jens nearly lost his footing as the saw pushed against him.

Jens scrambled back up. "Two," he hollered and pushed the blade back upward.

"One," hollered Björn, again showering Jens.

"Two." Jens pushed back.

The men cheered and laughed. From all appearances, the sawpit was in operation, although it appeared to be a very slow operation.

"One. Two." The boys' voices came, the scratch of the saw sounding in sync with them.

Soon the number calling ceased. The scratching continued, uneven, broken, hesitant, and mixed with heavy breathing. Shortly, Nils called, "Stop."

Sven explained while the girls watched. "A good two-man team is a sight to see. They can cut a hundred board feet in a day." He laughed. "Now Björn and Jens gave it a good go, but they have much to learn."

"I think they just need some growing up," Katrine said.

Sven smiled. "Ja, that would help as well."

The boys switched. Lars took the top-sawyer position, and Harald took under sawyer. They started a new cut about two inches inside Björn and Jens's cut.

"Go," hollered Nils.

The two immediately began sawing, taking long cuts. "One. Two."

After just two strokes, Katrine saw that it was no competition. Lars easily worked the saw. Harald mostly supplied weight pulling it down, and Lars helped heft it back up. In the same time as Björn and Jens, they cut double the length.

Nils declared they had done enough. "We see that it works," he cheered. He pulled out a bottle of brännvin and poured drinks for the men while the children gathered around. Lars, now fourteen, joined the men.

"Hey, this is a good day to celebrate," Gustaf Andreasson boomed. "We should have another."

"Ja, ja," Anton chided. "It is a long time until we go back to Boise City for more. This must last." He corked the bottle.

"Then I think I shall turn my potato crop into brännvin," Gustaf grumbled.

Frieda reminded everyone that it would soon be time for dinner. "You should all wash up."

"You children can use the hot springs," Anton said. "Get washed up good. Tomorrow is Sunday."

"I was going to ask," Jens said. "Th-this sawdust is itching bad." He ran a hand across his neck and wriggled a finger in his ear.

The children raced for the hot springs and were soon splashing about in the upper pool. Katrine looked for Björn to help with rocks, but for the first time, Björn insisted that Harald and Jens should join him in the lower pool. Katrine didn't understand. It was not much wider than four feet and was quite narrow. It served little more than a place to wash up. Even if they were boys, they had always played and soaked in the hot springs together. The upper pool was big enough to hold everyone.

It bothered Katrine so much that later, after returning home, she sought Mama Olafson. She found her with Torsten, cutting some lupine near the garden fence.

"Aren't they beautiful?" Margret held them for Katrine to see. "Here are some pink and lavender ones now. I thought I should bring a few inside."

"They are very beautiful, Mama Olafson." Katrine knew *blomsterlupin* were her favorite flowers. "Uh, I have a question." Katrine fidgeted, now unsure of herself. "Björn took Harald and Jens to the other pool. They didn't swim with us. I wanted to talk with them about the sawpit. Björn wouldn't talk with us girls at all."

Margret hesitated, pulling a few leaves off the bottom of a lupine stem. A smile tugged at her lips.

"Come with me. I should tell you and Mia some things." She seemed somewhat nervous but also happy. "Let's put these in water, and I'll see if I can't put Torsten down for a nap. You and Mia and I can have some tea."

Katrine put the lupine in a pail of water. Mama Olafson pulled the teakettle to the front of the stove, humming as she sprinkled some mint leaves into the steaming water. Katrine watched impatiently and wondered why she just didn't tell her and Mia already. Was there something bad about Björn?

"Björn is growing up, and so are Harald and Jens," she said softly. "Björn feels more comfortable not being with you girls now, at least not bathing with you. He's trying to be modest."

"But why? Mia and I have been swimming with him always."

She poured the tea. "I've explained that someday you both will become grown women and be able to have your own babies."

Katrine swallowed. She knew this of course, but what did that have to do with swimming?

"Especially you, Katrine." Margret took a sip of tea and then began telling of the mysteries of life for women and men.

Katrine listened intently. Mia seemed less interested, but for Katrine, according to Mama Olafson, all of this would happen soon.

When Mama Olafson paused, Katrine no longer knew what to think. Was all this really possible? She had a strange feeling that boys knew more about this than did girls, but she decided she would never ask, at least not Björn. And so what did it matter if the boys swam with her and Mia or not? They wouldn't be getting married—not for a long while, and she would probably marry Harald or Jens anyway. Björn was like a brother. She asked Mama Olafson her last question.

"But why does it matter?"

Margret smiled. "Björn knows it's not time for him to get married, so he does the proper thing of not swimming with you any longer."

That was not the answer Katrine expected. Was Björn thinking about other things? Katrine could not keep the new thought from bubbling forth, although she did not think it had anything to do with her or Björn—certainly not yet. "But how will he know when it's time to get married?"

Margret smiled. "First he has an obligation to his father with helping on their farm. His father will tell him when he has fulfilled that obligation. And then Björn will see to it that he is able to make a living because after marrying, he will be responsible for taking care of his wife and family. The Bible says he will know the right woman because he will be drawn to her. He will know it is the right time to leave his mother. An honorable man will wait until that time."

"Oh," answered Katrine. She remembered what she had told Anna about Lars some time ago, only Mama Olafson was sincere. "So then what makes a woman want a man?" Katrine asked nervously.

Margret softly laughed. "You will discover that in due time. Something special happens between a man and a woman when they come close together. She will want him even more, and she will stay with him even when times become troubled. And there will be troubled times, of that you can be sure, but if a woman marries the right man who believes it is the most important thing for him to take care of his wife and family, then no problem is too big."

"What if he's not the right man? What if he does terrible things?" Mr. Andreasson suddenly came into mind.

"There are times, but let's talk about that some other day."

Katrine silently agreed. For once she was happy she was still a young girl. In a way, she felt bad for Björn. He was thinking about things that just weren't so. She also could not imagine doing all the work he would have to do to have a homestead and family.

Chapter 30

THE FOLLOWING SATURDAY, Katrine and Mia hiked over the hill to visit the Wikstroms. When they arrived, they were surprised to find only Frieda at the cabin. She was busy as always, preparing meals.

"Where is everyone?" Katrine wanted to know.

"Anna and Linnea go to Adolphsons'," Frieda said. She pushed and patted some bread dough.

Of course she did, Katrine realized. "To see Lars."

"Ya." Frieda laughed.

Katrine liked when Frieda made bread. She was best at it and managed to make it light and airy, unlike the heavy Swedish breads. Maybe it was a German secret. She watched to see if she could determine the secret.

"Well, where are Björn and Laurens?" Katrine had hoped to play with them, as they often did on Saturday afternoons before visiting the hot springs.

"They go to the sawpit. Jens is with them. The men do some board cutting."

Frieda folded the dough and sprinkled on more flour. Katrine could still determine no secret.

"We were hoping to go to the hot springs." Katrine was not comfortable with going only with Mia. Although no one had ever encountered any danger, sometimes strangers used the old Indian trail, and there was always a chance of bears or a mountain lion.

"Ya, I fancy so. You children all come around just for the Vikstrom hot springs."

Katrine could not tell if Mama Frieda was joking or was serious.

"You all go when the boys come back." Frieda smiled. She continued folding and kneading the dough. "They should not be long."

"Maybe Mia and I can help you then," Katrine offered.

"Ya, of course you can help. You just get me that crock over there.

We split this bread up into some loaves and let them rise. Then we make apple cobbler." She pointed to a small pile of withered apples. "I'm tinking we can get a few apple slices for flavor. We add some green potato and lots of sugar. It will be fine."

Frieda split the dough and pulled off a large piece and handed it to Katrine. "Now you put this with the starter for next time," she said. Frieda nodded to a small crock on a shelf near the stove.

Katrine added the dough to the sourdough starter. It showed numerous bubbles. Maybe the starter was her secret.

Katrine realized that Frieda was becoming a much better cook. Maybe having Anna teaching and talking to the women during Sunday meetings was helping.

"Now we should have supper. You go tell those men should they want to visit the hot springs before eating, they best come now. They would work all night if I let them." She set the crocks with the rising dough to the side.

Katrine raced Mia toward the sawpit, eager to be of help and also happy that the day's work was nearing its completion.

They heard laughing and hollering as they drew near. Björn and Mr. Wikstrom were sawing. Jens and Laurens cheered their efforts. Sawdust flowed, and the blade flashed. Katrine realized Björn and Mr. Wikstrom made a good team with Björn as the under sawyer.

"Come," Mia shouted, waving. "Mama Frieda says supper is at hand."

With his hands in his pockets, Gustaf watched the sawyers. A look of mild disgust etched his face.

"Björn and my papa are doing good," Laurens said, turning to Katrine and Mia. "They are cutting a lot more than Jens and Mr. Andreasson did."

Jens smiled. "W-we had a competition."

Katrine noticed him wince as he turned.

"M-my pa and I are about like a mule and an ox on the same wagon, if you know what I mean."

"I do." Katrine knew all too well. "Come for supper. Mama Frieda says if you get back soon enough, you have some time to visit the springs."

Jens brushed some of the sawdust from his neck and back. "I'm needing that." He reached down for his shirt and revealed an ugly purple bruise on his ribs.

"You got hurt," Katrine whispered. "What happened?"

"N-nothing," Jens said.

But his eyes had flicked toward his father. Katrine's stomach turned queasy.

She turned back toward the cabin, followed by Mia, trying to comprehend what she had just seen.

Laurens caught up to them. "You should have seen them sawing today. Björn and my papa were the best." Laurens skipped along the track. "Mr. Andreasson yelled at Jens, saying he was no good. I didn't like that. I tried to help Jens, but we were no good together. I just got in his way. It was fun though, and Jens tried really hard. We still couldn't beat Björn and my papa."

The hollowness inside Katrine grew. Mr. Wikstrom and Mr. Andreasson came up behind them, engaged in some heated talk. Björn and Jens ran past, pushing and laughing. She and Mia quickly stepped aside to keep clear of their flying hands and elbows.

"Race you to the cabin," Laurens shouted. He started running, chasing after Björn and Jens. Katrine began running as well, with Mia close behind. They all crashed through the door to greet Frieda.

Björn stood smiling. "The bad part of sawing lumber is the sawdust," he said. He ran his hands through his hair, spraying some sawdust.

"Mein Gott, not in here!" Frieda complained. "You boys, all of you, go wash up!"

Katrine knew that was their intent—to get back ahead of the men and to reach the hot springs first.

When Anton reached the cabin, he greeted Frieda and then arched his eyes as he spotted Katrine and Mia. "Here I thought I was giving up two girls today, but you see who came out of the woods." He smiled broadly and held out his arms. "I didn't get a proper hug."

Katrine and Mia jumped into his arms. Mr. Wikstrom always made Katrine feel welcome; although this time after the hug, she came away with sticky sawdust.

"We were helping Mama Frieda," Katrine explained.

Anton patted Frieda's belly. "Well sure, in a few months it will be Mama Frieda." He winked.

Gustaf Andreasson stood aside, seeming a little perturbed, his bushy eyebrows pinched into a frown. "We should have snaps now, should we not, you and I?"

"Now, I'm getting to that, Gustaf. We have hardly put up our tools. I should think supper is not quite ready?" He glanced at Frieda, who shook her head. "Which is good because this is Saturday. Let the children go wash up. You and I shall go in a minute. In the meanwhile—" He rummaged around in a sack and took out what Katrine believed to be a small bottle of brännvin. He waved it toward Andreasson.

"Ah, that is good," Gustaf said.

The two men ducked out of the cabin.

"You heard Papa Vikstrom," Frieda exclaimed. "You girls should go to the hot springs."

"What about you, Mama Frieda?"

"I go when Anna and Linnea come back," she said, smiling. She ushered Katrine and Mia outside.

When Katrine reached the hot springs, she could hear the boys splashing around and laughing in the upper pool. Respecting what Mama Olafson had explained, Katrine waded into the lower pool. She splashed about and then lay down in the hot, shimmering water. She decided it was near heaven. She enjoyed soaking in the hot springs more than anything else in the world and wished she could do it every day.

"I wish Anna and Linnea were here," Katrine whispered. "It is kind of strange to be here without them."

"It's still nice," Mia said. She pushed back to where the water spilled into the pool, cascading off her head.

They continued splashing about. Katrine was happy for the chance to clean up after the long week. Nothing compared to the silky, hot water. She let the heat soak through her.

Soon Björn and Laurens came past the pool, already dressed.

"We're going back. You should go with us. We'll wait on the trail for you," Björn offered.

Katrine felt disappointed; she wanted to soak longer.

Mia began climbing out.

"Where's Jens?" Katrine asked, realizing he was not with Björn.

"He's still in the pool, but I'm tired. Besides, supper should be ready."

"I'll wait for Jens," offered Katrine.

"Good idea." Björn ran his hand through his hair and headed off.

"Wait for me." Mia clambered out and began drying off.

"We'll wait," came Björn's voice from farther down the trail.

Katrine waited a while for Jens, but he didn't come past. What was getting into him? She wondered if he had gotten out and slipped past where she didn't see him. She decided to check. She brushed off the water, dressed, and climbed toward the upper pool. Jens sat near the pool, dressed, kicking his bare feet slowly through the water.

"Are you all right?" Katrine asked.

Jens nodded. "S-sure. I'm just sitting."

"You're sure everything's all right?"

"Yes. You can go. I'll be along in a little while."

Katrine sat next to him. "How'd you get hurt?" she demanded.

Jens's eyes widened. His hands were in front of him in his lap, but Katrine had seen him move his left arm with some discomfort.

"I saw your bruise."

Jens shook his head. "I j-just fell down," he mumbled.

Katrine did not know anyone could be bruised like he was bruised just by falling down. She also noticed a pale bruise on his cheek. A crushing ache filled her chest. She knew how Jens had been bruised and why he avoided going back.

"Uh, it's not safe being here alone, Jens. I can wait with you, if you like."

Jens's face screwed up. He brought his hands to his head, slowly shaking it. "I-I'm all right," he blurted out again. "Don't wait." He looked up, shaking.

Katrine moved away and sat. "I'll just wait here, Jens," she said, rather determinedly. Inside she was breaking apart. How could a father do that to his son? What had Jens done so terribly wrong that he deserved this? Maybe Björn knew what had happened. Surely Björn must have asked about the bruises.

"Come, Jens, we need to go. Your papa will be angry."

"I-I'm coming." He glanced furtively around and stood shakily. They walked toward the cabin.

All eyes were on them when they entered.

"I was getting ready to come and find you," Anton said. "Around my home, even guests, you should not disappoint Mama Frieda and be late to her supper."

Katrine and Jens mumbled an apology. All through the meal, Katrine felt Mr. Andreasson's glare.

Chapter 31

SVEN BROUGHT TRILLIUM back into the yard from the Adolphsons' where she had been penned with their bull.

"Will she have a calf?" Katrine asked.

"We won't know for a few weeks," Sven replied, "but Mr. Adolphson's bull has sired calves every season."

"I hope Trillium has a calf. Then we'll have all the milk and cheese and butter we want."

Sven smiled. "That is our hope."

He took Trillium to her pen.

"Watch her. She may take a day or two getting used to being back and try to wander."

Nisse, now a good-sized pup, sniffed her and then raised his paw, seemingly uncertain of what to do.

"It's another job for you, Nisse," Katrine explained. "You have to watch Trillium just like you watch the chickens and the cabin."

Nisse was trained to stay around the cabin and warn of visitors or danger. He was becoming more able at doing so, and as he had done since the first day, he tended to be with Torsten, wherever the boy went.

On a normal day, at first light, Katrine dressed and slipped from the cabin. Nisse kept her company while she brought in water and wood. Usually Mama Olafson was already up fixing something for breakfast and heating a pot of hot water for coffee on the stove.

She mostly cared for the animals, particularly Trillium and the chickens. Sven had built a tight chicken shed from hewn logs and a lath of willows for both the door and part of the roof. The chicken cage had access from the back through which Katrine could reach in and shoo a hen off her egg.

During the day when Katrine first opened the pen, the chickens rose and stretched, fluffing their feathers, and one by one would leave the cages and begin scratching about the yard. She would throw out some

210

oats and leftover vegetables. The chickens scuttled about, pecking at the grain, eating the vegetables, and catching bugs. That was when she really had to watch Nisse because the pup thought she was playing, and he had a tendency to chase the chickens.

This morning she had just finished chasing the hens off four eggs and opening the pen when Papa Olafson came into the yard, leading Jack and June.

"Good morning, Katrine. We're going to go fetch the lumber that Mr. Wikstrom and I have been sawing all summer."

He harnessed the mules and hitched up the wagon. He trailed Jack behind. Katrine rode on the seat with Papa Olafson.

"What are we going to make?" she asked.

Sven smiled. "You shall see. It's a surprise."

Katrine's stomach fluttered. Papa Olafson often had her help, and she'd have to guess what they were doing.

At the sawpit, he positioned the wagon near the logs. Each was partially sawed through into four or five boards that were still attached at the butt. He unhitched the team and moved them away from the wagon. He then looped a rope around a log, hitched it to Jack, and skidded the log to the open end of the wagon bed.

"Now you hold Jack while I hoist the log."

Sven hoisted the butt onto the wagon bed. He then led the mule forward until the log had been pulled into the bed.

When he had loaded all the logs, he rehitched the team. "You watch that you don't sit on these logs. They could roll on you and pinch and break your foot before you could blink."

Katrine eyed the logs and kept her feet away as they started down the track back toward their cabin.

Presently, they stopped at a spot near their pond where Sven reversed the process and had Jack pull the logs free of the wagon bed. Mia and Torsten came out to watch. They made three trips before getting all the lumber back to the cabin.

Early the following morning, Sven loaded Katrine and Mia down with the mallet, auger, and wood plane. He carried the broadax and single-man saw. At the pile of logs, he dumped the tools and announced, "Well girls, we're about to build a smokehouse."

"Why not use a smoke tent?" Katrine was disappointed. "We could build other nice things from the boards."

"Well, if you don't say it very loud, we just might use our smokehouse for a bathhouse as well."

"A badstuga!" Mia shouted. "Like the one in Minnesota. Like the Eskolas'?"

A sauna. Katrine shivered. If so, Mia and she could bathe once a week, snow or no snow, and maybe her friends could come and visit her for a change.

"Now you girls keep this a secret from Mama. I'm calling it our smokehouse. Sure we'll use it to smoke our meats, but we'll all know it can be used for a badstuga as well."

The girls laughed.

"Why don't we tell Mama Olafson?"

"Oh we shall in due time, but remember, it took a long time for me to cut these boards. Mama might not think a badstuga is that important. She might have other ideas for the lumber."

Katrine believed that to be a more truthful reason. A bathhouse might not be the most important project.

Sven laid two courses of logs, similar to those that formed the cabin. He notched them deeply and rolled them into place. Then he began pegging in a footer and some studs. Katrine held the studs upright while he worked. By the day's end, they had built a frame about six feet by six feet square and about eight feet tall.

"Tomorrow we'll put on the boards. You girls can help me drill holes and peg them so the wind won't tear them loose."

During supper, Katrine hoped that Mama Olafson wouldn't ask about what they were working on, but she also hoped she would. She wanted to be the first to tell her that she was getting a bathhouse.

The next morning, after chores, they resumed work. Katrine and Mia held boards while Sven drilled and hammered or sawed.

By late afternoon, he had the roof beams on and they were fixing boards across the roof. They cut sod, similar to what they had done for the cabin, and laid it on top of the roof boards.

"Now you two girls find all the holes and fill them with mud."

While Katrine and Mia chinked the gaps, Sven built a bench across one end and then a smaller bench on top of it in the corner.

Finally, he began work on a door. He laid five boards on a cross bar and pegged them to it. He attached two more bars, one across the top and a second across the bottom. He used leather straps as hinges and affixed the door to the small structure.

"What do you think?"

"Can we try it?" Katrine asked.

"Tomorrow. We yet need to explain this to Mama." Sven winked.

In the morning, Margret came out from the cabin with Torsten. She seemed skeptical of what she saw. Torsten climbed onto one of the benches, seemingly very pleased at his accomplishment.

"I know what you be thinking, Margret," Sven said. "This is not just a bathhouse. This is a smokehouse. And remember, the girls and you can go to the creek or use the big tub. It is a bit trying for me. This will make it easier for all of us, and I can have peace and quiet while taking a bath on Saturday night."

"Well, it is finished, so I am in no position to protest," Margret replied. "Maybe next you can build me a new room or cupboards because we seem to have all the sawed boards we shall ever need."

Katrine knew Mama Olafson was not excited about the badstuga. Papa Olafson did not seem to mind. Indeed, he seemed quite proud.

"Ja, I can work on all of those things this winter when there's four feet of snow. I can't work on this in four feet of snow. And for certain, you'll thank me when you can use the badstuga in the deep snow."

"And what shall you use for a proper stove to heat rocks?" Margret continued.

Sven scratched his head. "A usual smokehouse would have a fireplace built outside the cabin with an opening to the inside for allowing in the smoke, but because we'll use it as a bathhouse, we'll have a fire pit inside the door." He waved at the pile of stones. "For baths, we bring hot stones in from the fire outside and dipper some water onto them. For the smokehouse, we build the fire inside and put on aspens and willow as we did for the smoke tent. The Indians do something like this."

"I shall be fine as long as you are the one walking into the snow to fetch the stones," Margret said. She relaxed and eyed the roof. "I think you should extend the roof a little and maybe build a shelf for our clothes. Otherwise, in the rain, they will get wet."

Sven smiled. "That shall be next."

Katrine could not wait to try the badstuga. It was a few feet from the edge of the pond, making it easy to get water, and making it easy to go swimming after sweating in the heat.

Sven showed how to scoop the rocks from the fire with some wooden paddles and carry them to the fire pit in the corner of the badstuga. He ladled some water onto the rocks and closed the door while the two girls huddled on the bench. The water exploded into steam that raced upward.

"When you want more steam, just sprinkle on more water."

Steam continued billowing upward into the small room, climbing to its uppermost reaches. The heat was greatest near the ceiling. On the lower bench, it was more tolerable for Katrine. She knew the boys would insist on the highest and hottest corner of the room, as they had frequently done back in Minnesota.

Katrine and Mia used willow branches to slap against their skin, which caused a tingling, refreshing shiver. When the water began running off Katrine's skin and the heat had become nearly unbearable, she opened the door, and she and Mia rushed out into the cold, invigorating air. It felt like a thousand pinpricks rushing across her skin, making her feel wonderfully alive. She waded out into the pond and splashed backward into the water, watching it close over her and seeing the sky turn into silvery bubbles. She bobbed for a moment and then quickly rushed back inside to the steamy, hot bath. She wanted to repeat it forever, but the stones grew cooler. At that point, she and Mia scrambled back to the cabin where they rubbed dry with a cloth.

"That's almost as good as the hot springs," Mia admitted.

"It's way better than swimming in the pond," Katrine said, "but I still like going to the Wikstroms' the best."

"You'd better not say that in front of Papa," Mia murmured. "He would be sad."

Katrine laughed. "He would agree, but I'll be sure to tell him how much I love the badstuga."

In the early morning, Katrine noticed two men coming from the east down the old Indian trail that came over the mountains from the South Fork. Travelers never came from this direction. Panic washed Katrine until she realized they were prospectors. When Nisse spotted them, he barked sharply. Each had a thick beard, wore tattered clothing, and carried little gear except for a rolled blanket. One carried a pick over his shoulder; the other carried a gold pan.

Sven noticed and came up from the garden, carrying his rifle. Margret stepped out and greeted them. They seemed of the friendly sort and hungry.

Visitors were infrequent, but whenever some happened by, Margret fixed them a meal. Katrine liked to listen to their stories, and although some had been to the camps directly north, none had been to the country to the east from where these men came.

Margret prepared a meal while they washed up in the creek. Although they contained the scent of dead things and worse, Katrine knew Mama Olafson would allow them to sit at the table. At least this time she had insisted they wash up. Upon returning, their odoriferous carcasses smelled only slightly better.

"Name's Randolph," the younger of the two said. "My partner's Dirk. We're mighty obliged."

Politely, Sven sat with them. For once his pipe seemed to serve a pleasant purpose. "So tell me from where you're coming."

"Oh, we been in the most treacherous place on this old earth," Randolph explained, pausing. He had a thick brown beard and a broken-down hat. One of his eyes was red, apparently injured. His partner, who was skinnier and had lighter colored whiskers, but equally thick, continued shoveling beans and potatoes into his mouth, hardly looking up.

"Never seen anything like it. All straight up and down. Can't go a hundert yards anywheres that's flat."

Sven leaned back. "Then what took you there in the first place?"

"Same as everyone goes there. Gold. We heerd there was some rich diggings on the Middle Fork. It were just too far fer us to turn around and head back to Warren's so we come up outer there this direction."

"Any gold?"

"Just a smidgen." Randolph cast a look toward Margret. "Say you wouldn't have any more bread, would ya? I've a hankering fer bread. Me an' my partner ain't seen anything like bread fer nigh on two years."

Margret nodded to Katrine. "We can spare another piece or two," she said.

"I'll be a paying ya," Randolph said. "That is if'n you'll take some gold dust."

"We can spare a meal," Sven exclaimed. "Besides we wouldn't have any means of weighing gold."

"Durn, a pinch is a dollar. We got several ounces. We insist." Randolph pulled out a pouch and set it on the table.

215

Katrine swallowed. A dollar was a lot of money. She cut two slices of bread and spread them with thick butter.

The men eagerly took the bread and began stuffing it down, smacking and licking their lips.

"No, sir," Randolph said. "Ain't had nothing this grand in a long whiles. Blessings to you, ma'am." He nodded toward Margret. His partner grunted.

"We have a badstuga," Katrine suggested. "Some visitors pay for a bath." Sven shot her a look.

The older man, Dirk, with watery blue eyes and thin face looked up, chewing as if contemplating a bath, probably something he had not seen in at least a year.

Randolph stroked his beard. "Well, that's a mighty fine idear. Never heerd of a badstuga. Did have a sweat bath once with some Indians on the Middle Fork. They was a friendly bunch. Didn't charge me a thing. Got some mountain sheep stew from them. We was pretty hungry by that point, weren't we, Dirk?"

Dirk slowly nodded.

"Strangest Indians I ever seed," Randolph continued. "We come outer a canyon above their huts, and they jumped us. I thought I'd lost my hair fer sure. Had these good-looking bows. Made out of sheep horn, I took it. Anyways, they got to jabbering and looking us over real good. I finally guessed they hadn't much seen a white man."

Randolph chased some gravy around on his plate with his remaining bread.

"And that reminds me of a real strange thing," he said, continuing. "When we was getting on nigh of winter last season, we run into a feller, another prospector. Name was Hailey, I think.

"Twern't that his name?" Randolph shoved a fork at his partner.

Dirk paused for just a second, looked up as if trying to figure out where he was, and then nodded. "Yep."

"Well Hailey, he said he seen a white man, not much older than a boy, was with some Indians. He said, and I swear this fer a fact, he was Swedish. Didn't know a lick of English." Randolph laughed. "Reminded me 'cause you're Swedes, ain't ya?"

Katrine went stone cold. Ice that had walled off her world shattered into splinters. She gasped for air. Instead of light, numbing blackness enfolded her. Only the faint image of her brother saying goodbye bled through.

Margret whispered, "Now, Katrine. Now, Katrine."

"What's the matter?" Randolph said. "Looks like she seen a ghost. You folks lose someone to the Indians? I heerd of it happenin'. But they's just as good as dead anyways when they turns Injun."

"Enough," demanded Sven.

"Well, I remembered what Hailey said 'cause you're Swedes. Ain't what I said, right, Dirk?"

"Yep. Only, we never saw nobody white with them Injuns," Dirk slowly said. He returned to eating.

"Dirk's right," Randolph replied. "If Hailey seen a white man, it couldn't a been with the Injuns we found. They was pretty miserable poor-like."

Katrine could no longer see—could no longer feel. *Erik.* He would be sixteen. It had to be Erik. At first, brilliant light had blossomed and filled her. Now it had been crushed. If Erik was an Indian, his soul had been lost. That explained why he had never come to find her.

Forcing herself to stand, wavering, she wandered outside. She was vaguely aware of Mia and Nisse following her. She found herself on the hillside where she had first found the trilliums. There were no trilliums now. Some deep purple larkspur bloomed amid yellow goldenrod. The grass had burned to auburn. A few aspen leaves had yellowed.

She sat, trying to absorb what Randolph had said, trying to find reason. There was none.

Vaguely Katrine was aware that Mia sat beside her. Her smaller hand had taken hers.

HARVESTING OATS 1865

Chapter 32

KATRINE FOLLOWED PAPA Olafson out to the oat field, which now rippled like waves of pale gold, the seed heads bowing and swaying in the wind. Birds flitted away. Papa Olafson pinched a kernel between his fingernails and showed it to her. There was no milk, and the indentation remained.

"Know what that means?" he asked.

"The oats are ripe."

"By gum, they sure are."

Sven unshouldered his cradle scythe and began swinging and cutting. Katrine watched for a moment while he worked. Then she stooped down, and similar to sheaving the rye, she gathered the long stems and bundled the oats, seed heads up, tying them with a few twists of straw. When Katrine had several sheaves tied, she gathered them together and stood them up, about three feet tall. She could not do the work Papa Olafson could do, but she knew any work she accomplished was work that helped him.

Sometimes Katrine envied that Mama Olafson and Mia were back at the cabin cooking and cleaning and out of the hot sun and wind, but she enjoyed being outside with Papa Olafson in the fields. The older boys in the valley were doing the same as she was doing, helping their fathers, and although she was not a boy, she was the oldest and most capable of helping. It had to be the way things were. In a way, she was proud that Papa Olafson depended on her.

Sometimes Sven came back to where she worked and helped her for a while.

"I need to give my arms rest," he explained, but Katrine knew he didn't.

Papa Olafson tied sheaves and shocked the oats twice as fast as Katrine could. When he caught up to where he was cutting, he quickly returned to swinging his scythe, walking steadily, swinging, swinging. Like music, the scythe swung through the grain, swishing, clicking

221

softly. Sometimes Katrine paused to watch, mesmerized by Papa Olafson's steady work. The oats toppled in curtains, catching the autumn sun in a long, glowing cascade as the stalks fell in a shower to the field. Papa Olafson reached and swung again.

The day grew long. Katrine bent and gathered and tied and stacked. Grasshoppers whirred away. Now the sun's heat dried her skin and hair. She breathed in the dust that caught in her throat. The stubble pricked red spots into her hands and arms. Papa Olafson was far away, swinging, swinging, a dark figure against the late afternoon sun. Flies bit her.

At last, his form grew larger as he came nearer. He shouldered his scythe. "Tomorrow we need to get an early start. We could be getting rain." His eyes swept the western sky.

Katrine trudged after him, hardly able to walk, her back aching, her hands chaffed and cut. As they drew near to the cabin, the aroma from the waiting meal soothed her, and she was suddenly thankful that Mama Olafson and Mia had remained behind.

Sven warmly greeted Margret and then hugged and kissed Mia. "How's my little angel?" He ran his finger down her nose as he sometimes did.

Katrine swished her hands in the cool water of the bucket before going to the pond for more. She scooped the bucket through the still, darkening water. She was Papa Olafson's best helper, but it seemed Mia was his little angel.

After a week of helping Papa Olafson cut and shock the oats, they had finished, and Katrine accompanied him to get the wagon from the Lundgrens. They drove it back into the oat field where Papa Olafson pulled it up beside one of the oat shocks in the corner.

"Do you think you can guide the mules to the shocks while I load?"

Katrine swallowed. "I'll try." She could if the mules didn't protest too much.

"Use the brake if Jack gets too cantankerous."

Sven swung his pitchfork into the shock and heaved a portion of it into the back of the wagon. After several more swings, it was loaded. Katrine flicked the reins and clucked at the mules to get them to move on to the next shock.

The day was again terribly hot and dusty. Sven sent up clouds of chaff and dust as he pitched the oats into the wagon. The bits and pieces went down Katrine's neck and dress and into her eyes and ears. She was thankful for not having to bend down any longer. Her back still ached. They stopped frequently for water.

After gathering a load, Sven took over the reins and brought the wagon back to the stock shed near the garden. There, Katrine helped him unload and store the shocks. They filled the shed to near overflowing.

Sven stood back and laughed. "Now we have no choice but to get this threshed so Trillium will have a shed again."

The following morning, Katrine and Mia followed Sven to the shed. He had earlier put down a puncheon floor for threshing the grain and had built a flail from a short pole and piece of flat wood, which he had attached to the pole with leather straps. He pulled down some oats and spread them across the floor.

"You girls can stomp the oats on that side of me, but watch out you don't get in the way when I'm swinging."

Sven swung and brought the flail down onto the oats with a solid thwack, sending up dust and chaff and separating the kernels from the husks and straw.

Katrine and Mia began stomping on the oats off to the side a safe distance away. Nisse must have thought it was a game at first because he ran about barking and chasing their stomping feet.

After threshing for a while, Sven took a wooden rake and raked away the straw. Katrine and Mia scooped it up and carried it to where they began building a straw pile. Katrine knew that straw was not as good for feed as was hay, but they used straw for bedding for the stock and for the chickens. In the snow, it helped keep the animals warm.

Sven repeated the process of flailing the oats and raking. Eventually a layer of what was mostly grain covered the floor. A puff of wind scattered some husks.

Sven raised a hand and smiled. "Let's see if we can start winnowing."

Katrine shivered with joy. If the wind hadn't been right, they would have waited. And although winnowing was hard work, harder than shocking, she looked forward to helping. There was something special about gathering the first grain.

She found the winnowing pans where Papa Olafson had carefully stored them and eagerly scooped up about three or four double handfuls of grain from the floor. Papa Olafson took considerably more.

Sven flipped his grain into the air. A curtain of straw bits and dirt was snatched away, and the grain rattled back onto his pan. He tossed again.

"You know this is somewhat like panning for gold," he said. "Gold is heavy, so it settles at the bottom of the pan. The water washes away the lighter material. Here, we use the wind to carry away everything but the heavier grain."

Katrine tossed her grain and watched the bits of husks and chaff drift away. The grain caught the sunlight and fell, sprinkling back onto her pan. She tossed again and again.

"This is a farmer's gold," Sven continued. "Not only can we sell or trade it, we can eat it. Let's see a prospector do that with his gold."

Katrine imagined that the clean oats accumulating on her pan *were* kernels of gold. In a way, she wished they were.

They drained their pans into a bag and scooped up more from the threshing floor. While it was exciting to see the growing bag of grain, Katrine's shoulders and arms ached terribly. Papa Olafson didn't say anything when she offered to fetch some water. She figured that he knew she had to rest more frequently.

On the way back out with the water, Mia followed and tried to winnow some grain. Katrine didn't mind. Any help meant less work.

Sven smiled at Mia's efforts. "Soon as I can, I'll build you girls a winnowing fan, and then you can both take turns cranking it. All I'll have to do is shovel the grain into one side and catch it out the other." He laughed. "Think about that."

At length, they had a large bag of cleaned oats and proudly carried it into the cabin. That night, Katrine began grinding the oat kernels in their hand mill, the same mill they used for rye grain and coffee beans. They would use the coarse meal for porridge. Otherwise, most of the oats would go to the livestock and chickens.

When she tired of grinding, Papa Olafson took over. He whirred away, churning out a steady stream of pale yellow ground oats.

"When we get more settlers, someone will build a grist mill, and this won't be such a chore. Maybe we'll grow some wheat then."

The following morning, they had their first bowls of porridge. Katrine believed that nothing tasted finer than porridge from the season's first oats.

At Sunday meeting, the men compared notes on their harvests. Everyone had oats, and some had barley coming in. After a moment of listening, Katrine didn't bother any longer. It seemed to be the same old farming news, and she had had enough of bringing in and threshing grain.

She visited with the women. They talked about Oscar and Torsten and Frieda's baby that was due in a few months. She looked around for something more exciting to do. The younger children played tag. None of the older boys were around. She decided they were probably down at the hot springs or wading in the river, chasing minnows. They frequently played together.

Heading for the river, she heard laughing and spotted Jens and Harald. Jens had his shirt off and his trousers rolled up. He stood in the water, swirling a pan.

Harald spotted her and asked, "Do you want to go to the hot springs? I'm going to go see if anyone wants to go swimming."

"Maybe in a while." Katrine was more intrigued with what Jens was doing.

"I'm going. It will be nice." Harald headed back past her.

"Where'd you get the gold pan?" Katrine asked.

Jens straightened. "A prospector coming by our place gave it to me. He said he wouldn't need it anymore." Jens picked at something in his pan and put what looked mostly like mud on a rock where there was more of the same.

"You're panning for gold!" Katrine exclaimed.

"Yes, and I'm finding some too."

Katrine hitched up her dress and waded out to where she could more easily see. The river ran cold. She climbed out onto a rock next to Jens. Her eyes caught the bruise she had seen before, appearing only slightly better. She was tempted to say something but didn't.

"So why'd he say he wouldn't need his pan anymore?"

"H-he was busted. He'd been up the Salmon River and didn't find much. He stopped by our place, and Ma gave him something to eat—him and his partners."

Jens bent over and scooped more gravel into his pan. He squatted down and began swirling it into the water.

"H-he gave Ma a gold nugget for the food, but Ma gave it back. P-Pete was his name. She said it wasn't fitting to take a man's last dollar. That's why he offered me his pan. Pa wouldn't have anything to do with me having his pan, so when Pete left, he put it by our creek where I would see it. I-I went and got it later, but I didn't want to t-try it out where Pa could see."

"Show me your gold," Katrine said. Her heart surged with the thought of Jens finding gold. So many men had come and gone through the valley, all intent on finding gold. Sometimes a prospector came through and paid for a meal with gold dust. Katrine imagined the things she could buy with it.

Jens kept swirling a moment longer. "It's hard to get." He picked out something shiny.

Katrine didn't think it looked yellow enough to be gold. She leaned over to where she could see. Jens swirled again. The sparkly pieces in the pan swirled with the water.

"I don't think it's gold, Jens," Katrine said, disappointed. "Papa Olafson says gold is yellow and doesn't swirl away."

Jens swirled again, studying the motion. "I suppose you're right. I was just hoping."

He stood up and dumped his pan of water onto the material he had scrapped onto the rock. It washed slowly back into the river, winking in the sunlight. "Maybe I'll look for a different spot."

"I think the gold's farther up in the mountains."

Jens shrugged and turned toward where Katrine pointed, taking a long look. "Yeah, maybe I'll go there someday."

Katrine saw the new bruises on his upper back—angry purple.

"You have more bruises," Katrine said quietly. Her world darkened. Jens looked so skinny. His ribs showed. There was no mistaking the new bruises.

"N-no, t-they're getting b-b-better." Jens glanced around.

"What about this?" Katrine touched his neck, and Jens winced.

He pulled back, and a shadow crossed his face. Katrine shook with disbelief.

"I'm sorry, Jens."

"D-don't. I-I'm all right." He pushed away and then softly repeated, "I'm all right."

Katrine wondered if she should say what she believed—wondered what she should do.

Jens waded to the shore, picked up his shirt, and began dressing. Katrine followed and watched as he tucked it in. He winced again as he did so.

"Why does he do it?" Katrine could not help asking. She knew it had to be Mr. Andreasson.

"W-what do you mean?" Jens asked. He studied Katrine. "I f-fell down. That's all."

"No you didn't, Jens. You were hurt, and I think it was your pa. I bet he was drunk."

Jens stopped pulling up his suspenders. He turned away, biting his lip, beginning to shake. "I-I'm all right," he insisted again. He turned back. A flash caught the wetness at the corners of his eyes.

Jens started talking. It was about his father. Some of it made no sense. Some of it, Katrine wished she did not hear.

"H-he doesn't hit Barbro or Joren. Just me. When he drinks. E-every time he drinks," Jens stammered, choking. "H-he says I'm no good. I was a mistake."

His eyes found hers, frantic. "What does he mean ... a mistake?"

Katrine shook her head. "I don't know. But you aren't a mistake."

"I try hard. I work hard. I get up before he does. Sometimes I fall asleep when I'm working. Th-that's the only thing I do wrong."

Jens sat and pulled his knees up and put his head in his hands. Katrine sat next to him and touched his shoulder, rubbing, not knowing what else to do. He quivered.

She realized that he really was skinny. She could feel his shoulder blades. She felt the knots from the bruises. Jens twisted away.

"M-maybe I won't stay here," Jens said. "I might just go to the goldfields. I've got a g-gold pan now. I'll teach myself how to find gold. My pa doesn't want me." His eyes sought hers again. "But I love my family. It would hurt them if I left." He was quiet for a long moment. His shoulders heaved.

"You can't go, Jens. Your pa would hurt Barbro or Joren."

Jens pushed away. "I used to think that but not anymore. He only hits me."

Katrine sat quietly.

"I don't think he means to hit me. He just drinks and starts yelling, and then somehow he finds me and hits me. He doesn't even know he's doing it."

"I think you're a good person, Jens. You're one of the smartest boys in class. You work really hard."

Jens turned to her. "You think so?" He was silent a moment, chewing his lip. "You are one of the smartest girls ... and prettiest."

"Really?"

"I've always thought so. I always fancied when I was old enough I would want to marry you."

A queasiness washed over Katrine. Never had she expected Jens to say something like that. She thought of him as a playmate—a friend. These were new feelings storming through her.

Jens turned and took her hand. "If I could, I *would* marry you, Katrine, but we're too young, and Pa wouldn't let me."

Katrine felt her world spinning.

"D-don't tell anyone what I told you," he said. "That I might go to the goldfields. If I did, it would only be to get enough gold for my ma and sister and brother. As soon as I got some, I'd come back and give it to them."

Something told Katrine that it was not true.

Mia approached them, calling, "Katrine, it's time for dinner. You didn't come. Papa sent me to look for you."

At dinner, Katrine carefully watched as Jens ate. He piled his plate full and sat between his brother and sister. He ate everything off his plate—potatoes, turnips, greens, venison, and biscuits. He went back for another helping. Katrine caught the glower in Mr. Andreasson's eyes, burning from behind his bushy eyebrows. Jens put a biscuit back and put some of his potatoes on Joran's plate.

Quietly, Katrine got up and went into the Adolphsons' cabin. She found a cloth and returned to the table. She rolled up some potatoes and a piece of limpa. Later, she caught up to Jens and told him she had left something for him in their wagon.

"Don't tell your pa."

Chapter 33

SCHOOL BEGAN AGAIN. Katrine felt good being back among her friends studying and learning new things. Lars seemed to miss school occasionally when helping his father, but he was fourteen. The others were all back, and now that Laurens was six and because Anna, Björn, and Linnea attended, they brought him as well.

Katrine was proud to tell everyone that the Olafsons now had a badstuga. She hoped some of them might come and visit, but she knew deep down that it was not the same as visiting someone with a hot springs. Everyone would rather soak in hot water than sit on a bench and sweat in a steam bath.

She watched Jens, who sat cross-legged with a slate in his lap doing math problems next to Harald. Jens never acknowledged the food she had sent with him from Sunday meeting. Instead, he seemed even quieter and skinnier, if that was possible. Jens was not like Björn, Harald, or even young Laurens who had some form and muscles. Jens was simply skinny. Katrine glanced at Joran and Barbro. They seemed as bouncy as ever. Katrine recalled the bruises she had seen on Jens's neck and shoulder. She wanted to know if there were more. Sometimes she caught sight of him stretching as if he were trying to relieve some unseen pain.

A flash of red crawled inside Katrine. Surely the Andreassons had enough food. Why was Mr. Andreasson hitting Jens?

She caught up to Jens during the break. He was sitting in the dirt, tracing a design with his finger. He smiled when she sat.

"Have you done any more gold panning?"

Jens shrugged, and his smile faded. "It g-got me into trouble."

Katrine had guessed that might happen.

"I took my pan up our creek and was digging in the gravel with Joran. We found some specks of gold—for real this time. Joran was so excited he ran back to tell everyone. He was hollering, 'We're rich, we're rich. Jens found some gold.'" Jens laughed. "When Pa found out, he was mad as a scalded skunk. He said I was wasting time. My job was h-helping him—not ch-chasing rainbows."

"He hit you again?" A chill washed Katrine.

Jens shook his head. "H-he j-just took my gold pan."

"He took it? It was your pan. Pete gave it to you."

Jens shrugged. "He said, 'What am I breaking my back for, j-just s-so you can play?'" Jens's eyes caught Katrine's. "Since then I haven't been able to find my pan. I think he threw it into the river."

They heard the gong that announced dinner. Jens stood and dusted his trousers.

Katrine's stomach tightened. "Maybe another prospector will come through someday, and you can get another pan."

Jens nodded. "Maybe."

Later, Katrine confided in Mama Olafson. "I don't think Jens is getting enough to eat. He's skinner than his brother and sister." She was careful not to mention the bruises and what she had been thinking about Mr. Andreasson. She also did not mention the gold pan because the oldest son had ample work in helping his father in the fields. There was no play except for some on Saturdays while cleaning up for Sunday, and then for only a few hours on Sundays.

Margret laughed. "He's probably shooting up tall like his father. The rest of him just hasn't caught up."

Katrine had not thought of that. Jens *was* thirteen. But then she shook her head. That could not explain all of it.

"He eats as much as he can at Sunday meeting. I've watched him. I feel bad for him. Can I take him a meat pie during school?"

Margret smiled. "That is for his parents, don't you think?"

Katrine wanted to tell Mama Olafson what was happening, but she could not bring herself to do so. "Maybe we can just make it a gift. We can give gifts to people, can't we?"

"Yes, we can. We are blessed. If it will make you happy, we can make him a small meat pie, but one meal isn't going to fill him out, and remember, because of his own pride, he might not want to take food from us."

Katrine had not thought of that. She swallowed. She knew what Mama Olafson now thought.

When Katrine tried to give Jens the meat pie, just as Mama Olafson had predicted, he refused it.

"I told you I was all right."

Katrine bit her lip. "It's just a gift, Jens," she said. "Mama Olafson made it special for you."

Jens shrugged. "Fine then, just this once. If my pa finds out, he'll skin me alive."

Later that evening, Sven took Katrine for a walk outside. "Mama told me what you did for Jens, and I'm thinking I know why."

Katrine felt stinging in her eyes. "He doesn't deserve it, Papa Olafson. He doesn't deserve it." Her chest ached.

"Nej, he doesn't," Sven replied quietly. He put his arm around Katrine. "There are some things in life you won't understand, sweetheart. It's a good thing what you did, but you're too young for taking a hand in this."

Katrine felt confused. Jens was not too young for what was happening to him, so how could it be that she was too young for taking a hand? "Jens isn't much older than me. He doesn't have a choice."

Sven paused before replying. "This is for his parents to work out. If Mr. Andreasson learns about this, he may not approve, and things could become worse for Jens."

Katrine's world darkened. Jens had suggested something similar. Had she made things more difficult for him? Hot tears squeezed from her eyes. She was confused, but she respected Papa Olafson. Jens's parents had to figure things out.

"Maybe we can invite the Andreassons over for a visit sometime," Katrine suggested. "Maybe when we need to borrow a wagon or something. They could see Nisse, and they could all stay for dinner."

"I would sure welcome them for dinner," Sven agreed and then laughed. "We hardly see them except at Sunday meeting."

Katrine wished Jens were her brother. The Olafsons would have taken good care of him. He would work hard in the fields and help Papa Olafson, and Papa Olafson would appreciate it. It hurt to realize that some children had good parents and others did not. Even so, they were supposed to honor their parents. How could they always do that if things were not right? Maybe someone would tell Mr. Andreasson. Then he could do the right thing as well.

She was thankful the Olafsons had taken her in, even when they frequently favored Mia. But of course they should. She was their real daughter. She knew they tried to make her part of the family, but she could not help sometimes feeling that she really wasn't.

Katrine thought of Erik and what the two miners had said. She had reconciled that Erik had become an Indian, if even the story was true. Papa Olafson explained that sometimes trappers lived with the Indians. The young man who had been spotted could likely be the son of a white man and an Indian woman. He insisted the man was not Erik.

"It happens frequently, Katrine," Sven had said. "Men are men no matter their language or skin. They long for the comfort of a woman wherever they may be. It should be no surprise."

Katrine had listened, trying to understand, but something hot inside her made her believe otherwise. Maybe if it was Erik, he had become lost. The two miners had said the country was nearly impassable. True, Erik was now a man and should be able to find his way, but maybe it was too far or too hard. She studied the peaks toward the east. Only their tops showed above the timbered ridges. She had paid little attention to them before. Stark and fractured, the ominous rock etched the far horizon. She could only imagine what the country beyond them was like.

The miners had been the only men who had come down the trail from the east. Others used the trail near the Wikstroms', but they went north of the peaks. She wondered what she could see if she took the trail. The thought tugged at her. Perhaps she would go to look sometime. She didn't care if Erik had become Indian. He was still her brother. She prayed only that he had not forgotten her.

Jackson's Skeleton

Chapter 34

IN HER FREE time in the evenings, Katrine began making straw figures from the oat straw similar to those she remembered making with her mother. Carefully she braided and tied the pale yellow strands, forming hearts and stars and goats. She began working on a large angel with a pointed crown and a red ribbon around her waist. With a tiny brush that she had made by chewing the end of some straw, Katrine painted the angel's eyes and mouth with purple elderberry juice. She couldn't wait to show Papa Olafson.

At noon meal the following day, Sven came in and sat while Margret brought him some soup with buttered limpa. Eagerly, Katrine laid her angel in front of him.

He frowned. "What's this?"

"It's an archangel," Katrine said. "For Christmas."

"Ja, that's nice." He pushed a piece of limpa through his soup.

Mia came to sit.

"Ah, here's *my* little angel. And what have you been up to today?" he asked Mia, smiling. He ran his finger down her nose.

"I've been helping Mama. We're going to make some *fattigma,* fried cookies."

"That's wonderful." Sven pulled Mia to himself and gave her a kiss. "You're being such a big help to Mama."

Katrine felt something crawling inside her. She wanted to leave the table. Afterward, she quietly put the braided straw angel aside. She found herself thinking about the ridge to the southeast.

"I think I'll see if I can gather some rose hips," Katrine said quietly. She found a flour sack and put some dried apples inside.

Margret didn't seem to hear Katrine's comment or notice her actions. She had turned her attention to Torsten, who was protesting something.

Mia reached him and picked him up. "Oh, you're getting heavy," she said.

Outside, Katrine walked rapidly toward the trail that led east behind the cabin. Nisse followed for a short distance, but she scolded him and told him to go back. He was trained to remain at the cabin.

Katrine's thoughts were on Erik. She had never taken this eastern trail for any distance. She and Mia had always gone the other direction to the Wikstroms'. Until the two miners came down it a few months ago, she had never given it a thought. She did not consider what the others would think when they found her gone. She was thinking only that if Erik lived, he was over the mountains in the direction of the trail.

Today the late autumn weather was warm, and the sky, brilliant blue. Katrine walked rapidly upward, not looking back toward the cabin. Pausing to catch her breath, she was startled by how high she had climbed. It hurt what Papa Olafson had done. She knew she was not the Olafsons' real daughter. Erik was her only real family. And since hearing the story of the white boy, the one who spoke Swedish, she knew in her heart the boy had to be Erik. But she could not understand why he had not come for her. He said he would. Well, she would go to him.

Katrine resumed following the faint trail upward. In places, it disappeared into the brush or tall grass. She determined which direction it likely ran by studying the landscape. The mountain crags rose beyond, more visible now. The trail had to pass over one of the ridges, but oh, how far it was. She struck out, following the direction she thought she should go.

The sun settled toward the western horizon. Katrine figured she had a best a couple more hours before it grew dark. It being northern country and late autumn, darkness came quickly, unlike during the long light of summer.

She knew she was being foolish and grappled with that truth. She knew the cabin lay generally downhill, somewhere behind her. She did not dare attempt to walk downward after dark. She could easily find herself turned around and in a dead-end gully or blowdown.

She glanced again toward the sun. The crags appeared a terribly long distance away and dauntingly rugged. Even Erik would find it difficult to come over them.

Then it occurred to her. *It was too far.* Maybe Erik hadn't come for her because it was too far. It wasn't because he had become a heathen and forgotten her. Maybe he was trying to find her and really was lost. An ache leaped into Katrine's chest.

"I'm sorry, Erik. I can't do it. You're too far," she whispered. "Maybe someday I can come and look for you."

Katrine took another look at the crags in the distance. Papa and Mama Olafson would be angry, but she wasn't sorry for trying. She felt a strange comfort knowing that Erik was somewhere beyond the mountains.

Katrine looked around. Below her, a rocky ridge ran downward toward the valley, appearing to fall suddenly away in a jumble of granite spires. She wondered about trying to go down in that direction before it grew too dark. She decided it was too dangerous.

She paused and looked back over the valley. There had been six families. Now only five remained, scattered about in its vast emptiness. Would there be even fewer come next spring?

She turned back in the direction from which she had come. A faint whistle reached her ears. She glanced around, not certain that she had really heard something. A crawling feeling raced up her back. Something had to be there, but she could see nothing. Maybe it had been a sleepy bird.

Then she felt as if there were a presence. Despite her growing fear, she turned and searched more intently beneath the trees. Whatever it was, it was below her, down the ridge, toward some ragged rocks.

Trembling, she slowly made her way downward. She might climb a rock to determine if she could see what had whistled. A warm breeze buffeted her.

Torn with desperate thoughts, she sobbed. "I can't. I have to go back." She turned back uphill, having gone only a few steps before she again heard a low, quavering sound. It could not be her imagination.

Frightened, she searched for the sound. She froze. Near the base of a granite outcrop, something appearing human was curled up.

An icy shudder raced through her. A body—the remains of a body—lay crumpled and partially bound with cloth rags; bones lay scattered about, and blank eye sockets in a grinning skull stared at her. A few patches of hair clung to the skull, and a rotten hat lay nearby. Heart pounding, nauseous, wanting to run, but telling herself the man's spirit had long abandoned its body, Katrine crept closer.

The skeleton had been stripped of flesh except for leathery areas that connected the ribs. Some bones appeared to have been gnawed. She frantically glanced around, now thinking of bears and mountain lions. A shiver raced down her spine. She had been foolish coming here alone.

The man's rifle lay near his side. A canvas pack rested against the rock behind him, tattered but mostly intact. A rusted gold pan told more of the story.

Gasping, Katrine turned and hurried back up to the trail. She glanced back toward the outcrop. The skeleton remained watching. She turned toward the Olafsons' cabin, almost running. She shook, watching now for any tiny movement in the shrubs—watching for the mountain lion she knew must be nearby. A buffeting wind pushed at her. She could not shake the possibility that this was where the lion lived—the very one that tried repeatedly to get to Trillium. How could she have been so careless? Her blood pounded in her throat.

Katrine found herself running, tripping. The sun settled lower, sending long shadows across the trail. Where was the trail? The country appeared different, unlike when she had first climbed the trail. Had she even come this direction? Frantically, she spun around, searching. Clammy desperation washed her. She had to be correct. *There. There's the line of jagged rocks.* The trail had come past them. But where did it turn downward toward the cabin?

Darkness rapidly gathered. The trail descended. Either she was correct or she was hopelessly lost. She gulped for air. She thought she recalled some of the trail, now shrouded in shadows. The cabin had to be somewhere below. She walked blindly in the dark, frantic. Then she caught a whiff of wood smoke. Shuddering relief washed her. She ran blindly down the trail. At last, she spotted a flickering light.

What would she say to Papa Olafson? How would she explain her absence? What had seemed so sensible and easy to explain on the mountain now seemed hollow and empty.

Looks of worry turned to concern when Katrine described what she had discovered. She struggled trying to describe the skeleton. She was glad she didn't have to describe her feelings. She could not overcome feeling that the man's spirit still lingered behind. Had it been the man's spirit that had called her?

They sat for a long while until Mia went to bed. Margret gave an excuse she wanted to comfort Torsten for a bit. The noise and excitement had been too much for him. She held the youngster to herself and walked about the cabin and then took him behind the curtain to where Mia slept.

Katrine found herself alone with Papa Olafson at the table with a single candle dancing its light about the cabin.

"I know why you were up there," Sven said. "I know what the miners told us." His mouth tightened.

Katrine sat quietly.

"I am sorry, Katrine. Your brother is not there. You have to understand we were over three hundred miles away in the lava fields southeast of here when we split up. Erik was twelve. He could not have survived on his own."

Katrine found herself trembling.

"I never want you to do anything like this again," Sven said.

Katrine hung her head.

"A long time ago, your mama and papa asked me to take care of you until they caught up." Sven leaned forward, his arms on his knees, catching her eyes. "I promised them that I would. As it has turned out, they can never release me from that promise. Dear Lord, I wish they could have—for your sake. But that being said, I no longer wish to be released, nor does Mama."

Katrine began shaking. The Olafsons had treated her well. These had been good times, the best they could be, considering. How could she explain these times also hurt? She wasn't their daughter. She never could be. She had no real family. How could she give up the hope that she still might have a brother?

"We do love you, Katrine. Mia thinks of you as her sister. And Torsten will always know you as his oldest sister."

Katrine pushed her fingers across the table, tracing the dancing candlelight.

"I'm sorry, Papa Olafson," she whispered. "I won't go away like that again."

"I believe you won't." Sven took Katrine's hands into his. "You are my daughter, Katrine, just like Mia is. I'll be your papa when you find it time to marry, and Mama Olafson will be your mama when you have your own children. Sometimes you may not believe that, but remember this night whenever you begin to doubt. I am not a man who does not keep his promises."

"I know that, Papa Olafson."

"Good. Then we shall put this behind us. Tomorrow is a new day. And from now on, it would please us if you called us Mama and Papa like Mia does."

Katrine rose to prepare for bed. "Uh, Papa Olafson ... I mean Papa ... what are we going to do about the dead man?"

Sven smiled. "Why, Katrine, I believe I will get my shovel and go up there and have a proper burial for him. You can come and show me where if you'd like, although I think I can find the ridge. You said he was near some tall rocks just off a narrow ridge."

Katrine thought about it for a moment. "What about Mia?"

"This time, I do not believe she is old enough."

Katrine wasn't sure she was old enough either, but she and Papa Olafson would be doing something very important together, and the thought warmed her.

Chapter 35

ALTHOUGH PAPA OLAFSON had said he intended to bury the skeleton, Katrine was surprised when the following morning he brought up Boots and Ornery, ready for riding. She did not expect that it would be so soon.

"We should take two animals, in case of trouble, and in case one of us needs to go for help."

It thrilled Katrine to be riding Boots by herself. The horse moved powerfully underneath her. She always respected the horse.

As they rode up the ridge, Katrine marveled at how the landscape seemed to change. The rocks and woods no longer seemed as foreboding. If there was a cougar around, it surely would not come for them now.

Within a few hours, they reached the ridge and turned down toward the rock outcrop.

"There." Katrine pointed. "He's down next to that tall rock."

"Ja, I see him." Sven dismounted and helped Katrine down. She sidled away from the skeleton.

"There is no reason to fear him, Katrine. His spirit is no longer here."

Katrine wanted to ask Papa Olafson how he was certain. She knew she had not imagined a whistle. Now that Katrine had found him, maybe his spirit wanted to watch what would happen. Maybe the spirit wouldn't want them to take anything. Katrine wasn't sure what Papa Olafson would do with the man's things.

Sven began digging. "You can gather his things. I won't need to dig very deep. The animals have already eaten what they could of him." He threw some dirt from the hole. "They won't be digging him up again."

Katrine gathered his pack, the rifle, and the pan. She thought of taking the pan back to Jens, but it was rusted and already had a hole in it.

Somehow she found the courage to gather up the scattered bones and place them near the rest of the skeleton. Nearly every bone had been gnawed. Probably by mice and squirrels, she figured. The larger marks were most certainly from coyotes.

"Find me some good limbs for making a cross," Sven said as he finished digging. "How unfortunate we don't know his name. We could have carved it into the crossbar."

"Jackson," Katrine said. "Why not call him Jackson?"

Sven frowned and then smiled. "Very well, Jackson it is." He pulled his skinning knife and began carving. When finished, he lashed the cross piece onto the base and buried it in a pile of rocks on the grave.

Katrine felt more at peace. Whoever the man really was, he was now at rest.

Later when they had returned to the cabin, Mia and Margret gathered with them at the table to hear about the day's journey.

"We brought his rifle and gear, such as it is," Sven said. He swung the man's pack onto the table. A portion of it ripped apart. "Katrine named him Jackson. Don't expect anything of his to be of much use. It's old and has been exposed to the weather."

He pulled some rotten clothing out of the pack, smoothing it. He found a frying pan, tin cup, and spoon. The man's knife had rusted. There was no ammunition.

"I expect he fired all his rounds trying to summon help. I found some casings lying about. I don't know why he stopped there. He was nearly down to the valley."

"I think he got cold and lost," Katrine said. "It was really steep below the rocks. I don't think he could get down from there."

"He might have tried to climb the rocks to see where he was and fell. I couldn't be sure, but it appeared that one or both of his legs were broken," Sven said. "Katrine found some bone fragments that we weren't even sure if they belonged to the man or some other animal there, but we buried them all just the same."

Sven pulled out two leather pouches from the pack. "Pretty heavy," he said, hefting one. He untied it, took out some papers, and then went silent.

"Gold ore," he said, eyes widening. He poured the chunks of rock onto the table. "That man found a rich strike somewhere."

He passed the pieces around. Katrine could easily see the bright yellow metallic specks scattered through the white rock. Some were masses as large as peas held together by bits of quartz.

"He was probably carrying it out to try to get assays," Sven said. "I don't know why he'd be coming this direction unless he knew about Fort Boise. He should have gone west toward Lewiston."

Sven untied the second pouch and dumped its contents out as well. It was much the same. Katrine's heart quickened at the sight of the gold.

"How much do you figure it's worth?" she asked.

"I can't say. I'm no expert on gold. I figure it's at least forty dollars."

A rush of needles washed Katrine. That was more money than she could imagine. It was no wonder people went to the goldfields to search for gold. She suddenly pictured men to the north pulling out chunks of rock with yellow metal like the ones on the table. It wouldn't take long to get rich with rocks like these.

Sven took the paper and carefully unfolded it. A section tore, but he pieced it together.

"You best read it, Katrine," he said. "You are the best at reading English."

Katrine pulled the paper to herself. The ink was faded and had been scrawled across the page in sweeping letters. It appeared hurried.

My Beloved Melissa,

I pray you are well. If you ever read this letter, you shall know what has become of me. After my year of travel and searching, I reached the Salmon River country and located a rich strike. There are samples in this pouch. I have recorded our claim at Washington in Warren's Camp. I named—

"It's too smudged, I can't read it," Katrine said. "Another part says, *located near,* and it looks like *1,200 feet,* but the rest is too smudged. I can only make out, *cleft rock.*"

Katrine examined the paper more closely, squinting. "Here, I can read the bottom part."

I feel the cold now. It is snowing. I have burned all the wood within my reach. I can no longer move my legs. The wolf is back. I shall not let it have the satisfaction of killing me. I am so sorry, Melissa. I did my best. I shall always love you,

Jackson

Katrine dropped the letter, trembling.

"It really says Jackson?" Sven frowned.

Mia picked up the letter and nodded. "It says Jackson."

Katrine sat for a long while. No one spoke.

"How do we find Melissa and give her the gold?" Katrine finally asked.

Sven shook his head. "Unless we know the city where she lives, we can't. What I can do is post a notice at Boise City. There was no one there when this letter was written, but maybe someone passing through will read it. Maybe someone can post it in Lewiston as well. Based on this, Jackson probably died the year we came to the valley. Maybe the year after at the latest."

"Where is Washington?" Katrine asked. "His letter says he recorded a claim."

Sven smiled. "Good thought. It's in Warren's Camp north of us. We can write a letter to the recorder in Washington. He will have a copy of the claim. It might have information on Jackson."

Margret rocked Torsten. "Well, Lord be. How strange is all this." She glanced at Katrine. "You were meant to find him, you were."

Sven nodded and stood. "In the meantime, we keep these things safe, Jackson's letter, his gold. I don't think Melissa will mind if we use his other things. I can use his rifle if I can clean off the rust."

That night, Katrine began writing some letters to the recorder in Washington and to Melissa, care of general delivery Boise City and Lewiston. Part of her hoped that Melissa would never get it. The other part hoped she would. She imagined that Melissa looked like Anna for some reason—light reddish-blonde hair, soft blue eyes. If Lars went away and left Anna, wouldn't Anna want to know what had become of him? Katrine shook at the thought.

To whomever this may apply,

If you are Melissa who knows Jackson, a man who went into the Salmon River country, please contact the Sven Olafson family that lives at the head of the valley north of Boise City and south of the Little Salmon River where there are some Swedish settlers. If you believe you know Melissa or Jackson please write to the Sven Olafson family or visit us.

Katrine Larson (Olafson)

Katrine folded the letters. She would take them to Mr. Adolphson for some miner or packer to take to their destinations. There would be no telling when, but without a doubt, her letters would be posted at some mail station for people to read.

Chapter 36

A COLD SNAP and freezing rain that turned to snow put an end to any more garden produce. Margret cut and brought in the remaining cabbages. Katrine and Mia helped dig the root vegetables—turnips, beets, onions, and especially potatoes. Katrine loved digging into the potato hills. Oily black leaves that were once vibrant green now draped the mounds and concealed any thought of life beneath. It was almost magical when she shoved the spade deep into the ground, turned the earth over, and released several light tan spuds. Squealing, Mia and Torsten snatched the potatoes that spilled out, rubbed off the dirt, and put them into a basket.

When they had filled a basket, they hauled it to the root cellar where Sven had cut a pit and lined it with straw. They set in the potatoes, threw some straw over them, and then began another row. In this manner, they filled the pit. As they would use the potatoes, they would dig down, pull what was needed from the hole, and rebury the remaining potatoes.

As before, the Swedes loaded sacks of cabbages, potatoes, and onions onto the mules for their semiannual trip to Boise City. They left behind a single animal for each family in case of an emergency.

This trip, Sven remained in the valley. He kept close watch on the others in case of unwelcome visitors and in the event someone needed help. Katrine rode with him on occasion to visit the other families.

It was a welcome relief when the men returned. In addition to staples, they brought new farm implements, household utensils, kerosene oil, cloth, and other necessities to manage the winter.

It reminded Katrine of Christmas day when they got their new supplies, but the return trip also signaled the ending of the seasons. Only winter and deep snow lay ahead.

Another storm raced through the valley tearing the last remaining leaves from the aspens and needles from the few scattered tamarack on the western mountains. Snow swept from gray-white skies, covering the meadows white and sifting through gaps in the cabin and around the door. Ice covered the pond and stilled the creek, creeping outward from the banks until only small sections remained open.

"The ice is earlier than last season," Sven remarked. "Might be some of the geese and ducks will get trapped and we can hunt a few."

"We can go ice fishing," Mia exclaimed. "Boots can pull the sled to the river."

Sven laughed. "That shall not be for some time. The ice won't be thick enough, and we need deeper snow to get over the rocks."

"I don't like it when it's only a little snow," Mia said, frowning. "Lots of snow is more fun."

Katrine agreed. It was no fun until the snow was deep enough for the skis or the sled. Now it just made for difficult traveling.

"I'm sure it's on its way," Sven said, eyeing the sky. He pushed past the girls, heading out into the evening to tend to the stock. "You girls help Mama."

Sunday after the storm and freezing cold, Katrine and the Olafsons made their way to the Adolphsons' for Sunday meeting. She wondered who might make it since the weather had been so cold.

The Lundgrens pulled in front of them where the creeks joined below their cabin, all piled into the wagon.

"It sure would be nice to have a wagon," Mia said. "The Lundgrens have everything."

"Now, Mia," Margret said. "We have what the good Lord intends for us to have."

"Well, I can't help but wish he had intended for me to have my wagon instead of giving it to the river," Sven said and laughed. "I expect we shall get one soon. Besides, a couple of more snowstorms and it won't matter."

"Then we will use our sled," Mia said. "The Lundgrens don't have a sled."

"That's because Papa is the best carpenter," Katrine added. But she wished they had a wagon as well.

Katrine enjoyed Sunday meeting largely because everyone could get together and share news. The Adolphsons usually had the most news because everyone coming and going into the mining camps stopped at their place. Now that the war was over, the news consisted mostly of mining and progress in the various mining camps. Katrine only had a vague idea where the camps were. She knew that Boise Basin was southeast, and the Salmon River mines were to the north. She wondered about the country to the northeast from where the two prospectors had come. Jackson had come from that direction as well and had gold that was still in the rock. Papa Olafson had explained that was what hardrock mining was about. Much of the news was now about hardrock mining starts.

Nils, especially, seemed excited with news of the hardrock mines.

"That means permanent settlements—churches and schools. More settlers will soon be coming into this valley. You shall see."

Today, the Wikstroms were absent. Katrine hoped that all was well. She knew they lived the farthest away and that the upper part of the trail near their cabin was difficult, especially if ice clogged the creek. With Frieda expecting, it was even less wise for her to travel. Katrine was disappointed. She enjoyed visiting with Anna and the others.

As usual, while the women fixed dinner, the men relaxed, smoked their pipes, and shared some snaps. Today, some of the children joined in a game of tag, chasing each other about in the yard. Katrine decided she wanted to go to the hot springs if only to wade in the hot water. She took Mia and Ingrid, and soon they were dangling their feet in the warm water. It would not be much fun when she pulled them out into the November cold, but now it was nice, sitting on a boulder in the sun. She noticed Harald and Jens exploring along the river as they often did, sometimes walking out across the ice. She thought about joining them but instead relished the warm water.

Pelle and Joran came to the springs wanting to play with Mia and Ingrid. The two girls dried their feet and soon scampered off with the boys. It was fine with Katrine. Sometimes she liked to be alone with just her thoughts, as she often did when she sat on the boulder behind the cabin in the clearing. Today was comfortably warm in spite of the snow and ice. Harald's and Jens's laughter filtered up from the river to her. She could hear the other children up near the cabin laughing as well, now chasing each other, accompanied by occasional yipping from Anka. She felt happy for all of them.

She studied the late autumn landscape, the deep green trees, a few aspens etched against them, and a few brown leaves too stubborn to fall off. White ice outlined the boulders along the river's edge and stretched out into the water, nearly choking it off in a few areas. Snow sparkled under the trees and carpeted the surrounding landscape.

She swished her feet in the water, enjoying the warmth. Tiny flecks of mica, stirred up from the sandy bottom, reflected the sun, breaking into a sprinkling of tiny stars. She watched as the mica sparks floated and swirled on the currents and slowly settled, sliding across her toes and then slipping back again to the floor of the pool. She stirred up more, kicking her foot across the bottom, watching the whirlwind of lights blossoming.

Katrine was half-asleep when she thought she heard yelling from downriver. She sat up. It sounded like Jens. He was calling at the top of his voice.

"Help me! Please, help!"

His voice grew louder. He ran in her direction, stumbling. Madly he waved his arms. Katrine started running toward Jens, her bare feet slipping on the slick rocks and ice. Jens was hysterical.

"Harald fell through the ice! Oh God, help me!" Jens cried. Jens's clothes were soaked.

A weight crushed in on Katrine. Jens collapsed in the sand, staring past her, not recognizing her. Tears streaked his cheeks. He trembled.

"He's in the river," Jens choked out his words. "I couldn't get him. Oh God, I couldn't get him." Jens stumbled back to his feet and continued running crazily toward the cabin.

Oblivious, Katrine ran downriver, a hollow fear and empty disbelief gripping her. She didn't know where Harald could be—only that she had to find him. Her feet slipped on the rocks. She stumbled, finding herself at the edge of the river, ice breaking under her, freezing water enveloping her. She scrambled out, tried to stand, and slipped again.

She saw where the boys' tracks wandered through the snow and in places out onto the ice. Pulling her feet under her, water streaming off, freezing, shaking uncontrollably, she stood and stumbled onward, now hearing faint voices coming from behind her.

A shelf of ice reached out across a calm elbow in the river. She began across it and froze in horror. Beyond her, the ice opened into black water, which led to a jumble of boulders where whitewater sucked through. A lump of color—Harald's brown vest and blue shirt—and his silent white face stared in her direction. She fell to the ice unable to breathe.

Men rushed past, yelling, crashing through the ice, splashing into the water.

Katrine felt Papa Olafson's arms about her, dragging her toward the shore. "Easy, Katrine, easy. Don't look."

But Katrine had seen. The black hole must have been where Harald fell through. The open water near the shore showed where Jens had unsuccessfully battled to reach him. Harald must have fought desperately, trying to get out. The hole had only opened larger. The current pushed him against the ice downriver, and the cold had numbed him until he could no longer fight. The ever-patient, unrelenting current had sucked at him, pinning him to the boulders, immobilizing him until he could no longer struggle, until he was unable to move, and he had lost consciousness.

Vaguely, Katrine was aware that she was being carried back toward the cabin. Her feet stung, and she shook violently.

Inside the Adolphsons' cabin, she saw Jens, a vacant look on his face, bundled in blankets near the stove. Olga shook and slapped him.

"Talk to me, Jens."

Jens remained unfocused.

Katrine's teeth chattered, and a pounding filled her head. Someone stripped her of her clothing and wrapped her in a blanket.

Astrid handed her a cup of hot tea. It vibrated and splashed on her. She gulped down some steaming liquid.

Others murmured. "He said the ice gave way on both of them. He couldn't reach him. He lost his grip."

Louise sat huddled, sobbing uncontrollably.

Jens buried his head in his hands, rocking back and forth.

Slowly, Katrine became aware of her returning warmth. When her clothes had dried, she dressed. Jens dressed much later. How could anyone not miss seeing the bruises that Jens displayed on his back and ribs?

Jens must have known that others had noticed. "It's w-when I fell through the ice," he claimed.

It snowed two days later when they lowered Harald's coffin into the ground on a hill behind the Lundgrens' cabin. Katrine thought it was a nice place. It was beneath aspen trees that overlooked the valley. Louise sobbed and shook while Magnus held her. Tears ran down Emma's cheeks as she held Oscar. Nils Adolphson said a few words and then stumbled through psalm 23: The Lord is my Shepherd. The other men and Lars shoveled dirt into the new grave. Katrine plugged her ears to stop out the sound of the dirt hitting Harald's coffin. They were the same sounds from when they buried Mrs. Wikstrom. No longer able to bear it, she turned and ran stumbling back to the Lundgrens' cabin.

Katrine sat alone, shaking, until the others crowded inside against the cold and snow. The women sat with Louise, talking quietly. The children said nothing. For a long while they sat until slowly, one by one, the families departed. Only the Olafsons and the Lundgrens remained. Finally, Sven patted Margret's shoulder, and they bundled up against the cold. Katrine whispered goodbye to Emma. Margret hugged Louise a final time and bundled up Torsten. They headed out into the darkness and blowing snow. Numbly, Katrine held onto Boots with Mia as the horse clambered back through the snow toward their own home.

For several days, Katrine moved about in a daze. Nothing made sense. She questioned why God could let this happen. This was unlike the deaths that had occurred during their trip from the east. They had made it to the valley. No one was supposed to die once they had reached the valley. Harald had been smart, a good friend, and a wonderful companion. Now he was a memory.

A few days later, the news came that Frieda had a baby boy. They named him Jon. During his christening, Nils remarked, "One life has been lost, another has begun. Let baby Jon know he is cherished and has a good place in this world."

Although Katrine knew it was of little comfort to the Lundgrens, Mr. Adolphson's words seemed appropriate. Nevertheless, she remained numbed by Harald's death, and she knew Jens, in particular, was troubled. It was as if Jens had sealed himself off from the world. He no longer smiled or even greeted her. In some ways, Katrine sensed Mr. Andreasson faulted his son and that Mr. Lundgren seemed to feel the same. What were they doing, playing on river ice? Why couldn't Jens reach Harald?

Katrine's thoughts turned to the two miners. She could not shake the possibility that Erik might be alive on the other side of the mountain, despite what Papa Olafson had explained. If her own brother was alive, she had to find him. She had promised Papa Olafson to never leave as she had done, but now she knew someday she would try again. She had to. There was nothing to lose.

Snow sealed the valley. The settlers got about on their skis, and when the snow packed down, they traveled by horseback or sled. School ceased.

Katrine did not see the Lundgrens at Sunday meeting. She and Mia and Mama Olafson went by once to visit. Mr. Lundgren already talked about leaving. He explained that nothing remained for them in the valley. Their cabin seemed empty without Harald. Katrine was happy to get back to the Olafsons' cabin.

Death was a part of life, and they had to carry on. Katrine found herself occasionally thinking of how when they started west there were thirteen Swedish families. People had died on the way. Mrs. Wikstrom died during the first winter at Fort Boise. Harald had died. Some babies had been born—Jon and Oscar and Torsten. Baby Robert had died.

The settlers gathered at the Adolphsons' for Santa Lucia. Katrine sensed that they tried to seem happy, but Harald's death made it difficult. No one needed to caution the youngsters about going near the river. No one mentioned fishing or skating. No one even ventured near the hot springs.

After supper, Katrine with her wreath of candles on her head, dressed in white, brought out the cakes. Her heart was not in it. She had so longed to be Saint Lucia, and now this. It was supposed to be the season of light. She bit her lip and tried to smile. Slowly the days would begin to lengthen until the longest day on Midsummer's Eve, but now only darkness seemed to surround the Swedes. Sometimes the darkness seemed to be gathering even more fiercely, pressing relentlessly in on them.

Katrine decided she had to be cheerful. Soon they would celebrate Christmas and rekindle their hopes. The seasons would slowly turn. Flowers would come back to the valley. Sunlight and summer would return.

Chapter 37

THE YEAR 1866 brought heavy snow. Katrine helped Papa Olafson carry hay out to Trillium and to Boots and the mules. She kept the path to the chicken coop tramped down. Other paths led to the woodpile, the stock shed, and to the springhouse. No one attempted to travel any farther than their own cabins until the end of January when the snow had packed down.

They bundled up for Sunday meeting. Boots and Jack pulled the sled. Katrine followed on her skis. She found she could slide along just about as easily. Sometimes she piled onto the sled with the others or grabbed ahold to go up a small hill.

Katrine and Mia studied from their readers on their own. Similar to when they first arrived in the valley, they gathered with Anna and some of the other children after Sunday noon dinner and reviewed lessons. No one said if Mrs. Lundgren would start teaching again or not.

Katrine missed the challenge of trying to learn new things and of reciting what she had memorized or written. Most of all, she missed being with the other children. She saw them at Sunday meetings, but it was different. At school, it was only Mrs. Lundgren and the other children—no babies or other adults.

Now when a storm passed, Katrine and Mia put on their skis and walked down the trail, packing it down. The Lundgrens had sometimes packed the trail from their place to the Adolphsons' by the time they reached the trail to the Lundgrens', but now it seemed the Lundgrens were no longer leaving their cabin. The snow remained quiet and unbroken along their creek.

This Sunday, Katrine skied the entire distance to the Adolphsons', following the sled. Some of the others came with their skis as well. They gathered and visited. Most of the children played near the cabin, but Katrine wandered down to the hot springs to dangle her feet in the hot water and to think about things. More importantly, she went there because she could watch Jens. Jens had begun walking down to the river by himself. He no longer played with Björn or the others. He stood looking out at the water, standing quietly, doing nothing.

Katrine joined him, not trying to talk to him but just to sit nearby. She began talking about things as if Jens was not present but as if the water and the trees could hear her. Once Jens looked in her direction and frowned, but he said nothing.

She talked about the miners who came through and told about the white boy living with the Indians.

"I think it's my brother, Erik," she admitted openly.

Jens raised his eyes.

"I might go to look for him," she continued. "I can't take a horse, but I can walk a long ways."

"Y-you'd h-have to stay in the woods at night," Jens said.

Katrine was surprised to hear Jens's voice.

"I can do that," she said.

"You might have to t-take a gun for wolves."

"Well, I don't have one."

Jens shrugged. He was silent for a moment. "I tried to get to him," he said softly, barely audible at first. His eyes pleaded for understanding. "We b-both fell through the ice. I was closer to the shore. I got out."

Tears began sliding down Jens's face, and he began shaking.

Katrine found her hand resting on Jens's shoulder. She could not believe what it told her as she felt his uncontrolled shaking.

"You tried," she whispered.

"It wasn't good enough," Jens said, pulling away. "I kept breaking through the ice. He was yelling for me, begging me to help, splashing in the water. Then he quit yelling. Only I could still hear him gurgling. He was looking at me the entire time. I couldn't do anything."

Jens was shaking so hard Katrine became scared. "Don't, Jens," she whispered. She didn't want to know how awful it had been watching Harald die.

"Somehow, I reached him. I grabbed him and began to pull. My feet slipped. I went under and lost him. He didn't seem to know I had even reached him. I was shivering so bad I couldn't hold onto him. My b-body wouldn't work anymore."

Jens gulped. "But he was looking at me the whole time, like … like he was somewhere else." Jens burst into uncontrolled sobbing for a long moment.

"I didn't know what to do. I ran for help."

"You did your best," Katrine said softly. His shoulders shook.

"M-my pa doesn't think so. Mr. Lundgren d-doesn't think so."

Katrine heard the dinner gong.

"It's time to eat," she said.

"You go ahead. My pa won't miss me anyway."

"You have to eat," Katrine insisted.

Jens pulled his knees up under his chin and stared out at the river.

"I'll bring you something," Katrine said, but she believed that Jens had not heard her.

Katrine raced to the dinner and ate quickly. Mama Olafson whispered for her to slow down. She forced herself to do so.

"Where's Jens?" Olga Andreasson addressed Katrine.

"He's sitting by the river. He didn't want to eat."

Olga's face quieted. "He should come and eat."

Gustaf had heard. "He'll come if he gets hungry enough."

"I can take him something," Katrine offered.

Gustaf shook his head and glared. "No, if he doesn't want to come and eat, he doesn't want to come. He sure won't get anything later. Maybe he'll learn some sense if he goes hungry."

Katrine swallowed. She did not acknowledge Mr. Andreasson but resumed eating. The entire dinner quieted. Finally, someone started asking about how everyone's stock had fared during the last storm. One person answered, and then the others joined in, talking about the weather, their animals, and how much hay remained. No one mentioned Jens.

Katrine quietly put some bread and potatoes into a cloth, rolled it, and hid it in her dress pocket.

When Katrine reached the river, Jens was gone. Icy fear swamped her. Frantically, she searched the riverbank and downstream. She saw no sign of him. She wondered if he had gone back to where Harald had died. Tingling numbness swept over her. She fought off thinking that Jens might have done something unspeakable.

Katrine started running wildly down the river. She wanted to call for help, but her lungs didn't allow it. She could hardly draw a breath. Her chest ached. Desperately, she searched downstream.

Nothing.

Dear God, it was happening all over again.

She came to the bend above the deep hole. Jens sat on a boulder staring out at the water.

Katrine began shaking with uncontrollable relief.

"I brought you some food," she said.

Jens nodded and took the bundle but didn't eat.

"Harald and I were friends. Only one time he made me mad," he said simply. "We did things together."

"Well, he's watching over you now," Katrine said. She had been doing a great deal of thinking about death and stumbled on. "Now he can only do things when you do them for him."

Jens eyed her. "You think so?"

"I think so. He wants to have fun, so you have to have fun for him."

Jens sat for a long while in silence. He began eating a piece of the bread. "Maybe you're right," he said. "At least when I do things, I'll think of him, and if he is watching me, he'll know that I'm thinking of him."

He wolfed down the remainder of the bread and began eating some of the boiled potatoes. "Thanks for the food," he said. "I'm glad you're still my friend."

A warmth flooded Katrine.

Chapter 38

IT WAS NO longer just talk that the Lundgrens would leave the valley. As the snow melted and spring approached, it became clear that they waited only for the trail to Boise City to open. Anna began teaching but did so at the Wikstroms' cabin instead of the Lundgrens'. Katrine was not surprised when Emma did not attend.

Katrine noticed that it was different when Anna tried to pick up where Mrs. Lundgren had left off. The boys' jokes and antics had abated. There were fewer giggles from the girls. An empty hole stood in Harald's place. Anna must have sensed this. She often had everyone start by singing a lively song, sometimes in Swedish. She picked the funniest stories from the readers for the boys to recite, encouraging them to use different voices and emotions. Often she took everyone outdoors to sit under the trees. They crowded under the Wikstroms' shed when it snowed and now when it rained.

Everyone tried to persuade the Lundgrens to stay. It was still unspoken, but Katrine believed everyone feared no one would ever come to join them in the valley. Their homesteads were too far from any town of size, and there was no road. Farming communities could not survive without a nearby town or wagon road. She thought that mining camps differed. People weren't expected to raise children in mining camps, at least not at first, but they were expected to raise children in farming communities.

The sole believer remained Nils Adolphson. "Any day now, a new family will arrive. You shall see."

Katrine continued to worry for Jens. She saw him infrequently. He missed school at the Wikstroms'. Barbro and Joran said he was helping Mr. Andreasson with work, but Katrine believed otherwise.

When Jens was at school, he would briefly greet her, but otherwise he remained quiet. Katrine knew he missed Harald and that he blamed himself. She realized Jens could just as easily have died. Maybe he was thinking it might have been better had he been the one who had died. She shook her head. That was a bad thought. Jens had done his best. People died. Mostly children died. It was the way that it was.

Katrine also closely watched to see if Jens still had bruises. She watched to see if he winced or limped when he walked. Finally, during one recess, she asked, "Is he still hitting you?"

Jens smiled weakly. "Sometimes, but now that the liquor is gone, things aren't so bad. He drank it all."

"Oh."

"He always tries to get some when he visits people, but I don't think they're giving him more than just one snaps." Jens spoke evenly, without emotion. "When he goes to Boise City though, that will change. He's been talking all winter about what he can sell. He won't let Ma use up all the turnips or beets. He wants to sell everything he can."

That explained another reason Jens went hungry. And knowing Jens, Katrine figured he was making sure Barbro and Joran got most of his food. They seemed fine to her. If anything, Jens was skinnier—even if he was shooting up in height.

"Pa's also been trapping all winter. That's why I missed school. We have to go miles in the snow every day to check for animals and then skin them. I've been hiding some of the furs I get. I want to buy things for Ma. If he doesn't know, maybe I can bring back some extra provisions. It will help until the crops come in."

At first, Katrine didn't know how to respond. Then, quietly she said, "I think that's a good thing to try to do, Jens. That's why I like you. You're a good person."

A pained look crossed Jens's eyes. "I like you too, Katrine, but we're too young. My pa would never let me leave the farm."

Katrine nodded. Jens had read more into her comment than she had intended.

Katrine and the others had gathered at the Adolphsons' place to say farewell to the men as they headed out to Boise City for spring trading and supplies. The Lundgrens had gathered as well. Everything they owned was packed onto their mules and horses. As the Eklunds had done, they left many of their belongings behind. They left their wagon and chickens for Sven. The river would be too high to even attempt taking a wagon back down to Boise City. But far worse than leaving their belongings, they left a grave in the valley.

"Where will you go?" Nils asked when they were prepared to head out.

Magnus shrugged his shoulders. "I will go to where I can build new memories and give Oscar a chance to grow up. This country is too uncaring." He glanced toward the timbered ridgeline. "I do not know for certain. I may go back to Minnesota. Maybe we shall stay in Boise City. Louise could teach there."

Katrine wanted to shout that she could teach here.

Nils shook his head. "Surely there can be some good from all of this. You and Louise and the children were like family to us."

Magnus nodded. "You have been good to us. You all have. It is this country. The snow. Few neighbors. No nearby town. We cannot live like this."

He pulled out, heading down the trail with young Oscar seated in front of him. Louise and Emma followed on other mules. The other fully packed mules and cows followed along. Their white dog, Sir, trotted after them.

Katrine watched as Papa Olafson headed down the trail as well with Mr. Wikstrom, Mr. Andreasson, and Lars. Only Mr. Adolphson remained behind—he and the older boys, Björn and Jens. They were taking as many goods as possible as well as Mr. Andreasson's furs for trading.

When Katrine realized Jens was not going, she knew that he would not be able to carry out his plans.

"It didn't work," he said, smiling weakly. "My pa needed me to stay. Now he will come back with whiskey."

Katrine should have known. Björn and Jens were expected to take care of the farms and remain vigilant while their fathers were gone. Katrine had the same duties while Papa Olafson was gone. What hurt the most was knowing that the Lundgrens would not be returning.

Katrine wondered how they could leave their oldest son buried on a hill to which they would never return.

As did everyone, Katrine eagerly awaited the return of the men, especially from the first trip of the year when they often brought back livestock. They always had something special for each family, which was delivered in person, and whenever Papa Olafson returned, he always had something special for Katrine and Mia and especially for two-year-old Torsten.

Katrine was disappointed. Papa Olafson did not bring back any livestock.

"I'll bring a shoat up next year. Every farmer coming into the country wants livestock. It is quite scarce. Besides, Trillium will have her calf in a few weeks. We need to make sure it survives."

Katrine knew there was always a chance Trillium's calf would be stillborn. It was the way of all things, but hearing Papa Olafson say it caused a chill. They had to have a calf. They needed milk, cream, and cheese.

At least they had chickens and eggs, and now with the Lundgrens' chickens, even more. They also had a nice garden. The apple trees were doing well, and Mama Olafson's Chinese chives were multiplying. Katrine acknowledged that their farm was not the best in the valley, but it fed them.

Then Sven brought out the special gifts—a new hairbrush and comb with a small mirror for both Katrine and Mia. Katrine's day brightened. He brought Torsten a nightshirt.

"Soon he will need shorts and shoes," he joked.

Going on three, Katrine doubted that Torsten minded. He was a talkative child, running about the cabin, getting into and under everything. Mia mostly watched him during the day because Katrine often helped Papa Olafson in the fields. However, whenever Katrine was in the cabin, Torsten seemed to seek her out, especially when Mama Olafson was busy preparing the meals.

"I was able to get these to replace some we've lost," Sven continued. He unwrapped some more apple trees. "And this." He picked out a smaller tree with waxy green leaves and handed it to Katrine. "This is for you, Katrine. It's a pear tree. It is doubtful it will ever bear fruit, but it should have pretty white flowers in the spring."

"For me?"

"You are the one who is my field hand. I just thought of you when the man showed me the trees."

Katrine hugged Papa Olafson. "Papa, this is so special. I will get some pears someday. You will see."

The last item Sven presented was a new teakettle that he had bought for Margret. She fussed over it and promptly filled it with water and set it on the stove.

During the noon meal, Sven again surprised Katrine. "We received a letter from the recorder at Warren's Camp."

Katrine took the letter, her hand shaking a little. The writing was neat and tight.

> *To Miss Katrine Larson, care of Sven Olafson, homestead near the big lake,*
>
> *I regret this letter has been some time in coming. I am recently elected recorder for Warren's Camp, and as we have had a very spirited filing of numerous mining interests, I have neglected to complete the research as you requested.*
>
> *A Mr. Stanly Jackson recorded on the sixteenth of September in the Year of Our Lord 1862 a quartz lode known as the Beloved Melissa in the then Washington Territory. That is of interest to us as 1862 was the discovery and location of Warren's Camp and the establishment of the towns of Washington and Richmond, the latter of which has since returned to the meadows from which it was hewn.*

Katrine's heart quickened.

Sven tapped his finger. "Then it is even stranger that Jackson would be coming over the ridge in this direction and not be going up the Little Salmon River."

"Maybe he was lost, Papa," Katrine said and then swallowed. "Maybe he died in the snowstorm just before we left Boise City." She realized if they had made it to the valley when they had planned, they may have heard his rifle shots for help.

Sven must have realized it as well. He shook his head. "It was the Lord's will, Katrine. We cannot reason why it was meant for us to arrive when we did."

Katrine resumed reading.

> *Unfortunately, the claim was not located in the general area of Warren's Camp but to the east of the South Fork of the Salmon River. I speculate that had Mr. Jackson survived, he may well have become the founder of a new mining camp. I currently know of no claims in that region. His claim is located, and I quote, "north of the black mountain at the north end of a narrow lake."*

Sven interrupted. "That explains it. He made a strike and went to Washington to file it. He returned to his claim to work it, and in coming out, he traveled this direction, thinking it was an easier trail to go to Fort Boise."

"You're right, Papa," Katrine agreed. It made sense that if Jackson was far to the east, he would not try to return to Warren's Camp.

> *The claim location description is recorded, and should you visit my office here in Washington, I shall make everything available to you.*
>
> *Because Mr. Jackson is deceased, his claim is considered to be re-locatable by others unless heirs to his property can affix such claim. He gave no other address than to indicate he was from Missouri.*
>
> *Thank you for apprising us of Mr. Jackson's death. If I should hear any information regarding his claim or of his heirs, I will notify you as appropriate.*
>
> *Sincerely,*
>
> *Mathew T. Watkins*
> *Recorder, Washington, Idaho County, Idaho Territory*

Katrine laid the letter down. "I wished we could have learned more about him. I don't think we can write a letter to every town in Missouri in order to find Melissa."

"It shall remain a mystery," Sven said. "We shall keep his gold awhile longer and pray Melissa will see one of our posts."

Chapter 39

KATRINE TURNED THIRTEEN. She went to the garden with Mia to pull weeds and to pick some green peas. It was always a good thing except when she had to pick worms and bugs. The chickens got some of the bugs, but they also scratched up the ground and the new seedlings or ate plants they should not be eating. Papa Olafson always said he needed a few ducks to balance things out.

The valley seemed strangely empty without the Lundgrens and Eklunds. Katrine thought about Harald. He was buried here, and his family had left. Katrine looked about herself. It was a beautiful place but an empty, beautiful place. If there were no people to see it, what did it matter? The people made it a home.

It came time for Trillium's calf to be born. Katrine and Mia were both standing by to observe. Sven helped reach in and pull the creature out. Katrine thought it looked like a half-drowned rat with a bag of blood and mucous. The calf started wriggling immediately, and Sven helped it to its feet. Joy flooded Katrine as the calf stood trembling, its big eyes trying to comprehend their first sight. A new life had arrived.

"Trillium has a calf," she exclaimed. "Think of that, Mia."

"What shall we name her?"

"Maybe we should check to see if it's a her or a him first," Sven said, laughing.

"Oh yes, maybe," Mia said.

"Well, I already know it's a her. That was the first thing I checked," Sven said. "Another cow is more valuable to us." He steadied the calf and led her to Trillium to start it nursing. It grabbed ahold immediately.

Katrine watched the wobbly-legged creature suckling. "She already knows how to do it," she said.

"Just like a human baby," Sven said. "That's good. Something special is in the first milk that the calf needs. If it doesn't get it right away, it never will, and it will die."

"Oh," Katrine murmured.

"What shall we name her?" Mia asked again.

"I named Trillium. You should name this one," Katrine said.

"Well, maybe we will name her Lupine. Mama likes the lupines."

Sven nodded. "By gum, Lupine she shall be." He gently pinched Mia's nose. "And if it were a bull calf, would you name it?" he asked.

"N-o-o. We would eat it when it grew up," Mia answered.

"Unless we decide to keep a bull for more cows."

"Will we?" Katrine asked.

Sven shook his head. "Maybe someday. We have to grow grain to get these animals through the winter. I'm afraid two cows, three mules, and a horse are about all I can feed at this time. But next season for sure we will get a pig to raise, especially if Trillium is good at making milk."

Katrine closed her eyes and imagined the hams and bacon and pork. "I hope she makes lots of milk."

"As long as you girls see she has plenty of good pasture and water, she should."

Already Katrine liked Lupine. It was a comfort having the animals. They were constant work, but they gave to the family. She closed her eyes, feeling thankful for finally having a milk cow.

A few days after the calf had begun nursing, Sven fixed a stanchion at one side of the pen with a feed bin on the other side that Trillium could stick her head through to reach while being milked. Margret milked Trillium the first few times and then said it was time for Katrine to try. Katrine had watched before at the Adolphsons' and even tried it, but this was their own cow.

"You have to show Trillium who is boss," Margret said. "Get down here underneath like so and shove your shoulder into her. She'll think you are Lupine wanting to nurse." Margret leaned into Trillium. "Now, you take two teats, one with each hand. Squeeze at the base with your thumb and finger and while clamping down, roll your fingers down, squeezing the milk out. Release and the teat will refill." Margret demonstrated, sending a stream of milk tinkling into the wooden bucket.

Katrine exchanged places with Mama Olafson. Trillium balked a little and tried to push away. Papa Olafson came up and showed her how to wedge Trillium's head between the rails when she reached to get grain. Katrine got set again. Then Lupine tried to get in to nurse as well.

"Get the calf out of here, and you'll have better luck," Sven said, laughing.

Mia wrestled with Lupine and led her away. Trillium didn't seem happy about that either and turned her head back toward Katrine, rolling her eyes.

"She'll get used to it," Margret explained. "She'll even start coming here every day so we can milk her."

Katrine shoved her shoulder against Trillium, into her coarse, hot hair. The cow shivered. Katrine inwardly cheered when she succeeded in getting a spray of milk to rattle into the bucket. She stripped a few times and then switched teats.

Katrine quickly realized that milking was not easy work, but she knew it was important work, and it made her feel responsible. And just as Mama Olafson had predicted, every morning Trillium came to the shed to be milked. Lupine continued to be a nuisance, and Katrine found it best to fence the calf out during the milking. She learned to leave enough milk for the calf. Even then, they now had plenty. It was not long until they began making butter. They acquired some rennin from the Adolphsons and started making cheese. Katrine found herself reflecting back to when she dreamed of having milk for cheese and butter. Now they had all they wanted. Come winter, Trillium would produce less milk, but Papa Olafson had explained that she should not go dry, especially if she had another calf in the future.

Just as Katrine had a new chore milking Trillium, there was increasingly more work on the farm. Papa Olafson split more rails to extend the fence around the ever-expanding garden, mostly for potatoes, which were becoming important for trading. He also extended his irrigation ditches that crossed above the garden and from which he drew water to run down small furrows into the garden. They now grew oats, rye, and barley, mostly for the livestock. They cut and stored more hay for the winter. The garden produced potatoes, turnips, onions, and cabbages, which they continued to pack to Boise City for trading. The rows of apple trees had lost their first season of blossoms and put up several inches of new growth. Katrine watched eagerly to see if any apples would form. Bees were scarce.

Midsummer's Eve approached. Katrine was especially excited because it was going to be at the Olafsons' this season. She and Mia and Mama Olafson had worked earnestly in the days leading up to the celebration. For days they had saved eggs and then boiled them up and peeled them. They boiled some new potatoes, pulled them free of their skins, added some diced wild onions and Chinese chives, and drenched them with thick cream.

"These will be the best boiled potatoes yet," Margret said as she finished the dish by sprinkling it with salt and pepper.

Lastly, Katrine and Mia picked strawberries and gathered nettles.

Sven cut a stout Midsummer pole. Katrine and Mia decorated it with pine boughs and flowers. Sven dug a deep hole, and when the other men arrived, they used a team of mules and ropes to pull it upright. Katrine thought it was the grandest Midsummer pole ever, especially with how the flowers dangled from its top and fluttered in the sunshine.

While people gathered and unpacked the children and food, Katrine momentarily forgot about the Lundgrens' absence. The Andreassons arrived, Jens, Barbro, and young Joran. The children unpacked the wagon. Jens started toward Katrine to greet her. Barbro and Joran attempted to unload a large basket of food; Joran slipped and dropped his end, and the basket spilled onto the ground.

Gustaf Andreasson cursed and yelled at Jens. "Pay attention. You should have been helping, not playing around."

Katrine backed away, feeling uncertain if she should stay to help or leave. Jens glanced around uncertainly and stooped to help his sister and brother.

"S-see you later," he called out.

The table was set. People gathered around the Midsummer pole, took hands, and began dancing and singing. There was no fiddle since Magnus was gone, but it failed to dampen their songs. It was true, Katrine told herself. It was the grandest Midsummer pole yet.

The meal was also one of the best. They had salmon, pork, and beef and lots of new potatoes. Katrine thought Mama Olafson's dish was the best of course, but each child claimed his or her mother's was the best.

They had the steamed nettles and rolls, and always the favorite were the first strawberries of the season with lots of cream and even some white sugar.

And then the brännvin flowed. People toasted their fortunes and their futures and each other. They sang the traditional drinking songs and told stories about Sweden.

Nils toasted the future. "We have had a few setbacks," he said. "We have lost some good neighbors, but we have good futures ahead of us. Now I shall share something.

"Lars and Anna. You have some news for us." He beckoned toward Lars.

Lars came up, blushing but radiant. Anna, dressed in her best calico dress and with flowers still in her hair from dancing about the pole, followed him.

"I hear that you have asked this young woman to be your wife. Is that true?"

Before Nils finished the comment, the others cheered and began chanting strands of a wedding song: Brudgum och bruden vilka i skruden.

Lars laughed. "Yes, sir," he said. "I have asked Anna to be my wife."

"Well, does that mean this is a wedding as well?"

Lars flashed a grin. "No, sir. We have some figuring to do and lots of planning. I want to get a nice cabin first and get some of my own crops growing, and I shall need your blessing of course."

Katrine knew that Mr. Adolphson knew all of this. Everyone knew it, but in the case of Lars and Anna, it was a formality. Everyone had known Lars and Anna would marry from even before they set foot in the valley. Now it was made public, and it gave reason for the community to celebrate. It gave reason for hope.

Amid more cheering and laughing, the children began chanting, "Midsummer's Eve is but a night, but it sets many a cradle to flight."

Nils interrupted, "That may be so, but just you make sure things are proper before you set any cradles to flight." Then he added, "We sure wouldn't mind if you didn't have us waiting another year."

Again there was laughing and cheering.

Nils raised his glass. "To Lars and Anna, *Skål.*"

Everyone, including the children with their sweetened mint tea, raised their glasses as well. "Skål."

"May God's blessings and all the good things of life come to you, and not that we are rushing things, we hope soon for a wee one as well."

"We aren't yet married," Lars protested. He blushed. Anna held onto him tightly, laughing. Katrine knew there was little chance of "hanky-panky," as Laurens had once said about his sister, but now it no longer mattered as much.

Although no one needed any additional reason, especially Gustaf Andreasson, more drinks were passed about, and the songs grew louder, although somewhat more slurred.

Perhaps with the loss of the Lundgrens, the remaining settlers needed to come together more closely. Katrine believed it to be so. They built a large bonfire near the creek where its light reflected from the water. The dancing and songs continued until the fire began to die. They gathered up the blankets they had brought with them and returned to near the cabin. There they gathered and told stories of trolls and elves to the youngsters yet awake. The older children huddled outside under the shed. Katrine stayed awake as long as she dared. She and Mia watched Torsten, who already slept. They pulled their blankets up around themselves and, with Torsten between, fell asleep against the hay.

Katrine woke sometime before daylight, dew soaking her blankets. It was not the cold dew that woke her but angry, slurred voices. One was Mr. Andreasson's, cursing. He had apparently found more to drink. The other voices were Mr. Adolphson's and Papa Olafson's. She listened as they escorted the yelling, swearing Andreasson away to where she could no longer hear his loud voice, only muffled and loud talking. The voices faded, and Katrine guessed Mr. Andreasson had passed out from too much to drink.

As it grew daylight, no one stirred for a long time. Katrine noticed that Björn and his sister, Linnea, and younger brother, Laurens, had slept near them.

Björn stirred and sat up. "Did you hear Mr. Andreasson yelling last night?"

"Yes."

"Did you hear what he said about Jens?"

Katrine grew numb. "No, is something wrong?"

"He called him a mistake. He said he was stupid and worthless."

A stabbing pain cut Katrine. Jens was anything but that. How could a father say such a thing?

"I hope Jens didn't hear. I wouldn't want my pa to say anything like that about me." Björn glanced to where Jens slept with Barbro and Joran.

The three seemed sound asleep.

Björn stretched. "Oh well, Mr. Andreasson probably won't remember a thing this morning." He stood and pulled on his trousers and shirt. "He got into Mr. Adolphson's whiskey."

"He did?" Katrine eyed Björn with some new interest. Björn seemed to have a knack for knowing things.

"You should have heard Mr. Adolphson cussing him out. I never heard such cuss words."

Katrine had not recognized some of the Swedish words, and now she knew why. She would have laughed had it not been so serious. "I can't say I recognized any of them," Katrine said with a smile.

Björn's face reddened.

As Katrine dressed, she noticed Lars's sister, Ingrid, and brother, Pelle, were also asleep nearby. She wondered where Anna and Lars were and then figured they were probably on the other side of the shed.

The dinner gong began ringing. Katrine needed no other invitation. She woke Mia and waited impatiently while she dressed. The women were hauling out huge platters of breakfast bacon, eggs, and biscuits and setting them on the makeshift table. There was little talk but lots of eating and plenty of coffee. That's when Katrine noticed Mr. and Mrs. Andreasson were absent. Papa Olafson had Jens to the side and was speaking quietly to him. Jens's look told Katrine everything.

Chapter 40

A WEEK AFTER Midsummer's Eve celebration, Katrine was with Mia in the garden. She caught sight of Jens on horseback in the timber.

She whispered to Mia, "I'm going to go pick some nettles to surprise Mama."

"But I'd like to come with you."

Exasperated, Katrine pointed toward the timber. "I can't explain now, Mia. Look."

"It's Jens," Mia exclaimed.

"I have to go and talk to him. You have to understand this is very important. I will tell you later, but you cannot let anyone know, so please agree. Keep Nisse here."

Mia nodded. She reached down and put her hands around the dog.

Katrine ran to Jens, reaching him, breathing hard. She did not have to ask any questions. She could tell he had more than a coat bundled behind his saddle. He also carried a pistol.

"Hello," he quietly greeted. "I'm glad you saw me."

Gingerly, he dismounted. Katrine could see his black eye. She knew what was going on.

"It's not good, is it?" Katrine said.

Jens began leading the horse farther out of sight to a sunny glen surrounded by newly greening aspens.

"I came to say goodbye," he said. "I'm leaving."

"I know." Katrine had known, and her heart was breaking.

"Don't tell anyone. He'll come looking for me." Jens winced.

"I'm sorry," Katrine said. "You're hurting."

He nodded. "It was pretty bad. I tried to get the bottle from him. He hit me hard."

They sat in the grass next to each other in the sun. They were secluded from the cabin in the distance. Katrine thought of the area's beauty, but at the moment she could not enjoy it. She felt hollow inside.

"Do you want to come with me?"

Katrine's heart beat strangely. "I-I can't."

"I know. I just wanted to ask. I'm going to have a hard time taking care of just myself anyway."

"Where are you going?"

"Up to the goldfields," Jens said. "I-I don't know where for sure. I've heard the miners talking about Florence and Elk City."

"You're fourteen."

"Well, I figure if I can find my own gold, no one will care how old I am."

Jens turned and looked deep into Katrine's eyes. She swallowed hard, and her heart began racing crazily.

"I love you, Katrine," he whispered. "But it would never work, you know, so I'm just saying goodbye."

Strange feelings flooded Katrine.

Jens stood and brushed the dirt from his trousers. "If I get rich, I might come back and give some money to my ma. Then she can take better care of Barbro and Joran. Don't tell her though in case I don't find any gold and in case I don't come back."

"Wait," Katrine said. She remembered Jackson's claim. "Don't go. I have something very important. Please don't go."

Jens stood, wavering. "Hurry then."

"I will." Katrine turned and ran to the cabin. She found a piece of ore from one of the pouches and raced back to Jens.

She handed it to him. "Take this. It was found by Mr. Jackson."

Jens seemed puzzled.

"That was the name of the dead man I found," Katrine said. "You remember the skeleton?"

Jens's eyes lit. "Yes, the skeleton." Jens examined the rock. He grinned. "You can see gold in it. Real gold."

"Yes," Katrine replied. "I got a letter from the recorder in Washington in Warren's Camp. Maybe you should go to Washington and ask to see Mr. Jackson's papers. They might tell where his claim was."

Jens brightened. "Maybe." He pocketed the piece of ore.

The ache returned. "Please take care of yourself, Jens," Katrine said.

"Oh, I will. I just wish you could come with me, but I know you can't," he said. "Besides, I know you like Björn, and that's all right. I wouldn't want you to wait for me just in case I do come back. I won't wait. Someday I'll meet a nice woman, and I'll get married. I'm just saying I wished it could have been you."

Darkness pressed inward on Katrine. She fought the ache spreading inside her.

Jens pulled himself onto his horse.

"Goodbye. I don't know if we'll ever see each other again."

Katrine felt the tears well within her eyes as Jens rode into the timber, heading north toward the gold camps. Jens was free now.

During Sunday meeting, Gustaf Andreasson at first tried to brush off the fact that Jens had left. "He's old enough to make his way. Like the prospectors we see going through this valley for the goldfields every day, just about. He just wants to see if he can get rich. He'll be back, he will."

A week later, Gustaf appeared more subdued. Olga Andreasson was found weeping. Barbro and Joran knew the truth.

"He never did a lick of good work," Gustaf said loudly. "He was always going off to sleep somewhere. He'll not be missed around here. I get just as much done now that he's gone." Gustaf piled more potatoes onto his plate.

Olga Andreasson got up and left the table, pushing at her eyes.

"You were hitting him, Papa," Barbro said.

"I disciplined him," Gustaf shouted. "He was disobedient." He looked around at the others seated nearby. Katrine looked away. No one spoke.

"Well, I have a duty to discipline my children, don't I?" he demanded more loudly.

Barbro whimpered. "He didn't do anything wrong, Papa."

Gustaf turned on his daughter, cursing. "How do you say such things in front of these people? You must honor me." He stood up, threateningly, clenching his fists.

Barbro sat quietly, not moving, not flinching. Young Joran, his eyes big, watched his father.

Sven and Nils moved toward Gustaf.

Gustaf frowned, and then his face relaxed. "Fine. So be it," he muttered. He sat down and took a bite of beef. "But I better never lay eyes on that boy again."

Katrine knew he never would. She suspected Barbro and Joran knew it as well. Their eyes were fixed on the ground.

Gustaf Andreasson suddenly pushed back from the table, stood, and walked away.

As far as Katrine knew, no one discussed the matter further, but it was clear that they had somehow come to an agreement to keep Mr. Andreasson away from any more brännvin.

Katrine wanted to talk about Jens, but she realized that she could never reveal what she knew. A deep hurt filled her. During dinner with her family once, she asked, "What do you suppose will become of him?"

Sven looked up. "I don't think what Mr. Andreasson did was proper. I would not behave in that manner if one of you became disobedient." He glanced toward Katrine and then Mia. "But then I do not believe that I shall ever have the trouble that Jens may have caused. We must allow Mr. Andreasson the right to raise his children the manner in which he sees best. We should not question him."

From how Papa Olafson said it and from the look on his face, Katrine knew differently. She wondered why he didn't say what he really believed.

After dinner, she wandered to her rock in the small meadow on the hill behind the cabin. She gazed toward the southern hill, still hoping she would see someone there but at the same time not believing it. *How can this be happening?* She knew the truth, despite what the adults told her. She thought of her own family. How terribly she missed them. To whom could she turn? Maybe adults had to say and do these kinds of things. If so, she was not sure she wanted to become one.

A few days later, Katrine accompanied Papa Olafson to the Adolphsons' with Trillium for breeding. She caught sight of the Indian pony on the hill behind the cabin, its red coat catching the sunlight. To her, the pony always seemed as if it wanted to run with the wind. Lars said it wasn't much good for riding yet, but he was packing with him. Katrine enjoyed watching the animal, somehow feeling a little freer, strangely thinking of Jens.

As if the pony knew that Katrine was watching, it shook its head and trotted off, disappearing into the aspens.

Katrine noticed that the Andreassons had come down the trail with their wagon fully packed.

Gustaf drew up and apologized to Nils and Sven.

"You don't have to leave," Nils said. "You can live through this."

"We can help," Sven added.

Gustaf shook his head. "It's wrong to expect help. For Olga's sake and my children's, I need to start anew. Maybe I'll stay in Boise Valley or go up to Garden Valley. They grow good crops there."

273

"We grow good crops here," Sven said. His lips tightened.

"My mind's made up," Gustaf replied. "If Jens comes through, tell him I never meant anything bad. It was the liquor. I've sworn off it. Never again." He took a breath. "Tell him he's welcome to have the homestead. Maybe when he's of age, he can find a good woman to marry and start a new life."

Astrid Adolphson came to the door. "Take these." She handed up a large bundle to Olga. Olga hardly acknowledged her. Astrid touched her hand. "Remember, the good Lord has a way of healing all things."

Katrine saw Mrs. Andreasson begin shaking, but still she said nothing. Mrs. Adolphson turned and disappeared back into the cabin.

Lars reached up to Gustaf. "I don't have much to offer, Mr. Andreasson, but you send word if I can help."

"I reckon you've all done enough. It was me that was wrong," Gustaf said. He glanced around again, settling on Nils and Sven. Never once did he glance in Katrine's direction.

He clucked to his mule team, and the wagon jerked into the ruts. Barbro and Joran rode behind on separate mules and led the livestock, two cows and a hog. They whispered goodbye to Katrine as they passed.

"I'll see you someday," she whispered back. "God's blessings."

Their gray-spotted dog, Rainy, followed.

Katrine wondered how Mr. Andreasson would get the wagon down the canyon, but she knew he was stubborn enough to figure a way.

"Probably float it," Sven told her later. "The trail is turning into a road now, and there are only a few places he'll need to ford the river."

Chapter 41

KATRINE WANDERED TO her rock in the clearing and sat, pulling her legs up under herself, smoothing her dress. The late summer flowers were blooming—the goldenrod, the pale lavender asters, and the deep purple larkspur. Some of Mama Olafson's lupine still bloomed. Papa Olafson was preparing to plant the winter rye. She had already helped him bring in the hay. Trillium would again calve in the spring. The seasons were turning. Soon another autumn and winter would be upon them.

She gazed upon the stark, empty beauty surrounding her. Three families remained in the valley, and no new ones had come. How would they survive another season? She didn't like being so alone. They weren't a community. They were survivors.

She shivered, thinking of the passing seasons. Anna and Lars would marry, come next summer. She no longer wondered whom she might marry. Unless someone new came, only Björn remained for her. That was if he was not interested in Ingrid Adolphson. Katrine felt a stab. She could not shake what Jens had said. It had sparked something deep inside her—something she didn't know was there until now. She was too young to be married, but she wanted to be—to someone who wouldn't go away. If something happened to Björn, there would be no one for her. She shook with the dreadful realization.

She thought about Björn. He was the boy most of them had always kidded her about marrying. She had always thought of him as she thought of her brother. At first, it had been a game among the young girls. Whom would they marry when they became of age? And the women would whisper who might make a good husband, planting ideas in the young girls' heads. The men more boldly would say, "Björn, that Larson girl, why she'd make a fine wife for you someday. You should be courting her for sure."

Those were the days when hope had glowed brightly—when they believed Adolphson's dream—that they would settle this part of Idaho

Territory and bring some of Sweden with them. Now the game had dimmed. As the families had dwindled, so had the girls' hopes. Katrine knew that a young man could go east and find a bride; a young woman could not.

At dinner, she could not hold back on all her thoughts.

"No one's ever going to come to the valley, are they?"

Sven arched his eyes. "Mr. Adolphson certainly believes people will. Perhaps this coming spring. Even I have seen more men coming through. It seems to be only a matter of time before some of them are farmers with families to raise."

"If not, Anna and Lars will begin a family," said Margret, smiling.

Katrine sighed. Even if Anna and Lars had a baby, it would be two more seasons until they were a family.

On Saturday, Katrine and Mia headed toward the Wikstroms' to visit with Anna and Linnea and to go swimming. The trail was well marked now but still nothing more than a footpath. Usually the girls had the hot springs to themselves before the men finished working in the fields.

Frieda greeted them with baby Jon in her arms. Anna and Linnea and Laurens gathered about, excited for their visit. Frieda set Jon down where he promptly scuttled toward Katrine. Now nine months old, he was close to walking. He reached for Katrine. "Ma ma ma."

"Not Mama. Aunt Katrine," Katrine corrected him. She picked him up, swinging him around, thinking as all girls did that someday she would have children as well.

She handed him to Mia, who was just as anxious to hold the baby.

Frieda served up some boiled potatoes with butter. "You just have someting to eat before you go to der hot springs."

Katrine thanked Frieda for the potatoes.

As always, Frieda cautioned them, "You watch for Indians. Maybe wait for Björn to go with."

When Björn was not in the fields working, he often accompanied the girls, but since turning thirteen over a year ago, he used the lower pool. Now that Katrine had grown older as well, she appreciated his modesty. Björn frequently brought the pistol and laid it nearby while he sat and watched—not so much because of possible bears or mountain lions but when there was reason to be more cautious, for example after a mining party had gone through and seemed to have more interest in the settlers than in their own business. Sometimes Björn walked to the top of the trail and sat and whittled on one of his carvings while waiting for the girls.

Once Katrine had caught Björn looking her direction before he quickly turned away. That's when Anna teased that her younger brother might make her a good husband. Katrine found herself thinking the same. Jens was gone. Harald had died. She was glad Ingrid did not live as close, but then she had realized that Björn saw Ingrid almost every Sunday as well. A knot tightened in her stomach.

They reached the hot springs and climbed to the upper pool. Although they were but a quarter of a mile away, Katrine found herself checking the surrounding trees and rocks, thinking of Jackson, for some reason, and of dead spirits. She shivered.

They had only splashed about for a short time before Katrine heard the clatter of hooves and riders coming down the trail. Frantically, she gestured toward the others. The girls ducked down, but Laurens, now seven, continued noisily splashing water over his shoulders.

"Shh." Anna grabbed him and squeezed him to the side of the pool. Katrine lowered herself farther, although anyone below could not easily see them.

Katrine's heart hammered. From the voices and sounds of hooves, she knew they weren't Indians. She guessed they were prospectors. Probably there would be no harm if they did notice the girls, but Katrine had learned to not take chances. Usually when the travelers spotted the cabin, they continued toward it, hoping to get a good meal.

Two men, ragged, riding trail-worn horses, lightly packed, came into view, staring in their direction. Katrine held her breath, watching. She pulled Linnea and Mia farther down into the water.

The younger of the two men appeared slender, wore a ragged hat and vest, and had scraggly, dark, short whiskers and hair. The older man was dressed similarly but had graying whiskers and hair. A queasy feeling surged through Katrine.

"Might be the place what I'm looking for," the younger man spoke. "That man was a farmer. Ain't many farmers near that ferry on the Salmon. None that are Swedes anyways."

"Doubt it's him," the older man said, coughing. He had a hawk-like nose and beady eyes that darted about. "That woman's long gone."

The two men passed below the springs, headed in the direction of the cabin. Katrine's bad feeling grew. They were not like the men who were flooding into the mining camps, many who looked shabby but were eager and had purpose in their eyes. These two rode stealthily, uneasily. The hawk-nosed man's eyes swept upward again. Katrine wasn't sure how he did not spot her.

"They frighten me," she whispered to Anna. She caught a strange look in Anna's eyes.

"We have to go," Anna said abruptly. She climbed from the pool and began dressing. "Laurens, go quick and find Papa and Björn."

Eyes big, Laurens stared back. "Are they going to hurt us?" He began dressing.

"Probably not. Just go and find Papa. Tell him about the men coming, but don't let them see you. Can you do that?"

Laurens nodded. "They won't see me." He pulled his suspenders into place, scrambled down from the hot springs, and headed through the timber toward the fields.

Anna addressed the girls, "Now, when we get near the cabin, we need to talk loudly. Let them know we are coming."

Katrine wondered why—wondered what Anna was thinking.

They headed down the trail. Katrine's heart pounded in her throat. When they came into view of the cabin, Katrine noticed the men's two horses just beyond it. The men stood outside with Frieda, who appeared distressed. Baby Jon was not with her. Katrine guessed he was inside in his cradle.

Anna abruptly halted and ducked down, whispering, "Linnea, you go around to their horses but stay out of sight."

"Why?"

"If I say to do so, I want you to spook their horses and make them run."

"I can spook their horses," Katrine whispered.

"No, I want you and Mia with me."

Linnea disappeared into the timber, taking a path behind the men. Mia hung back, behind Anna and Katrine.

"Come now, let's go," Anna said. She stood and continued out into the open, walking swiftly. Katrine hesitated before following, her throat parched dry.

"That was a good swim, don't you think?" Anna said loudly.

"Yes, it was," replied Katrine, feeling her comment was contrived and surprised she could talk.

"Papa should be right along. Supper is almost ready."

The two men spun in their direction. A wash of panic crossed Frieda's face. She waved for them to go back and then covered her eyes.

"Well, well," the younger man said. "Lookie what we got here." He pushed at his ragged hat.

The hawk-nosed man drew a pistol. "I got 'em, Cleatus."

Katrine froze. His glittery eyes settled on her and then swept to Anna.

"Relax, Hobarth, it's just kids."

Hobarth eased his pistol back, but his eyes remained fixed in Katrine's direction.

Katrine felt Mia trembling as they grew near. She hoped Mia did not feel her own shaking. Frieda appeared frantic.

"Mama, what is the matter?" Anna cried out.

"Now you girls don't get your petticoats in an uproar. It's all a misunderstanding. This here's my wife. I just come to fetch her home," Cleatus said, grinning.

A queer nausea swept over Katrine.

"She's not your wife," Anna countered. "She's married to my papa. They got married last spring."

Cleatus began laughing. "Well your papa's a bit late." He turned to his companion. "Ain't that right, Hobarth?"

Hobarth nodded. "They was just waiting for the judge to make it official when Frieda up and left. Way I understand it, she ran away with a hurdy-gurdy troop."

Cleatus shot him a look. "Didn't need a judge, Hobarth. We was already hitched. That was just a legal thing. Twern't that right, Frieda, lovely?"

Frieda stood, her eyes down, shaking.

He grabbed her chin. "Ain't that right?" he snarled.

Frieda nodded, trembling. Tears filled her eyes. Katrine could see she feared the man. Maybe she did run away, but if she had, Katrine realized that she had to, just as Jens had needed to.

Cleatus turned toward Katrine. "Now, young miss, if you don't want to see *your mama* hurt, you go fetch me a riding mule. My wife's coming with me."

Katrine began to protest that Frieda wasn't her mother, that she wasn't anyone's mother except Jon's. She suddenly worried about the boy, wondering where he was.

The look in the man's eyes told Katrine that he was deadly serious. She headed toward the corral where the riding mule was kept. She grabbed the saddle from the fence and, struggling, wrestled it onto the mule's back.

Anna was near hysterics. "You can't take my mama."

Hobarth laughed crazily. "*Your* mama? Judging your age, missy, she sure ain't your mama. She might be mama to another bastard here abouts but not to you."

Cleatus turned toward Anna and grinned. "Maybe you're right. Maybe I won't take your mama. Instead, I'll just take you. That might be a nice trade." He eyed Hobarth. "Hell, maybe we'll just take your mama and you. Where's your pa, anyhows?"

Anna was silent. Katrine also knew not to say anything.

"Won't say, huh? Bet he's out hunting. Won't be back for a few hours at best, right? If that's so, maybe we won't need to take you with us. Just borrow you a minute." Cleatus leered. "You wanna do that, Hobarth? I have my missus for later."

A horror filled Katrine as she began to understand their intent.

"He's coming soon," Anna said, desperation filling her voice.

"I don't think so," Cleatus said. He grabbed Frieda, wrenching her arm. "He's out hunting, ain't he? If he is, we got some time to visit, don't we? We can get to know your daughters real well."

"H-he's in the fields," Frieda cried out. "Don't hurt my girls."

Cleatus pushed her away. "Then you come along peaceful like. The girls will tell their pa that I came back for you and that you went along like a dutiful wife. Won't you, girls?"

He turned toward Hobarth. "Maybe we best get moving in case he's on his way. Hate to have to put a bullet in him. You can get yourself a woman in Boise City."

Hobarth frowned, his beady eyes remained fixed on Anna. "Tain't that a shame. I was sort of liking the looks of you, missy."

"You coming, Frieda, or do I have to hogtie you?" Cleatus headed toward Frieda.

Frieda rubbed her arm where it had been wrenched, nodding. "I vill come, Cleatus. Don't hurt my girls."

Hearing Frieda speak the man's name rocked Katrine. Unspeakable thoughts stampeded through her. She could now hear Jon crying as she led the mule forward. She dropped the reins and stepped toward Cleatus.

"You can't take her!" Katrine shouted. "She and Mr. Wikstrom have a baby."

Cleatus spun toward her and burst out laughing, "A new bastard, huh?" He shoved Frieda. "You went and laid with a man not your husband?" He shoved harder. "You sinning wench."

A blinding red overtook Katrine. She started for Cleatus, pummeling him. "You leave her alone," she cried out, pounding blindly with her fists. The man shoved her hard. She went down into the dirt and gravel, feeling a sharp pain.

Cleatus backed away and grabbed up his horse.

"You take the older girl then, Hobarth. It'll be a fair trade. My wife's been ruint anyhows." He reached for the riding mule that Katrine had saddled. "Throw her up here."

Hobarth grabbed Anna, but Anna immediately started swinging and jabbing. Katrine pulled back on Anna to keep her from being thrown into the saddle. Mia came into the fracas swinging a stick. Out of nowhere, Linnea showed up, kicking and gouging and sending up a ruckus.

Cleatus's icy voice cut through the melee. "You girls don't cooperate, your mama's going to be dead."

Cleatus held a knife at Frieda's throat.

"Stop, stop," Frieda cried out. She pushed Cleatus's arm away. "It's okay. I'll go with you, Cleatus. Leave Anna alone. Leave the children alone. I'll go with you."

"That's more like it." Cleatus pushed her away. "But I ain't taking no bastard kid with us."

"I-I can take care of Jon," Anna cried. "He'll be fine, Mama." She trembled.

Katrine stared in disbelief as Frieda mounted the mule and turned away toward the trail with the two men. Linnea came toward her, tears streaming down her cheeks. Mia held her tightly. Anna sat in the dirt, shaking.

Cleatus and Hobarth headed down the trail with Frieda and then cut off it toward the timber.

A sudden explosion rocked the stillness, followed by yelling from Anton and Björn. The horses bucked, and the two men grabbed to hold on. Frieda's mule began jumping and running, turning back toward the cabin. Frieda frantically held onto its neck. Cleatus and Hobarth turned back, trying to settle their rifles to return fire. A pistol shot split the air. They ducked.

Katrine spun and caught sight of Mr. Wikstrom raising his rifle again and aiming at the now running men. Björn stood next to him with a pistol held with both hands, steadying another shot. They both fired. A clipped tree limb fell about the head and shoulders of Cleatus. He frantically clawed it away and spurred his horse harder. Frieda came galloping back into the yard and fell from the saddle. The mule continued running.

In moments, Frieda was in Anton's arms. Broken phrases of Swedish and German tumbled between them. Björn came running and shouting, pistol waving. A strange feeling flooded Katrine. Björn appeared intensely serious, not a boy any longer. He paused when he reached her and fired a final shot after the fleeing men.

Young Laurens, out of breath, trudging along, caught up to him. He sank down to his knees, panting.

"What happened?" he implored.

For a moment, it seemed all was well. Anton took Frieda, stumbling, under his arms, into the cabin. Crying and soft talking ensued. That soon ended, and words Katrine had seldom heard came pouring out. Unintelligible pleading in German tumbled after. Anton's voice rose shrilly, threateningly, cursing. The children cowered in the yard.

"We should not listen," Anna said, crying. She held Björn and Linnea. Katrine held onto Mia. Laurens wandered aimlessly about and then went to the door. "Don't, Papa," he said in a scared voice. Anton thundered after him, sending him back with new cursing.

"It's not good," he whispered and sat next to Katrine, shaking.

After what seemed ages, the yelling diminished and then finally ceased. Frieda continued sobbing. Anton came into the yard and, spotting Katrine and Mia, turned on them. "What are you gawking at? You should not be here. Leave."

Katrine's world shattered. She scrambled to her feet, and grabbing Mia's hand, she turned and stumbled up the trail toward the hot springs. A terrible clawing being had erupted inside her. Dear God, what was happening? Björn's voice calling after her soon dimmed.

She ran, practically dragging Mia until Mia stumbled, panting. "I-I can't run anymore, Katrine," she sobbed.

Katrine sat hard. They were near the ridgeline above the hot springs and no longer in sight of the cabin.

The two girls gasped for air. "What did we do wrong?" Mia sobbed. "Why do they hate us?"

Katrine remained stunned at the events. She knew more than Mia about the ways of the world, but this confounded her. "I think that Mr. Wikstrom is just so upset that he doesn't understand anymore," Katrine whispered. "Come, let's go home. I think in a while he won't hate us anymore."

Shakily, Mia got to her feet, brushed off her dress, and followed behind Katrine.

Katrine grew more fearful with each step she took that brought her up and across the ridge. Cleatus and Hobarth could be anywhere. She had seen how they had grabbed for Anna. She had seen the looks in their eyes. She desperately tried to hide her fear from Mia, but she trembled as she walked.

Chapter 42

THE MOMENT KATRINE and Mia entered the cabin, they burst into tears. Margret immediately put down her dishes and wiped her hands. Katrine tried to explain. She did not want to tell about Mr. Wikstrom sending them home. Torsten watched with wide eyes. Margret reached out and took the two girls into her arms.

"There, there. The morning has a way of soothing our troubles. I should not think things are all that bad. You shall see. This is a grownup thing anyway, it is. Poor Mr. Wikstrom probably thought he was losing his wife again. After all, it is not that long past that he lost his poor Emma."

That seemed to explain things a little for Katrine. She knew if she were Mr. Wikstrom, she would not want to lose another wife or mother for his children.

The following Sunday meeting seemed strangely empty with only the Olafsons and Adolphsons. There was plenty of discussion among Nils, Sven, and Lars concerning Anton. They began speculating that he might leave the valley. A clammy ache filled Katrine. If he did, that would be the end of things.

"Well, someone should go pay him a visit," Sven said, "or soon, we'll be down to just the two of us."

"It should be you, Sven," Nils said. "You're good friends and so are your children. Maybe he'd listen."

"In time," Sven replied. "He ran the girls off."

"He was embarrassed."

"As anyone of us would be. Think about it. Having some scum of the earth show up and claim your wife is really his." Sven shook his head.

A couple of weeks passed, and still the Wikstroms had not come to Sunday meeting. Katrine worried. She especially thought about Anna and Lars. What about their pending marriage now? Would the Wikstroms really leave?

Eventually Sven said it was time to visit the Wikstroms. "Mr. Adolphson already visited. He said we should or that we would likely be facing winter with just two families."

When they arrived, Katrine decided Mr. Wikstrom and Frieda seemed themselves. They were friendly, and Frieda fixed a nice dinner. Mama Olafson busily helped. Papa Olafson and Mr. Wikstrom talked alone, out by the garden. During dinner, everyone was quieter than usual, but otherwise Katrine detected nothing different.

The following week, however, the Wikstroms again missed Sunday meeting.

"This is no good," Nils said. "We need everyone we have in order to survive here."

"We will reach through to him, we will," Sven said. "We just keep trying."

Katrine worked in the garden. Cabbages just now began to form heads. Each day, she and Mia picked the squiggly green cabbageworms. Each time they finished a row, they were surprised to find more. The chickens did well getting most of the insects but not all the worms. They also had to be supervised because they ate everything else as well.

It was a comfort to see things growing. The beets and turnips pushed partially up from the soil, rosy and plump. Potato plants were large mounds of beautiful, velvet-green leaves. Onions grew luxuriantly, their green tubular leaves bent like spears in the wind. They should do well trading this fall.

Katrine was surprised when Nisse went running past her and toward the trail behind the cabin, barking his visitors-are-coming bark. Then she heard Björn's voice. The Wikstrom children were coming down the ridge by their cabin.

Katrine's heart leaped, and she ran and hugged Anna and Linnea. She greeted Björn and Laurens. She wanted to hug Björn but hesitated. He smiled and arched his eyes. They were soon all lost in play. Katrine feared asking about Frieda or if Mr. Wikstrom was still angry. They took turns using the badstuga. Björn heated rocks and placed them on the hearth so the girls could splash water onto them for steam. The girls visited.

"It's not as good as your hot springs," Katrine admitted.

"I like it just fine," Anna said. "Besides, we had to come. We miss you." She explained that Frieda took care of them as before, especially young Jon. Her father did not talk much to Frieda, but Frieda still made his meals and mended his clothes. Anna admitted she did not know if they shared a bed any longer. If they did, it was, as she explained, only because it was the wife's duty and a man needed a woman. "At least Papa doesn't shout at Frieda. They just don't talk.

"It's after Papa leaves with Björn in the mornings to go to the fields that we talk with Frieda. She says not to worry, that life will go on just as it had before Cleatus and Hobarth showed up. But I know it's not true. She's sad. Frieda's sad."

The girls finished their baths. Björn and Laurens took their turn. Anna began helping Linnea braid her hair, and Katrine helped Mia.

"We do all the things we used to. We're tending the garden, and Björn and Papa are bringing in the hay and oats. We've even gone with Frieda and picked raspberries and mint leaves for tea together, but she's no longer telling stories like she used to. What can we do?" Anna asked.

Björn and Laurens had quietly joined them, listening.

Katrine was at a loss. "I think things will get better, I do," she whispered, but she had no reason for saying so. A dull disquiet filled her chest.

They talked and played a while longer, throwing a stick for Nisse. The boys chased minnows through the water. The girls talked about who would be Saint Lucia. They agreed it should be Linnea. She was next oldest. Katrine was sorry to see them head back home so early. Nisse followed for a distance until Katrine called him back.

At last, Sven and Margret rode alone to visit Frieda and Anton, leaving Katrine and Mia behind with Torsten. They returned late that afternoon. Katrine ached to know what the visit was like, but she was careful not to ask. She overheard Papa Olafson that night:

"She made a mistake, but that is all. I think Wikstrom has too much stubborn Norwegian in him. That's what I think."

The harvest was completed. The men took the crops to Boise City and returned with supplies.

School resumed. The children met at the old Lundgren place as they had done before. It made Katrine uneasy, thinking about Harald's grave on the hill.

Anton expressed his concern as well. "If Cleatus and Hobarth ever show up again, Anna would be too far from help."

Björn tried to joke about it. "The way Anna and Linnea were hitting those men, Pa, I think they're going to think twice about coming back."

Ever so slightly, a smile crossed Anton's face.

"Anna and Linnea were dead-set against them taking their mama," Björn continued.

Anton smiled more broadly. "Their mama? That was what they were hollering, wasn't it? Their mama."

Katrine and Mia rode Boots to school when able, just as they had done before. Lars arrived early each day with Ingrid and Pelle and built up a fire so that the cabin had warmed. Björn brought in his mule team and wagon with Anna, Linnea, and Laurens. Frequently, all seven children attended. Lars had completed school but now helped more with bringing his brother and sister and with helping Anna. With the Cleatus and Hobarth scare, he also kept a rifle at hand, but everyone knew the real reason he was helping was to keep near Anna.

Rarely anyone gave Anna trouble while she taught. There were the normal roughhousing, games of tag, bumps and scrapes, but during lessons, they paid attention. Katrine thought that maybe deep down each of them knew their futures were uncertain. None wanted to be the reason another family might leave.

School rarely lasted for more than four hours, and it met at most three times a week. They recited their lessons and read passages. Lars helped with arithmetic from the arithmetic book. They followed the same pattern that Louise Lundgren had established. After class, each student knew his or her assignment for the next day or week.

When the weather prevented attending, they studied on their own. The oldest girl in each household ensured her siblings had completed their lessons before next class. It became a matter of pride to see who could outdo the other.

Even so, Katrine felt empty. "It's just not the same without Mrs. Lundgren and Harald and Emma. Mrs. Lundgren knew so much about the rest of the world."

Mia did not reply.

"She could tell us about the places and people in our readers that Anna can't. And it's not as fun without Jens and Barbro and Joran."

Mia frowned. "I don't like it either. Maybe some new people will come."

It was in the early morning of a crisp October day when Katrine's time came. Mama Olafson was busy sewing when Katrine shared her news.

"I just cannot think of you as not being a little girl, Katrine." Margret shook her head and smiled. "Let me have your dress." Deftly, she let out the hem and tried the length against Katrine. It came to her ankles. "That should be fine," Margret said, singing a little song to herself as she worked.

Shortly, Margret held up Katrine's dress. "There, you now have a proper young woman's dress."

A warm glow filled Katrine. The day Katrine had waited for since understanding such things had arrived. She stood in near disbelief, admiring her longer dress. How long would it be until Papa Olafson noticed? Would he say anything?

After talking to Mama Olafson for a long while, she went and sat in her private glen thinking about it. What had happened to Frieda and what she had learned now had different meaning. She thought of Ingrid, her own age, and whether or not her time had come. Something told her otherwise. Ingrid seemed smaller than she was. What she really thought differently about were the boys. She could not help her thoughts—what it implied. She understood why they had started using the lower hot springs. She swallowed hard. Harald had died. Jens was gone. Only Björn remained. If he and she chose, they were capable of starting a new life together. The thought thrilled and frightened her.

She gazed across the valley, now dappled with autumn orange and yellow, thinking back on things when she used to be a little girl. How strange it now seemed. Things were different now. They would always be different now. She envied Mia a little.

Then she thought of herself as a mother. She saw herself holding a small child. It would be a few years yet, but how exciting it now was—and how terribly scary.

Chapter 43

KATRINE FLUNG GRAIN to the chickens and peered to the south as she frequently did. It was late autumn, almost winter. The tamarack and aspens stood naked against a gray sky. Only a few stubborn leaves clung to the willows and rosebushes. The cattails and grasses had long ago bleached in the sun. Several storms had moved through. The last had brought snow, but it melted except for on the surrounding peaks.

Mia came running up while Katrine fed the chickens. "It's a fine day," she said, sweeping her hands. "Maybe Papa and Mr. Wikstrom will get an elk." Nisse bounced around them, barking, probably thinking something special was going on.

"I feel like they already have one. Now they are trying to get two." Katrine tossed grain to the side where one of the gray and black chickens scratched around. She didn't know why she sensed they had an elk. Papa Olafson and Mr. Wikstrom had left two days ago and would be gone for several days. Katrine wasn't concerned with Papa Olafson being gone. They could protect themselves.

A movement in the trees caught Katrine's attention. She squinted hard. An icy chill rushed over her. It took just a moment before she realized whom she was seeing. *Cleatus!* He led a saddled mule behind his horse.

Frantic, Katrine pointed the man out to Mia.

"We have to tell Mama." She raced for the cabin with Mia close behind. Nisse chased after them.

"That man's come back, Mama. The one who tried to hurt Mama Frieda and Anna. He's sneaking through the timber."

Margret's face paled.

"What can we do?" Mia's brows were pinched.

"We have to warn Frieda," Margret said evenly.

"Should I run to the Adolphsons'?" Mia asked.

"I'll go," Margret said. "I can take the mule and get there faster. Torsten is old enough to hang on."

She began grabbing things, pulling a shirt over Torsten.

"You girls might be able to warn the Wikstroms if you go over the ridge. That man won't chance coming past us and will have to go the long way around."

Katrine understood. It was about five miles around the ridge and only two going over it. She and Mia had become so accustomed to walking over the ridge, it was almost as fast as riding around it—unless the rider cut up and over the ridge, but it was unlikely Cleatus would know that.

"I'll just have to stay out of sight awhile so he doesn't look around and spot me," Margret said. "Mia, see if you can see the direction he goes, but don't let him see you. He won't be traveling fast because he doesn't want to be seen. He doesn't know Papa isn't working in the fields, so he'll be trying to stay out of sight of the fields."

Margret quickly bundled Torsten into his coat and scarf. "Katrine, you saddle the mule for me."

"What do we do with Nisse?"

"Just close the door and make sure he's inside." Margret grabbed her own coat and scarf.

Katrine shook as she brought up the mule. She helped Mama Olafson mount and hoisted up Torsten. "Be careful, Mama."

Torsten seemed to think it was a great time. "We're riding," he kept saying, clapping his hands.

Shortly, Mia returned. "I didn't see him."

"That tells me he's not coming this direction, and for certain, we know where he's heading," Margret said. "You girls go and go fast. Run as much as you can."

Margret looked to the sky. "Herre Gud, Lord God, keep everyone safe." With Torsten in her lap, she turned the mule downstream and crossed the creek heading toward the timber in a direction that would keep her hidden.

Realizing they were on their own, that this was really happening, Katrine felt her world closing in. She checked that Nisse was safe. "We have to go, Mia." She began running up the trail.

She had only run a few yards before she realized she would wear out, especially running uphill. Mia already gasped for air. It reminded her of the last time they left the Wikstroms'. Dread filled her.

"Come, Mia, hurry," she said. "Walk fast." Lungs aching, she trudged onward.

Whenever taking the trail, she always worried about bears or mountain lions, but now the danger didn't matter. They had to warn Frieda.

Sweat stinging her eyes, chest heaving, Katrine reached the ridge and the burn scar. She bent over, gasping until her breathing slowed. Mia bent over with her. Katrine scanned the hill for signs of any bears. She saw nothing.

"Let's go," Katrine said. She began running again, not fast but steady. Mia kept up, but Katrine could hear her labored breathing.

"Walk now." She slowed and began walking. Her chest heaved for air.

The dense timber on the north side crept into view. Finally, they slipped down into the timber and neared the hot springs. Katrine heard Björn and Laurens talking. She didn't hesitate but called to them, hissing loudly, "That man's coming to get Mama Frieda."

She stopped at the edge, panting hard, chest aching, knowing the man could already be at the cabin, that they could already be too late.

Björn grabbed his clothes. "What are you talking about?" he demanded.

"Th-that man," Katrine gasped. "Cleatus. The one who tried to take Mama Frieda and Anna is on his way to your cabin. He's leading a mule with a saddle. He's after Mama Frieda. My mama went for help to the Adolphsons'."

Björn finished pulling up his trousers and slipped his suspenders over his bare chest. He didn't wait for Laurens but grabbed the pistol and checked the load.

"I'm hiking back and waylaying the bastard," Björn said stonily. "You warn Mama Frieda. Anna's not there, thank the Lord. She's visiting Lars. Tell Mama Frieda to take Jon and hide."

"Hide where?" Katrine asked, still gasping, stumbling after Björn.

"Up here above the hot springs. He can't climb a horse up here." Björn took a few running steps down the trail and then paused.

"Look, if you hear shooting, it's me. Don't come out after the shooting unless you hear another single shot. I'll wait awhile until everything is clear and then signal."

Katrine's heart pounded madly, catching the meaning of Björn's words. He intended to kill the man. Cold fear enveloped her.

Laurens caught up to them, carrying his shirt.

291

"Laurens, you help Katrine," Björn directed.

"Be careful, Björn," Laurens called after his brother. "Please be careful."

Katrine trembled as she watched Björn cross the creek and angle through the timber in the direction from which Cleatus would likely come.

They ran down the trail to the cabin and banged inside, startling Frieda and Linnea and baby Jon.

"You have to hide, Mama," Laurens cried. "That bad man's coming back."

Frieda appeared stunned. Linnea grabbed her. Slowly, Frieda straightened. "Where's Björn?"

"He went after him," Katrine said.

"Mein Gott," Frieda said. She whispered, "It isn't worth it." She stood, unmoving. "I don't want to hide. Jon's a little sickly. I don't think it is wise to take him out there."

"It isn't wise to stay here, Mama Frieda," Katrine shot back. "Björn will be safe. My mama went for help to the Adolphsons'. We only have to hide for a little while."

Frieda hesitated and then began grabbing some things. "Maybe you are right." She grabbed up Jon's blanket and some things from near the stove. Jon began fussing. "Bring those apples as well, Katrine," she whispered. "Just in case."

With Jon in her arms, wrapped in the blanket, she headed for the door. They all stepped outside.

"Well, well," Cleatus's voice broke the stillness. He came from the side of the cabin. The horse and mule were nearby. He leveled his pistol at Frieda.

"I'm back, sweetheart," he said, breathing heavily. "Let's do it right this time. I got you a riding mule so I won't be a mule thief."

"Don't, Cleatus, please. I don't want to go with you. I told you."

"Last time, you were agreeable to coming with me until that man you laid with showed up." He waved the pistol.

Katrine searched desperately around, trying to spot Björn. "We got help coming."

"Oh, you mean the little whelp you sent my way? He decided not to come."

"What did you do to Björn?" Frieda screamed. Linnea began crying.

"Oh, I 'spect he'll find his way back sometime. I took his pistol, so

I don't have to worry about getting shot in the back like he tried doing the last time.

"You should have taught your son not to be such a coward, Frieda." He laughed. "Oh, he's not your son, is he? He's just one of the brood you've been kidnapped into caring for. Well, you don't have to do that anymore. You're free now."

Jon began fussing and pushing to get down.

Cleatus waved his pistol at Frieda. "Just you, Frieda. I don't want no bastard that's not my own to take care of. Not like these 'uns." He grinned and swept his eyes about. "He has a passel of 'em, don't he? No wonder his wife died. He wore her out."

Cleatus grabbed the bridle on the mule and brought it up.

"Last chance, Frieda. Mount up. You don't have to die for his spawn. I'll treat you nice."

"No, you bastard," Frieda said. "I didn't marry you. You know that. Y-you just had your way with me."

"Shut up. We was married. It was common law. You was living with me."

Frieda began shaking. "You threatened to kill me. You tied me up."

Cleatus glowered at Katrine and the others. "I did no such thing. This is my loving wife, and I intend to take her with me." He grabbed Frieda.

Laurens immediately came running in, yelling, grabbing ahold of Frieda.

"You can't have my mama," he yelled. He began tugging on Frieda.

Deftly, Cleatus rapped Laurens over the head with his pistol, striking him with a hollow thud. Laurens dropped limp to the ground with blood welling from his scalp.

Linnea began crying uncontrollably. Mia clung to Katrine. Desperately, Katrine hoped Mr. Adolphson would show up. She feared for Björn and Laurens.

"More of you try it, you'll end up the same way. Now get on that mule, Frieda. I'm tired of being nice. You're going with me, or I'll be leaving you here to bury this spawn."

He aimed his pistol at Linnea. "How about if this one's next?"

Frieda shook her head, tears in her eyes. "Don't, Cleatus. You're right. You always were right. I'm coming." She handed Jon to Katrine. Jon reached for his mother.

"That's more like it. Now you're not going to try to run, are you?"

She shook her head. Tears wet her cheeks.

Cleatus swung into his saddle. He took the lead rope on Frieda's mule, tied it to the back of his saddle, and turned toward the trail.

"Now, I'm sorry for having it go this way, children. Really, I'm a very nice person. I just don't like it when someone steals my wife. You'll all forgive me for that." He tipped his hat and headed up the trail, leading Frieda.

Stunned, Katrine realized that he was heading north away from the direction Mr. Adolphson and Lars would be coming. She saw the sun flash from something he tossed. She ran to it. It was Björn's pistol. She picked it up and immediately aimed it at Cleatus and pulled the trigger. The hammer fell with an empty click. She heard Cleatus's hollow laugh.

When she turned around, Laurens was struggling up, holding his head, groaning. Linnea had some water and dabbed a cloth at his cut. Blackness began enveloping Katrine as she began running—running in the direction that she thought Björn would be. She ran blindly, chest aching.

"Björn, Björn," she called, sobbing.

"Stop, stop," she heard Mia's voice behind her. "I can't run like you, Katrine. I can't." Mia had begun to follow.

Katrine turned to find Mia slumped in the grass.

"We have to find Björn," Katrine choked. "He might ... might be—" She didn't dare say *dead*.

She turned back toward the timber now, unsure of what to do. A form stumbled into view.

"Björn?" Katrine ran toward him.

Blood stained Björn's face and wet his chest and arms.

He reached her. "I'm sorry, Katrine. He got her, didn't he?"

Katrine nodded.

"Bastard." Björn continued toward the cabin. "I'm going after him."

"You're hurt, Björn."

"Not as hurt as he's going to be," Björn spat.

At the cabin, Björn joined his brother, much in the same shape as he was in. He picked up the pistol. He laughed. "Might be his last mistake that he gave this back." He began shoving some rounds into it.

He poured some water and began washing himself. He shuddered strangely and almost sat down.

Katrine caught him. Something was not right. "You can't go, Björn. You're hurt."

"To blazes," he said. "I've been hit in the head worse than this. Just let me clean up a bit. I'm going."

Björn began washing again, then paused and shook his head. "J-just let me clean up."

Katrine knew he was hurting.

"Just you sit down for a minute, Björn. I can wash you up." Katrine led him to the bed. "Sit here," she commanded.

Björn obeyed.

Katrine began dabbing at Björn's head. A flap of skin was loose. She felt nauseous. Blood was everywhere. It had run down his back.

"I-I gotta go now," Björn pleaded.

"Just a little more."

Björn's eyes began drooping.

"Look, Björn, lie on your side. I can reach it easier."

Björn lay back and dragged his feet onto the bed. His breathing became heavy. His eyes fluttered closed. He shuddered and fell into a strange sleep.

Katrine knew sleep was the best thing. He had been hurt bad. Maybe his skull had been cracked. She found her own world swimming as she realized the danger that Björn was in. At least Laurens seemed all right. Jon was fussing, but Linnea was holding him.

The sound of voices brought Katrine alert. Outside it was dark. How could that be? She sat up.

"Are you all right in there?" Nils Adolphson banged into the cabin. "Someone strike a light."

Lars and Anna stumbled in behind Nils. Laurens found the kerosene lamp and lit it.

"We were afraid. We didn't want a light," Laurens said. He hugged his sister. "I'm glad you're here, Anna," he murmured. "Mama Frieda's gone."

Mia frantically looked about. "W-where's my mama?" Margret and Torsten were not with them.

"Shh, Mia. She's okay. She and Torsten stayed at the Adolphsons'," Anna explained. "We'll go there in the morning."

Anna reached Björn lying in the bed and began examining him. Katrine noticed that Björn slept fitfully, his chest rising and falling unevenly.

"That man came back and took Mama," Laurens began explaining. "I tried to stop him. He hit me. He hit Björn too. He's hurt."

Nils glanced at Anna. "How is he?"

"He has swelling, but I think he'll be all right," Anna said.

Nils bent over to examine Björn. "Time will tell. Too bad there isn't a snowbank around somewhere."

"The cold creek water might help," Anna said. "Come, Katrine, let's get some water."

On the way to the creek, Anna asked for more details. After Katrine had repeated the story again, Anna summarized, "So she really said they were never married and that she had been violated?"

Katrine nodded. "She was pretty clear."

"It wasn't her fault then," Anna said. "They weren't man and wife, common law or not."

Katrine tried to understand.

"She tried to explain the same thing to Papa, but they didn't have the right words. Now I've heard for myself. Mama Frieda did the best she could. She was never married to Cleatus. She was kidnapped and abused," Anna said weakly.

Chapter 44

Two DAYS LATER, Sven rode into the yard leading his two mules packed with an elk. Katrine helped him unload as best she could.

"You don't need to tell me about Frieda," he said. "I found out when we dropped off Mr. Wikstrom's elk."

"Is he just going to let that man take her?"

"No. I'm just here to unpack and resupply." He tossed his bedroll to the side and pulled off his horse's saddle. "Soon as Boots gets some oats and I get something to eat, Mr. Wikstrom and I are heading back out after him." His jaw set hard, and his eyes narrowed.

Katrine shivered.

When Sven sat down to some dinner, he explained that Lars had to run and fetch his father to simmer Anton down. Lars was now staying at the Wikstroms' with Anna and the children until Anton returned.

"How's Björn?" Katrine asked.

"Fine enough to be giving Laurens a fit for losing their skinning knife. I loaned them the one I had so they could start butchering Anton's elk."

"Maybe I should go and help." It was more than knowing that Björn was all right; Katrine wanted to see him.

"Nej, you'll need to be helping Mama."

Margret eyed Sven.

"I must go, Mama. I'm heading back out with Anton to catch that bastard." Sven took several more bites of stew and then stood.

"Oh, Sven," Margret whispered. She began packing some provisions. "Please be careful."

Sven hugged everyone goodbye, swung up onto Boots, and leading Jack, now packed with oats and his gear, headed back toward the Wikstroms' place.

Katrine stared after him until he disappeared from sight. She then wondered if he had even been home.

The day after Papa Olafson left, it snowed. Katrine doubted she would ever see Mama Frieda again. A stabbing pain filled her.

Katrine and Mia helped Mama Olafson butcher and smoke some of the elk. They dug the remaining roots from the garden and buried them in the root cellar. They threshed and winnowed some remaining grain. Torsten helped scoop some of it up and put it into the bags. They prayed silently for Papa Olafson and Mr. Wikstrom's return, and they prayed for Frieda.

Days later, Sven was back. He said that he and Anton had tracked them until they reached the Salmon River. From that point, it was any man's guess to where they could have gone.

"Maybe I was wrong about Frieda. I presumed she would have gotten away and come back." Sven shoved his coffee cup across the table.

Margret stroked his hand. "I think for a woman to get away from that man would be a miracle. Frieda's a strong woman, but even if she could get away, I do not know if she could have found her way out of that country."

Sven sighed. "Ja, maybe so. Now the peaks are covered with snow. I'm not sure anyone could find their way, even if they knew where they were heading." He took another swallow of coffee.

"How is Mr. Wikstrom?"

"About like any man who has lost two wives, I suppose," Sven said. He shrugged. "I don't understand. He knew he was taking a chance when he found her with that hurdy-gurdy troop. It is true that she may have been trying to get away, but for her to even want such a life says something." He looked up and noticed Katrine.

"You should leave us," Sven said. "I should not be talking in front of you about such private matters."

Margret sat down. "You know, Papa, Katrine is not so young anymore. Although this is unpleasant business, she should be aware of what the world can hold."

Sven nodded slowly. "Ja, that is why you stay in this valley, Katrine. You and Mia. You are my girls. I can take care of you here." He took a final swallow of coffee and stood.

"I best be checking on the stock and putting up things. This weather sure looks bad tonight, it does."

A cool rain mixed with snow whipped through the valley that night. Katrine later learned that Björn thought the scratching at their cabin door was the wind. When he found Frieda cold and shivering, he almost didn't recognize her. He first thought an animal was at the door until she called out his name. Somehow Frieda had enough of a spark of life that after a good hot cup of tea, warm blankets, and a good night's sleep, she pulled through and was soon up and taking care of her family as before. The following Sunday meeting was a great day of thanksgiving. Anton publically forgave Frieda of any and all sins, imaginary and future.

"I have wronged my wife. She sacrificed for her family in ways no woman could be expected to do. It was because of her love for me and for our children that she did what she did, and now she's come back to us. From this year forth, we will celebrate this Sunday as Frieda's day." He poured everyone a small drink of snaps, including the older boys. They toasted Frieda's health.

Katrine never heard how Frieda escaped or how she found her way back to the valley through the snow. Frieda only implied that no one need ever worry about any Cleatus spawn again. Katrine trembled at the thought. She remembered that Björn had blamed Laurens for losing the skinning knife. Then she recalled how Frieda had gathered up things from near the stove before wrapping up Jon. Katrine wanted desperately to share her thoughts with Björn, but the image of Frieda trying to protect the children—and not her own children—not once but twice was too strong in her mind. God would surely look the other way as well.

During the following weeks, snow continued falling, blanketing the valley. Sven gathered the cow and calf into the small enclosure near the stock shed that he had built and near where he stored hay. He also brought in the horse and mules. From now until April, the stock would subsist on hay he had cut and the small amount of oats.

Katrine took care of the chickens. They had their structure built on one side of the stock shed, and the cages were well in the back away from the snow.

Travel ceased after the heavy snows and the valley quietly became snowbound. For Santa Lucia, they gathered at the Adolphsons'. Nils and Lars had completed work on a large enclosed room, which doubled on occasion for meals and also a place for men passing through to throw out their bedrolls. Travelers often stayed the night, got a meal, and soaked in the hot springs, which was just about as good as a bath at a boarding house and in some respects, better.

Linnea was Saint Lucia and served each person a bit of cake. They exchanged small gifts. Katrine had crocheted several doilies and gave one to each family. Björn, who seemed always to be whittling, gave Katrine a bear that he had carved.

"*Gott Jul*, happy Christmas," he said.

Katrine couldn't help but give him a quick hug. It was a very special gift. She remembered the carved bear Erik had made her for her birthday long ago.

Björn pulled away and looked around quickly as if to see if anyone had noticed. His surprised look was accentuated by his dark eyebrows. He smiled.

"I'm glad you like it."

The Olafsons didn't stay long at the Adolphsons' because darkness came early, and as always, the stock needed tending. This night, on the return trip, the temperature dropped, and Katrine held Mia and Torsten close for warmth. Sven guided the mule pulling the sled, walking beside it. Katrine watched the stars overhead. She breathed out a fog and felt the tingle of the ice in her nose. The valley was again held fast in winter's grip.

Chapter 45

THE YEAR TURNED. Katrine thought often about her future and the others' futures in the valley. Would there even be anyone here in a few years? Three families of the six remained, and the six that made it to the valley were those that remained of the thirteen Swedish families that had originally headed west. She was the sole survivor from her family. Although she didn't want to believe it, she had begun saying that to herself. Maybe if she said it enough, she would begin believing it. The others did.

Come this spring, Anna and Lars would marry. In a year, there would be another family but from within. As of yet, no one had come up the trail from the lower valley to settle. The closest newcomers were a couple of hunters or trappers whom Katrine had heard built a rude cabin well north of the lake. They had no interest in farming and only came through to use the hot springs at the Adolphsons' and to get whiskey.

Katrine glanced around the Olafsons' cabin, taking in its familiar trappings, a rare moment because the kerosene lamp was lit, sending flickering lights across the rough-hewn walls, across their belongings, clothing, dishes, rough furniture, and the rocking chair where Mama Olafson sat with her sewing. Wind buffeted the walls, whistling around the crude window and door. Papa Olafson had intended to build a better structure, one that was larger, but like all the settlers, his days were consumed by farming. Although chores slowed because there were no crops to tend in the deep snow and cold, the livestock took constant attention. Otherwise, Papa Olafson was limited to carpentry projects he could do inside the cabin or on warmer days between snowstorms, under the lean-to. Katrine and Mia worked on a quilt, sewing squares and shapes that would eventually be fitted together to form a colorful pattern.

Snow had come before Christmas and continued piling up into the new year. It would continue deepening until sometime in March when the days would lengthen enough that the warming sun would overtake the snowstorms. It was also in March that the most severe storms hit, often leaving two or three feet of new snow. The only solace was that March snows were often chased by rain and warming weather, and the snow rapidly melted.

Katrine and Mia helped feed the stock, milk Trillium, and take care of the chickens. Boots and the three mules came to the yard each evening for hay and occasional oats. Sven turned the stock back out during the day. The animals tramped down trails in the snow under the aspens. Trillium and Lupine were kept penned because they were more vulnerable to the mountain lions than the horse and mules. Sometimes when the lion was near, Nisse would set up a racket, and the horse and mules would shake their heads, snort, and stamp. Sven would throw on his boots and coat over his long johns and head out into the night, often with Katrine at his heels carrying a flickering candle lantern. He usually took a shot in the direction of the cat, not expecting to hit it but to scare it away.

"That lion is more persistent this winter, it is," he said, lowering his rifle and turning back for the cabin.

"Will it ever leave us alone?" Katrine asked.

"Nej, I think not. We learn to live with the cougars the best we can and kill them if given the chance." He banged his way into the cabin, knocking the snow from his boots and hanging his coat from a peg. As usual, Margret and Mia waited to ask the results. Now nearly three and a half, Torsten wondered as well.

"Did you shoot it, Papa?"

"Nej, me and Nisse scared it away." He ruffled Torsten's hair. "Maybe we get lucky and someone comes and traps them. I don't have time. At least Andreasson was useful in that respect before he up and left."

Katrine swallowed. The Andreassons had been gone since autumn. She thought briefly of Jens who had gone to the goldfields.

"Maybe that is why the mountain lions are back. It's because Mr. Andreasson is gone."

"Ja," Sven replied. "So, Mama, because we are all wide awake, should we not have some tea?"

Margret smiled. "We should I think, and maybe someone should tell us a story." She eyed Katrine. As of late, Katrine had begun entertaining the family again with stories of Swedish trolls and elves.

"I shall tell you about Skurugata, the troll of Sweden Valley, and how he managed to hitch a ride on the Olafsons' wagon from Minnesota all the way across America."

The wind whistled and whipped about the cabin as Katrine bent low toward Torsten and began her story. The boy's eyes widened.

Mia giggled. "Don't make it too scary."

"Oh, I shall not. There are also elves."

No one attempted skiing through the snow immediately after a storm but waited a day or two for the snow to pack down. They then strapped on their skis and walked and slid along the trails until a good path had again been built. Usually they would hitch a horse or mule to a sled and drag it across the snow. When the Olafsons took the sled to attend Sunday meeting, Katrine skied along behind, enjoying the rush of air against her when she slid down the gentle hills and grabbing ahold of the sled if she needed help going up a hill.

The three families huddled at the Adolphsons', sharing a common meal, talking about life, sharing hopes for the future, and talking about farming. The three men and Lars talked about planting and tending crops and breeding livestock. The Indian pony seemed to handle the winter better than the other horses and mules; maybe they should try harder to breed it. They made plans to bring more animals into the valley. The Adolphsons had lost a cow in the last blizzard, and Nils talked about replacing it.

"Except for the deep snow, you won't see a better valley for raising cattle. Maybe I should bring in some beef cattle for the mines and take them out in the fall to sell," Nils said.

The others shook their heads.

"I don't like the risk," Sven said. "I'm a farmer. As long as I can grow enough crops and keep at least one cow, my family will be fine."

"I agree," Anton said. "I've considered some sheep, but the coyotes and wolves would get them, and those that survived would be killed by the snow while lambing."

"I'm bringing in a shoat, if some are available," Sven said. "Trillium's giving enough milk. I think we can spare some for a pig. I may have to plant more grain is all."

"And with all this snow, we might not get any grain," Nils said.

Both Sven and Anton eyed him. "And you are the one who tells us that Swedes can handle the snow."

"Ja," Nils said. "I just don't like losing cattle."

While the men talked in their group, the women gathered separately, guessing when Lars and Anna would have their first child, and when and who would be the next to marry.

The children played games, much the same as they did during school recess.

At last, spring warmed the valley. A few patches of snow lingered in the shade and in protected draws. Katrine began leading Trillium and Lupine out onto the greening grass and to graze back the winter rye. The sun sparkled, filling the valley with hope. Each day, Katrine snuck away to her favorite place on the hillside and peeked under the spruce trees for the first trilliums. She had watched the snakelike buds push up from the damp brown earth at the edge of the snow. Bright green leaves had begun unfurling. Today, half a dozen trilliums shone snow white against the dark shadows, their three petals spread like equally spaced white arms about their brightly burning yellow centers. Katrine breathed the warm, dank air, smelling the earth and new life and the promise of a new season.

"Now it is spring," she whispered.

The time for Trillium's second calf to be born arrived. Katrine and Mia both stood by again to help. It was a bull calf.

"Should we name it?" Mia asked.

"If you want to, but we may be eating him come this autumn," Sven replied. "It would be a good change from the elk and venison."

"Maybe we should keep the bull," Katrine suggested.

"I shall think on it," Sven replied. "But for us to have healthy stock, it is better to have a different bull for our cows."

ANNA AND LARS'S WEDDING

Chapter 46

THE CYCLE HAD begun again. Sven plowed from sunlight to dark. As soon as the fields were prepared, Katrine joined him to sow the seed—just enough barley and oats to feed themselves and the livestock. Katrine also milked Trillium and found her hands full with trying to keep the bull calf away. Margret put in the vegetable garden and pruned the apple trees. Mia tended the chickens. Torsten helped throw out the grain and called "chick, chick" to them. He then ran back to Mia when one of them ruffled its feathers at him. Wherever the girls were, Torsten was. And wherever Torsten was, there was Nisse. The dog kept them all in order, seemingly taking over the job of herding, and they had come to listen for his barks or whines that warned of visitors or predators.

The men, including Lars and Björn, headed out toward Boise City with the mule string fully packed with goods for trading.

"I think one season we should go north to the Salmon River mines," Nils suggested.

"And you won't get past the upper lakes until July," Anton said. "Remember, Sven and I have been there. You have another canyon to descend and then climb out of to get back into the mountains to the active diggings. You could make two trips to Boise City and back before getting to those mines up north."

"Maybe someone on the river would trade and take things into the mines from there."

"This season, we go to Boise City," Sven said, settling the discussion.

The pack train headed out toward the south. Katrine watched until the last rider had disappeared into the timber beyond the river's bend. She shivered, knowing they were alone again, but she was not overly worried. There had never been Indian trouble except for the lost stock three seasons ago. Miners and drifters were their greatest threat, as had been witnessed by Cleatus's visit.

The days drifted by until the men would return. Each day, Katrine looked toward the south. She couldn't hold back her joy when Papa Olafson at last came into view. Hardly had he dismounted than she, Mia, Torsten, and Mama Olafson were about him hugging him.

They were eager to see what he had brought back.

"Well, like last season, I wanted to bring us a pig," he said. "There were none to be had anywhere. The Chinese have them all for raising for the mining camps."

He began hauling his packs inside.

"That means we just have to make lots of butter and cheese. It was the Lord's will we had a bull calf for when we need him."

Katrine was disappointed but still excited at all the things he did bring back—salt, sugar, flour, salt pork, cloth, and kerosene oil. He even brought back a few pieces of candy.

The apple trees blossomed on Katrine's fourteenth birthday. She thought how special it was that the trees bloomed. Mama Olafson and she sat in the shade of the aspens at the corner of the cabin.

"It is no longer a question of whether or not you are a young lady," she said. "Soon a young man may ask you to marry. I'm not so certain I am ready for that day. For sure Papa is not."

Katrine sat very still. When she was young, she had been impatient, always wondering and thinking what it would be like. Now she was there and no longer wished to be.

"I'm not in a hurry, Mama."

Margret laughed. "If I recall, you were in a hurry not so very long ago, before I let down your hem."

Katrine laughed, remembering. No one had said anything about her dresses. It was something simply understood.

"My, how you have changed," Margret said, gazing up and down. "So tall and so very pretty. A young woman now. Your mama and papa would be so proud, as would your brother. Pray God is keeping them."

"He is." Katrine knew in her heart they were in God's hands. A day never passed without her thinking of them, but it was now her place in life to carry on. Only she had the opportunity to live her parents' and brother's dreams.

"I think I know a young man who might soon capture your heart," Margret continued, smiling.

Katrine swallowed. Of course she did. Björn was the only boy in the valley near her age. It would likely be him unless he became interested in Ingrid. Of late, Katrine had closely watched Björn to see if he was giving any hints.

"Perhaps," Katrine said, laughing.

Later, she found herself looking out over the valley from atop her rock. She wondered about love. She wondered about the feelings she had had for Jens. She liked Björn. They had always been good friends, but she had always thought of him as a brother and of Harald and Jens as playmates, although Harald had often seemed too studious. Katrine blamed his English mother. A stab overwhelmed her as she recalled Harald's death. And she missed Jens but in a different way. Maybe it was better for Jens now. She didn't think he would have made a very good farmer. But mostly, it was better because he was away from his father.

She had only briefly entertained the idea of marriage before, and none of the three boys had ever seriously been in her thoughts. It had often been someone else—someone she imagined who would come to the valley.

Presently, Björn seemed uninterested in her other than that they were friends. That was good. She was not ready and did not know if ever she would be. And like Mama Olafson had once said, Björn was still too young to manage a farm and support a family. But she wondered if he ever thought of such things. She wished he'd at least pay a little attention to her—perhaps tell her that he was at least thinking about the possibilities. Then an iciness enveloped her. Maybe he was not interested in her at all but in Ingrid. She kicked at the rock. She hated being in the valley. Her only hope would be that more families would come.

The days lengthened, and Midsummer's Eve celebration and Anna and Lars's wedding neared. The women had taken over. Katrine made the wedding crown. She crocheted one from cotton yarn, making loops and curves as she built it slowly outward with fancy holes and patterns knitted into it. Each trefoil loop ended with a small star.

"Now the easy part," Margret said. "We stiffen it up and sew it to Astrid's veil." Margret set a pan of water on the stove and melted white sugar into it.

"We don't have much sugar," Mia observed.

"We'll just make one less pie this autumn," Margret explained, "but Anna will be so proud."

When the sugar had melted and formed a thick, syrupy solution, Margret dipped in the crown. "We let it harden a little between dips," she explained, "forming it a little each time."

A dozen or so dips later, the crown sparkled even whiter and stood rigid. Katrine continued molding it to improve its shape.

"We shall hope it doesn't rain during the wedding," Margret said.

Saturday as they had so often done, Katrine and Mia headed over the ridge to visit the Wikstroms, but this time it was to help Frieda with Anna's dress. Frieda had an old light blue dance dress from which she cut some of the bustles and replaced them with white lace.

"It'll do, do you think?" Frieda held it up for Katrine's approval when she had finished.

"You mustn't let Lars see it," Katrine cautioned.

Excitedly, Anna held it up to herself. "It's beautiful. Thank you, Frieda." She hugged her.

Katrine knew that Lars and Mr. Adolphson had been busy with preparations as well. They had spent several days going to and from the old Andreasson cabin, chasing out the packrats, repairing the roof, bringing over some household items and tools, and in Lars's opinion, as Papa Olafson had jokingly shared with her, the most important thing— fixing the bed.

Eight adults and nine children gathered at the Wikstroms' place for Midsummer's Eve and the wedding. In many respects, this celebration would mark the end of a long journey, which had begun in Minnesota five years earlier.

After unpacking and laying out all sorts of food, everyone gathered at the Midsummer's Eve pole. Björn and Linnea had covered it with greenery and flowers. The women and girls wore crowns of bright pink, blue, and yellow flowers. Anna wore a crown of white flowers.

Perhaps they were more accustomed to dancing together. Perhaps the brännvin had not made its rounds as strongly. Everyone danced particularly well. The children danced their dances accompanied by their parents' clapping and singing. The adults, including Lars and Anna, danced to the children's cheers and clapping. The children, also joined by Lars and Anna, hopped around doing the silly frog dance, after which they ended in a tangle on the ground.

Somehow, Katrine found herself facing Björn. On impulse, she kissed him. After all, it was Midsummer's Eve—a time to be a little crazy. Björn's eyes arched up, and he blushed. Anna quickly kissed Lars. And Mia, seeing what was going on, kissed Pelle. Laughter from those closely watching flooded about them.

The singing and clapping began again, and they danced in the opposite direction, boys in one direction, the girls in the opposite, again tangling up with each other on the ground. Now it was an excuse of which the children took advantage.

They broke and tidied themselves for the wedding celebration. Anna put on her dress. Lars put on his father's black coat. His hair had been brushed back. Katrine believed he looked like a handsome prince from the fairy tales of trolls and elves, a prince about to win his princess. Anna appeared radiant in her blue dress that now sparkled with the added white lace and a wreath of wildflowers. Her hair had been braided above her ears and allowed to hang freely down her back. Astrid and Frieda pinned the veil with the crown into her hair. Both Lars and Anna now stood expectantly hand in hand in front of Lars's father. Anna's veil was pulled back.

Nils Adolphson read several Bible passages, mostly in Swedish. Katrine recognized that he talked about how a man and woman gave their lives to each other. She remembered what Mama Olafson had said. If a man truly gave himself to his wife, and the wife did so in turn, then no problem would be too great. She listened to the words as both Lars and Anna promised to care for each other. She could not help but think that it would not be very long in the future before she would be saying similar words. Her heart began racing.

Mr. Adolphson then announced that Anna and Lars were married and should kiss each other. They kissed. Katrine felt funny inside and could not see anyone else but Björn standing in place of Lars. She imagined herself wearing the white crown and feeling Björn's kiss. It was frighteningly real. She came to her senses when the cheering and clapping began. She sought sight of Björn, who seemed oblivious to her but ecstatic for his sister.

They gathered for the traditional Midsummer's Eve dinner. There were cakes frosted with white sugar and sprinkled with wild strawberries. The meal ended with a flurry of toasts and then broke as the women went to one corner of the yard and the men went to the other. Katrine noticed that poor Lars was being inundated with personal advice from the men as they smoked their pipes and enjoyed their brännvin.

"Now, Lars," Mr. Wikstrom said, "you should ..." The remaining words were lost.

Katrine guessed for once that Lars appreciated there were only three men.

Björn, Pelle, and Laurens had also joined in. She wondered what kind of advice the boys could give Lars. Clearly, their discussion was animated. It seemed Anka was even trying to give him advice as the dog busily bounced from one person to the other.

The women, likewise, had corralled Anna. Katrine had heard their advice before. It was toned down a bit because of the younger girls' ears.

"Now you come." The women escorted Anna back to the center of the yard and seated her in a chair.

"Here's for you, Lars." The men seated Lars facing the opposite direction in a second chair.

They began a song, clapping their hands and circling about Anna and Lars.

Shortly, Nils brought out a pitchfork and stuck it in Lars's hands. Frieda, Astrid, and Margret removed Anna's veil and crown and tied an apron about her middle. An ache sprang into Katrine's throat as she recognized Anna's mother's cream-colored apron.

Björn and Ingrid rushed in and took away the chairs.

Everyone now formed a circle about Anna and Lars. The couple danced inside the circle, embraced, and kissed. Their lives as husband and wife had begun.

The long shadows of evening approached. Most of the group took naps. Some of the children went to the hot springs to swim, Katrine and Mia among them. The older boys went to the lower springs. Although they were a distance apart, Katrine found herself sneaking glimpses in Björn's direction. A warmth enfolded her. She could not help but wonder if he was the one. She wondered what it would be like to be in his embrace. She shook her head. It would be Björn's decision of course. He could also choose Ingrid, she reminded herself again.

As night gathered, they returned to the cabin. It was time for the Midsummer's Eve bonfire. Everyone brought their blankets and gathered around. Lars and Anna lit the fire together and stood back watching as the flames climbed upward, illuminating the faces of those around, now sending dancing sparks upward into the gathering dusk.

They sat together telling stories—first one person and then the next. Katrine told about trolls on Midsummer's Eve who got confused and decided it must be daytime because the bonfire was so bright and of course ran away, fearing they would turn to stone.

At length, the bonfire began to die. Stars filled the night sky. Katrine found herself standing next to Björn, watching the dying embers. The youngest children were curled up asleep. Their parents sat about, talking, laughing, and even singing. Mr. Wikstrom's voice rose above the others. Katrine felt Björn's nearness and couldn't help but feel differently about him.

Anna and Lars had disappeared. Katrine wondered if there was room enough in the Wikstroms' cabin for them to spend their wedding night. She learned later that Lars drove the wagon and Anna back to the old Andreasson cabin, which was now the new home of Lars and Anna Adolphson. She worried a little. She had seen Lars drinking a bit too much whiskey. She knew Björn had had a few sips, but even though this was Midsummer's Eve and by tradition, everyone became a little carefree, it was still frowned on for the women to partake. She doubted Anna had indulged. Prudently, Katrine had declined as well.

Katrine decided it was not a bad custom for the women to abstain. After all, someone had to get the men home and hopefully keep them from making too much a fool of themselves. She was certain they remembered Mr. Andreasson. She remembered Jens and wondered where he was and how he might be doing. She wondered if even he would think to celebrate Midsummer's Eve. It would no longer mean anything to him. She bit her lip. People needed people. The wedding and Midsummer's Eve showed her that.

Mia and Linnea sat with Pelle, laughing and giggling and wrestling. She told herself that it could only mean trouble.

Chapter 47

THE SUNDAY MEETING after the wedding was as if it were a continuation of the celebration. The main difference was Anna gathered with the three women, and Lars gathered with the three men. Katrine moved from one group to the other. There were knowing winks and whispers. It appeared Anna was getting a good going over. She was glad she was not Anna at the moment. On the other hand, the men talked about farming. Lars talked about the calf he was raising and his garden. In disgust, Katrine returned to the circle of women.

Astrid advised, "Anna, you are sixteen already. By the time any baby arrives, you will be seventeen."

Björn happened to come up to Katrine. "I wonder if my sister's getting as much advice as Lars is getting," he said, arching his eyes and grinning.

"I believe he is," Katrine replied and laughed.

"Come, let's go somewhere," Björn offered.

Katrine felt her heart surge. They found a quiet place under the fluttering leaves of an aspen. Björn sat with her, his knee against hers. They talked. It was no longer like young children or playmates talking, or like brother and sister talking. Björn talked about taking over either the Eklunds' or Lundgrens' abandoned homestead. Katrine believed he must have been thinking about years from now when he would marry. She wondered if those thoughts included her. Just to be safe, she said, "You wouldn't want the Eklunds' place. Baby Robert is buried there. His ghost is still trying to find its way."

Björn laughed. "Maybe so, but look at it this way: he might like to have some company. Maybe ghosts get lonely."

They exchanged looks. Katrine realized the same could be said for Harald's ghost. She shivered.

Katrine found herself studying Björn's eyes, deeper blue than the other boys'. Deeper blue than Jens's she remembered. They lit

314

up with twinkles whenever he smiled or talked. And freckles. Björn still had a swarm crossing the bridge of his nose that crinkled when he smiled. He smiled a lot, but then Björn wasn't in pain like Jens had been.

Katrine felt strange again. A warmth flooded her middle like it had when she had visited with Jens.

A wondering look flooded Björn's eyes. He appeared to want to say something. He hesitated and shrugged. "It will be a long time though until I have my own homestead."

"Yes, I suppose." Katrine felt disappointed. She wanted to know Björn's thoughts and feelings toward her. She decided she would ask Anna. A sister should know those things.

It was not the best opportunity, but several weeks later, it was the only chance that Katrine had to quietly visit with Anna. After the wedding, they had briefly seen each other at Sunday meetings, but she could not get a word in edgewise and certainly not one alone. It was bad enough that Mia always wanted to be present.

After their noon meal, Katrine became rather direct. "Anna, I want to talk privately."

Anna frowned. "Is something wrong? Are you all right?"

Katrine tried to laugh. "Yes, I'm all right. It's just that you're married now, and I've been thinking a lot."

They sat near the river, pulling their legs underneath themselves, rearranging their dresses. Katrine could hear Ingrid and Laurens laughing as they played. Insects buzzed in the warm air.

Katrine hesitated. "Please don't laugh, but how did you know you were in love with Lars?"

Anna bit her lip and smiled. Then her eyes quieted. "I didn't for a long time, and what I thought was love wasn't."

Katrine wondered at Anna's comment.

"When I was your age, I felt I loved Lars, but it was nothing like how I felt about a year ago when Lars said he wanted to marry me. That's when I realized what love really was. And now that we're married, it's different again but in good ways."

"That doesn't make sense," Katrine protested. "Isn't love, love?"

Anna smiled. "Well at first when we came to the valley, people were already saying that Lars and I would someday marry. Truthfully, I didn't think of anyone else. I had a good feeling about Lars then, but the feeling was different. If someone else had come along ... I don't know."

"People had always talked that I might marry Harald or Jens," Katrine admitted. "Now there's only Björn."

"And what's wrong with Björn," asked Anna, laughing, "other than he's my brother?"

"Nothing," Katrine quickly answered. Almost too quickly. "He's fine."

"Well, Björn isn't perfect," Anna said, raising her eyes. "I could share a few things, but if you should fall in love with him, I don't think any of what I could say would matter."

Katrine felt her heart racing. "I just wonder if it would be the same between Björn and me if Harald and Jens were still here."

"And does that matter?" Anna asked softly.

Katrine missed Harald and Jens, but she pictured Björn, especially the way he smiled at her. Slowly, she shook her head. "No."

Anna recrossed her legs. "For me, getting married was always something off in the future, and Lars and I were just kids playing like all children do. After he said he wanted to marry me, I could only think of him, and I wanted to be with him every minute."

"I know," Katrine said, laughing.

"You know?"

"It was pretty obvious. Björn told me that as well."

"See, I told you Björn isn't perfect. He tattles."

Katrine became silent, thinking again, fidgeting. "Uh, I want to know things about men," Katrine continued. "I know how things are supposed to work, sort of. Mama told me, but I don't know much."

Anna raised her eyebrows and smiled. "Well, I guess I know a lot more than I did. Lars and I want to have a baby right away." She laughed.

Katrine swallowed. That was some of what she wanted to know.

Anna softened. "If it should be with you and Björn, you will have plenty of time before then. God has a way of guiding us in these matters."

Anna suddenly sounded like Mama Olafson. Katrine shook her head, disappointed. Of all the people, she had thought Anna would help.

"I talked to Mama Frieda a little," Anna confided. "She thinks differently than your mama and certainly Mrs. Adolphson, but don't worry about any of that right now. You still have a long while."

"I-I think I feel different about Björn now. Different from what I ever felt toward Harald or Jens. I just want to know if he feels anything about me. I think he does, but then I wonder about it."

"Oh, he does all right. I lived with him long enough to know that." Anna laughed. "You two just be careful."

Katrine felt her world blossom into brilliant colors.

Chapter 48

THE SEASON GREW long. Grasses had turned russet and auburn. The rye had ripened. The oats and barley rippled in waves of green. Margret's lupine that grew along the garden fence were a riot of purples and lavenders and pinks. Yellow coneflowers and spindly sunflowers lingered on. Aspens fluttered with hints of yellow on the hillside above the cabin. Blue jays argued, clacking among themselves, apparently angry at the squirrels that had begun cutting cones.

Katrine had visited Anna and Lars once at their new home in the Andreassons' old cabin. If Jens came back, it would no longer be his homestead. She wondered if he knew that his family had moved from the valley. Of the six original farms, only three had survived. Anna and Lars were beginning a fourth. The number of children had not changed in two seasons, and no one new had come to settle, despite Mr. Adolphson's letters and despite the increasing number of miners and packers moving through.

Katrine reflected on Midsummer's Eve. She and Björn had acted a little silly, as had everyone on Midsummer's Eve, but there had been no real reason to kiss him. Maybe Björn did care for her. Anna said he did. Katrine felt her heart quicken again at the thought. Maybe it was time for her and Mia to go visit Linnea and Laurens.

Katrine took the washbasin and headed outside to throw the dishwater on her pear tree that Papa Olafson had given her a year ago. New shoots from the summer were covered with waxy green leaves. She hoped that one season the tree would have blossoms. Pears grew in Boise Valley, but the extreme cold at this elevation either nipped the buds or froze the fruit. She watched as the water sprinkled down around the tree's trunk in the August warmth. A grasshopper, disturbed by the cascading water, whirred away on dusty wings.

She had been in the valley for over four years. Over four years, Katrine had scanned the ridge to the south. This day she did not. The nicker of a horse broke her reverie. A lone rider came down the hillside toward the creek. The man, maybe a year older than Lars, wore buckskins and at first appeared to be an Indian. Something inside of Katrine burst into showers of light. She dropped the pan and began running, crying.

The man slipped from his dappled gray horse, moccasined feet, long dusty-blond hair, piercing blue eyes. She ran into his arms.

"Katrine," Erik said as he broke from her hug. "I promised you I would come to find you. I believe I have done so."

She grabbed him again and could not let go. His wild animal smell surprised her, but she felt his solid form under his buckskins. He was not a ghost. He was real. Over five years since she had waved goodbye on the windswept plain, and her prayers had at last been fulfilled.

She laughed. "Erik. Erik. Erik."

Erik released her; his eyes found hers. They studied each other for a long while.

"You aren't the eight-year-old sister I said goodbye to on the prairie, are you?" He glanced up and down.

"And you aren't a twelve-year-old boy."

"I'm still your brother."

They stood laughing and hugging and laughing again until tears stained their cheeks.

Erik stepped back. Katrine saw his troubled eyes. His eyes had always been incredibly blue. A flicker of hurt shadowed them.

"I'm sorry, Katrine—"

"You don't have to tell me," she whispered. "I know that Mama and Papa are gone." It was the first time she had acknowledged the truth aloud.

Erik shook his head. "I tried my best, Katrine. I promise you I did. Papa died when he was hunting during the first winter. Mama died the following spring. I wanted to come for you then, but I was too young. I wasn't able. I buried them near the cabin we built. Someday I can take you there."

"Shh," Katrine said. "You have so much to tell me and the Olafsons. They've taken care of me. Let's go see them."

She took his hand and turned for the cabin below. Erik followed, leading his horse. Margret and Sven and Mia and young Torsten were already running toward them.

Katrine and Erik talked all that day, hardly pausing to eat, walking about the homestead, seeing what the Olafsons had accomplished. In bits and pieces, Erik told about his life with the Sheepeaters, and Katrine told him about life in the high valley.

They reached Katrine's quiet glen on the hill behind the cabin.

"I came here often, thinking about you, wondering if I would ever see you again," Katrine said. She studied Erik's eyes, reminding herself that it really was her brother. They were those same blue eyes.

"Well, you're seeing me," Erik said, smiling. He handed Katrine an animal skin. "Be gentle. I've been carrying this for a very long time."

Katrine carefully unwrapped the skin. At first she didn't recognize the shining blue and yellow glass. Then she remembered.

"It's Grandma Anderson's vase."

"Yes, and it was Mama's," Erik said. "We brought it all the way from Sweden and then with us on the wagon. I got it from the cabin last autumn."

Katrine's chest tightened, and her eyes misted. Carefully she turned the vase.

"Mama always said it had the colors of Sweden," Erik said.

"Sweden, yes, and I think it has the colors of this valley ... the yellow sunflowers ... the blue sky."

Erik glanced around. "I believe you are right," he agreed. "Well, it's yours now."

"Thank you, Erik," Katrine whispered. She kissed and hugged her brother. Carefully she wrapped the vase again in the skin. "I think I shall keep it for when I have my own home."

"You should." Erik smiled.

He then reached into a pouch he carried.

"I have something else." He pulled out the mussel shell necklace Shining Water had given him. "My Indian mother told me when I found you that I should give you this."

Katrine took the necklace and blinked. The idea that Erik called an Indian woman his mother unsettled her. She fingered the individual pieces of shell, their opalescence blues and pinks catching in the light. It had a strange beauty, but it was nothing she wished to own.

"I only offer it to you because Shining Water said for me to do so, but I also do not mind saving it. It reminds me of her." Erik opened his hand.

Katrine allowed the necklace to slip back into his palm. "Yes, you should keep it as a memory. The vase means much more to me."

Katrine studied Erik's eyes. There seemed to be so much in them now, some things said and many things unsaid. He often glanced away, staring intently for a moment before returning them to hers.

"What?" Erik asked and smiled.

"Lars and Anna got married a few weeks ago," Katrine said. She didn't want to say what she really thought.

"I remember them. I can't imagine them being old enough to marry."

"I'm courting with Björn, Anna's younger brother."

"Official?" Erik almost shouted. "You can't be. He's just a boy."

"He's older than me."

Erik laughed. "It's going to take some getting used to knowing everyone has moved forward by five years."

"So have you, Erik."

Erik nodded. "I have, but in many respects I don't believe I've gone anywhere. I think I'm still me at least."

Katrine and the Olafsons didn't wait for Sunday meeting. The next day, Erik rode with them to the Adolphsons' for a homecoming dinner.

It was a grand occasion. The women set food out, and Nils opened a bottle of brännvin. Jubilantly, they toasted Erik.

Someone asked about his life with the Indians.

Erik said, "I have five years to tell—three with the Indians. You will need to be patient." As if to emphasize his point, he took a bite of beef and slowly chewed it.

"The Tukudeka were my life," Erik explained and then began telling of the Sheepeaters. He talked simply but used his hands descriptively. Sometimes he used an Indian word. "*Baa` mo-ap* was their name for the water spirits."

"You should talk Swedish or English," Nils said, "not heathen talk." He laughed, but Katrine noticed Erik's eyes flash.

Erik frowned. "Sometimes I don't know the right word."

It was true, Katrine realized. Erik had some trouble with English. He had spoken very little English at the time they were separated. She realized he must have learned a good deal since leaving the Sheepeaters.

"You can go to school with us," Katrine said. "Anna is teaching. I believe before next planting season, you will be through the first reader and know lots of words."

Erik raised an eye but said nothing.

"How did you escape?" Nils asked.

A shadow crossed Erik's face. "I chose to leave *the people*, he corrected Nils.

Some of the others frowned.

"I met a prospector named Hank Hailey. I knew if Hailey had found his way into the river canyons, he could find his way out. Afterward, I followed the trail to Fort Boise."

Katrine remembered Hailey's name. The miners had talked of Erik. She had known it all along. The white boy had been Erik. Her heart raced. The others seemed not to remember the story.

"And we thank the good Lord you did so," Margret said.

"Yes," others agreed.

"Now, give Erik a chance to eat."

"Thanks," Erik said. He touched two fingers to his lips and then to his heart. He took another bite of beef.

Katrine noticed that most of them watched as he ate, as if he were a strange animal or something.

Presently, Anton asked, "So how did you figure your way out of Fort Boise? It's not easy finding this valley. Rivers don't run north out of there. We had Nils Adolphson guiding us."

Erik nodded. "I got lucky. I met some men who were packing mining equipment into the Salmon River country. We packed out of Fort Boise for a distance until we hit a river that took us to the divide where we left the gear. Afterward, I realized the river had to drain to the one Mr. Adolphson had told us about." Erik nodded toward Nils. "I remembered your letters that my father read to us and your descriptions."

Nils smiled. "I only found it because I was trying to get to the new gold camps."

"Well, Erik, we are happy you are here, we are," Sven said. He offered another toast.

People had finished eating. They continued to watch Erik. At last Nils asked the question that Katrine suspected everyone had in mind.

"So what are your plans now that you've found your sister and what's left of the rest of us?"

Erik spread his hands. He looked from person to person and smiled.

"I have family here. I believe I shall stay and make this my home."

People clasped hands and laughed and cheered.

"Well, one of our lost is returned. We shall always remember this day when Erik Larson came home," Nils exclaimed. They raised their glasses. "Skål!"

Lars lowered his glass. "I can't believe you actually lived with the Indians. You must know a lot about them."

"I do," Erik said. "Three years."

"It gives me an idea." He turned toward his father. "Maybe we should give Erik the Indian pony. See if he can do better with him than we've done."

Nils raised his eyes. "I believe you have something there, Lars. If anyone can handle him, Erik ought to be able to. What do you think, Erik?"

Erik asked about the pony.

Lars briefly explained about the horse thieves.

"Then it's a Nez Perce pony," Erik said. "The Sheepeaters did not have many horses, but I would do my best to try to train him for you."

"Nej, you can have him," Nils said. "Consider him a welcome home gift."

Later, Erik asked Katrine about the other families.

"There are only three families here. I remember more—the Jonassens, the Andreassons. What about them?"

"Only six families came to the valley. The others turned back or went to Oregon. The Stiles went to Oregon."

Erik slowly nodded. "It seems such a long time ago. Mark and I were friends. We buried him in the trail so the Indians wouldn't find him."

Katrine thought about telling him about the three families that had come to the valley but had since left. She hesitated. There would be opportunities later.

"It's not what I expected," Erik said, glancing around. "It will be difficult for so few of you to survive."

Katrine heard him say *you*. "Mr. Adolphson keeps writing letters. He doesn't know if more will come or not. But you're here, and Anna and Lars will start a family."

Erik turned and smiled. "I still can't believe it."

Erik began working alongside Sven. It went unspoken that he would do so, partly in payment to the Olafsons for the care they had given Katrine. He offered to live in a tent, but Sven and Margret would not allow it.

"Use the badstuga for now," Sven insisted. "When we're ready to smoke some meat, we can move you out. The girls insist on going to the Wikstroms' hot springs anyway."

Each day at noon, Erik and Sven came to the cabin for noon meal. Katrine kept reminding herself that Erik was real, looking into his face, seeing her brother there as she had last seen him five years ago. He did not look much different from that day when she had pulled slowly away in the Olafsons' wagon, only his hair was darker and he was a man. She remembered watching him, his blond hair disappearing, him standing next to Papa, now only a blurry shadow of memories—he and Mama. Both whom she believed now looked down upon her and Erik.

Erik also dressed strangely. His clothes smelled dank and musty like an animal den. They weren't unpleasant—just different from the smells of a cabin and the farm animals. He wore leather from animals he had hunted. Shortly, Sven must have decided he looked uncivilized because he gave him one of his shirts, a thin white one, to replace the tattered one he still had, which had belonged to his father.

Erik wore his long hair back, tied with a leather thong; otherwise, he was clean-shaven. Katrine noticed a scar under his left eye that she wanted to ask about. As when he was a boy, Erik was quick to smile or laugh, but often his smile or laugh seemed cut short as if he remembered that he should not be doing so. His eyes remained steady as if weighing his surroundings.

Shortly, Erik brought back the Indian pony from Nils and began working with him. Erik's gentle manner with the roan was not lost on Katrine. She could not help but wonder if the pony had been meant for him.

"What will you call him?"

"I believe I shall name him Hatchet. He gets along well with my mare, Misty. I think they will be good animals for me."

"Can you ride him?"

"I can now, after I quit trying to saddle him. I think that was what Mr. Adolphson did that made him skittish."

Katrine laughed.

At Sunday meeting, Katrine looked forward to seeing Erik united with the other men. As she often did, she put herself in earshot of their conversation, and as usual, they poured a glass of snaps. Erik took a sip and shouted skål with the rest of them as they toasted each other, all the while joking and laughing. Then talk turned to the fields and livestock.

"Erik, you should be taking up one of the homesteads," Nils suggested.

"Maybe this spring," Sven quickly interjected. "I need him for planting season."

Anton chuckled.

"I mean the man should have his own cabin," Nils clarified. "He can still work your fields."

"Yes, sir," Erik agreed. He nodded toward the others.

The men continued talking. All agreed that Sven was lucky to have an additional hand. Katrine noticed that Erik said very little. He smiled and shook his head occasionally with the conversation. His snaps was hardly touched. The warmth Katrine had felt began to fade.

Chapter 49

A FEW DAYS later, Erik packed Misty and Hatchet and headed to the old Lundgren cabin. Katrine insisted on going with him, although memories of Harald plagued her. During the time they had resumed school there, not once had anyone gone back to the hill to visit Harald's grave. She had caught some of them gazing in that direction, but they rarely talked about him. Now that Erik was moving in, Katrine wondered if she should say anything.

Katrine helped him settle his belongings. There weren't many—a few cooking utensils, a buckskin shirt, a hatchet, his bow, his rifle. Katrine recalled it had been Papa's rifle. She noticed the Bible.

"Our family Bible, Katrine," Erik said. "You have the vase. I have this." He set the Bible on a shelf near the fireplace.

After he had rolled out his bedding and started a fire, Erik paused and looked around.

"It's strange to have a roof over my head. I'm more used to the stars, especially after I left the people. For a year, I didn't have a lodge."

"Even in the snow?"

Erik laughed. "The first winter, I slept in sheds in Fort Boise from time to time."

"I wished you had stayed at the Olafsons'," Katrine said.

"It is clear I would just be a nuisance being in the badstuga all winter," he replied, "and it's right that I start getting my own place."

"But what can you do? There's no time for a garden or planting fields before winter," Katrine said.

"No, but I can start looking around, maybe fix some fence and work on a stock shed. I can tell the family before me didn't have much."

Katrine agreed. In a way, it was good. Erik would be settling and now building his own home.

"Come, do you want to look around with me?"

Katrine hesitated. She wondered about Harald's grave.

They walked down along the creek.

Erik pointed to the willows along the bank. "A lot of cottontail rabbits here," he said. "They've nibbled the buds." He touched a branch. "I'll be able to trap some."

Erik's eyes narrowed as he studied the ground.

"And here, Katrine," he said, "a mountain lion's tracks."

Katrine saw Erik touch where his medicine pouch was under his shirt. She shivered. She looked hard to see the mountain lion's prints where he pointed, but she saw nothing.

"The people call them night cats."

"I don't see its tracks," she whispered, feeling a shiver.

"Look closely near this stone. These rounded hollows, those are its pads."

"It's not a wolf?" She could now make out the toe marks.

"No, there are no claw marks, and the pattern can't be connected by an X." Erik drew two curved lines. He cocked his head as if listening.

Katrine had noticed before how Erik carefully listened for things. It seemed to annoy him when she made so much noise walking through the brush.

Erik had said, "Katrine, the world is alive. You should see that it is so and watch your steps."

Erik was different from the others, she now realized, but she respected what she saw in him.

At Sunday meeting, the men debated whether it was a good idea for Erik to have his own place or not. As usual, Katrine eavesdropped. She pretended to be playing with Torsten nearby.

"Ja, Erik, you need to start your own farm," Nils insisted.

"You're pushing him to get settled on his own, and then you'll soon be pushing him off to go find a wife," Sven said. "You forget that he is my field hand." He smiled. "Am I right, Erik?"

Erik nodded.

Anton laughed. "Maybe you don't need to fix that place up first, Erik. Go do like me. I found a wife right away, and now we've got a son as well. What about it?"

Erik grinned, but Katrine saw something flash in her brother's eyes.

"I agree, Sven," Nils said. "Anton's right. Let Erik be off. You've managed on your own with the two girls just fine."

"Ja, ja," Sven said in a sigh. "But surely you see Björn and Katrine.

I may soon be down to one daughter and one very young son." He eyed Erik again. "You should not rush off, Erik."

Katrine felt her heart skip a beat. They talked about her.

"Björn and Katrine?" Nils questioned.

Lars laughed. "It's not news, Pa. My Anna knows firsthand."

Katrine started to slide farther away with Torsten before they noticed her. Maybe they already had. She caught Erik's eye.

"You see, I am right," Sven said.

"Never mind about Björn and Katrine," Anton said. "I see Erik, and I see someone who should already be married."

"Ja, that's what I'm saying," Nils said. "Sven, you got to let Erik go and get that place of his properly built. You see he has done well with that Indian pony. He can go off and find a woman now."

"Can you at least give me until spring?" Erik asked and smiled a crooked grin to their laughter.

The men laughed and passed the brännvin. Katrine took Torsten's hand and headed toward the women. A funny feeling settled in the pit of her stomach. Papa Olafson had noticed. Maybe she and Björn *would* marry soon. Erik would have his own homestead, and then Papa and Mama Olafson would only have Mia and Torsten.

Later, Erik caught up to Katrine. "So they're wanting me to get married," he said. "But I suppose you already know that. I saw you and Torsten."

Katrine's face warmed. "I hope you do find someone to marry."

Erik was silent for a moment. "I'm glad you have Björn. Maybe he should move into the Lundgren place with me, and we can get it ready for you two for next year."

"Erik!" she exclaimed and blushed. "I'm fourteen."

"I'm funning you." Erik touched Katrine's hair. She pulled away but was strangely glad that Erik had said what he had.

"At least you have him for when the time is proper," Erik said. His eyes quieted, and his smile faded. She saw the strange look return.

In one respect, Katrine agreed with the men. She wanted Erik to work more on the Lundgren place as if he intended to make it his own homestead. She offered to help him fix it up, but he seemed satisfied with the way it was.

"It's a place to sleep," he explained. "I'm at the Olafsons' most of the day anyway."

There was another reason Katrine wished Erik would fix it up. As it was, it reminded her too much of Harald, especially when she walked past the old chicken coop or out to the pond where the now-abandoned muskrat lodge stood. Visions of Harald's body in the river penetrated her memories.

"Sometimes I don't think I can come here," she finally told Erik.

"Is it because of the boy that died? I saw his grave."

Katrine nodded.

"You should tell me what happened."

Reluctantly, Katrine did so and explained that she did not wish to relive the memories.

"I understand. It was troubling for me to stay at the cabin where I buried Mama and Papa. I thought their spirits were still there. But then I knew they weren't. A spirit the people call Sohobinewe Tso'ape was there—a spirit from the trees. Sometimes it was helpful. Sometimes it played tricks on me."

"I used to think there were elves and fairies," Katrine admitted. "I still sort of do."

Erik laughed. "There could be, but I'm talking about a spirit."

"You believed it was real?"

"Of course it's real," Erik replied. "I learned many things that we do not know that the people know."

Katrine shook her head. "I guess there are spirits."

"The Bible says there are," Erik said. "Some are good. Some are evil."

"Maybe I once heard a spirit. I thought it whistled," Katrine said. "It led me to Jackson's skeleton. After Papa and I buried him, the spirit went away."

"A whistle?" A shadow crossed Erik's eyes.

"It was more that I felt it."

Erik shook his head. "The first time Sohobinewe Tso'ape came to me, I heard him whistle. He visited several times. Once before Papa died. Also during my vision seeking."

Katrine began feeling odd. "The spirit was both good and bad?"

"Yes. Sometimes he foretold what was good. Sometimes it was something bad."

Katrine sat still, uncertain of her thoughts. "So the spirit that led me to Jackson may come back?"

"He might. You should always listen."

"Will it do something that is bad?"

Erik shook his head. "A spirit is not like that. It can only help you think or see things. You must be mindful, however, that it may suggest something bad."

Katrine believed she understood.

"So do you feel the boy's spirit here?" Erik asked.

Katrine felt slightly troubled. "No, I think Harald's spirit is gone now." She wanted to believe he was at peace.

"That was his name?"

She nodded. Troubling images washed over Katrine as she saw Harald's face in the river again. She tried to block it out.

Erik glanced around the cabin. "I don't really remember him. What was he known for? Something that was good about him?"

Katrine thought a moment. "He was a very good student. I suppose because his mother was from England and she was our teacher. But more, I guess. He was smart."

"Then maybe you could say he was the boy who knew things."

"Why would I say that? His name was Harald."

"The people would say calling his name now might cause the spirits to confuse him, and he might lose his way on the sky trails." Erik paused. "The people never say a person's name who has gone on to walk the sky trails."

"I suppose if it makes you feel better, I'll say it." Katrine smiled "The-boy-who-knew-things used to live here."

"That is good," Erik said. He brought his hand to his heart and absently touched his medicine pouch.

Erik stood and put wood on the fire. He filled a pot with water and set it on the stone stove.

"So, Katrine, when I first came back, you said I didn't need to tell you about Mama and Papa. How did you know about them?"

Katrine smiled. "I suppose they told me. I was on the hill behind the cabin, the place I showed to you. It was as if they were with me talking to me one day, and they told me." She looked at Erik. "Do you suppose it was them?"

"Of course it was. Did you ever feel me talking to you?"

"Yes."

"But I never told you I wouldn't come for you, correct?"

"No, never."

"And Mama and Papa told you to not worry anymore, that things were all right, didn't they?"

"Yes." Katrine shivered. That was exactly what she had sensed them saying. The thought was unnerving.

"You see," said Erik. "Not only do we have a spirit within us, sometimes our spirits go outward to talk to others. I know you came several times to me so I knew I'd find you. I knew in my heart that you were always here waiting. So I kept looking."

Katrine shook her head. "The Indians taught you that?"

"No, they showed me how to trust what I already felt. It was strongest on my vision journey when I was alone and praying." Erik sprinkled some coffee grounds into the boiling water. He smiled. "Then my name was Dugumbaa'naa Buih-nee'." Erik gestured quickly toward his eyes and toward the sky. "It means Sky Eyes."

Katrine laughed. "I can understand why they gave you that name."

"I was alone without food and sleep for a long while and prayed day and night for a vision. Then when I thought I had failed, the Great Mystery brought me my vision. From then on, mostly when needed, I could open myself to the spirits." Erik poured the coffee and handed a cup to Katrine.

Katrine thanked him for the coffee. She wondered if she should tell him that she preferred tea.

"You should tell me more about your vision," Katrine said. "What did you see?"

Erik shook his head and touched his chest. "It's for me to keep to myself," he explained. "After my vision-seeking, Gray Owl gave me my man's name. Gray Owl was what whites call a medicine man, a spiritual leader. He called me Wahatuwes Paadiha Nikkumpah, Two Elks Fighting."

"Really?" Katrine laughed. "Why? What does Two Elks Fighting mean?"

Erik shook his head again. He gazed about the valley and back toward the eastern mountains. "It seems like such a long time ago that I was with the people. It's been a little more than a winter is all."

Katrine shivered; she sensed Erik's longing and unease.

Erik glanced back. "I don't talk about it. The others would not understand. As it is, I've heard them call me godless. I'd appreciate it if you wouldn't tell the others what I've told you."

The next two mornings Erik did not come by the Olafsons'.

Sven looked in the direction of the Lundgren place. "He is all right, is he not?"

"I can go visit, if you'd like," Katrine said.

"No, he might be taking to heart some of the others' advice and fixing things up." Sven headed outside. "You can check the stock, Katrine. I'm trying to bring in more hay."

The next day, without apology, Erik showed up with some rabbits and a goose.

"I figured we should be putting up meat," he explained. "Winter's not too distant."

Sven and Erik exchanged glances but said nothing. Later they left the cabin and took the wagon to where the hay was curing in the field.

Then Erik was gone again. This time when he returned, he was riding Hatchet and leading Misty with a deer across her back.

"Hatchet is a better riding horse for me," Erik explained. "Misty doesn't mind packing, and she can carry more weight."

Katrine helped him butcher the meat and brine it for hanging and smoking in the badstuga.

"It's good that you have the Lundgren cabin now," she said, laughing. "You would have had to move out to smoke this meat."

"I could just as easily have put up a tent," Erik said. "But yes, this is easier."

Erik seemed happy enough when he brought in game, but when he went to the fields with Sven, Katrine recognized that his heart was not in it. He hunted more regularly and took game to Sunday meeting for the others. When Katrine visited him at the Lundgren cabin, he had several skins stretched on frames or tacked to the side of the cabin, similar to what the Andreassons had done. She recognized some mink and marten furs. He was hunting for furs.

Someone asked Sven what had happened to his field hand.

Sven shrugged. "He is a good hunter. That I will say."

But Katrine had noticed something else. Similar to how he handled Hatchet, when Erik did come, he spent most of his time with the stock, the horse, mules, and cattle. He led them out in the morning, and now that he had spotted fresh mountain lion tracks, he brought them back to the corral at night. She often observed him rubbing them down and patting them, sometimes even the cattle, and he talked to them. She realized that he spoke in the Sheepeater tongue.

The autumn harvest was finished. The grain had been gathered and threshed. The potatoes, turnips, and onions had been dug. Katrine overheard Papa Olafson talking about Erik to the others. When she attempted to listen in, they began talking about their upcoming trip to Boise City and what supplies they would need. She had caught his words, "prays to spirits."

Sven said nothing in front of her, but Katrine sensed a clash of their ways of life.

Erik declined to go to Boise City. She overheard Papa Olafson and Erik arguing. After the others had left, Erik resumed hunting. He brought in another deer, butchered it, and smoked it. Afterward, Erik returned to the old Lundgren place. He came to the Olafsons' and helped with the morning chores, especially with the stock. Afterward, he quickly disappeared.

With a growing hollow feeling, Katrine went to visit Erik a few days before the men were expected to be back. He was in the yard dressed in his buckskin shirt instead of the shirt he had received from Papa Olafson. He was strapping a bundle onto Misty—the furs, Katrine realized. Hatchet stood nearby with a riding blanket across his back.

"I'm glad you're here," Erik said. His voice sounded unsteady.

"You should have gone to Boise City with the men," Katrine said. "You could have gotten another shirt." She eyed his buckskins and tried to laugh.

Erik shook his head. "It would just have taken money away from what Sven will get for you and the family."

"But you—" Katrine stopped herself from reminding Erik that he was entitled to the benefits of the crop as well.

"Come in," Erik said. "Have some coffee with me."

Erik soon had started a fire. It was not lost on Katrine that the fire had been cold. She noticed that except for a few utensils, a chair, and a table, there was little to suggest someone lived here. She also noticed his bedding was stripped and missing.

Katrine felt her heart breaking.

"I'm going away for a while," Erik said. He put the pot of water on the fire.

"Were you going to tell me?"

"Yes, but I didn't want to come by the Olafsons', so I'm glad you're here."

Katrine stiffened as an icy wave hit her. "Where are you going?"

"There's a world out there I haven't seen, Katrine," Erik said. "I've always wanted to go to where the Salmon River meets the Snake. Then

I want to go to Lewiston and see a real city. I'll be back before the snow is deep."

"Why?" A knot grew in Katrine's chest.

"It's my time. If things are meant to be, I'll explain when I get back."

Katrine studied her brother's face. He had just turned eighteen. Of late, it seemed that much had been on his mind. When around her, he tried to be cheerful, but he seemed torn.

"Be careful." For some time, Katrine had been trying to place Erik's unease. It was after the men had talked about her and Björn and had suggested Erik needed a wife.

"I'll be careful. Besides, I have my watcher." Erik tugged out his medicine pouch from his buckskin shirt.

Katrine knew he always wore the small leather bag and that he often touched it as if thinking or praying. Most of the Swedes frowned on it. She had asked him what it meant. He implied it was his helper, but he never told her what was in it. It had something to do with his vision seeking.

Erik slid the pouch back inside his shirt and raised his eyes, smiling. "I'm going to bring you back something if I can. Something special that you'll like."

Katrine smiled. "What are you going to get me?" Her heart quickened. She realized he had no money, only his furs to trade.

"It's a secret for when I get back. That way, you'll have something to look forward to." Erik's eyes twinkled.

Somehow the fact he was leaving had loosed a noticeable joy inside Erik. The last tether had been to tell her. Katrine shivered at the realization.

Looking more Indian than white with his moccasins, his sheep-horn bow across Hatchet's shoulders, and a rolled blanket behind him, Erik turned down trail, leading Misty packed with gear. Then he was gone.

He said he'd be back, Katrine reminded herself. She choked back a sob. *So why did he take nearly everything he owned?*

334

BOW AGAINST SIX-SHOOTER

Chapter 50

KATRINE QUICKLY LEARNED that Erik didn't tell anyone else about his planned leaving. Papa Olafson took offense.

"He needs to relearn some civilized manners."

"He said he didn't want you to worry." Katrine tried to cover for Erik.

"Maybe it is just as well," Sven said and sighed. "I don't think your brother's much of a farmer."

"I know," she agreed and bit her lip. "He's a good hunter though."

"Ja, I will say that is so until all the game is run off. Then how will he do?"

At Sunday meeting, Katrine could feel the emptiness. Some agreed in quiet murmurs that it was for the best. She overheard Mr. Adolphson commenting that he was more Indian than white. Lars had given his father a cold stare, and Mr. Adolphson had shrugged as if asking to be proven wrong.

She left the men. Björn followed her.

"Erik's strange, Katrine," Björn said, pushing his hand through his hair. "I don't think he's one of us no matter how hard he tries."

A flash of heat caught Katrine. "He's one of us."

Björn paused, reaching out and catching her. "I don't mean like that. He's different is all, Katrine. He likes the wilds more. I think he's like what mountain men are like."

Katrine stood quietly. Björn was trying to comfort her, and she knew it. She also knew what he said was the truth.

"I-I'll take care of you." Björn stumbled on. "Don't you worry."

Katrine felt herself falling apart. It was the closest Björn had come to saying he wanted her. He was telling her not to worry if Erik did not come back. She wanted to hit him, and she wanted to wrap her arms about him.

She hugged him. "Thank you, Björn."

Björn mumbled something, blushed, and then headed back toward where the men visited. Some of the men had noticed and, grinning, poked at him.

Katrine joined the women. Anna greeted her, smiling. It was rumored that Anna was already expecting, but Anna had not yet told her personally.

Nothing else was said of Erik's departure. In some respects, it was as if he had never returned. He had been in the valley less than three months. Katrine found herself wondering each day, as she had done so for five years, if she would see Erik returning. He said he'd be back before deep snow. Winter fast approached. The aspens had shed their leaves. The tamarack stood barren. Only a few spindly brown leaves remained on the willows. Geese called to each other, winging their way south in long gaggles overhead.

The garden had been spaded. The apple trees and the pear tree stood naked except for a single apple still on a tree. This season they had their first apples, maybe a dozen. Katrine had left three apples hanging as the Swedish story told. Maybe the tree would be thankful and remember, and next spring there would be more. Maybe more trees would have apples. The barnyard elf and the birds might have to squabble over the remaining one, however. That night, it snowed heavily.

Katrine took Erik's job of pulling hay down and caring for the stock. In the deep snow, the animals generally remained near the shed. Trillium was expected to calve again in the spring. Lupine was full-grown and would be bred come summer. They had decided to try to keep the bull calf over winter. He was putting on good weight. They talked of trailing him to Boise City with a couple of other cattle for slaughter and sale in the spring.

Another snowstorm left a deeper blanket of snow. It was winter. Chickadees and nuthatches pecked at the remaining apple.

In another day, Erik came back over the ridge to the south, pushing through the snow, riding Hatchet, leading a different pony, a red and white spotted one, which was heavily packed. He hollered at the cabin.

All disagreements seemed forgotten as he unloaded. Sven helped him strip the ponies' tack and turn them out for some grain.

"You got a new pack horse. Where's your gray mare?"

"I traded her. This pony's younger and works better with Hatchet."

"What's its name?" Something troubled Katrine about Erik's

decision, but she could not place it. The mare had seemed a good match with Hatchet. Sven also appeared dubious.

"I'm calling him Leaf because he's a little skittish. I can train him like I did Hatchet though."

They helped Erik carry the packs into the cabin.

"You have a lot of things," Mia said, laughing and dancing about. "For us?"

Erik nodded. "For everyone."

Katrine noticed that Erik had gotten a haircut. She couldn't help but see how handsome he looked.

"In some ways, I've had a very successful trip," Erik said, smiling. "I traded my furs." He laid one of the bundles on the table and undid the straps. From it he took a folded square of checkered pink cloth and handed it to Margret. "For making dresses." On top of that, he placed some folded light wool. "For trousers." He set a third square of folded cloth on top of that—some striped blue and white cotton. "For a shirt for Sven, especially because he gave me one of his." He nodded at Sven.

Margret's eyes lit as she ran her hands across the cloth. "This is just like the striped material we had in Sweden. Oh, Erik, how wonderful. I can do lots of sewing this winter."

Katrine could not believe how happy Erik seemed as he continued to hand things out.

"For Torsten." He gave a package to Margret. "He should grow into this pretty soon."

Katrine thought she could see tears in the corners of Mama Olafson's eyes as she unwrapped a boy's beige shirt and shorts.

Torsten, his eyes big, danced about. "For me?" he called. He grabbed the shirt from his mother.

"But how?" Margret asked. "Surely a few furs and a horse wouldn't trade for all of this."

"They didn't," Erik said. He began fishing more items out of a second pack—dried peaches, oysters, a small bag of white sugar, and a large canvas bag of coffee beans.

Sven reached for the coffee. "Praise the Lord. We've already split our last pound." He rolled some of the dark brown beans across the palm of his hand; their aroma filled the cabin.

"And now please don't mind, but I told my sister I would bring her something special." Erik handed over a wrapped package.

Katrine felt a shiver and, smiling, pulled the paper off. Inside was a white apron with a scattering of pink flowers on it.

"A store-bought apron," Katrine exclaimed. "Not made of pieces of clothes or anything." She held it up to herself and swung about, dancing.

"I have a feel you may need that sooner than you believe," Erik remarked.

Katrine blushed, and the cabin filled with laughter.

"Björn's a good man," Sven said, nodding. "I think the time will soon come."

Katrine swallowed. She could not believe what Papa Olafson had admitted. She glanced at Erik. He nodded, smiling.

During dinner, which included some of the dried peaches and coffee, Erik told about Lewiston.

"Largest city I've ever seen," he explained. "More people there than all the people I've ever met."

Katrine realized how few people she had met in her life as well, especially since coming to the valley.

"The shops were like nothing I'd ever seen. There were stores full of all sorts of things. Some had boots and shoes and hats. Some had mining gear and horse tack. Some had all sorts of rations—that's where I got the peaches.

"I think the best thing I saw was the store that had already made-up clothes. Shirts, dresses, underthings—just everything you could imagine. That's where I got Torsten's shirt and his short pants." Erik glanced at Sven. "I would have got you a shirt, but I wasn't sure of size."

"I like my Margret to make mine, by gum," Sven said. He patted Margret's hand and smiled. "The cloth you brought is gift enough."

"And I'll make you one too, Erik," Margret said. "From the looks, there should be plenty of material."

"That would be fine, but a muffler and coat are all I need. Buckskin is warmer than a shirt."

"Just the same," Margret said. "You need a new shirt."

Erik shrugged and continued his story. "Then I wandered into a saloon thinking it was a place that served meals with rooms upstairs."

"You didn't," Katrine said and giggled.

"Don't worry, I only wanted a room," Erik said. "However, the saloon did remind me of Adolphson's place, except I think Adolphson has about the best snaps around and more of it."

Katrine frowned, wondering if Erik had had some personal experience in the saloon after all.

"Ja, it's getting to be a regular trading post with room and board, it is," Sven said. "But you couldn't have traded for all this with just a few hides."

"Nope," Erik said. "It happened when I stumbled into the saloon. A man saw me come in. I had my bow with me. 'Whagh?' he shouted. 'We got us a real live wild Injun among us.'" Erik laughed. "I can't say it like he said it. He made it sound pretty ridiculous.

"'Bow and arrawhs and everthin'. Whar's your war paint?' he said. He had the entire place laughing at me." Erik leaned back and spread his hands. "I about up and left, but another man asked if I knew how to use my bow or if I just clacked the bears over their snouts with it. By now everyone was gathering around me to see what was going on.

"I said I was fair with handling my bow.

"'But can you hit anything?' the first guy asked, and everybody laughed again. Then someone said, 'It sounds like a contest to me.'

"Before I knew it, I was up against a man with a six-shooter—Reynolds was his name—and I was supposed to knock some apples off a shelf. Whoever hit the most apples was the winner.

"A guy came up to me and looked at my bow. He must have known a thing or two because he said he'd bet with me that I'd win, and that he'd split his winnings with me. Pretty soon everyone was betting. A big Irishman held all the money.

"They led me out back and set this shelf up on top of a fence. It might have once been used for holding whiskey bottles because it was like a box and had a brace across the front of it. It was now being used for shooting contests because I could see holes in it. The way Reynolds eyed it, I knew he had faced off with people a time or two in front of it. It was clear he fancied himself to be a good shot.

"The trick was they balanced the apples on top of some whiskey bottles so we could see them, and if you hit a bottle, it was a miss, and of course, the apple would fall off.

"Someone wanted to give Reynolds another drink and give me a fighting chance. Someone else said I should get the drink so as to give Reynolds a chance. The betting just kept going. I didn't mind because I didn't have any stake in it other than if the one man won, then I might make a dollar or two.

"Reynolds went first. He hit the first apple and didn't budge the bottle either. My arrow glanced off a bottle, and the apple fell off, so he was ahead by one. Everybody figured I would lose, so the bets went up.

"He hit his second apple, but I got one as well.

"We both missed our third shots.

"Then he busted another bottle, but I hit the fourth apple. The bottle fell over, hitting the bottle next to it. The apple didn't fall off but rolled behind the wood brace.

"Reynolds had three apples sitting on bottles to choose from. Everyone believed the best I could do was three apples, so the bets went up.

"He busted a bottle, and the apple went flying. They inspected it. and his bullet didn't hit the apple. Now I had a chance. I hit my third apple. There was one apple left sitting on a bottle. Everyone decided the worst Reynolds could do was tie. If he missed, I'd win.

"He hit the apple. Everyone for him started cheering. They decided it was a tie and started to set up some more apples. It was Reynolds who said I still had a shot remaining. It was the apple behind the brace. He said I could fit an arrow through the gap and hit it. It was not much of a gap.

"Some guys in favor of me protested that it wasn't fair. I said I didn't mind. They said of course not because I had nothing to lose. I asked them if I could bet on myself. They laughed. 'Well, laddie, you shan't have nothin' to bet,' the Irishman holding the money said. 'I have my bow,' I told him. The man that was backing me said it was worth ten dollars. Odds were two to one against me, but if I could somehow fit my arrow through the gap under the brace and hit the apple, I'd stand to win twenty dollars. Of course if I didn't, I'd lose my bow."

Erik paused. "My Tukudeka uncle made me my bow. I had far more to lose than ten dollars."

Sven shook his head. "So you put your arrow through the brace into the apple."

Erik laughed. "That's right. I had no intention of trying to fit it through the gap. A Tukudeka bow can drive an arrow through a tree. The guy who looked at my bow knew it and knew I could put an arrow through that wood."

Everyone laughed. Katrine danced about with Mia and Torsten.

"Well, this has been like Christmas, Midsummer's Eve, and Easter all rolled into one," Margret said.

At Sunday meeting, Erik related the stories of his travels again, especially for Björn, Laurens, and Pelle. Erik talked about crossing the

Salmon River on the ferry with his ponies and how the boat rocked and the decking sank and the boat filled with water.

"It's nothing like the ferries on the Snake. The water might be low, but it's fast."

"I crossed when it was high," Anton interrupted. "The operator told me he had just opened and that I was lucky. I might have had to wait a couple weeks for it to drop.

"But luckier than just getting across, I met my Frieda on the other side. If not, I might have gone all the way to Lewiston, same as you." Anton winked.

Erik tightened his jaw. "I *did* go all the way to Lewiston, but I wasn't so—" He quieted.

Katrine realized what had been on Erik's mind. The others now understood as well.

Afterward, Katrine tried to console Erik.

"You've got Björn," he said quietly.

A day later during evening supper, Erik announced, "I did a lot of thinking while on the trail. If I'm ever going to acquire cows and put in fields, I need money. I'm going up the creek the next draw over and put in a camp and a trapline."

Sven raised his eyes. "We have crops to trade in the spring, and I could use a hand getting the stock through the winter. From the looks of it, this might be a bad one."

"Yes, sir," Erik said. "But I don't see us bringing in enough cash for me to buy my own livestock. In the meantime, I'm eating your food, and there's still a market for furs."

Sven ran his hand through his hair. "You should have considered that before you bought all the presents."

Erik bit his lip. "I suppose you're right."

The silence made Katrine want to say something. She could not. An ache filled her.

Sven glanced out the window and then back. He set his jaw. "But if anyone can do it, Erik, you can."

"I'll come by once a week or so," Erik said. "Help with the stock and such."

"I sure will miss the fresh duck and rabbit," Margret said.

"That's another reason for me to come by once a week," Erik said, smiling. "I'll miss your cooking."

"But how will your ponies make it in the snow?" Katrine asked.

"Don't forget I lived with the Tukudeka." A shadow crossed Erik's face. "I've had more experience tending ponies in the winter than I care to remember." He brightened. "Besides, there's a small hot springs a couple miles up the draw where I plan to camp. It should keep the snow off the hillside a bit."

"A hot springs?" Mia beamed. "Can we come and go swim?"

Erik laughed. "It's only a trickle. But maybe someday someone could make a pool."

Katrine immediately thought about telling Björn.

"If there's too much snow, I can leave one of my ponies here. *If* there's enough hay," Erik added.

"Ja, you helped me put up the hay. That is fair enough," Sven said, "but it will get skimpy before the snow goes."

"Come spring I should have enough furs to trade for a couple of calves, I would think," Erik said.

"Do you have traps?" Sven asked.

Erik hesitated. "I'll have no trouble the way I trap."

Erik got up and started packing some provisions. "If I correctly recall, this is the venison I brought in." He wrapped up a good portion of the smoked meat.

Later Katrine caught up to him. "I wished Papa hadn't said that."

Erik shrugged. "It just means Sven appreciates my help. But I'm right on this one, Katrine. By trapping, I'll be able to trade for stock."

"How long will you be gone?"

"This time, maybe two weeks. I need to set up a camp. Afterward I should be by about once a week, mostly to help with the stock. After a trapline is set, it takes tending every few days."

Katrine quickened her step to keep up as Erik threw his pack onto Leaf. "How can I find you?"

"You shouldn't need to, but you can follow my tracks." Erik pointed to the southeast. "Over the ridge, through the small notch, you should be able to see the steam from the hot springs."

Hollow desperation filled Katrine. "Take care of yourself."

"I'm not leaving. I'm just trapping," Erik said, smiling. He hugged her goodbye.

Chapter 51

In two weeks, Erik was back. He brought several rabbits and some venison.

Margret fussed over him. Katrine realized how much a part of their life he had become and how good it was for him to be back. Laughter filled the cabin. He looked good. More importantly, he seemed happy.

Katrine and Mia both hugged him. Torsten wouldn't leave him alone until Erik promised he would tell him a story about Indians later on. Nisse raced around, wagging his tail, jumping, and barking.

"Did you see some Indians?" Torsten asked, eyes big.

"Not this time. They live nearby though."

Katrine eyed Erik to try to determine if he was just telling stories. She was not sure.

Sven simply said, "Ja, we got cold weather now. You can help me put a side on the shed. Snow pushed some of the boards off."

After noon lunch, Erik joined Sven in the yard and worked on the shed, drilling new holes, whittling pegs, and driving them home to fasten the planks.

True to his word, that evening, Erik told stories. It reminded Katrine of when he first came to the valley, as if the stories were all stored up inside of him just waiting to be told. Some of them she had a hard time believing. Katrine tried to tell Swedish troll stories in return, but Erik's stories of the mountains and the Indians were far better. Torsten in particular begged for more.

The next couple of days, Erik helped Sven take care of the stock and make repairs around the farmyard. He then headed out again, promising to be back in about a week.

On his return trip, he brought in a brace of rabbits.

This time, he apologized. "This is all I could bring. The deer have gone over into the canyons to get out of the snow."

Like before, Margret fussed over him and the rabbits. "You sure have a way about you hunting."

"I like eating," Erik said, grinning.

"Ja, so do I," Sven agreed. "You sure are welcome to keep on hunting, you are." Sven asked how trapping was going.

"It is good," Erik said. "The fur animals are attracted to the hot springs and the creek. I've got mink, fisher, and marten. I even killed a wolverine. I wouldn't have, except that it insisted on helping itself to my trapline."

Katrine listened to them talking. She thought it was now well with Erik and Papa Olafson.

Erik remained the night and the next day spent the entire day helping with the stock. Katrine loved how he took care of the animals—even the cattle. It was as if they awaited his return. Both Sven and Erik talked of feeling another storm heading their way.

"I probably won't be down until Christmas," Erik said. "If this storm hits like I'm thinking it will, I might have to hole up for a bit."

Katrine swallowed. She remembered him promising about once a week. He had only been by a few times.

Christmas morning arrived. Erik had not shown up. Katrine was disappointed but not surprised. The snows had been deep—far deeper than previous winters. Sven did not hesitate to share his concern that the stock would quickly consume the hay and oats and that he as well as the others might lose animals.

Margret handed a shirt to Sven that she had made from the striped cloth Erik had brought back from Lewiston. Katrine gave out socks she and Mia had knitted.

They had roast goose, gravy, potatoes, and limpa for Christmas dinner. Mia burned some tallow candles mixed with kinnikinnick berry wax that she and Katrine had collected. They sang some songs.

Katrine heard Erik about the time they began cleaning up. He came banging into the cabin covered in snow. Everyone clambered up, but Katrine reached him first. There was general laughing and hugging.

Sven shook hands. "Those boards came loose again and now, we have a mountain lion prowling about. Maybe you should stay here and do some trapping."

Erik laughed. "I'm sorry." He explained, "The snow's a bit deeper than I expected. I wanted to come sooner, but I had trouble finishing one of my lines. I didn't want to leave some animal in a trap to get eaten by a coyote or some birds."

"Ja, ja," Sven mumbled.

Erik joined them at the table. Margret brought out the food again. Everyone tried talking at once.

"Tell a story," Torsten begged.

"With all this wonderful food your mama has made us, I think it should wait," Erik said.

"Ja," Sven said. "Now we are all here, we can have a good Christmas. Tomorrow we can fix boards," he reminded again.

Erik eyed Sven. "I'll be happy to help you put those boards back up and maybe show you how to set a trap for that cougar. However, if you get a lion, you get to club it and skin it."

Katrine frowned.

After Christmas dinner, Erik brought out one of his packs and handed out red hair ribbons to both Katrine and Mia. "I saved these back from when I went to Lewiston."

He handed Torsten a horse he had whittled and painted with red ochre. Torsten took it and danced around the cabin as if he were riding.

Erik handed Sven a pair of new suspenders. Sven smiled. "I sure could have used these before now," he said.

Margret brought out a shirt she had made for Erik from the same cloth she had made Sven's shirt.

"There was just enough material," she explained.

Erik tried it on.

Chapter 52

THE NEW YEAR came. Sven pushed aside the shutters and gazed out.

"All this snow. The cattle can't even find grass under the trees. I'll for sure run out of feed before spring."

Katrine knew there was nothing she could say or do.

"I don't know how your brother can live out there in the woods buried to his ears," Sven continued. "To blazes, even the Indians have sense enough to go to the canyons to get out of it. What's he feeding his two ponies anyhow? He should come out here and give me some help."

Margret sat with him and touched his hand. "We'll manage," she said. "Thanks partly to Erik, we have plenty of meat."

Sven nodded. "We might have plenty more if I have to slaughter the steer."

Katrine wished he had not said that.

These days they rarely made it across the snow to Sunday meeting. Erik had come down the mountain only twice since the heavy snows hit. Katrine felt overjoyed this Saturday when he did. He came on snowshoes, still waiting for the snow to firm up so he could cut a trail for his ponies.

"Give it another week," he said, taking off his pack and brushing off the snow. "If I was coming and going, all the time, I'd learn how to use those skis of yours. You get around pretty well on them."

"I can teach you," Katrine said. She felt overjoyed to see her brother.

They visited and laughed. Torsten begged Erik silly to tell stories until he finally broke down and did so. Erik helped Sven bring in wood, chop ice from the pond, and feed the stock, but it was clear there was little else that he could help with. Sven worked on his tools for planting season and his harness, but it was nothing for which he needed help.

The following morning, Erik and Sven hitched the sled, and they headed to Sunday meeting. Katrine followed on her skis and convinced Erik to try a pair. He seemed to try to walk too much and not slide.

She laughed when he fell.

348

"I'm faster walking," he said, getting himself up, dusting off the snow.

"You're supposed to keep your feet still and push and slide," Katrine explained.

By the time they reached the Adolphsons', Erik was managing to keep upright and slide along. He even took Torsten on his back for a short distance. "You're old enough to put a pair of these on yourself," Erik told the boy.

"Can I, Papa?"

"When we get back, you can try Mia's," Sven said. Then he muttered, "I best get started on making another pair, I see."

All four families had gathered, including Lars and Anna from the old Andreasson place. It was closer than either the Olafsons' or the Wikstroms' but still a difficult walk.

"You need skis," Erik told them.

"We have some and can get here just fine on them," Lars said. "It's going back up the hill where we have trouble. Sven's supposed to build us a sled."

"I can't keep up with building everything for everybody," Sven complained.

The sun shone strongly, and despite the cold, the children played outdoors, wandering down to the hot springs to find bare patches of ground around the springs or to stick their toes in the steaming water. Some wandered along the river, but none went onto the ice except along the quiet of the shoreline. A pair of eagles roosted in a snag across the river. Katrine watched the eagles awhile until Björn and Pelle said they were going back to the cabin.

They now gathered in the original cabin where often Astrid served meals to travelers. Nils had continued to add to his place, increasingly developing it into a supply station. He had built a separate building with several rooms for the travelers, and he had added back rooms to his own cabin for his family. The original cabin was completely used for serving meals.

The women and girls brought out coffee and, shortly, the noon meal. Afterward the men broke out their pipes and a glass of snaps. Lars and Björn joined them. The women retired deeper into another corner of the house with their own gossip. Pelle, Mia, Ingrid, Linnea, and Laurens snuck away to play, leaving only the youngest with the women. Katrine had noticed Mia giving more attention to Pelle lately. Katrine tried to listen in to the men's business as generally she did. Besides, Björn was with them.

The news was the same for the other settlers as it was for Sven. They wondered how to get the stock through the increasingly heavy winter.

Anton said he had a calf and cow stranded. "Björn and I skied out to them with a sled load of hay. We'll take out more when we get back. I just might run out of hay before the ground clears though."

"Bring the sled down when you need more," Sven said. "I'll split what hay I have. If we both run out, we shall all share the burden and then decide on which animals to slaughter."

The men talked almost too quietly for Katrine to hear.

"Lars, you should consider coming back to our place," Nils said. "There's nothing you can do at your place. I have room. It might be easier."

"Ja, you already showed you know what to do with your spare time," Anton laughed. "You can only do that once at a time."

There was general laughing. Sven poured the brännvin. "To Lars and Anna. Skål." The men raised their glasses. "Let's pray for health to Anna and the wee one on his way."

Lars grinned and then fidgeted.

Sven cleared his throat. "You have ample room, Nils, but I'd suggest that Lars and Anna stay with Anton." He nodded toward Anton. "More hands might help you get your stock through. You're up that valley in the most snow. You said you already have some stock to get out of it."

"I do," Anton said. "When this packs down, if it ever does, Björn and I'll get them back to near the cabin."

"If a mountain lion doesn't find them first," Nils said. He pushed back and sighed. "I think you're right, Sven. As much as I'd like to have Lars and Anna about, I agree it makes more sense for them to be helping Wikstrom. How about it, Lars? You and Anna go to the Wikstroms'. Spring is going to be a long time coming."

"I would welcome having them," Anton said. "Björn may not like being back out on the floor sleeping with Linnea and Laurens, however."

Both Björn and Lars shrugged as if they knew their input mattered little.

That was the last Sunday meeting for two weeks. Another heavy storm hit. Erik came back after the third week. He apologized.

"The snow coming over the ridge is deep. It took me a few tries to break a trail and pack it down. As soon as I did, it snowed again, but I got Hatchet and Leaf out this time."

"Ja," Sven said. "Maybe you should go back to the Lundgren cabin and give up trapping for a while."

Erik shook his head. "I have not done as well as I had hoped. I've moved camp farther up the creek for a bit. I had to go to where the animals are."

Sven nodded. "So stay here awhile and help with the stock."

"I can do that."

Katrine could see that Erik seemed uncomfortable with saying that he would stay.

Erik helped with the stock for a week. He stayed at the old Lundgren cabin again and came up to the Olafsons' each day. The snow packed down, and the settlers finally cut trails between their cabins. Erik got around on the skis occasionally, and when travel became easier, he apparently took it as a good sign because he took his ponies and headed back to his trapline.

Shortly after Erik returned to his trapline, the temperature plummeted. It was all the Olafsons could do to keep heat in the cabin. It reminded Katrine of the bitter cold at Fort Boise. She helped Papa Olafson feed the stock. The grain was now running low.

"The grain is the only thing we got to give these animals enough fuel in this cold," Sven explained. "I may just go ahead and slaughter the steer. I wanted to see if we could get him through a winter and fatten him up."

He threw a scoop of grain into the bin. Trillium and Lupine pushed at it, shoving the steer out of the way. Sven threw another scoop farther down the bin, giving the steer a chance.

Katrine brought in some armloads of hay, spreading it for the animals. "Is there anything we can do?" she asked.

"Keep them inside the shed like we've been doing. Make sure they have clean bedding. Keep water in their barrel. This cold has to eventually break."

"Do you think Erik's ponies are handling the snow all right?"

Sven's jaw tightened. "I can't worry about your brother's ponies. He chose to go off up that creek, saying he knew how to get stock through the winter. Now we shall find out if he really can."

Katrine shivered. The only thing that kept her from worrying even more was knowing that Erik had survived with the Sheepeater Indians in similar conditions.

Back at the cabin, Katrine flexed her fingers over the stove until they tingled with pain. She put them under her arms. Her nose and ears stung as well. Mama Olafson had some hot tea for both of them.

Katrine knew they had sufficient rations, partially thanks to Erik. They had plenty of cut wood. It was the stock that might not make it.

It snowed again, a deep, heavy snow.

Chapter 53

Katrine woke to the smell of smoke, different from the cooking fire. She sat up trying to make sense of the difference. A crackling noise came from above her. Thick smoke filled the cabin and burned her lungs.

"Fire!" Sven hollered. He was up, scrambling around in the faint morning light. "Get out."

He was moving past Katrine before she fully realized what was happening. Mia scrambled up, coughing. Torsten wandered around in his nightshirt, calling mama.

Fear gripped Katrine. Nisse was trying to crawl underneath a bed.

"Get out, Margret. Get everyone out and to the stock shed."

Pandemonium had broken out. Margret had ahold of Katrine.

"Come, Katrine. Take Torsten's hand."

Katrine saw that Mia had ahold of Torsten as well. They stumbled and coughed in the smoke. It billowed about them more violently.

Sven opened the door. It was as if the gate to hell had opened. Flames erupted across the ceiling and exploded near Katrine's bedding. She felt the heat sear into her and take her breath. She choked, coughing, gasping for breath. Somehow her hands found her carefully wrapped bundle. She found Nisse. She grabbed him and stumbled from the cabin with Mia and Torsten into the snow.

Sven madly threw things out.

"Get out, get out," Margret shrieked.

Instead, Sven stumbled back into the cabin and dragged more things into the snow. Katrine saw him fling his rifle out. She picked it up.

The entire roof was engulfed in orange flames and billowing smoke. Surely the snow would stop it, Katrine thought. But it was as if the fire burned from underneath the snow, burning from the inside, hollowing it out.

Sven ceased trying to enter the cabin. He stopped and stared with the rest of them. The fire burned brightly, consuming the kitchen area, crackling with an unearthly roar. A loud crack filled the dim morning air. Sparks rose in a red column, twisting and turning. Wood popped and splintered, sending a shower of burning pieces across the floor. The roof sagged, and snow slid into the cabin, hissing. The fire winked out except for some flickering orange near the door.

Sven ran toward the cabin with a shovel in his hands. He began shoveling snow. Katrine scooped snow with her hands toward the flames as well. The flames sputtered. More snow slid from the roof. Hissing, billowing clouds of white filled the air. Black clouds continued pushing out from the cabin door.

Sven reentered the cabin, now bending to get inside. Smoke billowed out in torrents. He coughed uncontrollably and fell to his knees at the door. Katrine and Margret both pulled at him, dragging him back.

Margret sobbed. "Enough, Sven, enough."

Katrine helped Mama Olafson lead him to the shed from where they watched, unable to move.

A flicker of flame reignited. Sven returned and threw on more snow. He continued now to shovel snow into the cabin and against the walls. With each shovelful, hissing and billowing white erupted. Finally, coughing uncontrollably, he stopped.

Katrine couldn't tear her eyes away. Somehow she expected to see the remains of the cabin again erupt into flames. Every time the beast seemed defeated, it came back to life. She reached down and hugged Torsten. He had his arms wrapped around Nisse. Mia hugged him as well. All were stone silent.

"See if you can find your brother," Sven said quietly, turning toward Katrine. His eyes smoldered.

"No." Margret shook her head. "Erik can do nothing."

"Ja, well if he had been down at the Lundgren place, he *might* have been able to do something."

Katrine swallowed hard. She knew Erik could have done nothing unless he had happened to be spending the night in the badstuga.

"I'll go, Papa," Katrine whispered. "Erik can help us."

Margret got up and began sorting through things. "Does Katrine even have proper clothes for going through this snow?"

Sven said nothing. He returned to the cabin and began pulling more things from the smoldering ruins.

Katrine found herself headed in Erik's direction, following his old tracks, walking and pushing along on her skis, struggling slowly up the hill. She had a coat pulled over herself and her boots. Somehow Sven had managed to throw some of their clothing out of the cabin. Katrine's and Mia's boots were near the door and had not burned.

Midday, she topped the ridge and could not help but pause and survey the somber beauty of the country about her. The sky shone brilliant blue, stark against the dazzling white that was broken only by scattered deep green firs. From the ridge, she could see the thin tendril of black smoke in an otherwise cobalt sky. Maybe the others would notice the smoke and come to help.

She pushed off the top, stepping and sliding downward along Erik's old trail. She spotted him leading Hatchet and Leaf up out of the timber, tramping ahead of them on his snowshoes. The ponies struggled, blowing vapor, hopping through the snow, following.

"The cabin burned," Katrine choked.

"I knew something was wrong. Every day I pray to the Great Mystery. When I turned this direction, I saw the smoke."

They hugged each other.

"Is everyone safe?"

"We all got out. Mama and Torsten are coughing bad. Mia got burned but not bad. I burned my hand."

Erik took her hand and looked. "Keep it covered with cloth," he said. "Maybe we can get some pine sap to put on it."

Katrine turned and struggled back to the top of the ridge with Erik and his ponies close behind. It became easier sliding back down along the broken trail.

"Wait for me," Erik muttered.

The ponies broke through the soft snow, floundering but following.

They reached the burned cabin by late afternoon. Katrine could not help but catch the anger in Papa Olafson's eyes when he saw Erik. He did not shake his hand. The family had moved some things into the badstuga and other things up to the stock shed. Mama Olafson had a small fire going on the hearth in the badstuga and had the coffeepot on it.

Katrine figured Mama Olafson was happy they had the bathhouse now. She had complained before that it was a waste of lumber. Although it was too tiny for all of them to sleep inside, at least the children could. Katrine wondered how Erik had slept there. Maybe his cramped quarters had more to do with him moving to the Lundgren cabin than the desire to begin his own homestead.

Margret hugged Erik. "I'm so happy you've come." She poured some coffee. "I didn't expect you until tomorrow."

Nisse wagged his tail and jumped up to greet Erik. He reached down and petted the dog.

"Erik saw the smoke and was already on his way," Katrine said. She noticed Papa Olafson glance at Erik, but his jaw remained clenched.

They ate a little. Sven didn't talk of a plan to rebuild the cabin or how to go about it.

"I can go and get Mr. Adolphson to help us," Katrine offered.

"Tomorrow, maybe," Sven replied. He handed his dish back to Margret. "No, I'd rather you fetch Lars instead. He'll be less needed than either Adolphson or Wikstrom. They have stock to tend." His eyes narrowed, and he glanced in Erik's direction.

Erik's face remained steady.

Sven rose and headed out the door with Erik following.

"Just tell me what you need," Erik said.

Sven didn't answer.

The following day, Katrine made her way toward the Wikstroms'. No one had used the trail since before Christmas. The snow was deep and soft, and she found the going even more difficult than her trip to get Erik. The skis sank, and she could not push or slide any distance, just walk. Slowly, she traversed back and forth to get up the small valley, fighting to move her skis against the deep snow. Her chest heaved and ached. She was exhausted and hardly able to move her feet by the time she reached the Wikstroms' cabin.

The surprise and joy quickly turned into subdued concern. Lars began packing his things as Björn helped. Frieda inspected Katrine's burned hand and redid the bandages. Anna packed rations to replace some of what the Olafsons had lost in the fire.

Lars said he was ready. Anton stopped him. "You're not going tonight," he said. "Even though Katrine has come over the ridge once, it won't be good in the dark. Besides, there might be more snow."

Katrine hadn't noticed, but she could now see the heavy underbellies of clouds swirling in from the north.

"You're safe here, Katrine," Anton said. He had seen her concern. "We will look at things in the morning."

Katrine felt relieved. She was too exhausted to attempt a return trip. The cabin was crowded, but the two new rooms offered some sanctuary for the children and for Mr. Wikstrom and Frieda. Now Lars and Anna shared one of the rooms, and the children shared the cabin floor.

That night, Katrine could hear Mr. Wikstrom's and Frieda's hushed voices as well as Lars's and Anna's. Words from Mr. Wikstrom's room seemed strained. She heard Erik's name mentioned. Lars's and Anna's voices were also strained at first, and then things quieted. She soon heard hushed laughing.

She glanced at Björn, who lay awake on the far side of Linnea and Laurens. He whispered, "They haven't been married that long." She caught the flash of Björn's smile, and a funny feeling washed her.

Quietly, he got up, came over, and sat next to her.

"You worry about Erik, I can tell," he whispered.

Katrine wanted to cry.

"He's a good brother," Björn continued. "He will have his own life though, I can tell. Didn't I tell you already that he liked the wilds?"

Katrine knew it as well. Her chest ached. She nodded as she felt his arm about her shoulders. He pulled her near.

"I'm going to ask if I can go with you tomorrow," he whispered. "Being near you makes me feel good."

Katrine felt comforted, but she found she was shaking. Björn admitted what she had felt as well.

"You're cold," Björn whispered. He rose to put a piece of wood into the firebox. In the pale light of the stove, Katrine could see his form. He looked strong—a man. She felt fiercely drawn to him, and then the thought scared her.

He came back and held her for a moment longer. "Is that better?"

She nodded. "Thank you."

Then something strange happened. Björn pulled her closer and tighter. He looked into her eyes as if he wanted to say something. Katrine felt her world spinning. Slowly, Björn released her as if something else had occurred to him. He stood.

"Good night."

Quietly, he returned to his bed. Katrine felt cold and terribly empty, despite the cabin's warmth.

It was snowing in the morning, soft, swirling flakes. Anton had been correct—more snow. They ate breakfast.

"I think we can make it," Lars said. "It's a light snow, and it's only about two miles."

"It's four," corrected Katrine,

"Not over the ridge," Lars replied.

"You can't go through the deep snow over the ridge," Katrine said. "Go around with me on your skis. It's faster."

Lars appeared skeptical and then agreed. "I suppose you are correct."

"I intend to go," Björn said. "I can help."

Anton shook his head. "They'll have enough on their hands without another mouth to feed."

"We're taking them rations," Björn reminded him. "With me packing some things, we can take even more."

Frieda glanced from Björn to Katrine. "Björn should go. More hands can put up a cabin in less time."

Katrine thought she might understand something else.

"He and you got those cattle back, and there's no sign of that mountain lion."

Anton hesitated and then nodded. "Ja, you go, Björn. I would go, but I think you and Lars can do better. And if I know what's what, that Erik can go hunting and feed everyone."

Frieda bundled up more rations. When Anton frowned, she smiled. "I can make more."

Lars led the way. Katrine followed. Björn brought up the rear. They pushed along on their skis, sometimes walking, sometimes sliding a step or two. They all carried heavy packs, mostly food.

Chapter 54

By NOON THEY had turned up the creek. Katrine soon smelled the charred wood. The nightmare of the fire washed over her. She felt strangely relieved to see Mia, Torsten, and Mama and Papa Olafson, as if something worse could have happened while she was gone. She noticed that Erik and Papa Olafson had cleared an area to the side of the cabin and dug down to barren earth. They were laying a completely new foundation.

They took a few moments to greet each other. Margret hugged her. "We worried the storm had caught you. Erik said he knew you were fine."

Katrine glanced at her brother. Erik shrugged and touched the small pouch around his neck.

Shortly, they sat down to a meal inside the stock shed. It was the only place that afforded enough room.

"If the weather holds, we can have the walls up in no time," Sven said. "I thought about pulling apart the smokehouse, but then there would be no place to get completely out of the snow."

"We managed before in the snow," Margret said. "There is good lumber on that badstuga, there is."

"If you are thinking about that winter near Fort Boise, I swore never again," Sven said. He glanced at Björn. "I wasn't expecting you. We might have trouble keeping a roof over everyone's head."

"I don't mind where I sleep as long as I can keep dry," Björn said.

Sven shook his head. He glanced at Katrine. Katrine guessed that Papa Olafson knew the reason Björn had insisted on coming.

"We will figure it out. Tonight, the men can sleep in the shed. Margret, you may not have room enough, but maybe you and the others can manage in the badstuga."

"You just want me to admit the badstuga is a good idea," Margret said, scowling but with a slight smile.

"It is, is it not?" Sven said.

Katrine could tell Sven was on edge.

"All right, we shall make it work with you and me in the shed just as well. Where we sleep is the least of our worries just as long as we can be warm and dry."

Sven continued talking. He now made his plans clear for a new cabin. "I'm not building on the old site. It will be easier to salvage what's still good and put it into a new home."

"Lars and I can skid logs," Björn suggested.

"No, I think Lars and I shall skid logs," Sven said. "You and Erik can see if you can shovel out the sawpit and cut some lumber from all those saw logs we stockpiled."

"I'll look at it in the morning," Erik said. "And because we are going to be cutting lumber, Björn and I can stay at the Lundgren place. It's closer to the sawpit than here."

Sven started to protest and then nodded. His jaw tightened. "Ja, but every day you cut a log. Bring the lumber by in the evening. You have something to eat, and then you go back."

Katrine felt disappointed. She wished Erik had not suggested what he had. She might see Björn but unlike she had hoped.

Work began immediately. Sven and Lars broke a trail to the ridge where they cut timber and then skidded the logs down to the building site. After dragging the first log, there was a good trail in the snow for the mules, and the logs moved much easier through the snow than across dry ground.

It was not until the third day that Björn and Erik showed up dragging their first bundle of lumber across the snow.

"It took longer to dig out the pit and get it working than we planned," Erik explained.

"We went to the Adolphsons' for the saw," Björn added.

Sven frowned. "I was preparing to send Katrine to check on you to see if you were still alive."

Katrine realized Papa Olafson had forgotten about the saw.

When the logs were ready, Katrine skied to the Adolphsons', and Björn fetched his family. As they had done during the summer, the families gathered to raise the walls. They used a tripod and pulleys to hoist each log, setting it into the notches of the logs below until the walls were eight feet high.

"I plan to use studs and lumber to build the upper floor," Sven announced. "A real house."

What had begun as an emergency cabin had rapidly become a winter project involving nearly all the Swedes. Frequently, either Frieda or Astrid brought food and sometimes the younger children to visit. It became like Sunday meeting.

Katrine went one day to visit Erik and Björn. She fixed a noon meal of venison, corn bread, and hot coffee while they worked. It was strange to be back inside the Lundgren cabin.

"Thanks," Erik said as he sat down.

"We should have thought of this a while ago." Björn began cutting into his venison.

"Thought of what?"

"Having you come over and fix us noon meal," Björn said, arching his eyes and laughing.

Katrine blushed. She couldn't help but notice the cabin appeared in disarray. Bedding was on the two rope-frame beds, but other things were strewn about.

"Don't look so dismayed," Björn said. "We're still alive. Erik's a good hunter too." He took a swallow of coffee.

Erik laughed. "It's how I'm used to living ... Only here, I have a roof."

Both Erik and Björn ate quickly. They had not made trips to the building site every day as had been planned. Some of their time was consumed by caring for the horses as well as themselves, and dragging logs the distance from the sawpit to the Olafsons' took hours.

Katrine had seen the tracks up the hillside and across to where the sawpit was on the other side of the ridge. Now they were cutting lumber all day, every day. Painful memories from when the men first tried the sawpit, from when Jens and Björn challenged Harald and Lars, flooded Katrine. Now it was Erik and Björn, cutting all day, every day.

She sat quietly, watching Erik and Björn finish eating, wondering about the past years, wondering about her future.

Erik rose. "Well, I guess I can go get that other log dragged down." Björn stood as well.

"Don't you have some business to attend?" Erik asked. He headed out the door. "I'll see you up there in a bit."

Katrine was beside herself. Björn and she were alone. Awkwardly, Katrine asked if he wanted more coffee. She brought over the pot and poured some. Björn sat with his cup in his hands, watching her.

"Remember when we were all on the floor at my place, and I got up to fix the fire?" Björn asked.

Katrine vividly remembered.

"I wanted to kiss you, but I didn't. I've thought a lot about it, Katrine," Björn admitted. He set the cup down and stood. He pulled her to himself. "I love you, Katrine," he whispered. He leaned closer.

Katrine felt his soft breath as he hesitated, and then she felt his lips. She melted in his warmth. Her heart began beating wildly. This was a real kiss—not a child's game. She tried awkwardly to kiss him back. "I-I love you too." Her feelings raced crazily.

He wrapped her into his arms more tightly.

"I don't know if it will work. I can't leave my father yet. I just wanted you to know."

The feelings storming through Katrine were nothing like she had ever felt. Her heart hammered. She could not believe the words she was hearing. This was Björn holding her and telling her that he loved her but then wondering whether it was possible or not.

"We have to wait," Katrine managed. She didn't want to wait, but she wanted Björn to know it was manageable as well as proper.

"I don't know if I can," he whispered and laughed softly. He rested his forehead against hers, peering into her eyes, studying them.

Katrine knew she loved Björn. She knew it deep within her soul. She didn't know if she could wait either. It scared her.

"What do we do?" Katrine wondered.

"I can tell my father the truth," Björn said simply. "I'll talk to Mama Frieda as well. I'm sure she understands more than he does. We could all see it with Anna and Lars."

"See what?"

"That they were in love."

They both laughed.

"But did they kiss?" Katrine worried about what she and Björn had just done.

"All the time, whenever Pa wasn't around." Björn laughed again. "And they hugged each other, and rolled around together, and went to the hot springs together. I'm not sure how they lasted."

Björn quieted and kissed her again more softly. "I just wanted you to know. Now I best go help Erik. We have lots of work to do. Maybe you can come by once in a while."

Katrine knew she would.

The house began taking shape. Erik and Björn had sawed their last boards and dragged them to the site. They now joined Sven and Lars drilling holes and pegging boards. Katrine helped as always with the meals, the wash, and daily cleaning. Both Katrine and Mia had begun sewing new clothing in their spare time. The days now lengthened. When work was finished, they gathered for dinner. Afterward, Erik told stories. Sven listened passively, but Torsten increasingly climbed into Erik's lap whenever he did, laughing and giggling. Nisse curled up with them as well. Katrine gave up on her troll and elf stories. It was only Erik to whom Torsten now listened.

Hints of spring now wafted on the air. In the early morning, the snow had crusted so heavily a horse could walk across it. The Swedes returned to Sunday meetings at the Adolphsons'. Hope became renewed.

The Olafsons' house neared completion. Just as Sven had desired, they built the upper portion from sawed studs and lumber. The floor was also sawed lumber. They were now drilling and pegging the boards onto the roof braces. Sven promised to get some glass windows on his first trip to Boise City.

Except for final touches, the house was completed and was much larger than the original cabin.

"It is the house I always dreamed about, it is," Sven said proudly.

They moved their surviving belongings back inside.

"When the weather warms and I can get more rocks, I'll work on the fireplace."

"Just make sure you don't use any sticks and mud," Margret said.

"Not this time. All rock and clay, or nothing."

Björn and Lars returned to the Wikstroms'. Katrine was saddened to see Björn go. Ever since the nearness of his embrace, her life seemed incomplete without him. She wondered though. What was Björn really thinking? Would he talk to his father? And would he talk to Papa Olafson? He only hinted that this coming Midsummer's Eve would be a special time.

Erik had worked without pause, getting the logs cut, hauling them from the hillside, and sawing them into lumber. Sven hardly acknowledged his effort. It deeply bothered Katrine. Björn was not the man that Erik was. Erik had done the bulk of heavy work, especially dragging and bucking logs into place for sawing. Although Björn never complained, and he worked the same long hours as did Erik, Erik had the strength to do the cutting. Björn did for short stints but was usually the under sawyer.

Erik returned to his trapline for a few weeks until the snow pulled back and revealed the matted brown meadow grass. Water ran from the meadows into trickling rivulets that joined in the rushing creeks.

"I have enough furs," Erik explained one day when he came riding up with Hatchet and Leaf fully packed. He returned to the Lundgren cabin. Katrine visited him there. She wondered if anyone would ever know it as Erik's cabin. He rarely came by the Olafsons' any longer, only to help with the stock. Katrine still marveled at his work with the animals.

One day he announced, "Boots should have a colt in early summer."

Sven appeared surprised.

"Hatchet got along quite well with her last autumn."

"Well, I'll be—" Sven gulped.

TORSTEN AND THE SHOSHONIS

Chapter 55

THE DAYS LENGTHENED. The snow receded, leaving barren meadows. Only the mountain peaks still glimmered with brilliant white. The geese winged their way back north. Ducks clustered on the ponds. The men began plowing, cursing the muddy earth, turning it one furrow at a time, sowing seed for oats, rye, and barley.

Katrine thought of visiting Björn at the Wikstroms'. She could not keep him out of her mind. Maybe this Saturday she and Mia and Torsten would ride over to visit. Her heart quickened at the thought. Torsten would be five in a few months and now ran about the yard, playing with Nisse, following Sven to the fields, watching the new chickens, and exploring. Torsten was good at hanging onto a horse and could ride over with them and visit as well.

At noon meal, Margret asked where Torsten was. "Go tell him we're eating."

Sven already sat down to some soup. He pushed his spoon around in it. "In a couple weeks, maybe we can go to Boise City and resupply. We've been mighty skimpy since the fire."

"I can't find Torsten," Mia announced, returning to the house. "And where's Nisse?"

Katrine felt an icy wash of fear. Usually the boy quickly showed up. She shouldn't worry, she told herself, but this feeling was different.

"He and Nisse are probably out with the new calf," Sven muttered. He dunked a piece of limpa into his soup.

Katrine left the house. She ran toward the calf pen. No Torsten. She called his name.

Now Mia joined her and Mama Olafson. They wandered about, checking all the places the boy would be. Sven saddled up Boots and rode out. "You tell Torsten when he shows up he'll be hearing from me. I'm going to look for him. He knows he's to never leave sight of the house."

Katrine approached Mama Olafson. "That's not like Torsten. He's never done anything like this." Katrine was beside herself. To where could he have gone? She thought of the pond and raced toward it, heart hammering. Torsten liked watching the ducks. Margret and Mia followed.

Topping the rise, out of breath, Katrine quickly surveyed the pond. She was relieved not to see him, but dread filled her. He might be in the water.

She walked the edge, looking.

Margret caught up.

"You keep looking. I'm going for Erik," Katrine said. "Last time, Papa blamed him for not being here. Now he's here. I'm going."

Katrine didn't wait for Mama Olafson's answer. She caught up the riding mule, Ornery, who was near the corral fence.

Margret reached her. Katrine mounted and swung the animal downstream toward Erik's cabin, putting it into a fast trot.

"Be careful," Margret called after her. "I-it might be Indians."

A clammy knot rose in Katrine's chest. It could be. They would be moving through the valley now. A young boy would be a real prize. She shook her head. *Dear God, don't let it be so.*

She raced Ornery down the trail, probably faster than the mule had ever traveled. She prayed Erik would be around. He didn't spend much time at the cabin. He was often out hunting. The look of his fields was not much encouragement that he was taking much interest in farming, despite that he still talked of taking his furs to Boise City and trading for livestock.

She pulled up and swung down, running toward the cabin. Erik came out.

"Torsten. He's missing," she sobbed.

Erik gave her a quick hug. He ducked inside and quickly returned with his bow and rifle. He threw a blanket onto Hatchet.

"How long has he been missing?" Erik swung himself onto his pony.

"We noticed at noon meal." Katrine climbed onto Ornery. "We looked for a while. Papa is still out looking. We can't find Nisse either. I came to get you."

"We'll find him," Erik said. He clucked to his pony.

"I-is it Indians?" Katrine asked.

Erik looked hard at her. "I won't say it isn't." He touched his medicine pouch.

A chill washed Katrine. She felt an uncontrollable dread. She followed as fast as possible behind Erik.

When they reached the house, Papa Olafson had returned. He tightly held Margret and turned pain-filled eyes in their direction. Katrine feared that Papa Olafson had found Torsten's body.

Sven shook his head. For once, he took and shook Erik's hand. "Thank you," he whispered. "I've looked everywhere I could think. It's like the earth has opened up and swallowed him."

Erik nodded. He scanned the surrounding hills carefully, frequently returning his eyes to the eastern ridge.

"Do you think he took the trail to Wikstroms' for the hot springs?" Katrine asked.

"I saw no tracks," Sven replied.

Erik said nothing but began looking carefully about. "Where was the last time anyone saw him?"

Katrine tried to think. She had seen him near the calf pen. Nisse had been with him as well. Mia could not remember for certain—maybe when they were down near the creek. Margret said she had last seen him near the chickens where he went first thing in the morning.

Erik walked down along the creek. He walked back toward the calf pen. Katrine watched. His eyes had become like when he had been examining the mountain lion prints at the Lundgrens' place. She'd seen it before. He knelt, examining something.

"What do you see, Erik?" Sven demanded.

Slowly Erik stood. "Sven, you should recheck the trail to the Wikstroms'. Go a distance up it." A shadow had crossed Erik's eyes. "Meet me back here afterward. I need to look around some more."

Sven nodded and glanced around. He checked his rifle before remounting and heading back up the trail behind the house.

Margret began crying. "N-o-o," she sobbed.

Erik walked to the fringe of aspens to the south and east of the house. Katrine followed him. He paused several times and studied the ground and then the surrounding hillsides. Katrine saw nothing.

"It might be Indians all right. They won't be back if they have what they want," he said quietly.

Katrine felt her world going black. She shook uncontrollably.

Erik grabbed her. "Listen, Katrine. You and Mia stay with Margret in the house. Don't go out, even if you hear what you think is someone calling for you or calling for help."

369

Katrine tried to grasp what Erik was saying. How could this be happening?

"Get the pistol. Keep it on yourself. Use it if you have to."

Katrine knew to what Erik referred. Gulping for air, eyes stinging, she nodded.

"It may be that Torsten saw them, and he's hiding. They might be watching us."

Needles moved up Katrine's scalp. "W-what are you going to do, Erik?" She sobbed.

"I'm going after Torsten."

"W-what about telling the others? The Adolphsons?"

"The Indians have picked us, not the Adolphsons or the Wikstroms," Erik said. "Sven will be back in a few minutes. Tell him what I told you. Tell him to be vigilant, but don't let him follow me." Erik swung back onto Hatchet. "I'll explain when I get back."

Erik reached his hand down to Katrine. "Promise me."

She nodded, her chest heaved in pain. Erik moved away toward the east at a quick trot. Katrine watched as he slipped from sight.

Shortly, Sven returned. "Where's Erik?" he demanded.

Katrine slumped to the ground. "He's going after Torsten. He didn't want you to follow."

"Herre Gud," Sven muttered.

"He thinks it's Indians, Papa," Katrine cried. "M-maybe Torsten's hiding. D-don't go looking for him. If they are out there, they'll kill you and still take him."

"And they won't kill Erik?"

"No." She shook her head vigorously. "They won't even see him." Katrine realized why Erik insisted on going alone. "H-he's like them."

Sven stiffened. "So how long do we stay hiding in the house?"

"Until Erik gets back." Katrine knew the next question, but Papa Olafson didn't ask it.

"Best to go in the house then, Katrine. Take in some water. If they are out there watching us, they'll not do anything, especially if Torsten is hiding. They'll wait. If they have Torsten … then—" Sven's face crumpled. He buried his face in his hands.

Katrine could not bear the sight. She got the water. Papa Olafson left Boots saddled and near the door. They gathered inside in silence. Mama Olafson had quit crying. She now held onto Mia.

"Let's put some water on to heat, Mia," she whispered.

They sat at the table, keeping their thoughts quiet. They knew Nisse was dead—killed by one of the Indians to keep him from barking and from warning them. Torsten was gone. The house seemed incredibly empty. Sven went out once to look after the stock despite Margret's protests. They kept the fire burning but lit no lamp.

Katrine had dozed. Papa Olafson's voice woke her, but at first she didn't recognize it.

"I wondered how Magnus and Hans could leave this valley, especially when leaving a child buried behind." Sven groaned and pulled his head into his trembling hands. "Maj Got, why did I ever come here?"

Katrine felt scared, more scared than she had ever been in her life. She wished Erik was with her. She wished she could see into the woods. Darkness shrouded the land—darkness to do whatever anyone wanted to do, to find a small boy, and to escape over the mountains to the east and to never be seen again.

Mama told her to sleep, but terrible thoughts kept Katrine awake. Mia slept fitfully. Sven kept company with Katrine, keeping a small fire going and his rifle leaned up against the table.

Morning came. Katrine looked out. Nothing had changed. It seemed exactly the same as it had the night before. She wondered if whatever had been out there was now gone.

"If they were watching, do you think they're still out there?"

"Nej," Sven answered. "If Erik is right and they have Torsten, he's following them by now, and they've probably headed over the mountains. If Torsten had been trying to hide all night—" Sven didn't finish.

Katrine knew what he was thinking. Torsten had but his new shirt. Temperatures still dropped to well below freezing at night.

Margret seemed in a stupor. She went through the motions of making something to eat. No one ate.

"I'm going to have another look around," Sven said.

Katrine remembered what Erik had said. She didn't think it would matter now, and she didn't try to stop him.

Margret protested but without avail. Sven switched his saddle to Ornery and headed out.

In a daze, Katrine realized it was now up to her if they were attacked. That was why Erik had her get the pistol.

She watched the hills, particularly those to the east, although there were few openings in the timber. She watched all day until her eyes stung.

371

Sven returned in the late afternoon. "I found pony tracks," he said. "I should have never listened. They have Torsten. Get me some traveling rations. You are all going to the Wikstroms'. I'm getting Anton to go with me after my son. If I have to go to hell and back, I'm going."

Katrine felt her world growing blacker. That meant abandoning their house. The stock could fare for themselves, but Indians burned cabins, she knew. Desperately, she thought about the Wikstroms. Had they already attacked there, unbeknownst to them, and taken Laurens or baby Jon?

They began rounding up some belongings. Katrine glanced again toward the eastern ridge.

Faintly visible, a horse and rider crossed an opening in the timber. Her heart caught. For a moment, she thought the Indians were returning. She stared. Erik was there coming their direction. He appeared strange, the manner in which he sat. She realized why. Torsten sat in front of him.

She let out a cry. "It's them!"

She could hardly get the words out. She began running. Sven saw her and caught her. They watched as the two made their way nearer, topped the ridge, and came down and across the creek. Erik paused in the yard and swung Torsten to the ground. The boy seemed oblivious to what was going on. He giggled and ran to his mother and hugged her.

Erik dismounted. Sven was all over him, demanding to know what had happened. Erik said only that the situation was resolved. "I've been riding all night. I could use some coffee."

They made their way into the house, and Torsten climbed onto Erik's lap as if nothing had happened.

"Where'd you find him?" Sven demanded.

Erik said quietly, "Torsten should not be hearing some of this."

Torsten looked up. "I went with the Indians, but they didn't hurt me."

Erik laughed. "And so I see that you are fine."

It was later when Torsten slept that Erik explained. "A party of Shoshonis happened to be through. Either one of them enticed Torsten out of the yard, or they found him in the woods. They killed Nisse so the dog couldn't warn us. They didn't take Torsten forcefully."

"What do you mean? How? For what reason?" Sven demanded. His eyes narrowed.

"You heard Torsten. He said he went with the Indians. He said they didn't hurt him. He was too afraid to tell you everything. You've impressed on him never to leave the house—never to go out of its sight, correct?" Erik insisted.

Sven worked his jaw. "It's impossible, Erik. Why would he have done such a thing?"

Katrine was thinking dark thoughts—all the Indian stories that Erik had told Torsten. She swallowed.

"For whatever reason, Torsten may have wandered into the woods, but he willingly went with them. It won't be the first time a child wandered away and was taken by Indians."

"Were you involved?" Sven demanded.

Katrine wondered how Sven could even suggest a thing.

Erik stiffened. "I used to live with the Tukudeka," he said evenly. "I'm not an Indian."

"What are you then?" Sven demanded.

Katrine could not believe what she now heard. She bit her lip to remain calm. She knew that Papa Olafson lashed out in desperation.

Erik shook his head. His eyes didn't waver. "Truthfully, Sven, I don't know what I am anymore."

Sven started to speak but then shook his head and looked away. "How did you find him?"

"One of the Shoshonis who found Torsten believed he was an answer to a vision he had. Torsten was a gift from the Great Mystery, and they were going to take him to live with them.

"I didn't know that of course. I assumed the worst, so I followed them until they stopped for the night. I could see Torsten with them, talking away. At least one of the Shoshonis knew English. He wore a cross that Torsten played with. I knew then that he was not in trouble. I walked into their camp and introduced myself."

Katrine almost laughed.

"At first, I didn't know if I'd walk back out. They were on me in an instant. Torsten came up to me and grabbed me.

"We sat and talked. The man who had the vision would not let Torsten go. I shared my own story." Erik spread his hands. "You see, Sven, when I showed up in the Tukudeka camp as a boy years ago, the Tukudeka believed that I was a gift from the Great Mystery. This is what the Shoshoni brave who took Torsten believed—that Torsten was a gift. I told them that, unlike me, Torsten had parents and sisters who loved him, and they would not understand it if he did not come home. The

Shoshoni brave who had the vision about Torsten, had not lost a child who needed to be replaced, but instead, you now had.

"Visions are very powerful among the Indians. They could not understand how the man's vision was incorrect. We spent a long while talking. I told them something that happened to me when I was with the people. The Tukudeka and Shoshoni are related. They knew of my people and listened to me. I told the man that because I truly was a gift from the Great Mystery, I knew these things. I explained that his vision was about something that had not yet happened and that now he was being tested. I offered to fight for Torsten to prove that what I said was the truth. Finally he seemed satisfied, especially when I gave him my rifle as proof of my story."

Sven shook his head. "Your rifle? How could that be proof?"

"I prefer not to say, but I can assure you that if I had not convinced the man with my story, I would not be here, and Torsten would be on his way to becoming a Shoshoni warrior."

Sven clenched his fists, opening and closing them. Softly, he said, "I am indebted, Erik. Thank you for my son."

It was a few days later when Katrine visited Erik that she knew things had changed.

"You won't tell me either?" she asked.

Erik shook his head. "Forgive me, Katrine. There are parts of my life I cannot share."

She sat quietly, a fear beginning to envelop her.

"Are you not going with the men to Boise City anymore?"

"Yes, I'm going." Erik smiled. "I have good furs to trade, and you still don't see any cattle grazing about this place, now do you?"

Katrine wondered about the sincerity of Erik's comment.

Chapter 56

GRASSES NOW GREENED the meadows. The streams filled to near overflowing. Wildflowers began appearing among the aspens and leafing willows. Katrine marveled at the buds on the apple trees. The chives that Margret had received from the Chinese and planted near the doorway had survived the fire and now unfurled flattened leaves and globes of starry white flowers. Shoots began appearing in the new gardens. The men prepared to head to Boise City with their remaining root crops, eggs, and dairy products.

Torsten seemed unharmed by the events of a few days past. Katrine thought often about it. Torsten missed Nisse and could not understand where the dog had gone.

"Sometimes things happen to animals, especially when they wander away. That is why you are never to wander from the house."

Torsten seemed to understand. "Nisse won't be back, will he?"

"No, but Papa says when someone has more puppies, we will get one."

Once when Torsten asked where Erik was and if he was going to visit and tell stories, Katrine realized a little more of the truth. The boy may have wandered off in search of Erik. The fact the Shoshonis happened upon him had turned out to be a strange chance. They rarely saw Indians in the valley and had experienced but one loss to them. Katrine now suspected that the Indians were often around and had simply chosen not to be seen.

On Saturday, Katrine asked Mia if she wanted to go to visit the Wikstroms' hot springs.

"You mean go visit Björn," Mia said, laughing. "You're just like Anna. She always went to Lars's to go to their hot springs, remember?"

Katrine's face warmed. "We can do both."

Mia skipped along. "Yes, and maybe when I'm older, I'll do like Anna and go to the Adolphsons' to their hot springs to visit Pelle."

"I hope you do."

But Katrine also wanted to visit with Frieda. She remembered her talk with Anna. Though it frightened her to hear the answer, she wanted to know if she should even be thinking about marrying and if Björn had ever said anything.

They reached the burned area and cautiously looked about for the sow bear, especially to see if she was there with cubs. Although the bears preferred the lower meadows in early summer and later the burn area when there were berries, bears could be anywhere digging for grubs or bulbs. She also carried some wheat rolls that Mama Olafson had baked. Bears could smell food a long distance. Fortunately, this day the bear was somewhere else.

Katrine strode ahead, anxious to get to the cabin and hopefully to visit with Björn. Increasingly, she thought of him.

Mia lagged behind, causing Katrine to become exasperated.

"Fine, you just catch up at the Wikstroms'," Katrine said. She hurried on and was several yards ahead when she came into view of the hot springs. She stopped.

Björn stood, splashing water toward Laurens, laughing.

Katrine remained staring until Mia caught up. "What are you doing?" she hissed, panting for breath.

"It's Björn and Laurens," Katrine whispered.

"I can see that."

Katrine had not fully seen Björn since he was a boy. He had changed, as had she, she realized.

"Then come," Mia said. "It's not as if we never swam with them."

Katrine hesitated. She could not help her thoughts. She knew under the right circumstances that she could now become a mother, and Björn, although unknowingly, suggested that possibility. The strange feelings grew more intense.

Mia continued down the path. "Hi, Björn. Hi, Laurens."

Björn snapped around and then quickly sat down in the pool.

"Hello, Mia," Björn greeted. He slipped farther down into the water. "Where's Katrine?" He arched his eyes.

Frustrated, Katrine followed after Mia. "Hello," she called. "We came to visit."

Björn didn't move but blushed. A strange look crossed his face.

"We'll see you at the cabin," Katrine said.

As she continued down the trail, Katrine heard him loudly talking. "Why didn't you warn me? She could see me."

Laurens replied with something like, "And so, everyone knows you're going to marry her."

The angrier-sounding words and splashing that followed were muted, but Katrine caught a distinct yelp coming from Laurens.

They reached the cabin. Frieda was inside with Linnea and Jon, mending clothes. They greeted her and Mia warmly.

"Put on some water for tea," Frieda directed. "This is a blessed day. I have my Katrine and my Mia."

"Yes, and your Linnea," Linnea added.

Frieda smiled. "Of course."

Katrine quickly sat down. Her thoughts flashed back to Björn.

Frieda gestured at her mending. "Those men go through clothes too fast. That Björn, I just mended this shirt. He and Laurens are up at the hot springs."

"We said hello." Katrine felt herself blushing.

"Ya, they are swimming. I figured I could catch up on my mending. It might be the only chance I get." Frieda laughed. "I used to have Anna help do all the mending. Now it is Linnea and me."

Katrine squirmed. "How did you know you were in love and should get married?" she asked. There was no easy way to ask the question.

Frieda looked up, pausing in her stitches.

"I mean, Mama Frieda, when you met Mr. Wikstrom, how did you know? How did you know that you loved him and that you should marry him?"

Frieda glanced at Mia and Linnea. "You two girls should go to the garden. Pick me all the peas you can find. While Katrine's here, we can shell them."

Linnea appeared a little surprised. "There aren't any peas yet."

Frieda laughed. "Maybe there are eggs to gather then. Do you know what I mean, Mia?"

"Yes, Mama Frieda, but you can just ask us to go play so you can talk to my sister about Björn. We would understand. She came here to see him anyway."

Katrine's face warmed.

Frieda laughed. "Thank you. Take baby Jon as well."

Mia picked up the youngster and left the cabin with Linnea.

Frieda shook her head, smiling. "Katrine, you make me think of days when I was younger." She absently studied her stitching and then said, "For Papa Vikstrom and me, it was much different. We needed each other. We had faith we would come to love each other as we grew to know each other after we got married."

"But how'd you know?" Katrine felt confused.

"I knew he was a good man when he told us hurdy-gurdy girls straight away that he was looking to marry. He was hard to understand, but we figured it out. I'll never forget. We were heading into some mining camp. He stopped in the middle of the trail on his horse and explained he was a farmer with four children and that he'd like to have at least five. At first I thought he was talking about wives." Frieda laughed.

"Eventually we understood what he wanted. He explained he could not promise much, that he was just beginning to break sod. But then he said, 'I can promise that I will take care of you if one of you would like to be my wife.'"

Katrine laughed.

"I knew I had no future as a dance-hall girl—it seemed exciting enough—but I wanted a family, and I had that Cleatus after me." Frieda frowned. "I told Vikstrom I'd go with him. Love came after."

Katrine shivered. It was not anything like she thought it might be.

"And then I almost did lose Vikstrom when that Cleatus accidentally found me. Thank the good Lord I didn't. After that, I knew I was in love with Vikstrom. I know I always will be, despite his sometimes stubborn Norwegian blood."

Katrine smiled. Most everyone blamed Mr. Wikstrom's stubbornness on his Norwegian ties, but Katrine had seen enough of it among the other Swedes, especially in Papa Olafson, to figure it was also in their Swedish blood.

"Uh, I saw Björn at the hot springs today," Katrine admitted. "It made me feel funny."

Frieda laughed. "So this is what this is about."

Katrine squirmed.

"You want to know if your feelings about Björn are okay."

Katrine nodded.

"I should say so," Frieda said. "It's how I feel about Vikstrom. Otherwise no woman would ever marry and chance dying to have a man's baby."

Katrine wished she hadn't asked.

She thought about how she felt—the time she and Björn embraced and now at the hot springs. The feelings were for more than what took place between a man and woman. She knew what she felt when Papa and Mama Olafson held each other. She also saw it when Mama Olafson cared for Torsten, fixed their clothes, and put dinner before them.

"I understand. They're the feelings that my mama talked about that would happen to me someday," Katrine admitted. "I was thinking something might be wrong with me. I think that's how I feel about Björn."

"You're in love for sure," exclaimed Frieda. She came and hugged Katrine.

"To think, a while ago I was a hurdy-gurdy girl. Then I had Vikstrom and four children. And then I had Jon, and pretty soon, I betcha, I'll have a Katrine. Oh, I'm so happy."

Katrine heard Björn and Laurens coming into the yard, and then they came stumbling into the cabin. They were in their undergarments and demanded their trousers. Frieda handed them over.

Once dressed, they gathered about the table where Katrine sat.

"We were talking," Frieda said.

Katrine blushed. She wondered if Björn had an inkling about what they talked.

"So?" Björn's eyes swept over Katrine. "I can talk too, can't I?" His eyes lit up; his face crinkled into a smile again, and then it changed into the look that Katrine had seen more frequently—the one that made her go weak inside.

"Of course you can, Björn." Frieda rose. "Come, Laurens, we're going to go help Linnea and Mia in the garden."

Laurens started to protest.

"You can visit with Mia." Frieda led Laurens toward the garden.

Katrine found herself now seated alone across from Björn, something quite unexpected. Her heart again began beating strangely. Björn's hair was still wet, but he looked entirely different now. She still pictured him the way he had been a short while ago. She felt different than she had ever felt when being around Björn.

"I-I'm sorry about seeing you at the hot springs today," Katrine whispered, but she knew she wasn't.

Björn shrugged. "You startled me is all." He smiled, catching Katrine with his deep blue eyes and his still-wet blond hair. "Warn me next time."

"Do I have to?" Katrine couldn't help herself.

Björn started laughing and couldn't stop for a minute. "O-only if I don't have to warn you and Mia." Then he was suddenly quiet. "I-I mean it would only be fair." He now blushed.

Katrine thought about it, causing an excited feeling within her. She shrugged. "I don't mind."

"R-really?" Björn laughed, shaking his head, grinning.

"You'll just have to catch me when I'm not watching out." Katrine laughed.

Björn's face fell. Katrine felt warm inside and even more strongly drawn to Björn. She now believed he had meant it when he had said he loved her. It had not been something children said.

Chapter 57

A PARTY OF miners came through and said that only a few snowbanks remained along the river canyon. The men prepared for their trip—Nils, Lars, Björn, and Erik. Sven and Anton remained behind. Although it was not stated, the Indian scare had tempered them. Because Anna was now expecting her first child, she returned to her father's house during the time Lars would be away.

"If they ever put a road through and we can drive wagons back and forth, we'll all go," Sven promised.

Katrine hoped so. She remembered the tiny group of ramshackle buildings that first winter. She wanted to see the city that was now supposedly there. She wanted to go into stores where all they sold were shirts and dresses. Katrine asked Erik if he would buy something for himself this time. He at least deserved a hat. Erik simply laughed.

Ever since Erik had brought Torsten back from the Shoshonis, Katrine had noticed Erik spent more time with her. He didn't talk about his future, however, as much as he talked about hers, and he frequently asked about Björn.

"You're just days from being fifteen. Björn's sixteen," Erik said.

"I know. Everyone knows," Katrine replied. "I think it depends on what Mr. Wikstrom wants."

At noon meal before Erik left for Boise City, the same conversation came up again. Sven said the same thing. "You are my daughter, Katrine, but Björn still has an obligation to his father."

Sven then turned to Erik. "What about you, Erik? You say you are going to Boise City to trade your furs for a couple of calves if you can get them, but your garden doesn't show much work."

Katrine felt embarrassed for her brother.

Erik grinned. "I'm more of a see-what-grows kind of farmer."

Sven's jaw tightened, and he rattled his knife onto his plate. "Both of you. I think it's time I shared some things." Sven pushed back from the table. "When your father said he was bringing your mother out here—God rest their souls—everyone told him not to do it. We said for Ruth's sake, stay in Minnesota. I, more than the others, wanted Jon to come. Despite that, I knew—we all knew—that Ruth wasn't very strong. In truth, it mattered little what we thought. She would have nothing to do with staying in Minnesota anyway."

Katrine swallowed. She glanced at Erik. Erik gave no indication that he had known.

"When your father made the decision to stay back on the Snake River, we both had bad feelings about it. That is why he sent you with us, Katrine, to be his family's future. Before that day, he had dreamed every day of his own land and a new life for both of you. That was all he ever talked about—until Ruth grew so ill."

Sven faced Erik. "He wanted the farm for you, Erik. Just as all fathers, he knew that Katrine would someday marry and have her own home. But your chance for a good life would be that farm." Sven pushed his hands across the table. "I promised Jon that I'd care for you like my own daughter, Katrine, and I prayed to God every day that Jon and Ruth would show up with Erik and take you back and bust sod in this valley with the rest of us."

Sven's fingers trembled. Katrine now realized how much it affected him and how much Erik had disappointed him.

"Both you and Erik have become family to us. I don't want to see either of you go. Erik, you have the chance to carry on your father's dream. You would honor him by doing so. Katrine, your mother's dream was to see you grow up and marry and have children. That's every mother's dream. You could soon have that chance. I won't hold you from it."

Katrine wrestled with Sven's words. He had given his permission, but Erik had been denied. Sven demanded of him to remain a farmer.

As Erik headed down the trail with the fully packed mules, he reached down and took Katrine's hand. "I tried, Katrine. I swear to God I did."

"You were twelve, Erik." She gently released his hand.

Katrine missed Erik and Björn while they were gone. Patiently, she worked in the garden. The apple trees were thick with pink and white blossoms, and their fragrance rose to her as she pruned and watered them. Her pear tree had two bundles of white blossoms. Bees busily visited from one blossom to another. The badstuga had returned to being their smokehouse and bathhouse. After the long winter, it again felt good to wash up. Soon the summer heat would return. She could not keep her thoughts from Björn. Although Papa Olafson had said yes in a roundabout way, maybe Mr. Wikstrom would say no. Frieda had given no indication that Björn had talked to either her or to Mr. Wikstrom, and Katrine knew that Mr. Wikstrom had already lost Anna. He would be reluctant to lose his oldest son as well.

She thought about Anna. She was beginning to show now. She and Lars anticipated that the baby would arrive in August. Katrine marveled at the thought of a new baby. Too many people had died or left the valley. This would be a new life given to a new family.

Katrine watched the southern hill each day, knowing the men would not be back for a few days, but yet she always hoped. Each time it reminded her of watching for Erik as she had done over many seasons.

At last, she spotted Erik returning. Björn was with him leading their fully packed string of mules. Erik rode Hatchet. His other trailed behind. Four calves scampered along with the other stock. Her heart leaped at the sight.

"They're coming, they're coming!" she called.

Margret, Mia, and Torsten tumbled from the house, running a short distance toward the riders. After hugs and kisses and turning out the stock, including the four calves to the calf pen, they gathered inside with the packs.

Sven joined them as they began unpacking the staples—coffee, tea, sugar, cornmeal, and wheat flour. There were beans, dried peas, and lard. As usual, there were small gifts—hair ribbons for the girls and new cups. There was more cloth. Mia had a new pair of shoes, and Katrine received a hairbrush set from Erik. Katrine believed other things remained hidden.

"I got me two calves," Erik announced. "There is a third one for you, Sven. You can pick whichever one you like. The other is the Wikstroms'. Björn and I will take their goods over shortly."

Erik laid out the seed for planting. "All yours, Sven," he explained.

"Where's yours?"

"I got some apple tree seedlings."

Katrine smiled. "You have to have apples for a proper homestead."

"Ja, but you have to grow grain to get your stock through the snow up here," Sven reminded them.

"I know," Erik admitted. "I decided because of the fire, other things were more important."

Erik swung a new cast-iron oven up onto the table as well as a frying pan, some tin plates, and utensils.

"It's more important to grow crops," Sven insisted again. "Margret and I could do without like we've done before."

Margret frowned. "Hush, Sven. Erik has done a good thing."

Sven remained silent for a long moment. He softened. "Ja, I admit he has."

They sat for a moment, taking in all that they had traded for. Sven nodded. "Both Erik and Björn have done well for us, Mama. I think they should always go to Boise City."

Erik stood. "Come, Björn, let me help you get headed for your place."

Katrine watched as Björn swung into his saddle and, leading the mule string, headed toward his home with his family's share of the goods. Erik followed.

Chapter 58

Katrine knew the moment whenever Erik arrived in the mornings. She could hear the stock welcoming him while she took care of the chickens or milked the cows. Afterward, he joined the rest of the family at the table for breakfast and to discuss the day's plans for work. There was always plenty—plowing, harrowing, planting, or cutting fence rails.

Mia and Torsten greeted Erik joyfully.

"I saw the blue herons along the creek this morning," Erik said as he sat. "Sure enough they're nesting."

When Torsten's eyes grew large, Erik added, "Of course you will wait for me until after work, and we will go and watch them."

"Midsummer's Eve is coming soon," Mia said. "What do you think the news will be? We already know Anna is having a baby."

Erik raised his eyes, but before he spoke, they were interrupted by the sounds of a horse coming into the yard.

"*Hej*, the Olafsons."

Katrine nearly dropped her mug. The voice was Jens's. She jumped up and raced out, followed by the others.

"Jens, Jens, it's really you." Katrine found herself gazing upon a young man as tall as Sven but slender. She remembered his darker eyes and darker blond hair—even darker now, but it was Jens. It was his same smile.

She caught herself from running up and hugging him.

Margret did hug him. "Jens, you've grown up!" she exclaimed.

"Well, I'll be a troll's uncle." Sven shook hands and laughed. "Are you coming back to take up an honest life?"

Jens's eyes darted about and settled on Erik.

"This is my brother, Erik," Katrine exclaimed. "He made it." Then quietly, she added, "Our parents didn't."

"To blazes, I remember you, Erik," Jens said. They shook hands. He frowned. "I'm sorry about your parents."

Katrine and Erik nodded.

Jens laughed. "Erik. Think of it. We used to pretend we were hunting Indians on our way out here."

Erik smiled. "Well, you might say I've done some of that rather recently."

They exchanged looks and laughed.

Jens hugged Mia. "And this is little Mia."

"I'm thirteen, Jens, and I'm not so little in case you can't notice things." She smiled at him with an impish look. "It's only been two years."

"And baby Torsten." Jens bent down toward the boy.

Torsten held back.

"No, you wouldn't remember me."

"Come in. You're in time for breakfast."

They gathered at the table again, pulling up an extra stool. Margret set out another bowl of porridge.

"Tell us where you went," Sven said. "You know your parents left."

Jens busily ate as if he hadn't seen food for a while. "Yes, I know. I've received a couple of letters from my ma. Pa died." He gulped some coffee. "It's why I'm coming through. I'm going to Garden Valley to see Ma and my sister and brother. Pa got a homestead up the river there. Barbro and Joran are still with Ma."

"You should bring them back here, you should," Sven said.

"Lars and Anna took up our old place," Jens said, shaking his head. "I stopped by the Wikstroms' and saw everyone."

Katrine swallowed. She wondered if Björn had said anything. She had immediately felt conflicted when she caught sight of Jens. The same strange feeling she had had when she saw Björn the other day had flooded her.

"I'm not sure what I'll do. I think Ma will want to stay where she is. I'll probably go back mining."

Jens pushed back. "My ma wrote me and told me something I never knew. My real ma died when I was born. I don't know if Pa and my real ma were even married. It doesn't matter now, but that might be why Pa always said I was a mistake."

Katrine swallowed hard. Jens was a bastard. She felt badly. Jens had unknowingly paid a price for his parents' mistake.

She didn't want to hear anything more. "How are you doing mining?"

Jens caught her eyes with the same pained look she remembered when he had said goodbye.

"I won't lie. It's hard work. Some days you can eat. Other days you can't."

"Which is why you ought to come home and take up a homestead," Sven said.

Jens shook his head. He glanced briefly again at Katrine. Katrine wondered if he thought about her.

Margret picked up the bowls. Sven packed and lit his pipe. Katrine regretted that soon Jens would be on his way. She wished she could find a reason to make him stay. Too many of her friends had left the valley. Jens was the first of those who had left to return, even if for a short visit.

Margret brought more coffee.

"Oh, yes," Jens said. "Here, I brought this back." He pulled the piece of gold ore from his pocket and handed it to Katrine. "Thanks for loaning it to me."

Katrine examined the piece, marveling again at the visible gold. "Did you find Jackson's claim?"

"No, I talked to Matt Watkins and looked up the paperwork. The location information was vague. After my first year, I gave up looking. I only looked that long because Mr. Watkins couldn't believe how rich the ore was. He said if he didn't have a job already that he'd be out looking for it as well."

Sven interrupted. "We never did hear anything back about Melissa."

"Then Jackson's ore should be yours," Jens said, somewhat excited.

Sven shook his head. "We lost Jackson's ore in the fire."

"That's a shame," Jens said. "I heard about the fire." He glanced around the house. "Your house is really nice."

"We were just thankful to get out alive," Sven said.

Jens drained his coffee cup and rose. "Mighty obliged for breakfast and to see everyone. I might stop by the Adolphsons' on my way down the river. Good to see you again, Erik. I still can't believe it."

"Maybe you and I can share some stories someday of that country you prospected," Erik said quietly. "On your return trip."

"Sure," Jens said. "For what reason?"

"I met a prospector who found something there."

Jens's eyes widened. "So maybe I can chase another rainbow?" He laughed.

Erik nodded. "If you really wish to be a prospector."

Katrine knew it was time. The silence felt awkward. She also knew what the others still thought.

"No one blames you," Margret said quietly.

Jens's eyes flashed. "Ja, thank you. I best be off." He hugged Margret and shook hands again.

Katrine followed him out the door. She guessed the others knew there was something between them because they did not follow.

Catching up to his horse, Jens paused and turned and then pulled Katrine to himself and gave her a quick kiss.

"For old times," he said.

She gasped at the overwhelming feelings. She wanted to say something but couldn't.

"It's all right, Katrine," Jens said. "I know you have Björn. I told you when I left that it was good. I'm happy for you."

He swung into his saddle. "Besides, I'm a wandering prospector now. It's hard to explain, but I'm not into farming. My heart belongs to the mountains."

All too vividly, Katrine knew what Jens meant. Strangely, she felt she was looking at Erik. "I'll always think of you, Jens. Do like Erik said and visit us."

"I shall. He has a story to share." He turned toward the trail.

"And do see the Adolphsons," she said.

"Yes, I believe I should like to at least say hello to Ingrid."

Despite what Jens had said, Katrine could not ignore the ache in her chest.

A few days later, Katrine took Ornery and rode out to visit Erik at his cabin. She had quit worrying about him making it more of a home. She had realized that Erik had no reason to do so. Björn had told her how he had tried in Boise City to find a woman. There were no women who had not already been spoken for. There were no emigrant trains coming through. Now it was single men, survivors mostly of the Southern Uprising, looking for a new life. Most were heading into the goldfields to make a quick fortune, with intentions of returning east or maybe of buying a place of their own. Few intended to remain miners. Erik explained to Björn that those who intended to get rich quick often left it at the saloons, gambling tables, or with women of the night.

Katrine wished for something better for Erik. At least he had brought back two calves. He had been working on fencing a large corral and a stock shed. He also had a small garden with potatoes. Otherwise, as before, he worked with Sven in his fields.

Truthfully, she wanted to ask Erik if Björn and he had talked about her on the way to Boise City. She wondered if he had said anything about Midsummer's Eve.

She was dumbfounded when she rode into Erik's yard and discovered Björn's horse. Her heart immediately began racing. She couldn't help it.

When she entered the cabin, both Erik and Björn were seated in an animated discussion but quickly rose and greeted her, smiling. Katrine felt overwhelmed.

"I came over to help Erik haul some poles for fence. We were just having something to eat."

Katrine wasn't sure if Björn was telling the complete truth.

Erik hugged Katrine. "It's always good to see my little sister."

They talked for a few moments, and then Erik flicked his eyes between Katrine and Björn. "Uh, don't you and Katrine have some business to attend—what we discussed on our trip?"

Björn laughed. "It could be."

Katrine felt her heart beginning to race as she remembered the last time they had been alone.

"I'll get that load of poles dragged down," Erik said.

Erik left the cabin. Katrine listened to the soft thud of hooves as his pony moved away.

She stood staring at Björn. Katrine swallowed. Björn smiled uneasily.

"I guess you saw Jens," Katrine ventured.

"You did as well."

"He looks good."

"Yes. I'm sure he will go back to mining, however," Björn said.

"He told me the same, and he was happy I had you," Katrine said. "And what were you and Erik talking about when he said, 'discussed on our trip'? Does it have anything to do with Midsummer's Eve?"

Björn laughed. "Maybe."

"Tell me." Katrine couldn't stop herself from bouncing on her toes.

"Come here first." Björn held out his arms. Katrine fell into them, feeling his kiss, feeling his strength as he pulled her close.

They moved, clasping onto each other about the cabin, rocking, kissing.

"I love you, Katrine," he repeatedly murmured.

"I love you too, Björn."

His kiss was firm, eager. She felt his heat and found herself melting into his embrace. She fought for her breath. She didn't want to move but just to be held.

All too soon, he separated from her. The coolness of the room enveloped Katrine.

Björn arched his eyes and laughed. "Laurens used to always catch Anna and Lars whenever they were doing anything and tell them there better not be any hanky-panky." He took Katrine's hand and kissed her fingers.

Katrine could no longer stand not knowing. "Did you talk to your father?"

"He knows what I'm thinking, and so does Mr. Olafson."

Katrine bit her lip.

"Erik suggested that if it works, and it is all right by you, we could live at our place at first, now that there are two rooms."

Björn must know something, Katrine decided, although he was not disclosing everything. Her heart began hammering again. Then she began to feel odd, imagining things—imagining always being together with Björn, being beside him.

"And then when able, we could move to the old Eklund place."

"Maybe we can go to where Erik is trapping and build our own cabin," Katrine suggested. "There's a hot springs there."

"There is?"

"I meant to tell you. That's why Erik could keep his ponies there last winter. Some of the springs kept the snow off the hillside."

Björn grinned. "We should go look. Maybe we could build a pool. I wasn't looking forward to not having our hot springs."

"I wasn't either," Katrine said. She laughed.

Björn caught Katrine's eyes and smiled. He pulled her to him, kissed her again, and embraced her. She felt his heart hammering against hers and his quickened breathing. She wanted to hold him forever, to feel his strength and his arms about her as she folded into him, marveling at the mystery she could feel.

He pushed gently away and grinned, shaking his head. "I best go help Erik or we really will get ourselves into trouble. Erik and I do have lots of work to do."

Katrine felt an incredible surge within her. This was real. She wasn't dreaming any longer. Björn wanted her. She wanted him—if only they got the proper blessings.

Chapter 59

KATRINE TOOK WATER to her pear tree. The two clusters of white blossoms danced in the bright light. It was hardly four feet tall, just a spindly sapling. Maybe its flowers foreshadowed Björn's promise that something special would take place during Midsummer's Eve. She knew that sometimes foolish things happened as well. "After all," Mr. Adolphson had said, "at least one night a year, people should be able to be forgiven for being a little foolhardy." There was reason for the children's chant: "Midsummer's Eve is but a night, but it sets many a cradle to flight." It was a time for magic and love, and she was in love. She shivered thinking about Midsummer's Eve.

The day came. They gathered at the Adolphsons'. Katrine watched Erik to see if he seemed to be having fun. He joined in the dancing about the pole and ended up laughing and tangled with her and Björn. Afterward, he joined in the toasting and storytelling.

The meal was one of the best ever—smoked salmon, beef, boiled eggs, wheat biscuits with butter, new potatoes, and for desert, a pound cake with wild strawberries and cream.

Then Björn stood, a glass of brännvin in his hand. He toasted the Adolphsons for hosting the Midsummer's Eve celebration. He toasted his father and Frieda for his life with them.

He toasted Margret and Sven.

"You have been like mother and father to me. Now, Mr. Olafson, this is a proper request. I'm asking you for permission to ask Katrine to be my wife."

Katrine began shaking. She thought she knew Papa Olafson's answer. He had hinted before, but what if he said no?

There was a moment of silence before Sven rose and addressed Björn. "I will be happy to call you my son," he said. "You and Katrine have my blessings."

Cheering and laughing broke out.

After the cheering died down, Björn addressed his own father again. "And, my father, I'm also asking you for your blessings—that I have fulfilled my obligations to my family."

Mr. Wikstrom stood up. Again, Katrine wondered if he might say no.

"I could not have been blessed with more able help from you, Björn, but I believe with Frieda and Laurens, this old Swedish farmer with that bit of stubborn Norwegian blood in him just might be able to see you on your own."

More cheering and laughter ensued.

"You have my blessings, son, to make your life with Katrine. I believe there shall be little difference. She's practically been my daughter since we got here anyhow—she and her sister, Mia, at my place always."

He raised his glass to the laughter. The others cheered and toasted Björn.

When it quieted, Björn turned to Katrine. He took a deep breath. "And so, Katrine, I have proper permission. I'm now asking you if you will marry me."

Katrine could hardly believe Björn's words. "Yes," she whispered. "Yes!" she shouted.

Cheering erupted as somehow Katrine, numb with feelings, found Björn's arms and felt his embrace.

Someone said, "All we need is to ask God's blessing, and they would be properly married now."

"Like Anna and Lars," someone else murmured. "They should not wait."

Nils stood up. "As is proper for the man most responsible for all of you coming to this valley, I shall do just that. Bow your heads please." He cleared his throat. "Almighty God and Father who has seen us come to this valley and seen our struggles, our triumphs, and our weaknesses, we ask you for your blessings on Björn and Katrine for whatever their futures may hold, and if it is your will that they not wait too long, none of us shall hold it against them."

Katrine noticed that Erik seemed to hold back, but when she caught his eye, he was smiling. He had Torsten on his shoulders so the boy could see during the toasting and announcements.

"My sister is going to marry Björn?" he asked.

Erik replied, "It sure looks that way."

Everyone moved to the Midsummer's Eve pole. Anton began singing a familiar Swedish folk song. Björn and Katrine danced together about the pole, twisting and swirling with each other. The others danced one direction and shouted in unison, "God's blessings on you." They danced the opposite direction and came together clapping and shouting, "God's blessings for children." Once more they danced the reverse direction. "God's blessings for long, joyous lives."

Katrine glowed with happiness. Björn held her tight. It was real, she told herself. He was promised to her, and she to him, in marriage.

The celebration continued long into the evening. The Midsummer's Eve bonfire was lit. Tired from the dancing and singing, Katrine sat with Björn watching the orange sparks ascending into the dusk. Erik sat nearby.

"I'm happy for you, sister. And I'm happy for you, Björn," he said. He shook Björn's hand.

"Thank you, Erik. I'll be happy to be your brother."

"I believe you already are," Erik replied.

They laughed and embraced.

Maybe it was Nils Adolphson—Katrine didn't remember—but someone suggested they go to the hot springs. Maybe it was the snaps. Katrine didn't know, but she found herself with Lars and Anna and Björn climbing the trail behind the cabin. The others remained curled up near the bonfire or heading back to their homes.

Katrine felt unbelievably free and giddy.

The four of them somehow found themselves soaking in the deep, lower pool, talking, and dreaming about life.

Lars turned to Björn. "I think you should not wait either."

Björn laughed. "I'm not sure I can."

Katrine felt overwhelmed but a little scared. They had nothing. They were young. How could Björn start a new life with her?

"Come, Anna, I think you and I should head back. I don't know whether or not the hot water is good for our baby."

"Certainly it is. How many Swedish mothers-to-be don't have long saunas whenever they can?"

Lars laughed. "Well, maybe we should get a head start before it is too dark."

Katrine turned away as they climbed out and disappeared down the trail. She could soon hear their hushed talking below them.

"Come, you two. We'll wait a minute for you," Lars called back to them.

"All right," Björn said. He immediately turned to Katrine. "You have made me the happiest man in the world, Katrine," he said. He leaned over and kissed her. "I'm not sure I will be any happier, even on our wedding night."

Katrine returned Björn's kiss. Katrine's heart hammered hard in her chest. Björn's strength surprised her as he embraced her. The fire she felt racing from within made her shake.

"We will have our lives together. Think of that," Björn said. He pulled away. "Maybe like they suggest, we should think about marrying soon. What would a few months matter?"

"I will marry whenever you wish." Katrine found herself longing for his embrace again. She realized before this night that all the feelings she had imagined did not match what she had just felt.

"We better go," Björn whispered. "Even if tonight is a night to be a little foolish, I'm thinking we have been foolish enough. We should not overdo things."

Katrine laughed. They climbed out and dressed in the dimming light. Katrine knew she would soon be with Björn for the remainder of her life. The thought thrilled her in a way she had not experienced before.

"Hey, we're coming," Björn announced.

"We're waiting," Lars answered back. Katrine heard both Lars and Anna laugh.

Katrine and Björn quickly caught up, and they headed together back down the trail. They reached the dying bonfire.

"Where were you?" Laurens demanded. "You'd better not have been doing any hanky-panky."

Chapter 60

KATRINE RODE WITH Papa to the Adolphsons' to pick up some supplies. It had gradually become a way station. Increasing numbers of prospectors and pack trains stopped for goods, to get meals, to use the hot springs and, frequently, to spend a night. Katrine was mildly surprised to see two wagons and two teams of six mules out front. It seemed like a dozen people were swarming about.

"I'll be a troll's uncle," Sven exclaimed. "Someone has brought in wagons. Well, that changes everything, it does!"

Something about some of the people gave Katrine a funny feeling. She noticed one of the men limped.

"By gum, am I seeing who I think I'm seeing?" Sven kicked Boots into a gallop. "Why, it's Magnus and Louise and their children."

Katrine could see them now. An incredible joy washed over her. She could hardly breathe.

They reached the yard amid laughing and cheering and clapping.

"You are in time to celebrate with us," Astrid exclaimed. "The Lundgrens are back, and they've brought a new family with them."

Katrine noticed what appeared to be half a dozen children and a blond-haired man with his redheaded wife. For a second she thought she was looking at Emma Wikstrom again.

There was an incredible ruckus about the place. Katrine quickly caught bits and pieces. The family was the O'Donnell family.

"Ja, I ran out of Swedes to invite, so I had to settle for some Irish folks," Magnus said.

Sven frowned and stroked his chin. "They're Americans—are they not?"

"Ja, but I'm not sure how to handle this," Nils said. "They're Catholic."

Sven shook his head. "Well, why not, Nils? Louise is English. Wikstrom has a German wife. Why not a passel of Irish Catholics?"

Nils raised his eyebrows. "I always prayed for more settlers, but this … I never would have guessed."

Katrine could hardly wait to catch up on the news. She visited with Emma, now thirteen. A couple of the younger O'Donnell children kept her company; she guessed they were twins.

"My papa and mama weren't happy in Oregon," Emma explained. "We just about arrived there when Papa decided he was coming back. Mama missed teaching us. They were sad that Harald was buried here. I was too."

"I'm so, so happy you're back. We have so much to catch up on," Katrine said.

"Yes, I heard your brother, Erik, found you."

"I'm so happy," Katrine repeated, finding herself shaking, finding what was happening unbelievable.

"We know Erik is living at our old cabin. We might find a new place, but we just got here. We wanted to be here for Midsummer's Eve, but the road is still no good." Emma pulled at her braid. "I have a new baby sister. She's one. Her name is Elizabeth."

"Anna and Lars are going to have a baby," Katrine added.

"I heard. I also heard you're in love with Björn. I knew you were."

Katrine pushed at Emma.

"I kind of like Sean," Emma said, nodding toward one of the red-haired O'Donnell boys about her age. "He talks funny though."

Katrine sat a long while, talking and talking. She could hardly wait to tell Mia and Mama and Torsten. Suddenly, her entire world had been showered in sparkling bits of sunlight. It was as if a myriad of blossoms on the apple trees and pear tree had all unfurled at once in an incredible riot of color and happiness.

Farewell to the High Valley

FAREWELL TO THE HIGH VALLEY

Chapter 61

AFTER THE NEWS of the Lundgrens and the O'Donnells and after the following Sunday meeting, Erik did not show up at the Olafsons'. Katrine went to visit him, afraid of what she might find. His belongings were packed and in front of the cabin. Had she not known better, she would have guessed he was returning the cabin to the Lundgrens.

"I expected you, Katrine," Erik said.

An ache leaped into Katrine's chest. She had guessed this day would come, but she had always held hope that it would not.

"You have to go, don't you?"

"You know I'm not a farmer," Erik said, trying to laugh. "And I'm not good at pretending to be one either. Come inside. I still have some hot coffee."

They sat at the table. The cabin looked neater than Katrine had ever seen it.

Erik laughed. "I fixed it up a little. It was the least I could do for you and Björn."

"Why do you think we'll live here?" Katrine teased. "The Lundgrens are back."

"I've talked with them. They are talking of a new homestead adjacent to the north. There were too many memories. Plus, they want to build with real lumber."

"But we might not live here either," Katrine said.

"You will for a while, at least until you can build a cabin up the valley where my trapline was."

Katrine laughed. "Björn and I have plans for making a pool."

"I know," Erik said. "He and I have talked. It will be awhile. In the meantime, I fixed the shed for hay, and the corral is sturdy and will keep your two calves safe."

Erik glanced around. "The potatoes are sprouting. At least I got that part right." He laughed. "I think you and Björn will do just fine."

"You will miss the wedding."

"I'm no good with weddings. Besides, according to the Tukudeka, you two were married a few nights ago. Adolphson asked a blessing. You publically acknowledged your love for each other. What else is there to do?"

Katrine blushed.

"Don't tell me," Erik said and laughed.

"So will you go back to the Sheepeaters?" Katrine asked.

Erik shook his head. "Not for now."

"I always thought you'd go back. Why not?" Katrine could not fathom his response.

Erik swallowed and looked away for a moment. "I would have been married in the eyes of the people as well when I was sixteen, the same as Björn. I turned away on my wedding night. She's now my brother's wife."

"Oh," Katrine whispered. She had never imagined it might have been possible for Erik to fall in love with a Sheepeater woman. "Oh," she said again, unable to comprehend, unable to clear the image.

"I knew if I married that I could never leave the people," Erik continued. "I had promised you I would come to find you."

Katrine felt her magical world beginning to spin. Erik had given up what she was about to have in order to find her. She began shaking. "I'm sorry, Erik."

"Don't be," Erik said. "We each have our lives to live. I'm so very thankful I was able to see the life you will have."

"Will you be all right?" Katrine asked. "Shall I tell the others goodbye for you?"

"I've said goodbye to most of them," Erik said. "Sven gave me his blessings despite our differences. He admitted he did not understand all the ways of God but that he knew I followed my heart. I couldn't tell Torsten. I'm sorry. You'll have to do that for me."

"I will," Katrine said.

Erik smiled. "Here. Give him this." He handed Katrine one of his arrows. "This is the arrow that won the contest for me last fall."

He got up and retrieved the Bible from the shelf. "I left this for you as well. I know the oldest son should have the family Bible. I hope you understand where I am going that it may not be cared for properly. I also know you will have a family before me, and you and Björn are best suited to take care of this."

Katrine's face warmed. "What makes you so sure? You might soon meet a wonderful woman, and Björn and I might wait a very long time."

"Nope." Erik shook his head with a smile. "You will be like Lars and Anna. For sure when you are seventeen, you will have a child."

Katrine shook her head. "What tells you?"

"You just mark my words, Katrine, and remember when your son comes to you, you shall tell him his uncle, Two Elks Fighting, will be by to see him one day as well."

Katrine frowned. "Two Elks Fighting." She glanced around, biting her lip. "I see now. Your vision. Even before you found me, you knew." Katrine fought the realization.

"Yes." Erik nodded. "I tried, but it is something I cannot change."

Katrine grabbed Erik. She couldn't let go of him. Her chest heaved. "I'll miss you." She found tears in her eyes.

"The Tukudeka have many beliefs, many that I now share. Remember this. Each morning, you pray to the Great Mystery. Always you pray for your family. You remember those who walk the sky trails. You remember those who walk with you. You pray for those who will come to live. Life is a great circle. It does not end."

Printed in the United States
By Bookmasters